# bad boss

## A RED ROOM NOVEL

### LANA SKY

**Bad Boss**

**Bad Boss** By Lana Sky



This is a work of fiction. Names, characters, businesses, places, events and incidents are either the products of the author's imagination or used in a fictitious manner. Any resemblance to actual persons, living or dead, or actual events is purely coincidental.

Cover Design and Interior Formatting by Charity Chimni
Editing by Charity Chimni
Alpha Reading by Jessica Rita Rampersad

# acknowledgments

Thanks so much to everyone who supported this draft along the way, including the many beta readers who provided encouragement! Please keep in mind that this story includes dark, graphic, and explicit content matter that may not be suitable for readers under the age of 18—or for readers who are uncomfortable with the following subject matter: explicit sex, and graphic depictions of violence.

Even if, in theory, it sounds appealing, strangling your boss with one of his priceless silk ties is a bad idea. After all, jailhouse orange is a hideous color, and I highly doubt attempted murder is conducive to earning the raise I've been after for the past year and a half.

Telling myself that usually gets me through a day without killing anyone—at least when my phone *isn't* buzzing with a barrage of incoming text messages. The gist of them, which sent me rushing to the office in the first place, spells out a familiar scenario—*Bellamy's on the warpath.*

Given the milieu of horrific scenarios that might entail, I can only pray for restraint as I race into an empty elevator on the building's first floor. Then, all hope for a good day vanishes as a new message flashes across my phone's screen—*He's throwing things again.*

I grit out a sigh. What damage lies in wait this time?

Just last week, he threw his cell phone through the glass doors of an upscale restaurant. It took four hours of negotiations with the owner, on my part, to convince him not to make the incident public. To reward my efforts, Bellamy ordered me to purchase a phone "stronger" than the last. As if the darn thing should have survived an impact with a sheet of glass.

To my credit, I didn't take my own outdated flip phone and shove it through his eye socket—though even the world's most hardened judge couldn't blame me if I finally *did* snap, considering that Graeme Bellamy puts the "ass" in bastard. As head of the prestigious Atelier Noir, the company I work for, he also happens to put food on my table.

We straddle a strange, fine line—the dangerous one between hate and a grudging sort of respect. Even though I initially became his assistant out of a desire to avoid homelessness rather than to pursue a career in corporate America—or fashion, for that matter—three years later, I'm still here because of him.

For all his *quirks*, Graeme Bellamy also puts the "star" in bastard, and spit-shines it while he's at it. At the age of thirty-two, he is already one of the most influential men, not only in his native UK, but also worldwide. With his claim to fame being the steward of a lingerie brand, the rise to power seems doubly impressive. As a fashion pioneer catering to some of the richest women and men in the world, Atelier Noir is expanding far beyond silky bralettes.

If only its owner possessed a personality comparable to the brand's comfortable attire. While his sister, Stella Bellamy-

Ashton, curates the fashion side of the business, he is solely responsible for aggressively growing their market share to astronomical results. Admittedly, to those who view him from afar—namely any warm-blooded woman within a five-mile radius—Graeme Bellamy is a god. But to those who know him personally?

Devil is almost too polite a term.

"Where in the world have you been?" Branden, a sales analyst, snaps the moment I step out of the elevator and into the lobby of the twelfth floor, better known as hell. The wing contains Mr. Bellamy's private office and houses the boardroom where he conducts most of his business—aka the fiery pit. "Was, 'Bellamy's on the warpath' not urgent enough for you to hustle, Evie?"

Dressed in a navy suit with a black tie partially askew, Branden Anderson looks as though he barely survived his last tussle with the devil. His short, light brown hair is wild and unkempt, his brown eyes wide with fear. The expression touches my soul, and his brusqueness is instantly forgiven.

Surging past him, I steel myself for the nightmare I'll find up ahead. "What happened this time?" I ask, mentally bracing for the worst-case scenarios—someone is nursing a concussion, courtesy of one of Bellamy's hand-held devices. Or he broke something again. Or he punched another politician in the face. All those possibilities threaten to trigger a panic attack—but I've dealt with worse.

"The proposed merger with that Eastern European distributor fell through," Branden explains while smoothing the front of his blazer. "He's furious." His crisp British accent cracks, revealing the Scouse Liverpool twang that he secretly spent thousands of dollars on voice lessons trying to disguise.

The devil must be in quite the mood. I've only seen Branden this disgruntled when *another* business partner bailed out of negotiations at the last minute, and Mr. Bellamy inadvertently tried to decapitate him by throwing his cell phone against a wall.

He has a habit of doing that, and I am almost certain another device is about to meet its violent end. *Damn.* My only form of protection is my bag—thankfully, I've learned, since my very first day, never to walk within a yard radius of Bellamy without some sort of shield.

"That bad, huh?" I eye the way Branden's hands shake as he attempts to smooth his hair and wince in sympathy.

"Worse. You best be on your guard," he tells me, but his gaze finds the bag slung over my right shoulder, and he sighs. "Though what am I saying? You're the only one who can calm him down."

Calm, being the relative word.

"Wish me luck," I say while warily approaching the boardroom door. Its smooth surface reflects just enough light for me to make out my appearance.

Thanks to the unceremonious wake-up call, I look like shit. My hair is an unruly mess, barely tamed by a hair tie and three bobby pins. No concealer in the world could disguise the circles under my eyes, and the only makeup I had the energy to apply was a streak of ChapStick along my lower lip. Oh hell, I'm breaking all the rules today—Mr. Bellamy demands a polished appearance at all times, but he can kiss my ass.

Just as soon as I finish spanking his.

The moment my hand brushes the doorknob, I work to school my expression. Tighten that upper lip first. Narrow my eyes to minimize the exhaustion second. Finally, I test my breath against the back of my free hand.

All clear. As I push open the door, I become Ms. King, the devil's assistant, and the only person in the world capable of surviving one of his temper tantrums unscathed—or so the rumors claim.

That assertion is put to the test as what I assume is a silver letter opener ricochets off the wall, inches from my head. *Bang!*

In anticipation of the next airborne object, I seek out my assailant—the man seated at a massive desk who rips a cell phone from his ear and promptly throws it into the nearby wastepaper basket. It's barely made a thud amid a wad of crumpled paper before he's wrenched open his desk drawer and withdrawn a spare—my suggestion after the last ten device mishaps.

"It's you," he growls. Despite my resolve, it takes every ounce of steel that my military father instilled within me to keep from flinching as two ice-blue eyes find me the instant I step over the threshold. God, this man is gorgeous—it's just too bad his temper is equally impressive. His fingers tap a dangerous rhythm against the edge of his desk as he hunts my frame for any flaw to level an insult at. When he spots my bag, the malice in his gaze detonates. "You're late, Evelyn."

I wince. Bellamy's usually musical British accent is crisp and flat this morning. Branden had under-exaggerated. Bellamy isn't on the warpath as much as he's strolling down massacre lane.

"Get Morris on the phone," he commands without letting me say a word. "And if that bastard tries to push you onto his secretary, so help me god—"

"Done," I chirp, as any good general might. It takes me ten steps to approach his desk. With honed practice, I shrug my canvas bag from my shoulder and withdraw my first line of defense. "But not until after you eat breakfast."

"Evelyn…" He scowls while I unzip the posh designer lunch box and withdraw a fresh banana, a steaming container of oatmeal, and exactly a quarter cup of granola. I make a show of arranging them neatly alongside a stack of documents and dig into the lunchbox for a spoon that I brandish in his direction as well.

"Eat," I tell him, my voice monotone, my face expressionless. "Then I'll call Morris, and we'll head to your first meeting."

His upper lip curls from his teeth in a vicious snarl. "Are you bloody serious right now?"

God, this man. His stare can cut through someone like a razor—and still inflict awe beneath the violence. It's the blue irises. They suck you in like a riptide, and you're drowning before you even have the sense to struggle. If only the rest of him wasn't equally mesmerizing. Maybe then it might have been harder to forgive him for being such an ass.

But no, his face is disgustingly handsome—all chiseled cheek-bones, complete with a strong chin. He has that suave, shampoo commercial-hair thing going on and a nose that seems plucked right from some Italian Renaissance statue. Not that I could blame the guy for his looks, but seriously...

Whatever beauty the powers that be couldn't cram into his face during his inception, they shoved into every inch of his lean, six-foot-and-some-change frame. The bastard even has a mole on his neck that doesn't diminish his looks any.

He's basically a grouchy, six-foot-tall Adonis shoved inside a tailored suit.

"I'm not hungry," he snaps, still fixing me with the same glare I assume sent Branden running for cover. "Though I am quite parched. For blood. Get Morris on the phone... *now*."

I hate when he does that—growls. Somehow he manages to seem professional doing it, but it's a damning sign, none-theless. It's already time for phase two, and with my eyes on that ripe banana, I withdraw the second weapon in my arsenal from my canvas bag.

"Unfortunately, exsanguination isn't on today's agenda," I announce while flicking open a leather-bound day planner, though I already know every appointment inside and out. During the past three years, this thing has become my Bible —the codex to all things Graeme Bellamy.

And he has just ten minutes to simmer his temper back to acceptable levels before the next topic on his itinerary.

"Your first meeting is at ten sharp," I recite without looking up. His guttural sigh is my assurance that he's listening to every word, however. "A hearty breakfast will keep your blood sugar from crashing to the point that you curse out everyone in the boardroom," I point out. Maybe it's not necessarily a medical condition, but a lack of regular meals seems to correlate directly to the severity of his moods. "After that, it's another meeting down at the Uptown offices to go over the new designs from Stella. Then it's an hour with Dr. Thorton. And then—"

"Have you become automated now, Evelyn? Like everything else in this damn day and age," he interrupts. "How do I turn you off?" He makes a show of pushing my banana aside to adjust his already neat stack of papers—but at least his nostrils are no longer flaring. A good sign, but not good enough. With another practiced flick of my wrist, I dig into my bag again.

"We scheduled only five minutes for breakfast, so be quick," I remind him while nodding at his container of granola. "While you eat, you can take your vitamins, and then it's straight into the car. James is waiting," I suspect, naming his personal driver.

"Oh?" His scowl deepens. "Remind me, Evelyn—is it you who pays my bills or vice versa?"

Ah, a *Me Tarzan, you worker,* quip. It's not quite as alarming as one of his *I could fire you in a heartbeat and have you replaced before the damn thing can even begin to pump again,* threats. Time to draw my last weapon and let the cards lie where they may.

"Fine then," I say with feigned casualness—but, as predicted, when I palm my cell phone, his entire posture changes—suddenly, he's a lion crouched on his seat, unsure whether to pounce on his prey or retreat. "But the lunch is with *Gloria,*" I add, invoking his mother's first name, a woman fearsome enough to have raised a devil. "Of course, I can just call her and tell her you'll have to reschedule. I'm sure she won't mind..."

I let the threat dangle while my thumb brushes the cell phone. It's a tense wait. He glares for nearly a full minute before finally snatching up the banana and ripping it open in defeat.

"Lunch will remain as scheduled," he says after a ravenous bite. "And you can still get Morris on the phone... *Now.* If you plan on remaining employed, that is."

"I do," I simper in a deadpan tone. "In fact, I would like to discuss the particulars of my employment at your earliest convenience."

He raises an eyebrow. That got his attention. "It isn't like you to be pushy and overbearing in one morning, Evelyn," he snipes. "Submit your request in writing, and I'll schedule you in."

He's joking—I think. In any case, I'm too desperate to salvage this morning to push for the raise talk just yet. Thankfully, I see a glimmer of hope on the horizon—he's no longer growling, and we're back to terse politeness and thinly-veiled insults.

I try to hide my small smile of triumph as I scroll through my contacts for one Richard Morris, the head negotiator for Atelier Noir. What transpires next is a fascinating study in multitasking, as Mr. Bellamy somehow manages to devour his breakfast in five minutes while simultaneously tearing poor Mr. Morris a brand-new pair of "bloody fucking balls" via a conference call.

I make a mental note to salvage the carnage by sending Morris a gift card, in Bellamy's name, of course, once he's cooled down, and I've barely finished jotting the note in my planner when Bellamy withdraws from his desk and rises to his feet.

"Damn, we're already running late," he declares after glancing at his wristwatch, as though I didn't suggest the same thing minutes earlier. "We should go. How do I look?"

I bite my lip at the question. We are the only two in his office, but—as always—he preens as though he's on the world's stage. His shoulders go back, his chin jutting high into the air, his gaze stern and focused like a laser. There's no denying the obvious.

"You look perfect, as always," I declare with a grudging bit of honesty, "but we should really get moving."

Normally, the reminder would send him storming from the office, shouting orders. Today, he... lingers. With one hand, he smooths the front of his pristine navy suit while the other sweeps a few wayward crumbs of granola from his desk. A tendril of alarm shoots through me. If I didn't know any better, I'd say he was stalling.

As if sensing my train of thought, he cocks his head and jabs those stern blue eyes into mine. Then he turns to stare from the floor-to-ceiling window behind him.

"A decade ago, this company was a floundering label with no prospects. I'm the one who took charge of the board from those lazy, money-grubbing bastards my father had installed. I'm the one who spearheaded a new direction of innovative design. I'm the one who..."

"Staked a claim on the heart of high-end fashion and uniquely melded style with a business acumen," I recite, spewing a line more or less from the company website. It's the kind of blather I'm used to including in emails when trying to browbeat a positive news story from a journalist. Oddly enough, though vain he may be, I rarely have to pump this kind of fluff into Graeme Bellamy himself. He isn't the type to require a pep talk.

So why now?

"If image wasn't so damn important in this city, I would have kept our headquarters in the old warehouse near the docks," he grouses, naming the very spot his great-grandfather had founded the company nearly a century ago. "I can't deny that this location is impressive."

He's right, though he doesn't sound happy about that. It's a breathtaking view. From this height, a gleaming swath of the city lays before the office building like a kingdom ripe for the taking.

And, as long as we stay on schedule, it is.

"Sir?" I glance at my watch as well and mark exactly six seconds before he turns and strolls past me for the door.

"Evelyn," he snaps, as though calling a dog to heel.

And we're back on track.

Out in the hallway, a still-shaken Branden is rewarded with a terse, "Good morning, Aiden," for his trouble before Mr. Bellamy commandeers an elevator that takes us to the lower level.

As the elevator doors open, I take five seconds to ready myself. It's always chaos in the office this early, with plenty of opportunity for someone to do or say something to piss off Bellamy and ruin ten minutes of hard work. Again, I glance at my watch. We have exactly five minutes to spare. Ready. Set. Go.

"Good morning, Mr. Bellamy!" The greetings come almost as soon as he steps out onto the polished marble floor of the main lobby. The open, modern design cost thousands to implement—all sleek metal and polished surfaces. A throng of workers, dressed to the nines, is clustered nearby, and the moment they spot Bellamy, they stand at attention. Luckily for me, his still surly expression warns most of them off, but a few lines are muttered regardless.

"Good morning, Sir."

"How are you, Sir?"

"Thank you for the flowers, Mr. Bellamy," a perky blond in a beige pantsuit gushes as we pass. I'm close enough to notice how Bellamy's eyes curiously cut in my direction.

"Birthday," I mutter. "That's Catherine Howard, and you—through me, of course—arranged for roses, her favorite flower, to be hand delivered to her desk last Wednesday. As the head of the legal department, it pays to keep her happy."

"I hope you had a lovely day," Bellamy says at normal volume while reaching out to shake her hand. He sounds so sincere that one might think he remembered to send the gift himself.

Regardless, the distraction only costs us two and a half seconds, and we still reach the front of the building on time. Then, all my planning goes to shit. The traffic is murderous for a Monday morning, and James, the driver, does his best to navigate the shitstorm of taxis and town cars, but I calculate that we'll be at least seven minutes late. Seven whole fucking minutes.

*Deep breaths.* Like any beast, Bellamy can sense fear. Therefore, I disguise my irritation by flipping open my planner and scanning the details with a religious focus. My boss, on the other hand, isn't as subtle in disguising his emotions.

Now that no one else is there to witness his tantrum in full swing, I notice that he's clenching his jaw and fiddling with his tie—two warning signs that an explosion is in the works without immediate intervention.

"This meeting," I start, thumbing quickly through the details. "It's with one—"

"Adrian Riley," Bellamy fills in, his tone murderous and his accent delectable. So much is conveyed through the sinister utterance alone, and I suspect that poor Richard Morris was just a proxy for the true source of Graeme Bellamy's latest case of manly PMS.

Adrian Riley. Right. I run through my mental database of all things related to Atelier Noir and come up blank. *Wait, what?*

I blink, rack my brain... once again, nothing. Even my notes for the meeting merely state the time and address. Strange. I know everything about Bellamy's life. I know about Gloria and when to wire her weekly allowance of hush money. I know about his sister Stella, who is currently backpacking through Germany on a quest for "self-enlightenment," and apart from that...

Well, that is pretty much *it*, as far as his personal life goes. Graeme Bellamy has no wife, only a handful of ex-girlfriends —all of whom kept their distance... mostly—and no children or friends to his name. Adrian Riley is a mysteriously round puzzle piece that doesn't fit into the neat, square grid I've meticulously studied.

"Do you know him?" I ask, already wrapping my fingers around my pen. I wait to jot down whatever details he might rattle off, but Mr. Bellamy merely grits out a harsh sigh and glares from the window.

Another daunting sign. If there is one thing, out of many, that Graeme Bellamy is *not*, it is secretive. Moody? Yes.

Hostile? Always. Obsessive? Compulsively so. Ruthless? Check, check, and triple check. But guarded? No... never.

My mind spins as I watch my pen rest against the page of my planner. The rapidly spreading ink mirrors how my nerves unravel. Discovering something new about someone as predictable as Graeme Bellamy is not a good sign, to say the least. In fact, it's a terrible fucking omen.

The knowledge haunts me as James barely escapes a traffic citation to bring us to our destination, only five minutes behind schedule. It's not ideal, but I'm still counting it as one positive in an already shitty day.

In preparation to race into this meeting, I shove my planner into my bag and wait for James to circle around to open the door. From the corner of my eye, I notice that Mr. Bellamy is... damn it, he's still scowling. According to my watch, this current tantrum has lasted for twenty-plus minutes. Even on a bad day, Bellamy usually simmers down after breakfast when the promise of another meeting gets his cold blood pumping.

I can only think of one reason why that might not be the case this time—Adrian Riley. The mystery of this impending appointment is too great to resist. When James finally opens the door on Bellamy's side, I risk clearing my throat enough to ask, "So, Mr. Riley. Is he a potential client?"

That would make sense. Bellamy's been on the hunt for more shares of retail lately. Perhaps this man owns some boutique I've never heard of despite spending months researching potential sales avenues?

"No," Bellamy tosses back curtly as he steps onto the curb. My free hand is already reaching for his briefcase, and I juggle it with my own bag as I hurry out after him.

"A business associate, then?" I try next. The owner of some silk or textile empire, perhaps?

"Something like that," Bellamy grunts while snatching his briefcase from me, once again throwing me for a loop.

I try to remember back to the day I first made a note of the meeting, but in a blur of various appointments and the overall hectic quality of Mr. Bellamy's daily schedule, I can't pinpoint an exact moment. Already the perfectionist in me senses something fishy.

While keeping pace with Bellamy, I yank my planner from my bag, open it, and once again scan the entry for Monday, 10 a.m.—meeting at the McNair Law offices.

Glancing at the brick building directly ahead gives me the impression that said offices are nothing special. The front sports a carefully manicured lawn that seems out of place this deep into the city. Fenced-in trees create a shaded walkway toward the front of the building and an entrance formed of glass doors framed in gold.

Scurrying along in Bellamy's shadow, I take note of every pristine speck of white marble that forms the floor of a grand entryway. Wood-paneled walls create a soothing yet elegant atmosphere, and a beaming receptionist is already waiting in the lobby to lead us toward a row of elevators.

"Good morning, Mr. Bellamy," she says warmly while glancing him over with a flick of her eyes. "Mr. Riley is expecting you. Right this way, please."

Despite her friendly greeting, Bellamy looks even more surly, and my anxiety swells toward mayday levels. *Breathe,* I tell myself as my sweaty palms almost lose their grip on my planner. One name. One meeting. One mysterious man who may or may not be a potential associate.

"Is there anything I should know before we go in?" I question, low enough for only him to hear.

His initial reply is a grunt. Then a tersely uttered, "You're good at reading people. Do that and tell me what you think."

He lurches forward, leaving me to scramble to catch up. All the while, my mind is reeling. I don't know if I'm more surprised by the blunt directive—which has nothing to do with my usual role in his meetings as a note-taker-slash-referee—or if I'm just caught off guard by the fact that he noticed an actual quality of mine. *And* pointed it out without utilizing an insult.

*You're good at reading people.* Maybe I am, but so is he. Rarely does he request my personal opinion on a business associate. So why now? Though the building mysteriously looms overhead, I try to focus.

Part of this job meant being proactive—and not overreacting to every little detail that happened unscheduled. It would be best to write this off as an unexpected new bit of information and store it for later. I've barely finished thinking the thought when the elevator doors open to a hallway draped in ebony.

The harshness of the scenery is only undercut by another smiling woman wearing a pantsuit in a matching shade. She's gorgeous—absolutely stunning. With her black hair slicked back in a professional bun, her small smile should seem charming and disarming. Key word being *should*. After years of mingling in the fashion industry, I recognize a cutthroat woman when I see one.

The type already poised to attack.

"Mr. Bellamy," she greets, overlooking me entirely.

Bellamy merely scowls, seemingly disinterested in her beauty. "Is he in here?" he demands, jerking his head toward a closed door a few feet down.

The woman smiles wider and nods once. "This way."

Her hips twitch in tandem as she leads Bellamy to the door and palms the knob. "Adrian," she calls sweetly after opening the door a crack, "he's here."

She opens the door to display a chicly decorated office and the man sitting at a polished oak desk situated before his own breathtaking view. Adrian Riley, I presume, a suspicion that's bolstered by the way Bellamy's entire body tenses up and his eyes take on a particular shade of blue I personally dubbed *hostile navy*.

"Riley," he says, clipping the name into one harsh syllable.

"Bellamy." The answering voice is as rich as verbal honey. The man it comes from is equally impressive. Dressed entirely in a black suit, he cuts an imposing image against the backdrop of the overcast sky and gray buildings of the city.

Loose blond curls frame a gorgeous face formed of breathtaking bone structure. He's tall, I notice once he stands and unfurls his limbs to extend one hand in our direction. Bellamy makes no move to take it.

"It's been a while," Mr. Riley adds, as though oblivious to the slight. His smile widens as he lets his hand fall and focuses on me. His blue eyes are as disarming as those of my employer. Even the assured way he carries himself seems similar—though Graeme Bellamy rarely cracks a grin, and this man is all perfect teeth and suave charm. Goodness, they're like night and day. Even Mr. Riley's voice is the opposite of my boss' gruff responses, as he asks, "And you are?"

"Evelyn," Mr. Bellamy cuts in. "My assistant. I would like to have her present during this meeting. I hope that isn't a problem."

"Evelyn," Adrian Riley repeats, drawing out my name. His eyes flick over me, raking up and down. If I weren't so well-versed in the business world, I'd assume he was checking me out—but he wasn't. With that single glance, he'd just sized me up. "I recognize you, after all. Always accompanying your boss to his many promotional events. Three years. His longest-serving assistant, in fact. Our Graeme always did have exacting standards few can meet."

*Our?* The familiar word choice throws me off and highlights even more just how different this meeting is from Bellamy's usual rash of meetings. No... This is personal.

"It's good to finally make your acquaintance, Evelyn." In three strides, Riley crosses the room to stand before me and extends his hand again. His fingers are long and manicured, though not in a way that warns me that he isn't willing to get them dirty. Maybe it's the faint bruises along his knuckles that give him away. Perhaps he does boxing in his spare time?

I stare too long, and Mr. Riley clears his throat, his brilliant grin still firmly in place.

"Um... Evie," I choke out while taking his hand and giving it a firm shake. "Evie King."

"Ms. King. Charmed to make your acquaintance." Mr. Riley turns to command the center of the room with little effort, and I rush to heed my sole directive—read him. He's almost as tall as Bellamy. Nearly as intimidating even—there's something about the way he stands, his gaze fixed, that warns me he's more than a formidable match to any business opponent.

But no one can come close to Graeme Bellamy when he's in one of his moods, and unfortunately for Mr. Riley... he is.

"Let's begin, shall we?" Bellamy runs his hand along the front of his suit, smoothing out every nonexistent crease and wrinkle. Rather than make him seem nervous, the motion has me gritting my teeth in wary anticipation. *Oh no.* It's going to be one of *those* meetings. I may have never owned dogs, but I certainly know a pissing contest when I see one.

Adrian Riley merely nods in agreement and returns to his desk. As if following some unseen cue, the door to the office opens, and a woman enters—the same woman who met us near the elevators. She carries herself with enviable confidence, like someone very much aware that the eyes of every nearby man with a pulse are watching her—Bellamy included. Her tanned skin glows, her dark hair framing her flawless face.

"This is Dahlia McNair," Mr. Riley says by way of introduction. With a wave of his hand, he indicates her shapely form while her green eyes simmer in the spotlight. "I hope you don't mind if she sits in as well. Consider her my legal counsel."

There are only two free chairs. I don't know whether to stand or claim one for myself, but Dahlia breezes past both to take up a post behind Mr. Riley. Though she places one hand supportively on his shoulder, her gaze is fixed directly over my surly boss.

Rather than object to her appearance, Bellamy just strides over to the nearest chair and takes a seat, setting his briefcase down beside him. He's barely straightened his posture before jerking his chin toward the empty chair. "Sit, Evelyn."

Biting back a sigh, I obey, and pry open my planner. My pen is ready, and with my free hand, I tuck a stray piece of hair behind my ear, prepared to take notes. Curiosity has me riveted to the impending conversation before I can help myself. Adrian Riley. Apart from magically springing up in Mr. Bellamy's daily schedule, that name still sounds familiar. *Riley. Riley.* I'm so busy trying to pinpoint how I recognize it that I almost miss the words the man in question directs at my boss.

"I must say that I was surprised when you expressed interest in the merger outright," Mr. Riley begins in a controlled tone. "From what I remember, you aren't one to share. Considering the gravity of your current success with Atelier Noir, I had assumed you'd be eager to have me take what is obviously a lesser priority of yours off your hands. That offer still stands, of course—"

"Well, you proposed an interesting prospect, and I never back down from a challenge," Bellamy bites back. "Why sell? Two highly successful clubs on different continents may seem impressive to some, but one coalesced entity? It would expand our range of clientele and introduce Atelier Noir to the forefront of those who might be interested in our wares. Even if my club is a 'lesser priority,' I can still see the benefit of a promising business venture when one presents itself, and I am always willing to use my success as an example to others. After all... From what *I* remember, you always wanted what I had. This way, at least, we both benefit." He lets the potential hang on the air while I scramble to decode their cryptic banter.

*Club*—not business. Obviously, they aren't talking about Atelier Noir, but it isn't like Mr. Bellamy doesn't have a million other ventures to choose from. I doubt they're referring to the charities, though. Or the real estate he sometimes dabbles in. In my three years of working for him, I've never heard anything about a club mentioned. The third ominous surprise in one day. This can't be good.

"I was of the same opinion," Mr. Riley admits drawing my attention back to the two men. He continues to smile as he laces his fingers together, inadvertently cracking each knuckle. "You've done well in your corner of the world, but together... We could take both of our interests, as well as the club, to new heights of prestige."

"Ideally," Bellamy says.

Watching their exchange is a bit like keeping up with a tennis match. My head keeps bouncing back and forth from player to player. On the other hand, Dahlia seems perfectly content to divide her time between casting admiring looks at Adrian and curious ones at Bellamy. There's an air of unfinished business underlying this whole meeting, and I feel like everyone, but me is on the same obscure page.

"I'm glad we're in agreement," Mr. Riley says. "Though, before we make any rash decisions, you should come by the club. See how things are done on this side of the pond. Are you free anytime this week?"

"Evelyn," Bellamy snaps. I can't help thinking that it's merely for show. The only person more well versed in the life and schedule of Graeme Bellamy than myself is none other than Graeme Bellamy. Still, I take my time scanning the planner for any evening activities. Apart from the few hours he spends each night staying late at the office, there are none. Not that I'm stupid enough to mention as much out loud.

Like always, I take my cues from his posture—the stern set to his jaw warns me against giving an honest answer. Ironically, it was easier to know what Graeme Bellamy wanted without actually listening to what he said. You merely watch and decode him the way one might some peculiar, abstract piece of artwork that the artist thought he was so damn smart for thinking up.

"I'm sure with a few calls, I might be able to rearrange some appointments," I reply instead, facing Adrian Riley directly. "Who should I contact to arrange a date?"

If I'm not mistaken, Mr. Riley's smile quirks even wider. "You can contact me personally," he says, his voice warm. "Anytime. Here is my card."

"Thank you." I have to stand and approach the desk to take the small business card he offers. It's white and exceptionally designed, with his credentials printed in black ink. I do my best to scan it for pertinent information, all while convinced that Bellamy's eyes are boring a hole through the back of my head.

Goodness, I can feel the tension crackling off him, piercing and electric.

"Until next time," Mr. Riley says as I step back. Only then does the suave smile drop, revealing the expression lurking underneath. He's not as easy for me to read as Bellamy, and I can't quite decide what emotion glints within those eyes. Smugness? Boredom?

A heavy hand falls over my shoulder before I can reply. "*I* will schedule the meeting," Bellamy declares from behind me. I know, without even turning around, that he's still scowling, his eyes that ominous shade of blue. "Evelyn," he barks before withdrawing his hand from me. I turn to find him already strolling out into the hallway, briefcase in hand. By the time I catch up, he's barged into an elevator.

I expect to find him still surly and glaring, but the Bellamy who reaches out to strike the button for the ground floor almost looks... normal, and something about that makes me uneasy.

"That was a short meeting," I say before taking my place at his side. I glance down at my watch and have to choke down a gasp. I'd blocked out an hour for this meeting in my planner. It barely lasted fifteen minutes, leaving a whole forty to spare.

"Too long," he grunts while adjusting his tie. I notice his gaze drifting from my face down to my throat. Goodness. It's like he's trying to see whatever Adrian Riley had in me. By the time he finishes his swift appraisal, he's frowning. "I'll pick the time to meet with him again."

His eyes are on the business card that I surreptitiously tuck into my planner before snapping it shut.

"Alright. But, um, is he a friend of yours? So I know how to categorize his details into your contacts, I mean."

Bellamy's eyes narrow into navy slits. "Don't. Just tell me what you thought."

"I, um..." I rack my brain, trying to summarize my observations in the least dramatic of terms. "It seems as if you two know each other, though I'm guessing you weren't close friends—"

"An understatement," he snaps. "What else?"

"It seems like he was being honest about the merger," I admit, recalling Riley's grudging acknowledgment of Bellamy's business prowess. "Though I'm not sure what you two were even discussing." If I was hopeful that he might enlighten me, I'm woefully disappointed. His jaw clenches, and despite him supposedly bringing me along for my skill for observing people, I can't get a read on him. My only take-away is a sinking feeling that I've said the wrong thing.

Seconds later, the elevator door closes, trapping us alone. I spend most of the day with this man, but this time feels different. Tense. Suffocating. I find myself shifting my weight from heel to heel, suddenly aware of how tight my blouse is, and how form-fitting his slacks are. I can't breathe, and as the floors tick by, I become more lightheaded. It's almost like he waits until the very moment the doors open on the first floor to speak to me again with witnesses present.

"I'll handle it. Anything concerning Adrian Riley from now on, you will leave to me," he commands before pulling past me for the entrance.

It may just be a few words, but I marvel at the strange occurrence. Graeme Bellamy and I do not converse. Ever. He dishes out orders. I rein in his bullshit. Somehow we manage to get through it all with barely ten words spoken to each other at any one time. Rarely do I see him like this—unguardedly honest without an insult to hurl.

Once again, Adrian Riley is shaking everything I know about Bellamy and Atelier Noir to their very foundation. By the time I scurry out onto the street and climb into the car, I'm convinced it's not a good thing. Events that happen unantici-pated rarely are, in my opinion.

Craving the monotony of a neat, predictable schedule, I flip open my planner and review today's events again. For some reason, my eyes always seem to return to the same appointment, and there's an odd taste in my mouth when I glance up and find that we're in front of the Atelier Noir headquarters and not the café where he usually meets Gloria.

"Did you forget something?" I ask, while scrambling to follow as he opens the door and steps out. The moment I set foot onto the curb, he reclaims his seat and slams the door, right in my face. The window lowers almost in slow motion, just enough for him to fling a terse statement at me from over the glass.

"Cancel my appointments and take the rest of the day off. I'll be going to lunch alone."

"What?" I can't stop myself from halfheartedly tugging on the door handle. Shocker, it's locked.

Bellamy isn't even looking at me. "Let's go." He jerks his chin in James' direction, and the car pulls away, leaving me with my thoughts reeling.

Abandoned, I can only call after him, "Just eat something with a healthy glycemic index!"

For the sake of the rest of us, I hope he listens.

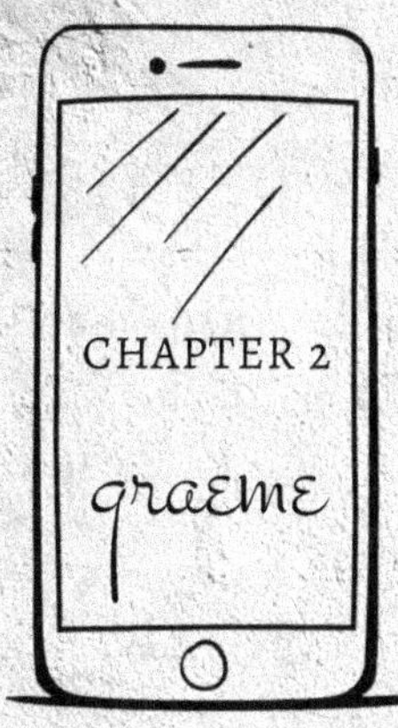


Lunch is an American concept my mother bastardized to describe an allotted amount of time during which she can torture her chosen prey for information. If she wanted to eat, she called it *Tea*. In all fairness, she learned from the best—all the prior Bellamys who schemed and plotted before her. She taught me most of what she learned, yet I never underestimated her.

Turning the tables on her favorite pastime, however, is as simple as trapping a wild animal—using bait and a small cage.

The moment I enter the dining room of the café, she's already frowning, seated at her favorite table by the bay windows. When I join her, she doesn't even waste time on niceties before stating the obvious as her gaze cuts toward the nearest exit.

"Where is Evie?"

"Why hello, Mother. It is quite nice to see you as well." I sit, reach for the silverware roll on her end, and unfurl it. Setting aside the utensils, I flick the napkin into the air and then present it to her by the corners. When she doesn't accept it, I toss the bloody thing onto her place setting. "Business meeting ran long. I hope I didn't keep you waiting."

I had. In fact, to ensure a long wait, I made James circle the block twice before running over a business proposal I'd brought from the office. As a result, I'm nearly an hour late, and I don't give a single damn.

Her lips part, but before she can say a word, I reach for the pitcher of water in the center of the table, pour a glass, and shove it pointedly in her direction.

"Do drink something other than liquor, Mum," I suggest. "I can still smell your mid-morning brandy."

"Don't be cheeky, darling." She cranes her neck to peer over my shoulder. "Is Evie in the loo? It isn't like her to let you galivant around *unsupervised*—"

"I'll have you know that I told *Evelyn* to clear off for the day," I admit, irritated by the lengths I've gone to in order to rob Gloria of her precious ally.

Predictably, she gasps. "A day off? That's unlike you, darling. Though, she most definitely deserves one after all these years. I wonder what she's doing at this very moment? Perhaps she's enjoying her own lunchtime meeting with a handsome young lad."

I wince, though I'm not sure why. It can't be jealousy at the thought of her with anyone else. Perhaps it's merely annoyance at the idea of wasted time. Given what I pay her, Evelyn King doesn't deserve a day off.

Though, if she were here now, she would fawn over my current opponent, spewing some trivial details about my mother's life that no one but her cared enough to remember. Lost in thought, she'd bite her bottom lip—the very mouth that some crass associate had once deemed *Fuckable* under his breath when he thought no one was listening. I should have punched the bastard then, but Evelyn intervened and before I knew it, the meeting was over with a deal signed—one highly beneficial to Atelier Noir. It was her defining skill, that social charm. Like the good referee, she would interject whenever the mood became even slightly tense and prod me to eat a slice of damned toast because of the bloody hypoglycemia. The toast would be undercooked, but I'd choke it down anyway, if only to keep her from severing her lip entirely.

She thinks she has me deciphered, but the golden rule of business is to always stay one step ahead. However, there are some things about my family that even Evelyn King isn't privy to learning.

"Enough about Evelyn." Fixing Gloria with a stare, I launch into the most pressing issue. "I'm sure you'll be pleased to learn that *he* contacted me this morning."

"W-Who?" She coughs and snatches up the glass of water I served her. After two sips, her eyes begin to stream, and she sputters even more. It must have gone down the wrong pipe.

Good. I've caught her off guard.

"Your son. I know you've been sending him money," I add, springing my trap.

"D-Darling—"

"Correction—I know that *Evelyn* has been sending you money that you've been sending to *him*."

"Graeme." She swallows hard, and her hand flies to her throat to clutch the pearls strung there. They aren't genuine, as she was forced to sell the real heirloom by "drastic circumstances after being left by your bastard father and forced to raise three children alone." To hear her tell it, she wore the fake ones supposedly as a reminder to herself of her strength in the face of adversity. In reality, she wore them solely for appearance's sake and was too damn frugal to buy a new pair.

"Graeme, darling, I..." Her eyes lock with mine. With a heavy sigh, she drops the startled act and rolls her eyes at the ceiling. "Did Evie tell you?" she demands, her tone wary.

Her fingers drift toward the handle of her teacup. *This* is the mother I know—a woman who wouldn't hesitate to hurl the porcelain tea service across the room should things not go her way.

Regarding her question, I frown. "You know damn well that she wouldn't. And why would she? It's been two years since she started funneling money to you—" In addition to what I set aside for her daily expenses at that. "Did you think I wasn't aware?"

"Well, you haven't complained until now, darling," she grouses while clawing at a menu. "I *am* your mummy, after all—"

"Back then, I didn't really give a damn," I admit. "It was only when *your* son had the gall to contact me for more that I decided to put an end to your little game."

"Oh. That." My mother pales, straightening in her seat. She's twisting that damn string of pearls around her neck so tightly I half expect her to asphyxiate before the end of this blasted luncheon. *That* would certainly save me the hassle of cutting her off. "Graeme... darling. He is your brother."

"I'm not convinced of that," I say, crossing my arms. The rude gesture draws attention to our table—something Gloria can't stand.

"Graeme." She forces a strained smile and races to pour herself another cup of tea from the kettle. "Here, darling. Just have a cuppa—"

"In fact, I'm still unsure of whether or not I really am your son," I declare over her. "Some days I wonder if you snatched me from some other woman's pram just to keep my bastard 'father' tethered to you for a few years longer—"

"Graeme, darling, he was going to be *evicted*," she says in a hushed whisper. After a quick glance around to ensure no other patron is within earshot, she leans across the table. "Do you really want to see him on the street?"

I meet her imploring stare without hesitation. "Perhaps."

"Graeme!" Gloria gasps and raises a hand to shield her partially-opened mouth as if I've committed sacrilege.

"Maybe then he might decide to stop taking the piss out of me and make something of himself."

"Language, Graeme! You make him sound so awful," Mother admonishes with a pout. But we both know my assessment is on the polite side of the truth. "You used to be so close. As thick as thieves. Remember when you used to run around with that other little boy, one of the nanny's, remember? Aiden, I think his name was—"

"It wasn't," I snap without correcting her.

"You two were so competitive, always seeing who was the fastest, the strongest, who could make the most friends. You'd always work yourself into a tizzy over it."

"I don't remember," I insist. The last thing I need is for her to reconnect with Adrian Riley. She might decide to hand him even more of my money next. Or perhaps she'll conspire to give the bastard Evelyn King on a silver platter. I saw the way he looked at her. Hell, I wouldn't put it past him to hunt her down on her supposed day off, eager to seduce her for his own ends.

Luckily, a few minor facts bar said fantasy from becoming reality. For one, Evelyn isn't the sort to fall for superficial compliments, *but* if the bastard offered to let her organize his wardrobe by shape and color instead?

Only God knew what she might do.

"Graeme, are you alright?" Gloria is staring. I have my hands curled into fists, my teeth gritted.

"Besides," she continues, "Evie sends the money to *me,* and you haven't had a problem with it until now. I don't see what's the fuss if I happen to loan a family member a few pounds—"

"You know that son of yours?" I start coldly. "The one you love so much. The one who stole everything from the family home that wasn't nailed down? The one whose bastard chav mate got Stella up the duff before running back into whatever corner of London he'd crawled out of? The one who can't even be arsed to ring you on your birthday, but certainly never forgets the day his rent is due—"

"Now, now, darling. You know that I hate when you talk like this." Gloria directs her nervous glance at an old couple who keeps pausing mid-meal to gawk in our direction. "I know that you and Alexander have your... differences—"

"*Differences* doesn't even begin to describe it. I wouldn't give a damn about what your son is up to if he wasn't such a cock up, dragging *our* family name through the mud."

Like with that damn club.

In fact, I choose to remind her, "You do remember when he went out and purchased a rumored brothel, do you?"

"Graeme!" She presses a hand over her mouth.

"Then," I snarl, "he had the nerve to saddle me with the debt and threatened to drown Atelier Noir—your family's bread and butter—under a wave of scandal. Do you remember that?"

I sure as hell do. The anger that thought alone brings up is too much to even be directed at Gloria. Today, at least.

"I know how protective you can be, darling," Gloria remarks with a sigh. "But Alexander is your blood. Family. It means more than any old fortune."

"You can keep your damn money," I tell her before pushing back from the table. "For now."

"You always were a good lad, darling." Her hand finally leaves her throat and settles atop a cream-colored menu. "I could always send my *own* money to Alexander," she says. "Whatever I can scrounge up out of the measly bit of severance money I get from your father, that is. I'm sure he'd love to have me grovel before him like a pauper."

"Oh, I'm sure you'll make do out of the ten thousand pounds a month," I retort. "You might have to give up the early morning brandy, however."

She winces, but doesn't counter now that she's gotten her way. Instead, she waits until I start to stand before launching into another unwelcome topic. "So... dear Evie. Were you as dreadful to her as you were to me when you found out?"

I force myself to sit back down. "I told you that I was already aware of it." *So don't go running to her for sympathy,* is the part I hold back. The last thing I need is for Evelyn King to start second-guessing my finances.

"It's because you know she'd be on my side, and you can't stand not being the center of her attention," Mother suspects with a smug grin. "You always were the jealous sort, so protective of your favorite toys."

"Whatever helps you sleep at night, Mother."

"She's a good girl, that Evie," my mother adds, and something in her voice catches my attention. It isn't like her to sound so bloody... genuine. "And... I know that she may not be a countess or distantly related to a duchess like that Persephone girl you dated last—"

"Penelope," I interject.

"But she is a sweet girl. Perhaps if you weren't so picky when it comes to your women..."

"Then what, Mother?" Before I can help it, I picture her, Evelyn King. Blond hair that when pulled back, exposes her slender throat. Blue eyes that could get a man's dick hard with a single searching glance. Round face with a pert button nose. The body of a goddess hidden beneath her polished attire. Any bloody fool with eyes would find her ideal.

But sex is temporary, and a competent employee is hard to find. Evelyn more than fulfills her position, despite her inability to cook anything remotely edible. I can't lose her over an instance of mindless lust. Business before pleasure is a motto that hasn't failed me yet.

"I see the way you look at her sometimes," Gloria remarks with a sly grin. "When you think no one's watching, and it isn't lost on me that you insist *she* alone accompanies you to all your meetings. Oh, I remember when you were a child, and you used to drag around that horrid little stuffed animal. What was it? A cat—"

"A lion, though I don't see why this is relevant."

"You wouldn't go anywhere without it," Gloria continues with a smirk. "On the outside, you seemed so serious and surly, especially for a child, but I remember when your sister ripped the poor thing's head off, you nearly strangled her—"

"Mother."

"Then, rather than fix the toy, you locked it away in a chest somewhere. In fact, I'm sure it's still there on the family estate, gathering dust." She sighs wistfully. "Darling, you were the only child I'd ever seen who would rather deny himself what he loves than lose it to someone else."

"Frankly, I'm surprised you can recall anything about my childhood," I snap. "Given how often you had to retire early after one too many breakfast brandies."

"You treat Evelyn the same way," she says over me. "Like a toy you can stuff in your trousers when no one is watching—but she isn't. If you aren't careful, she might walk away on her own, and then where would you be?"

*Fuck.* My brain takes her words literally—Evelyn King in my trousers—and I have to grit my teeth as an image of such flits through my skull. I shake off the thought and bite out, "Frankly, she's the only person I trust to keep her damn wits about her, and not be swayed by likes of you *or* Alexander."

Or Riley. He'll expect me to hide her away in some proverbial chest, out of his reach. He wants me to panic in response to his obvious interest in her.

I won't. If he intends to make Evelyn King my weakness, I'll turn her into my *weapon*.

"It doesn't hurt that she's attractive, I suppose," Gloria remarks. "Maybe one day you might look up from your stuffy meetings and realize that."

"Mother, the only thing I find attractive about Evelyn is her ability to string a sentence together that doesn't, in effect, request money." I stand and make out a waitress hurrying in our direction. "I'll leave you to your lunch. Should you choose to drown yourself in wine today, rather than your typical martini, order a bottle of their finest, on me." As the breathless waitress approaches, I reach into my breast pocket for a business card and toss it onto the table.

"Put whatever she orders on my tab," I tell her before turning to the door. I don't have to look behind me to know that my mother is more than willing to accept my offer.

After all, her affection is completely transactional in nature.

It is a Bellamy family trait.

My first unscheduled "afternoon" off in three years unfolds the same way I figure anyone else's might—I head up to the office and straighten Bellamy's desk before inquiring about any new messages left for him with Ann, his secretary—completely out of my own curiosity. Unsurprisingly, none of them are from Adrian Riley.

For *fun*, I spend the next two hours organizing my planner, and by the time I stumble into my apartment, it's only four-forty-five—about fifteen minutes earlier than when I usually arrive home.

The moment I walk in the door, I spot the end table placed against the nearest wall, taking stock of the items neatly arranged on top of it—first, the framed picture of me and Dad, the vase he saved from his tour of Vietnam, and finally a single plastic rose I couldn't bring myself to throw away. Last is Mom's cheap clown figurine and a barely-alive ficus plant I was attempting to revive with daily infusions of tap water.

Those few objects are all I need to tether me back to reality after hours spent chasing Graeme Bellamy.

After all, this is the reason I put up with the bastard in the first place—to afford enough money to support myself with no one's help—even if it means sacrificing my sanity. Telling myself that doesn't erase the glaring fact that paying for this new condo is bankrupting me. To be fair, the expense was a small price to pay for peace of mind after a thug looking for my brother, Danny, tracked me down and tried to break in. Long story short, unless I want to lose another security deposit, or wind up on the street, I need a raise.

And I somehow have to convince Graeme Bellamy to give me one. Despite this morning's dustup, I still have hope that I can somehow wrangle him into a new contract before the week's end.

And before I lose what's left of my mind.

For now, I'm supposedly off for the rest of the day, right? After kicking off my shoes and munching on a nuked burrito fished from the back of my freezer, I head into my bedroom and set about cleaning out my closet. I double-check that everything is properly organized by color, season, and style, rearrange my shoes by height, and I've forgotten all about Graeme Bellamy and his mysterious meeting by the time six-thirty rolls around.

*Six-thirty.* It's when Bellamy finally leaves the office and heads to the gym to work out for exactly two hours. On a normal day, I'd meet Maria, his maid, about an hour before she gets off and "help" her turn down his bedsheets as well as place a satchel of lavender on his pillow before he arrives home. Lavender supposedly promotes a calm and restful sleep, and I've been determined to ensure that Graeme Bellamy enjoys its full effects for all our sakes.

Considering I have the "rest of the afternoon off," I don't have to do those things tonight. Instead, I gather my fresh laundry and safety-pin each pair of socks together. Then I shelve the items in my fridge by expiration date while attempting to ignore my neighbors—the two above are shouting while the family down below is blasting some film involving what I think is a high-pitched chipmunk singing show tunes. I've only been in this place a few weeks, but I'm already uncomfortably aware of the other tenants' habits. For instance, in exactly two minutes, the couple upstairs will loudly break off into separate rooms and slam the doors while the family downstairs will cut off the movie to signal bedtime.

The itch to escape the inevitable leads me to grab my jacket and head for the door. Normal people take walks on their days off, right? I let the resounding thud of two slamming doors and the high-pitched whining of the children down below make my decision for me. It's a brisk climb down three flights of stairs and out onto the street, where I find the evening traffic cutting a lazy flow through the quaint brownstones that dot this part of the city. I chose this building specifically for the security. It's impossible to enter without being buzzed in by a resident.

I can't let myself miss my old apartment with the breathtaking view and the bakery right across the street. Or the proximity to the office that made it only a quick ten-minute commute to work rather than a forty-five-minute sprint across a subway line and four blocks.

This location does have some merits—it's not long before I find myself in a place where rich socialites stroll the sidewalks with their teacup-whatevers while anxious bellhops attempt to flag down taxis for their wealthy patrons. When I glance up ten minutes later, it's entirely by coincidence that I find myself standing outside of a posh high-rise formed of sleek metal and polished glass—The Royal Suites.

"Evening, Ms. King," the doorman says, holding the door open with a smile. "You're always right on time. If only I had just a fraction of your dedication."

It would be rude to ignore him, so I happily approach. "Evening, William. I'm not here on business tonight."

At least not until habit completely takes over, and it's impossible to stop myself from squeezing into the next elevator going up, and riding it all the way to the top floor. There, I run into a frantic woman muttering Spanish under her breath. When she sees me, her brown eyes threaten to bulge right out of her head. "Oh, Ms. King! I thought you weren't coming. I... I tried to do those little things, but I—"

"Good evening, Maria," I say, feeling a real smile shape my mouth for the first time that day as I extend my hand for the black key card she yanks from her apron. I continue past her and approach a gleaming silver door at the hall's end. One swipe of the key card and it opens, revealing the entryway of Graeme Bellamy's penthouse.

Unlike my own hectic living arrangements, he's dwelled in this building for as long as I've known him. There's a picture of Gloria on a glass end table beside a leather chaise in the living room. The chicly modern furniture hasn't changed much in three years. Lucky bastard. I doubt he has to keep half of his belongings in storage, just in case of another last-minute move. Staying ahead of Danny and his debt has basically been a part-time job—meanwhile, his sibling quietly manages half of a billion-dollar fashion empire while backpacking across the world on whatever wellness journey has struck her fancy. Am I jealous? I don't know, maybe, but I don't give myself time to put a name to whatever emotion pings in my chest as I climb the metal staircase leading to the upper level.

The last door at the end is already ajar. When I enter the room, I find that Maria has done her best to turn down the dove-gray sheets, but I remake the bed anyway and grab a satchel of lavender from the stash I keep in the hall closet. With only ten minutes to spare, I arrange his outfit for tomorrow—the same gray suit, red tie, and patent leather he wears every Tuesday. Then I hurry back downstairs and leave, tucking the key card into a nearby ficus plant for Maria to pick up tomorrow morning.

As I head toward the elevator, I glance at my watch. Eight-forty-five. Unless there was unusually heavy traffic this evening, Mr. Bellamy should have been on his way up right about... now. I decide to play it safe by heading for the stairs, and by the time I reach the lobby, there's only the smiling doorman to greet me, and Mr. Bellamy is none the wiser.

"I thought I told you to take the day off yesterday," Mr. Bellamy admonishes when I enter his office.

I try to hide my guilt by running a hand down the front of my cream blouse and tweed skirt. His eyes track the motion, and I'm sure he's noting the many ways my appearance doesn't live up to his high standards.

If only he wasn't so damn perfect in comparison. His clothing doesn't display so much as a wrinkle. His hair is lazily slicked back as if he's been tearing through it absent-mindedly while reviewing this morning's reports. *Damn.* I hate the lurch that shoots through my belly at the thought, and I blink my gaze away while I try to form a coherent reply.

"I did," I finally insist before meeting his expression.

His eyes are a stern shade of blue, though he's wearing the outfit I left for him down to the black loafers. It's funny how the crisp, professional look dispels some of the hostility cast by his scowling expression. Almost.

"I took some time for myself," I reiterate. "I had fun. What makes you think otherwise?"

"Fun. Hmph." Grunting, Bellamy tosses a folder across his desk and snatches a pen from the neat row in his drawer. "My boxers were color-coded to my slacks and arranged according to thread count," he says. "Maria doesn't have that level of... dedication."

"Maybe she picked up some new tricks?" Before he can counter me, I reach into my bag and withdraw today's breakfast—an apple, a cup of oatmeal, and a freshly-buttered piece of multi-grain toast. "Eat. I've already set up the boardroom for this afternoon's corporate meeting. I've had Ann type up the itinerary, and perhaps later, we can talk about my contract—"

"Good. I'll tell *Ann* to meet me there," Bellamy says, cutting me off. He glances up and drills his gaze into mine to bolster the effect of his next words. "You won't accompany me today."

"W-What? Why not?" There's a whine in my tone that I can't suppress. At the thought of more "time off," my palms feel slick. "I really don't need any more—"

"I'm meeting with Adrian Riley again tonight. You will accompany me, but I need you to wear something—" He gives me a quick appraising with a sweep of his eyes. "Elegant," he declares, settling on what I assume is the politest term he comes up with. "You can model the new collection, no expense spared. I've even arranged for you to work with a personal stylist at the flagship boutique. Please consider it a gift."

The concept instantly puts me on guard. A *polite* Graeme Bellamy is a rare creature only seen when his usually smoldering temper has reached near glacial levels. When normal people start kicking in doors and punching walls, Graeme Bellamy throws around the word "please."

"Elegant," I repeat, glancing down at my current ensemble. "As in a pantsuit?" I picture the sleek one worn by Mr. Adrian's associate, Dahlia. Something tells me that without her ample attributes, such an outfit wouldn't have quite the same effect on me.

"More like a *dress*," Bellamy scoffs as if the word were some deadly disease. "I've made you an appointment with our head stylist. Nine a.m. sharp. Pick out something suitable for..."

"A business meeting?" I guess, going off his "dark" suggestion.

"No." He frowns and seems to chew over his next words before spitting them out. "Something fit for a *casual* gathering at a private club."

"A club? Like the club you and Adrian Riley spoke about?" My eyebrow shoots into a wayward fringe of hair before I can help it. Graeme Bellamy and "club" are subjects that don't even belong in the same sentence, unless separated by some clinical word or phrase. Something like "Young Billionaire's Club," "Super Rich Club," or "Asshole Boss' Club."

I wait for him to fill in the blank, but rather than rudely bark out some form of clarification, he rolls his eyes instead. "Give me the damn granola."

Right. I've been holding his breakfast hostage during our conversation.

I start forward and lay out the items neatly on his desk. He sinks his teeth into the apple just as his personal secretary,

Ann, pokes her head through the doorway. Meek and petite, Ann Delany is the one person in the world I've ever seen Mr. Bellamy show some sort of restraint with.

"I'm sorry to interrupt, Mr. Bellamy, but one of the executives mentioned something about needing to take an emergency flight out of state in a few hours, and they wanted to know if you could push up the meeting to... now—"

"Bloody hell." He tosses the apple aside and lurches to his feet. "I'm coming," he tells Ann, who promptly scurries back into the hall. "And you—" He fixes his gaze on me while straightening his tie. "You leave. James is waiting out front."

"Why can't I just go shopping after I get off?"

He hesitates, and I watch his Adam's apple bob with a twisted mixture of anticipation and admiration. He can seem so dangerous like this. Thoughtful and quiet, almost like a normal, breathtakingly handsome man who isn't driven by ruthless ambition. My mind wanders dangerously, imagining how that stern jaw would seem in a context outside of this office. Like in a bedroom, with those lips forced to occupy something other than a sales pitch...

"Because," he declares, snapping me back to reality. "I don't need you to be your usual self tonight. I need you to be—" He swallows again, seeming to fish for the right words. At the same time, his eyes track over my face and then downward, raising goosebumps as they go. "Like *them.*"

Who, exactly? He doesn't say. Instead, he storms off. Only when he's halfway to the boardroom does he glance back and mutter, "If I could be there, I would. Take this seriously. That's an order."

Dismissed, I can only stand and watch him follow Ann. Once again, I'm forced to navigate my day without the one person I'm being paid to babysit. He didn't even finish his breakfast—a fact that I know will come to bite us all in the ass later when his sugar drops and his already infamous temper turns feral. I'm tempted to nag him into taking at least a bite of granola. I've only flinched toward the desk when his voice reaches back to me, as sharp as a whip.

"Go *now*, Evelyn."

Gritting my teeth, I force myself to leave his office and march toward the elevators. By the time I exit the front entrance, James stands beside the Mercedes, ready to ferret me away. "Ready, Miss?" he questions as I clamor onto the back seat.

I'm *not* ready. Nothing good happens when things don't go according to schedule—and not once, or twice. This is the fourth time in two days that Graeme Bellamy has acted out of character. Hell, he's even been erratic if I wanted to get dramatic about it.

First, Adrian Riley.

Then, his unusually long temper tantrum yesterday and my unrequested time-off.

And today... this—sending me away in the middle of the day for a shopping excursion?

Of course, he's entitled to keep his secrets. He's allowed to order about his employee any way he sees fit. He can skip breakfast if he wants to—good for him.

But if there is one thing that Graeme Bellamy cannot do...

It is expect me to stand idly by and *not* get to the bottom of it.

My mind is spinning as James cuts through traffic and arrives before a chic boutique on the opposite side of the city, the flagship location of Atelier Noir. I suspect the distance isn't a coincidence—Bellamy wanted me far out of his way this morning. I can't decide if the "club attire" mission was contrived or legitimate as I enter the boutique stocked with impeccable clothing stamped with the Atelier Noir brand.

A beaming saleswoman dressed in a black dress approaches me. "Ms. King? Mr. Bellamy called to tell us that you were coming. Welcome! He's already had us prepare a few selections for you."

"Selections?" I don't like the sound of that. My anxiety is only heightened as the woman leads me through the store and toward a room lined in red velvet where what I assume is a changing area is cordoned off by a scarlet curtain. There, hanging on a far wall, is an array of clothing so exquisite that my palms sweat at the thought of trying them on—silk, satin, lace...

I've seen concept sketches of the garments, of course, drawn up by the company's head of design, his sister Stella— though, like a true masochistic perfectionist, Bellamy reviews them all himself before sending them off to be refined.

Seeing the actual creations in person is another matter entirely. Perched on a table nearby is a selection of black heels, and... no, it can't be. I shake my head and blink a few times, but the items don't disappear.

"Is something wrong?" the saleswoman wonders.

I shake my head. "N-No, nothing."

Other than the fact that Graeme Bellamy apparently went so far as to select *underwear* for me, in addition to the clothing.

As if on cue, my cell phone buzzes, and I withdraw it only to find a single command flash across the screen:

*Show me each item as you try it on.*

Then, seconds later, a far more clarifying statement—*This isn't a request.*

My palms feel sweaty, and the world starts to spin. He couldn't possibly mean... Could he? I'm shaking so badly I can barely type out the words—*Are you, as my boss, commanding that I strip for you?*

His reply, and its swiftness, takes my breath away. Barely a second later, I'm staring dumfounded at the words—*If that's what it will take for you to comply. Fine. Think of it that way.*

I'm so stunned I promptly drop my phone on the floor. While the worried assistant chases after it, all I can do is stare into space with a single thought running through my mind on a loop.

That son of a bitch.

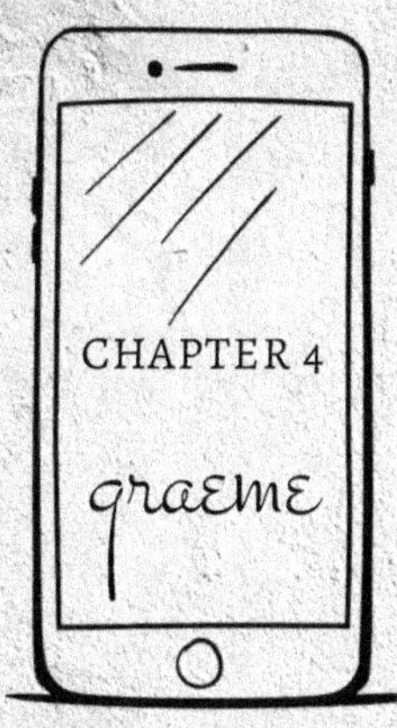


D amn Evelyn King and her fucking pouty bottom lip. The sight of her haunts me—or, to be exact, my cock. I feel like a blasted teenager, locking my thighs together during my next series of meetings, just to keep my own lust in check.

*Enough.* I slam my hand onto the desk before me merely to snap some sense back into my brain. Tonight has nothing to do with seeing Evelyn out of those matronly blouses for the first damn time. It is about keeping her protected. If Riley makes the mistake of thinking my interest in her is merely physical, then he won't have any interest in using her as a cudgel in his childish game of revenge.

At least, it's my gamble.

After back-to-back appointments, I return to my office to find the remains of her bloody breakfast on my desk. I start to pitch the oatmeal into the rubbish bin, but at the last minute, I snatch up a fork and take a bite. It's awful, as per usual, but with every forced swallow, I can smell her scent, still lingering in the air. Roses.

*Damn her.*

Ignoring the dry texture, I down the whole thing, determined to write off the headache pounding behind my temples as a result of that damned hypoglycemia she loves to cite so much.

It has nothing at all to do with the lack of reply to the text message I sent her nearly four hours ago. It has nothing at all to do with the annoying suspicion that she somehow escaped James and is busy micromanaging my life from some nearby broom closet. It has nothing to do with the way Adrian Riley undressed her with his fucking eyes like she was some kind of tart on display for his amusement.

In irritation, I circle my desk and peer beneath it, half expecting to find her crouched there, clutching her precious little planner for dear life.

The fantasy gives me an idea—the next time she disobeys me, I'll burn it. Or perhaps use it as a carrot to get what I want—her, stoically by my side, well beyond the reach of anyone. Least of all, Riley.

"Mr. Bellamy?" I turn to find Ann in the doorway, twirling a lock of brown hair around her finger. "Do you need me for anything else?"

"No," I tell her, turning my attention back to my desk. There's a proposal to look over. Accounts to check. Bastard gits to placate on the board. There is no time to pull my mobile from my breast pocket and hunt the text messages for a certain reply.

Nothing. My thumbs fly, drafting a new message in seconds. *Answer me. Now.* I hit send and drop the device onto my desk. Not even a minute later, it buzzes with an incoming message.

*This isn't necessary. I have my own clothes.*

Like the navy blouse with pearl buttons Riley's goddamn eyes practically bore a hole through.

"Bloody hell..." I have to suck in a breath and release it slowly just to prevent my thumb from striking the call button. Evelyn would anticipate a ring, during which she could easily browbeat me into letting her have her way. Instead, I type —*If you leave that store without a dress, I will deduct the cost of the most expensive item from your paycheck, are we understood, Evelyn?*

Seconds later, the mobile vibrates, and I flick open a picture of what seems to be red velvet curtains. I assume it's the inside of a dressing room. Cheeky. Another line of text appears before I can respond. *I must pick one of your options.*

Wisely, the statement isn't framed as a question. More like a taunt. For all her enthusiasm when it comes to managing my life, Evelyn King doesn't appreciate being micromanaged in turn. Something I'd anticipated.

*I gave you plenty of options,* I retort, but her reply comes so swiftly that she must have expected it.

*Why not just choose one for me?*

I don't tell her the truth—*Because I know you would quit.* I take my time, staring out the window while thinking up a reply. Why supply Evelyn King with a limited selection of clothing to choose from, down to the most intimate of details? If I wanted to be honest with myself, I'd admit that having Evelyn accompany me is part of a subtler plan of sabotage. Adrian Riley thought that by parading me into his office and flaunting the idea of a merger, I'd fold and let him take the lion's share of my brother's mistake. He thought wrong.

Tonight, Evelyn King will serve as a weapon. I need her honed. I need her sharp. I need her in bloody tailored satin whether she likes it or not. Riley won't be able to ogle her body without seeing my goddamn brand draped all over it.

*Humor me,* I tell her, and then I toss the phone aside, prepared to spend the rest of the afternoon managing accounts. I open the laptop, usually shoved to the farthest corner of my desk, and shuffle the documents, only to be distracted by my vibrating mobile. I reach for it with one hand and open the incoming message. I expect another whining missive from Evelyn. Instead, I find a picture—three pairs of women's undergarments, all of them black, elegantly displayed on a strip of red silk. *Which one?* She's captioned.

Cheeky woman. Evelyn King, queen of propriety and order, doesn't like to be on the receiving end of her own brand of management. Her annoyance is all the more amusing when paired with the fact that I know the prudish, uptight façade is all an act. I once saw her tell a man who groped her to go fuck himself in French, all while keeping her face in a mask of bland politeness. Apparently, she wants to play a battle of wills.

With an hour to kill before my next meeting, I'll oblige her.

Pushing back from the desk, I observe each garment in grainy detail. One pair is a simple brief and a matching bra—part of a French-inspired collection with imported lace Stella insisted we release last season. Beside it is a bit more feminine design with a fringe of lace lining both the knickers and the bustier. While the last...

I suppose the saleswoman I'd tasked to compile my selection had assumed that picking clothes for a "female associate" meant something much more intimate than the title implied. One set is purely lingerie, formed of a bra that doesn't have a chance in hell of supporting much, and a matching strip of lace that only distantly resembles knickers.

Gloria's words choose to haunt me—*It doesn't hurt that she's attractive, I suppose. Maybe one day you might look up from your stuffy meetings and realize that.*

I have bloody eyes. I know that she turns heads every time I bring her into a blasted meeting with some horny associate. Yet...

Given her value as an employee, I had enough sense of mind to keep our interactions strictly professional. Until now. My jaw goes slack at the thought of her in the spring collection, and I can't stop my mind from conjuring images of what lurks beneath those thin strips of material. My cock stiffens, and I suspect it, rather than my brain, is in control as I type out a reply. *The one on the left. The thong,* I add by way of clarification. *Hurry up.* Out of pure curiosity, I add, *Unless, of course, you aren't as dedicated to your performance as I thought.*

Five minutes pass without a reply, and I regain control of my senses enough to attempt to return to my work. Four briefings later, and still, nothing. Have I rendered the great Evelyn King speechless? I've only begun to entertain the thought when an incoming message illuminates the screen—*So, do you want to see what they look like on?*

A sound tears from my throat so suddenly that Ann runs into my office, her expression concerned. "Are you alright, Sir?"

"Fine," I bite out, trying to discern what the hell that sound could have been. A cough? It damn well wasn't a laugh. Evelyn King isn't one for humor. The moment Ann leaves, I scan the message again. Taken out of context, the words could be interpreted as a come-on. Coming from anyone else, they damn well would be.

Evelyn King, on the other hand, doesn't flirt the same way she doesn't laugh, smile, or show any ounce of human emotion other than annoyance when defied and satisfaction once she's gotten her way. No, this is a challenge, one that a good employer would ignore. Knowing her, she's counting on that show of restraint.

But Gloria hadn't been entirely coy by suggesting the woman was attractive.

She is, which makes her a target ripe for exploitation by Adrian Riley. He'll home in on her like a heat-seeking missile, and I plan to circumvent him, no matter the cost. The good news is that if the clothing alone makes her feel out of her element, I'm on the right bloody path.

*If you must, then by all means, try them on,* I tell her, watching the words appear on the screen. The corner of my mouth quirks at the thought of her reaction. She'll bite her lip and scowl. Then she'll ignore me, grudgingly accept the simplest items offered and show up twenty minutes later to nag about the importance of lunch before shoving that damned planner in my face to remind me of my next appointment. *Your hypoglycemia, Mr. Bellamy. You know how you are when you skip meals...*

The screen lights up. I glance down. I... stare.

Evelyn King scowls back at me, wearing nothing but a lacey bra and matching knickers. She must have gotten a sales worker to take the photo. I can see the velvet interior of a dressing room behind her, along with a row of three hooks, each displaying a closed garment bag. She does her best to cover what the bra doesn't with her hands, but the undergarments can't hide...

That I've overestimated her size, for one. The brazier straps hang loose on her shoulders. The knickers ride too low over delicate hip bones. Enhancing the overall effect is the way she's glaring at me, her eyes narrowed, her lips... she's bloody pouting. Who would have known that the flawless Evelyn King was even capable of looking remotely sullen?

I don't know why the thought of it makes the corner of my mouth lift higher. I scan her body, trying to ignore the urge to tally up the things I had never really noticed beneath all those damn blouses she wore. She has breasts. Decent ones. Add to that slender hips and thighs. Only on the third pass of her do I finally notice the line she's captioned the photo with—*You might want to reconsider your option.*

I think not, Evelyn. *Dress next,* I tell her, trying to remember which designs I had selected for her to try on. Frankly, I don't give a damn as to the style or color. All that matters is that she fits the atmosphere of the club—an environment about as far from Evelyn King's comfort zone as the earth is from the sun.

Ten minutes later, I'm interrupted from business once again as three photos arrive in sync. In one, Evelyn is wearing what I assume is the most conservative of the selected gowns—a black cocktail dress with a modest neckline. I write it off based on her neutral expression alone—too safe. The next one seems promising—a cream dress with a hem that brushes her knees and a scooped neckline to display those breasts she apparently loves to hide. Her frown is an encouraging sign. But the third option...

I notice her posture first. She stands stiffly, her arms held tightly to her sides, her blue eyes wide with a mixture of revulsion and discomfort. The gown is red, sinfully tight with a plunging V-shaped neckline—part of the new collaboration with an emerging Italian artist set to debut next year.

And if you cut off the head, this woman doesn't resemble Evelyn King.

*This one,* I tell her. Sure enough, she replies before I can set my phone down again.

*Is this an official assignment?* I assume that's her cheeky way of asking, "Is that an order, Sir?"

*It is,* I reply. *Put it on my tab and return to the office.* After a moment's pause, I add, *And yes, I remember the Perigrine meeting at one,* using her obsession with schedules to my benefit for once.

When minutes pass without a response, I attempt to prepare for that damn aforementioned meeting. I've barely begun to rise from my desk when Ann appears in the doorway. "Your next appointment is here, Sir."

I force myself to nod. "Show him into the board room." Ann takes off, and I stall by smoothing my papers into a pile, straightening the edges. It is a moot point, as Evelyn will likely come in after me and tidy up what I've already done. Still, the task prolongs the moment I'll have to face that damn Perigrine alone. The flagship store is in another borough, and in this traffic, Evelyn won't arrive in time to catch the meeting.

Which is fine with me. Without her there to nag about blood glucose levels, I might actually get some bloody work done.

Ten minutes later, I'm seated across from Andrew Perigrine, the majority shareholder in one of the most prominent PR firms in the states. He's droning on about numbers, stakes, and statistics rather than jumping to the main reason he required to meet with me—a merger. I draw my mobile from my pocket to check my messages while the bastard rambles. There's the quarterly report from the finance office to scour.

Ann's sent me an updated list of my latest appointments for the next month.

And Evelyn King is glaring at me through the screen.

A polite man might delete the picture of her—though Evelyn will most likely comb through the device later and do it herself. That fact alone makes her humiliation fair game at the moment. I can't decide if she's lost weight or if her posture makes her seem so thin. I could encircle one of her thighs with my hand. Not that I'd want to.

Not that she'd let me.

"Did you hear what I said, Bellamy?" I glance up to find Peregrine watching me with one eyebrow raised.

"Something about the prestige of your clientele?" I say, taking a stab in the dark.

"Oh. Well, yes." Placated, the man continues to rattle off his company's many accolades while my gaze returns to the screen of my mobile. And Evelyn bloody King.

My last message had been more than clear, and I know her well enough to suspect that she won't outright disobey a direct order. However much it makes her seethe, she'll wear the damned dress. Rubbing that fact in was merely for my own enjoyment.

*Did you buy the red one?* I ask.

Her reply is so crisply phrased that I can practically hear her clip the words out loud. *I feel the black would have been a better choice... but yes.*

There's no reason not to take her at her word—but my thumb seems to strike the next keys of its own accord. *Proof.*

She's silent for five whole minutes of Perigrine's blather. I've begun to turn my attention back to the actual task at hand when her reply finally illuminates the screen—a snapshot of a white clothing box she must have balanced on her lap. Folded inside is the red dress and nothing else. I assume the arrangement is for dramatic effect. Evelyn King isn't happy. But she's also dutiful to a fault.

*And the undergarments? Where are those?* I expect a quick photo in response, but all that appears are eight little words I never expected.

*Change of plans. I'm better off without them.*

"And then we'll... Bellamy?" Peregrine stops short as my mobile crashes loudly onto the conference table. I can't even salvage the scowl I can feel my mouth curling into.

Trust Evelyn King to have the last bloody laugh.

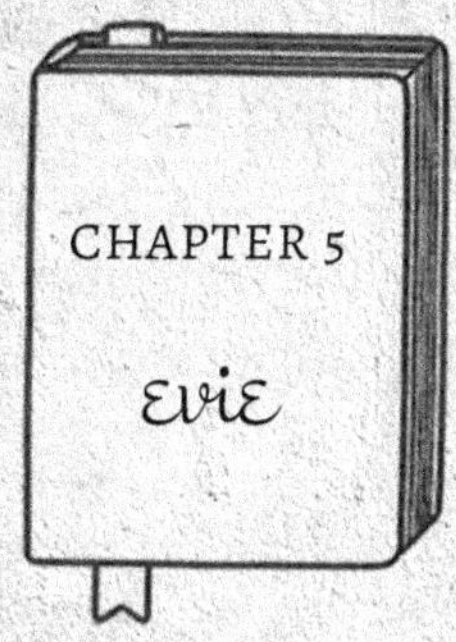


My heart skips a beat as James brings the Mercedes around the front of Atelier Noir headquarters. When I eye the imposing, gray building, I feel the same apprehension I felt the very first day I showed up, wearing a blouse two seasons out of style with a smudge of lipstick on the corner of my sleeve and a month's worth of poor sleep evident beneath my eyes. In the three years since, I thought I'd finally left that girl behind—trading her in for a newer, harder model who didn't take shit from anyone, not even Graeme Bellamy himself.

With one swipe of his platinum credit card Bellamy almost took it all away—along with my underwear. All because of some fucking meeting with Adrian Riley, one I was obviously not privy to know anything about. If I were smart, I would have demanded a raise then and there as compensation for this latest humiliation. No bother—somehow, someway, I'll make him play.

I let that simmering resentment drive me out onto the curb with my planner tucked carefully under one arm. It could be just another trip to the office if it wasn't for the heavy shopping bag dangling from my other hand. The implications of the past few hours finally sink in as my arm registers the weight—he is actually going to make me wear that dress.

He's making me accompany him to a club, containing only god knows what.

*He* is making *me*—which simply isn't how things typically work in the world of Graeme Bellamy and his dutiful assistant, Evelyn. I tell *him* what to wear and how to wear it. I tell him what time of day to arrive. What events he has to attend. When. Where. Why.

It's what he pays me to do, after all. Not this. I don't like *this* —him... bossing *me*. A nervous swallow contracts my throat, and I shake my head to combat the unease. Regardless of the feeling, Evelyn King doesn't back down from anything or anyone—not anymore.

Ignoring the curious stares of those I pass, I take the elevator up to the top floor and barge straight into Graeme Bellamy's office with my head held high—in theory. In reality, I creep through the doorway, my heart pounding with every step, only to find that the man himself is nowhere in sight.

Oh, thank god. I glance over my shoulder to find that Ann isn't even in her usual spot in the waiting room outside his door, either. Rather than wonder why that might be, I close the door behind me and attempt to get my bearings. Unsurprisingly, his desk is a mess—papers scattered in a haphazard stack and his pens lying strewn across the polished surface. He must have been in a rush for his next meeting—which he wouldn't have been if I were there. Dropping the shopping bag on a leather chair placed nearby, I run my fingers along the desk's surface. I've only begun to reach for the nearest document when a trickle of cool air brushes my neck.

"I thought I told you to meet me once you've *changed*, Evelyn."

I flinch and turn to find Graeme Bellamy standing a few feet behind me, his eyes a glacial shade of blue. Before I can compose myself, he nods toward the shopping bag and then jerks his chin to the door. "I suggest you do so. Now."

Ignoring the command, I scan every inch of him. At a glance, I can tell that he's skipped lunch, probably breakfast as well, judging from the alarming tilt of his chin. His jaw is clenched, his gaze honed and focused. But...

He's looking at me wrong. All wrong. Well, he's actually *staring*, for one. His eyes perform a slow crawl from the top of my head down to my chest, and an unfortunate feeling comes to life in their wake.

Maybe it's residual shock? After all—even though it was under duress—I stripped for him and modeled a thong via images. Images that are still on his phone. Images that he could blackmail me with later.

Dear god, what had gotten into me?

"I hope you requested a smaller size," he remarks while straightening his tie. His voice contains no inflection—he could have been commenting on the weather. Not my clothing size. Not my *breasts*. Both of which he had become more than familiar with within the past hour. In an almost comical silence, he cocks his head and glances at the "smaller" items in question. I turn away as my cheeks catch fire. I will *not* allow myself to regret what transpired in the dressing room. He asked. He received.

I complied...

Maybe the impulsiveness stemmed from the fact that he didn't do things like this—challenge me. Order me around. I know how to react when he sulks. Or when he threatens, glowers, or simmers like the devil.

In this instance? I'm woefully out of my element.

But I won't back down without a fight. "I did," I say, hating how high-pitched my voice sounds. "But I think I may need them specifically tailored. To properly accommodate my size, I mean."

Abruptly Bellamy clears his throat, and I don't know why I relish my brief bit of triumph so much. I've knocked him off balance for once. Good.

"I'll arrange it."

"What?" It takes everything I have in me to face him again and not flinch.

"I'll arrange to have the items tailored to you specifically." His eyes are as steely as ever, narrowed with focus. "Change and freshen up. We'll go to dinner, before..." He can't seem to mention anything about a club. Instead, he shakes his head. "There, we can discuss things."

Discuss. Things. *Things* such as Adrian Riley, mysterious clubs, and his sudden demand for me to wear gowns worth more than my rent, maybe? Or perhaps that raise I've been dancing around? I try to bite back the questions as I snatch up the shopping bag. Jutting my chin into the air, I stroll past Graeme Bellamy, out into the hall, and enter the single bathroom at the edge of the adjacent waiting room.

With the door closed and locked, I fish the gown from the bag and hold it up to my chest. My scowling reflection reveals my feelings perfectly. Oddly enough, I don't hate the dress, per se. It's something I would never wear, though I'm familiar enough with Bellamy's past girlfriends—many of whom had graced the society spread of magazines on Mr. Bellamy's arm, wearing his precious designs—to know that it's his style. Satin. Expensive. Well-tailored. The man has taste—even I can give him that.

Sighing, I strip off my blouse and skirt and tug on the dress. It's halfway up my hips when I remember the goddamned underwear. Or lack thereof... I don't know what possessed me to buy the set he chose anyway, tucked away at the bottom of the shopping bag. The thong taunts me, its silken tag gleaming in the artificial light. I'm sure he made me wear them as a joke—some chauvinistic way of proving that he, Graeme Bellamy, owns me, no matter how many breakfasts I might nag him to eat or closets I may organize.

He could only wish. I do cave, however, and wear the bra. Even in a smaller size, the straps hang loose on me. Unlike the bony, stick-thin but still well-endowed women Bellamy tends to date, some benevolent surgeon has never enhanced my chest with silicone. Not to mention the fabric is so damn thin that I can see my nipples through it. Dark. Erect.

An embarrassing reaction that *isn't* because of Graeme Bellamy.

That statement plays like a mantra as I pull the gown's straps over my shoulders and zip it up one-handed. The one item I apparently had no say in is a pair of dangerously high black heels that the saleswoman had picked out without comment. Once I've touched up my makeup and finger-styled my hair, the outfit is complete—*avant-garde* humiliation.

When I fold my clothes neatly into the shopping bag with the abandoned scrap of underwear, I do my best not to show fear as I exit the bathroom. Already awaiting my walk of shame, I find Bellamy in his office, his back turned to me, his eyes on the view of the city in that sleepy pre-rush-hour traffic.

He stiffens as I approach. "Well, Evelyn..." He turns. He continues to stare. He frowns.

In two strides, he's crossed over to me, his jaw clenched so tightly it actually seems like polished marble. Without warning, he reaches out and snags the black bra strap intertwined with the dress' red. "Seriously, Evelyn, it's like you're *trying* to be insufferable," he grouses. "Lift your arms."

My heart stalls as his heat bites through my skin. I don't know whether to slap him or... *really* slap him. "W-What?"

"Your arms." He gestures with his free hand until I warily oblige. Then, without loosening his grip on the bra strap, he maneuvers himself to stand behind me and snatches up the other strap. "These things tend to be versatile, Evelyn," he explains, right before his fingers drift down... Too low. The pads of his thumbs graze my shoulder blades as they slide beneath the back of the gown. Goosebumps prickle my flesh. My heart stops beating. I stop breathing.

His touch is felt in snatches through the lacy material of the bra—manicured fingers hunting for something alongside the tiny fastenings. I feel two of his fingertips meet, hear a small click, and suddenly one of the straps is looser than before. He does the same to the other side, grunting under his breath as the mechanism resists him for a few seconds.

"It's a new design implemented specifically for convenience," he mutters. It takes two firm tugs on the bra's frame before he gets his way. I'm swaying on my feet by the time he steps back.

"Turn," he tells me. I gape over my shoulder to find that he's even making a circular motion with his finger. When I don't move, he circles me himself. In the blink of an eye, he's in front of me, his breath basting my throat, his gaze fixed much lower than it should be. He reaches for my shoulders, and I finally regain enough control over my body to jerk out of his reach.

"What the hell is wrong with you? First your erratic behavior the past few days, and now this." I don't even recognize the breathless voice that comes out of me. I feel along my side only to remember that, given his current position between me and my things, he's holding my bag hostage, along with my emergency stash of protein bars. "I think you need to eat something *now*," I tell him, pointing a shaking finger in his direction. "Or I'm not going anywhere."

"Seriously, Evelyn." He cocks his head and approaches me before I can stagger back. His hands graze my shoulders... and then dip beneath the neckline of the gown, hunting for the straps. With a well-timed flick of each thumb, they come off altogether. Frowning, Mr. Bellamy holds them out to me, and only then do I register the unspoken meaning hidden within that gruffly uttered "seriously"—*Seriously, Evelyn, as if I would even deign to grope someone like you.*

I'm still gaping when he tosses the discarded bra straps onto the desk after I don't move to take them. His hands come for me again, tugging at the red satin until the front falls smoothly. He doesn't avoid any erogenous areas, instead sweeping his palm along the side of my ribcage to readjust the bra. His face, however, is the pure picture of suave professionalism.

For a second.

Then, it's as if a shadow falls over those flawless features. His eyes narrow as they skim over my shoulder and along my exposed throat. A muscle in his jaw twitches. I swear I feel his fingers slip, drawing a gasp from me as they ghost along the bare skin right beside where the straps fall. My brain plays a dangerous game, imagining what those same fingers would feel like if they drifted lower, beneath the material of this dress and...

"There," Bellamy declares while stepping back, apparently satisfied by my appearance. "Now we can go."

He strides for the door, but I remain frozen in place. Too many thoughts clamor in my mind for me to make sense of any of them. Graeme Bellamy just put his hands on me. He saw me partially naked.

Admittedly, one of those events was entirely my fault. Regardless, I inhale and exhale a harsh breath. My world is changing—rearranging—and I'm not sure whether or not this is really all some distorted nightmare.

"Evelyn." Bellamy lingers in the doorway with his back to me. I half expect him to snap his fingers to complement the harsh tone.

For the first time, I realize that he's already changed into a deep, ebony suit—the one he usually paired with a navy tie to offset the color of his eyes. He's opted for a gray one tonight, once again changing his predictable routine.

"Dinner," he reminds.

The commanding way he says it finally makes my throat work again. "Have... have you lost your mind?" I'm actually concerned. Without a decent breakfast or lunch, his blood sugar is probably reaching dangerously low levels. For all I know, he could be delirious.

"No. The only thing I am in danger of losing now is my *patience*, Evelyn." He flicks his collar before marching out into the hall.

I watch him, digging my heels into the polished floor. "You need an energy bar," I say with a note of challenge in my voice. "I'm not going anywhere until you eat something. *Now.*"

Without glancing back at me, Bellamy reaches into his pocket, angling his body so I can't miss the small energy bar he withdraws from his pocket. With a flick of his wrist, he tears the package open and then rips off a bite with his teeth. "Come," he barks after swallowing.

My mind is in a daze as I stagger after him and into the elevator he summons to take us to the lower floor. When the elevator doors open, we draw eyes from every breathing organism in the lobby. The receptionist pauses mid-phone call to gape while a group of executives heading to the door freezes open-mouthed. Ironically, the focus of their attention isn't Graeme Bellamy, who cuts a disgustingly handsome figure in his suit, despite the half-eaten snack bar in his grip.

No, this time, they're staring at me—Evelyn King, the current object of the CEO's scorn.

He *must* hate me, for some unknown vengeful reason. These past two days are punishment for something—some slight I don't remember or some insult I committed against him. Believing that was so much more comforting than the alternative—Graeme Bellamy is acting out of character because he knows something I don't. Something about Adrian Riley and this club. Something that has him... anxious.

I try my best to combat the thought as I follow Bellamy into the Mercedes. James attempts to beat the rush hour traffic, but we get stuck in the thick of it only a few blocks from the office. Amid the resounding barrage of honking horns and drivers shouting from car windows, I almost don't notice when Bellamy speaks.

"You can stop pouting now, Evelyn," he tells me gruffly. With one last bite, he finishes his snack bar and tosses the wrapper aside. "As promised, I will explain."

"Really?" I sit straighter, folding my hands over my lap. So many pressing questions jockey for precedence over my tongue. Before he can speak again, I pick what seems to be the most vital of mysteries to unravel. "So, who is Adrian Riley?"

I'm holding my breath, though I don't realize until his eyes cut in my direction, and I choke out a startled exhale. It could be a trick of the waning daylight, but the expression on his face almost looks... human for once—uneasy.

"An old family *acquaintance*," he says. It's not exactly an in-depth bio, but it's enough to satisfy my curiosity. For now. "We have a long history, Riley and I—"

"History? Wh-what kind? If you don't mind my asking." Were they childhood friends, perhaps? Though, honestly, I can't picture Graeme Bellamy as a child. That would require him to have, at one point in his life, been vulnerable. Innocent, even—which is far from how he looks now.

Blue eyes ablaze, he watches me for a moment. "Let's just say it isn't exactly a pleasant one."

"Ah." I nod, mentally filing away every nuance in his expression and every word. "And this club? You're thinking of some kind of agreement…"

Bellamy jerks his chin to glare out of the window. "Think of it more like collateral. I won't get into the specifics of it now," he says, but before I can argue, he adds, "Just know that it isn't typical of my other business ventures."

An atypical club. I glance down at the plunging neckline of my dress. Little by little, his erratic behavior is starting to make sense—and at least now I can link it to something with definite proof. Adrian Riley and his strange club.

"So, this meeting…"

"It's an important one," he admits, sighing. "Frankly, that's all I feel you should know for now. At least on that subject."

Fair enough. The request won't save him in the long run, of course. I will eventually get to the bottom of this, but something in his expression makes it easier to back down. For now.

"Then, after tonight, everything will go back to normal?" I can't ignore the hopeful tone in my voice at the prospect. *Normal. Order. Freedom from this chaos.* "By that, I mean, a regular schedule and no impromptu shopping trips, and time to discuss my contract?"

As if sensing my anxiety, Bellamy shifts in his seat and strokes his jaw with his index finger. "Perhaps."

It's not exactly a promise, but I latch onto it anyway.

Twenty minutes later, James deposits us in the front of a posh building in the heart of the Upper East Side. *Elegant* is the only word that can even remotely describe the brick façade graced by a ruby-red awning. Two waiters in matching black suits stand beside the entrance and spring into action to open the doors when Bellamy and I approach.

Crossing the threshold is like wandering into a parallel realm as a million implications sink in—I've never been with him to dinner before. Never like this. Never... alone. The dining room is spacious, with dimmed lights casting an intimate ambiance. Waiters and waitresses dressed in demure black uniforms do their best to blend into the background while guests wearing business suits or designer couture sip on glasses of wine and chardonnay.

"Bellamy. Reservation for four," Bellamy declares to a smiling host who promptly leads us through a maze of black tables topped with cream tablecloths.

"Four?" The question barely leaves my mouth when my gaze falls over the couple seated a few tables away. Adrian Riley sits with his head cocked, mouth lowered near the ear of his table companion—the same woman who met us in his office, Dahlia. She laughs at whatever he says, her eyes sparkling as they flit in our direction. With his mouth set in a permanent half-smirk, her companion copies her, his gaze ghosting over me.

"Bellamy," Riley calls out to us, his voice easily carrying across the room. "So glad that you could join us."

His charming smile is magnetic, his expression nothing but a mask of politeness—an appearance that serves as a stark contrast to Bellamy's reaction. If I'm not mistaken, he growls. The sound travels down my spine, resonating in the satin of this damn dress. I feel his discomfort in my bones with every step we take toward the table. To those who don't know him as well as I do, the way he shakes Mr. Riley's hand could almost seem friendly.

Not feral.

"I was able to clear my schedule at the last minute," Bellamy says before running his palm down the side of his slacks. It's a subtle gesture of hostility that I'm sure no one at the table misses. Regardless, Mr. Riley's smile only seems to widen.

"At the last minute," he repeats softly. His eyes drift in my direction and settle over the front of my dress. "I hope you weren't *too* inconvenienced, Ms. King."

I dig my nails into my palms to reinforce my dad's old mantra. *Stiff upper lip, Evie. Never let them see ya sweat.*

"Not at all," I manage to croak.

"Lovely."

My cheeks catch fire as Adrian Riley flashes yet another dazzling display of white teeth, but the expression sets me on edge in ways I can't explain. Maybe it's the elbow that Mr.

Bellamy rams into my side as if to reinforce the gist of our prior conversation—use my skill of observation.

"This is Dahlia," Riley says, gesturing to the beautiful woman beside him. "Though I believe you met earlier, at the office."

She smiles demurely and casts us a searching glance from beneath her eyelashes. "Hello. It's a pleasure to see you again," she says, her eyes on Bellamy. "I am a frequent patron of Atelier Noir's European distributors during my visits overseas."

"I must say, the quality has improved drastically over the years," Mr. Riley interjects, his upper lip quirked.

As my brain processes his words, I feel my cheeks catch fire. Is he implying what I think he is? Looking at him and Dahlia, I can't tell a damn thing. They hold themselves with a professional, though impersonal posture, that makes it hard to discern whether they are strangers, or more intimate partners than client and lawyer...

A few more polite introductions go around, but the moment Mr. Bellamy reaches for a chair and pulls it out for me to sit, it's like he's picking up the gauntlet that Adrian Riley himself set down by inviting him here. When Bellamy takes the seat beside me, I sense the tension boil over like water in a kettle.

"So, Bellamy," Mr. Riley says from across the table. "I trust you've settled okay in the States."

"Quite," Bellamy says tersely. He even manages to force his lips into the semblance of a smile, but there's no real warmth in it. "I'm beginning to think that perhaps America isn't as bloody obnoxious as I was once led to believe."

Even the waitress who ambles past our table senses the barely concealed dig. She covers her mouth with her hand and glances away, but Adrian Riley merely laces his fingers together over his elegant place setting. In an instant, his smile falls, revealing a guarded expression that one might cautiously deem "thoughtful." "Oh, there is plenty that America has to offer," he insists. "This city especially. I think you'll completely change your mind once you see what we've done with the club."

"*Your* club," Bellamy corrects as he reaches for a bundle of silverware expertly rolled within a square of black linen. He unfolds his napkin and lays out each silver utensil beside his plate, finishing with a gleaming steak knife which—by coincidence or fate—happens to point directly toward Adrian Riley. "*My* club is being managed without incident in London."

*A club in London?* I do my best to hide my shock and reach for a pitcher of water resting in the center of the table. I pour myself a glass and take a hasty sip before silently offering the pitcher to anyone else. Dahlia shakes her head, but Adrian Riley raises his glass, his mouth curved into another dangerous smile.

"If I may."

"Of course." I pour him a moderate amount while Bellamy's gaze bores a hole through my cheek. If I didn't know any better, I'd think... *No way.* He can't be jealous. Right?

"It's funny you should mention the London club," Adrian continues after a sip from his glass. "From what I've heard, it's been running exceptionally smooth. Though there is one rumor I've found of particular interest..."

Bellamy glances up. "I didn't know you were one to partake in gossip, Riley."

"Of course." Adrian chuckles, but he knows as well as everyone else at the table that the remark wasn't a friendly bit of banter. "This information comes from a reputable source," he says smoothly. "Depending on who you ask. This source seemed to be of the mind that you would welcome the chance to sell, what with your company's reputation to uphold."

"Is that so?" My entire body stiffens at the distinct, guttural murmur.

Graeme Bellamy has exactly two settings when it comes to voice volume. The normal rich baritone he typically converses in—and then the *growl*—that husky, lowered octave that makes every hair on the back of my neck stand on end. "And did this 'source' seem to think I'd easily sell my stake and let you take off with the lion's share?"

He's still smiling, but the grotesque motion of his lips doesn't soften the harsh undertone of his words any. I've only seen him like this once before, when Gloria mentioned inviting the "family" over for Christmas. I'd assumed then that he just hadn't wanted to spend time with Stella. Now, I'm not so sure. Adrian Riley seems to be dancing around someone's identity on purpose. But who? And why?

"I have to say that I'm surprised by how dutifully you've accepted this responsibility, Bellamy," Adrian says softly. The fingers of his left hand capture the gold ring on the pinky of his right, spinning it around the digit. "You wouldn't strike the average person as the type to be the proprietor of a tawdry *gentleman's* club."

"A what?" My mouth falls open. Water spills out. As I sputter, Bellamy snatches up my silverware and rips off the cloth napkin.

"Here," he snaps, shoving it into my hands.

"Thank you." I do my best to dab at my mouth while staring down at the table's polished surface, but I can't seem to catch my breath, no matter how many coughs I smother into the cloth.

The room is spinning. Adrian Riley's words are buzzing through my head. *Gentlemen's... club.*

"A wise businessman merely goes where the opportunity takes him," I hear Bellamy retort, but his voice is almost a murmur now. So deadly soft. After three years, routine is enough to overcome any shock. He needs to eat something —*now*—for all our sakes.

Glancing up, I flag down a nearby waitress. "I'm ready to order. The steak," I tell her, "Rare. With um..." I reach for a menu and hunt for the starchiest, most fulfilling items that can skyrocket a man's blood sugar in minutes. "A baked potato. French bread. Fresh squeezed orange juice—"

"Flounder for her," Bellamy cuts in. "Grilled, strawberry salad on the side." I'm left dumbfounded as he snatches the menu from my hands and places it on his before handing both to the waitress. Fish and some version of veggies is my go-to meal whenever we wind up at a business lunch. I'd always thought he'd been too focused on the task at hand to notice. Apparently, he had.

From across the table, Adrian Riley watches the exchange with what I'm starting to believe is a permanent half-smile. "We'll have the same," he says without even bothering to ask Dahlia her choice, not that she seems to mind the slight. I'm starting to suspect this outing isn't about food at all. It's about power. Adrian Riley and Graeme Bellamy are wrestling over something—the beautiful stranger seated across from me, and I are merely spectators brought to ensure the match doesn't get too bloody.

"My apologies for the delay, Ms. King," Mr. Riley says smoothly. His eyes stare straight into mine, and I could almost swear he was genuine.

"It's nothing. I... I have hypoglycemia," I blurt while Bellamy promptly stiffens beside me. "Sorry for interrupting."

But neither man rushes to take up the previous conversation topic in the ensuing silence. Instead, Adrian Riley mentions the Parisian art scene, and Dahlia perks up as they launch into a friendly debate about the classics.

When our food arrives, I snatch up a slice of French bread, slather it with butter and drop it onto Bellamy's plate before he can argue. To my immense shock, he grabs it without comment and takes a bite.

The bulk of the dinner passes in relative silence as we move from the meal to sampling a bottle of the finest wine.

"I love your dress," Dahlia gushes to me. I recognize the polite attempt at conversation, but I can't take my eyes off the two men watching each other from over their place settings. Bellamy cuts into his steak, smearing blood across the plate. Stabbing at a thick chunk with his fork, he places it onto his tongue and devours it in a single, ravenous bite. In contrast, Adrian Riley sharpens his steak knife between the tines of his fork without cutting into his food.

Neither man breaks eye contact until the moment the check arrives.

"I've got it," Bellamy declares, snatching for the check holder.

"Relax." Adrian Riley laces his fingers together. "It's already covered on my tab, Bellamy," he admits. "The bill is merely a formality."

The exchange once again devolves into a heated round of unbroken eye contact. Ignored by both, Dahlia runs her fingers through her hair while I scan Bellamy's plate, tallying up each and every remaining item. There's more than half of his steak left. He barely even touched the potato. The toast is missing only one bite.

My hand shoots into the air to flag down a passing waiter. "Can I get a to-go box, please?"

"You've disgraced me, Ms. King," Adrian Riley declares so apologetically that I flinch. "Feel free to take your time and finish your meal. We do not mind." He glances at Dahlia, who nods dutifully.

"I... It's alright," I stammer. "I'm full, really. It's just... very important for me to make sure that I eat on a *regular* schedule to stave off any dangerous side effects. For the sake of those around me, at least."

A grunt comes from my left—Bellamy's eyes are glacial when they cut in my direction, picking up on my not-so-subtle tirade. *That's enough.*

"I'll just make sure to finish the rest of this later," I tell Adrian. Ignoring the glare issued by the man beside me, I carefully shovel both his leftovers and mine into the takeaway box the waiter brings seconds later. By then, Adrian Riley has already stood and extends his arm to help Dahlia to her feet.

"I do hope to see you at the club, Bellamy, Ms. King," Mr. Riley says, nodding in my direction with yet another smile curling the corners of his mouth.

"Of course, you do." Bellamy flashes a cold grin in return. "We'll meet you there." We remain seated when the two leave, the picture of elegance as they drift across the dining room. The moment they're out of earshot, I flick open the lid of the to-go box and snatch out the toast.

"Don't even waste your breath arguing," I tell Bellamy before shoving the food in his direction.

He's still scowling, but accepts the offering anyway and takes a bite. He chews slowly, each motion of his jaw exaggerated. I'm sure that Adrian and Dahlia could have safely arrived in China by the time Bellamy finally swallows and stands. "Come on."

We exit the restaurant to find James already waiting, and with every step toward the car, I sense something harden up in Bellamy like solidifying ice. I'm alarmed to realize that even the food didn't help. He's on an island unto himself as James navigates the Mercedes toward a bustling part of Uptown.

When I finally manage to tear my gaze away from him and glance out of the window, my eyes widen, and my heart begins to thump uneasily in my chest. We're in one of those secluded, posh sections of the city where everything seems to sparkle, and every establishment is blockaded by a security guard. It's a playground for the Graeme Bellamys of the world while the rest of us contend with the average hole-in-the-wall bar or club. Something tells me that even this so-called "gentleman's club" doesn't fit the typical stereotype that name implies.

"We're here, Sir," James announces warily.

I glance around. We've been in the same spot for the last ten minutes. At first, I'd assumed we were merely stuck in the thick of traffic, but no. James is already parked alongside the curb. Looming above us is a polished building encased in glass, reflecting the lights of the city in a beautiful mosaic. I can't make out a name or a sign to give the building an identity, but when Bellamy finally wrenches open the door on his side, I assume we've reached our mysterious destination.

As I follow him out, my mouth falls open for the second time this evening. "Posh" would be too common a word to describe this place. Breathtaking, maybe? Beautiful? Foreboding?

I can't decide as I scramble after Bellamy and tiptoe in his shadow. Two men in nondescript black suits stand on either side of the main entrance. They give Bellamy a quick once-over but make no move to bar his entry, and he shoves on a glass handle and barges inside.

The lobby alone is tasteful enough to have been described as a "club" entirely on its own. A distinguished one, perhaps, where the patrons lounge on leather furniture beneath vaulted ceilings and stare at their perfect reflections in the sparkling white-marble floor.

I'd always been ready to name Atelier Noir's corporate complex as the most impressive building I've ever seen, but this place quietly shoves those assumptions aside.

"Mr. Bellamy! Ms. King." Dahlia stands to greet us beside a massive reception desk. Affixed to the wall behind her are two interlocked golden letters—R.R. They're a strange set of initials. I would have expected A.R. Maybe he named the club something other than after himself?

"So glad that you could make it," Dahlia continues. She's even more stunning in this more-muted lighting, standing tall in her slinky black dress that makes *mine* resemble something from my Granny's old muumuu collection. Her dark curls spill down her back, and her smoked-out green eyes glitter as they drift from me and settle over Bellamy. "Adrian is waiting for you. This way."

I glance over at Bellamy, but his expression reveals nothing as he falls into step behind the beautiful Dahlia. She leads us to a set of elevators and indicates the button to ascend to the upper levels.

"Adrian has put me in charge of you, *personally*," she admits, her voice toying with the words. "I would have loved to have given you a tour first, but he made it seem as though your meeting was imperative—"

"Yes," Bellamy rudely interrupts. "I believe it's best if we get our... business done and over with. The sooner, the better."

Dahlia nods with a knowing smile, but doesn't say anything else until the elevator finally arrives at a floor and the doors open. "This way."

We travel down a long corridor until Dahlia digs her heels in before a closed wooden door polished to shine. "He's expecting you," she tells Bellamy, but when her eyes fall over me, she frowns. "But I'm not sure..."

"I'll meet him alone." Bellamy shoulders past her and barges into the office, ruining the somewhat dramatic effect that being led in by Dahlia would create. Nonetheless, Adrian Riley stands in the center of the room with his back to the doorway, ready to greet him. He cuts an imposing figure, and despite meeting him not too long ago for dinner, I still find myself impressed by the way he stands silhouetted against the backdrop of a grand office. The desk is polished oak, and fully-stocked bookshelves line the walls.

Right then, everything makes sense—dinner was a formality. This meeting is the true main event—an arena Graeme Bellamy seems determined to dominate. He squares his shoulders as he steps forward, crossing over an antique Persian carpet.

"I'll take good care of her," Dahlia croons to him sweetly before closing the door before I can see how Mr. Riley reacts to the abrupt entry. Alone in the hallway, with the sickly-sweet scent of Dahlia's perfume in my nose, I'm finally forced to reconcile the bits and pieces of my surroundings that I've ignored until now.

The elegant atmosphere. The scantily-dressed women. The handsome men. The gold lettering in the elevator that spelled out a moniker that surely couldn't be the name of a place that someone like *Graeme Bellamy* would ever associate with.

Dahlia scans my face as if aware of every thought circling my brain and then some. Her red lips part into a feral grin, and I suspect she gets great pleasure in drilling home the truth once and for all. "Welcome to the Red Room," she says sweetly. "Would you prefer cognac or a nice cold beer?"

"I'd prefer the truth," I blurt out.

Rather than take offense, Dahlia's smile widens. "About?"

All I can do is shrug. "Everything."

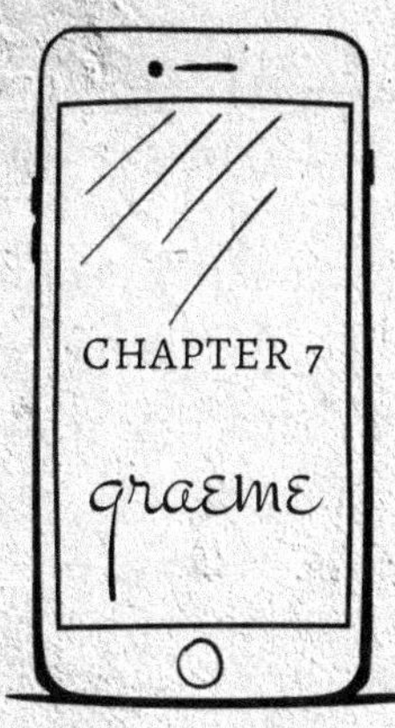


"You know what I find amusing, Bellamy?" Adrian Riley starts once we're alone. "You haven't spoken to Alex in what? Five years? Seven? And yet he was *still* able to predict your reaction—*except* for the rejection of the merger." He cocks his head to observe me in the lighting thrown from a hanging chandelier. "He seemed convinced that you would dump your share in what you so eloquently described as '*his* mistake.'"

"Minds can change," I retort coldly. "Like most men in business, I've since learned to prioritize making money over pride."

"Pride," Adrian repeats, his brow furrowing. "Is that what you call it..."

"Now let me tell *you* something that I find amusing, Riley," I interject. "The fact that you would make room in your schedule merely to discuss my delinquent brother. You know, my mother has plenty of vices for you to exploit. Shall we discuss her next? I'll even offer up the first target for you to strike. How about her alcoholism? Now there's a start…"

Riley chuckles and runs the fingers of his left hand along his lapel. "A mother's loyalty is much harder to sway than that of a 'delinquent' brother," he says with a small, infuriating smile. "Frankly, I have no desire to take *that* route to reach you. Now, about this proposed merger—"

"Ah yes," I say, cutting over him. "This merger. I find it intriguing how the offer only comes *now*, seven years later, when originally you seemed content to let Alexander flounder after you manipulated him into your trap."

"Funny." Riley's amused expression falls flat. "I don't seem to remember it playing out in quite that manner."

A bloody damn lie. "Well, regardless of your murky memory on the subject, consider any form of merger completely off the table from this moment on."

Rather than scowl in defeat, Riley smirks once again, unshaken. "I think you will soon reconsider that position, Bellamy." He turns and approaches his desk. After rummaging through a drawer, he withdraws a stack of documents that he casually sets down. Coincidentally, they face in my direction, allowing me to easily make out what appears to be an old newspaper.

The images of two children dominate the center page beneath a decade's old headline—*Multi-state Kidnapping Saga Comes to an End.*

From Riley's satisfied grin, the words might as well be some sort of smoking gun.

"Unless you're accusing my company of partaking in a kidnapping ring, I don't understand the connection," I reply.

His smirk widens. "You don't?" With a seemingly casual swipe of his hand, he nudges the document closer.

My gaze goes to one of the children featured a second time— a girl with a crooked smile and blue eyes. Familiar eyes. Even with years shaved off her appearance, it's uncanny just how quickly I recognize Evelyn King—except the name crammed beneath the image, in small print, reads, *Evelyn Browning*.

"I think your investors might take offense to the fact that your righthand woman was involved in such a scandal."

"Kidnapping?" I sardonically reply, but I can't keep the anger from my voice. *Damn.* My hand curls into a fist to keep from snatching the damn paper and scouring it for clues. Apart from her schooling and employment credentials, I hadn't thought to delve into the childhood of Evelyn King.

But Riley had. What the hell had he found?

"Have a seat, Graeme," he says, indicating a chair nearby with a wave of his hand.

I don't move so much as a bloody muscle. The bastard takes his time arranging his chair before sitting down regardless. He folds his hands in front of him, allowing his thumb to toy with the ring on his right hand. "I'll admit it. I'm impressed at how well you manage to run the London club, even after uprooting to America."

"Is that so?" I grit my teeth to hold back a nastier retort. I'm sure that by saddling my black sheep of a brother with a monumental debt, Riley thought he'd put enough shame on the Bellamy name that it would take decades to outrun. What I wouldn't give to have seen the bastard's face when his scheme failed.

"You've even attracted some rather... prominent figures to join under your branch," he adds, frowning. "I can't deny that some of those names have caught my interest."

Ah, and there it is—the root of his sudden interest in a "merger." "Why?" I ask, glancing around the wide office as if searching for some list tacked on the wall of nefarious schemes he has in the works. "Run out of American socialites to exploit?"

Riley chuckles even as his eyes narrow into a glare of calculation. "Something like that. I never did run in the circles you seemed privy to, Bellamy. Some of us are forced to use our wits in *addition* to a strong family name to get things done."

I don't challenge the insult. Instead, I meet his gaze fully, refusing to so much as blink. Here he is—the Adrian Riley I know and loathe. Without the suave, polished exterior, he is the same scheming git he's always been.

Some things never change. A good businessman stakes his livelihood on those rare, stubborn variables.

"As I've mentioned before, I'm not interested."

"So you've said, but like *I've* said, I'm more than sure you'll change your mind," Riley assures me. He pulls out a drawer on his end of the desk, rummages inside it, and withdraws a file that he tosses onto the polished surface alongside the newspaper. "I may not have had much luck enticing many members of the royal family to join my establishment... but I am acquainted with a few individuals whom you might be interested in *befriending*."

He flicks open the file and drags his finger along the neat stack of documents contained within, spreading out a series of profiles. I recognize most of the names at a glance—mainly the corporations they represent. Oil. Industry. Politics. Riley has certainly been lucrative in collecting new lives to exploit for his own gain.

"I took the liberty of investigating Atelier Noir's interactions with a few of these associates," he says, unashamed of that very fact. "It stands to reason that you might be interested in smoothing the path toward a closer relationship."

I make my expression steel, refusing to give the bastard even an ounce of emotion to feed off. "And what would you get out of it, Riley? Though, I'm sure you can't wait to get your hands on whoever might sign in *my* guestbook."

Riley shrugs. "The truth is that we both could benefit should we merge the two clubs. I'm merely offering a truce."

"A truce," I scoff. "And what exactly would this little truce entail? Two separate businesses, each run by two different presidents? That doesn't seem to be a very cohesive form of management."

"Oh?" Riley raises a dark eyebrow. "Naturally, there would be only *one* president..."

I scoff. "And let me guess. You already have a man in mind for the job."

"To be honest, Bellamy, I didn't think you would *want* the position, given the lengths you've gone to minimize the connection to your own club." He strokes his chin thoughtfully.

"Unlike you, I don't feel the need to exploit my own power for personal gain."

That insult manages to strike where all the previous attacks missed. He sits straighter, and his palms flatten against the surface of his desk. "Is that so? You don't feel the need, or you simply don't have the *nerve*?" He chuckles when I don't answer and leans back against his chair. The thumb and forefinger of his left hand hook the corner of his lapel, smoothing the sharp edge. "Evelyn King," he states, launching into a fresh line of attack. This one slips through my defenses—I can't disguise the clenching of my jaw. Damn it. I wasn't counting on the bastard to fixate on her so soon.

"What about her?"

"I will admit that I was perplexed by her at first," he says, lacing his fingers together again. I'm not naive enough not to suspect that he hasn't kept an eye on me ever since I arrived in New York. Digging into Evelyn King's background would have been his first task. "She's young," Riley adds. "She's inexperienced. At first, I thought you kept her around for more than just business, but she isn't your type." He strokes his jaw with the pad of his thumb as if processing his own suspicions. "And then it struck me..."

I have to pry my gritted teeth apart to find enough leverage to speak. "What did?"

"*That's* why you chose her. She's not a threat. She's untainted by any other prominent boss or company. There's no risk when the moment comes that you throw her away. If there was one area in which you were always predictable, Bellamy, it was self-preservation."

"Is that so?" It's my turn to play the role of a conceited bastard. I run a hand along the inside of my right wrist, fingering the edge of a silver cufflink. Evelyn's damn voice is in my head, prattling on about the dangers of blasted hypoglycemia—damn Gloria for ever mentioning that bloody term around her. *Your blood sugar, Mr. Bellamy. You turn feral when you're hungry.* "Or maybe the truth is that I knew the moment I hired her that you would dig tirelessly until you found something to exploit, only to come up with *nothing.*"

Of that, I was bloody certain until five minutes ago. It was almost disgusting how clean she is—Evelyn King spent her whole life walking the straight and narrow. She didn't have so much as a traffic citation to her name. The daughter of a military man, she'd maintained perfect marks and graduated at the top of her class. Her previous places of employment didn't keep good enough records to discern much from. As far as a man like Adrian Riley was concerned, she was an unappealing target.

Until now. My eyes keep straying toward that goddamn paper. *Kidnapping.* The word alone conjures too many sordid, horrific conations to consider. Even the thought of someone hurting her makes me...

"As I mentioned before," Riley says, his head cocked with an air of superiority. "Some of your investors might take offense to you being linked to such a scandal. The daughter of a well-known gambler and thief so intrinsically linked to your business interests might make them second-guess your judgment, Graeme."

"And I'm sure you wouldn't hesitate to inform them," I snarl in reply.

*Fuck.* The man looks too smug for my liking. He continues to stroke his chin, his expression unreadable. "Perhaps..."

"And let's say you *were* telling the truth, as you yourself already guessed it isn't like she's indispensable. Frankly, I've been meaning to let her go for a while now. Anything you might try would merely give me an excuse to act on that desire."

It's a risky move to play my hand so early, though if Riley takes the bait, I can't tell. Without giving a shred of emotion away, he rises to his feet.

"I suppose it's a good thing that I didn't ask you here to talk about Evelyn King then," he says. I'm of half a mind to take his change of the topic as a sign of concession—but I don't. "I'm merely asking that you consider the benefits a merger would bring to both of our mutual ventures. We can always discuss the finer details at another date."

"I'll consider it," I say, forcing the words out. My feelings for Adrian Riley aside, the bastard did hold some interesting cards in his deck. Writing him off outright would be counter-intuitive. Making him sweat is far more enjoyable, regardless. "I say we conclude this meeting."

I turn for the door without giving him a chance to respond. In three strides, I reach for the doorknob. I grip it firmly. Turn...

"Oh, and Bellamy?"

And there it is—that smug bit of inflection. Once again, the polished exterior cracks, revealing a hint of the manipulative tyrant lurking underneath. This is the same man who tricked my brother into ruin with little more than a wink and a handshake—like hell would he let me keep the upper hand so easily. Tension laces my entire body as I glance over my shoulder. "What?"

"You were right about Evelyn King. By all appearances, she does seem like the perfect assistant for someone with your... quirks. At least, on the surface."

"Oh really?" I drop the attempts to feign politeness. He's treading a dangerous line, and I'm more than willing to attack any part of him that strays out of bounds. "How so?"

"Everyone has a small area of weakness upon which one only need apply leverage." He lets that statement hang in the air, weighed down with a barely concealed threat.

I do my best to shrug it off and turn for the door again, throwing it open. "As I mentioned, I've been meaning to cut her loose any day now."

Maybe it's the truth, and I've had more issues with Evelyn's work lately than I care to admit. Only god knows why I hear Gloria's voice echo snidely in my head, *Darling, you were the only child I'd ever seen who would rather deny himself what he loves than lose it to someone else.*

"Until next time, Bellamy," Riley says. His final words reach me before I slam the door shut. "Oh, and I had Dahlia show Evelyn to the club. It's in the basement. I hope you don't mind."

His arrogant laugh chases me out into the hall.

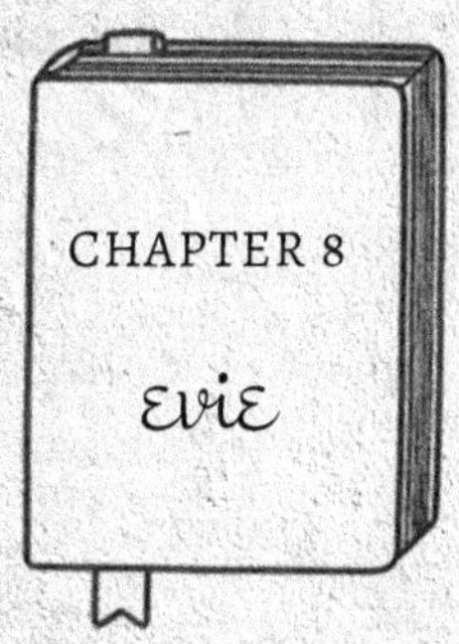


The one word to describe Adrian Riley's mysterious secret club is *loud*. Loud in color. Loud in style. Deafening in elegance. It's so many facets of charm, sensuality, and fun rolled into one brilliantly presented package—like a diamond dressed in gold and placed beneath a spotlight.

"You're impressed," Dahlia declares as she slides a glass of cognac down the counter toward me before taking a sip from the rim of her martini. "The reality is much better than your first impression, right?"

I feel myself nod. Impressed is an understatement. I don't know where to look first, so my eyes bounce from a smirking Dahlia to the elegant bar behind her. Then the well-dressed patrons spread out amongst leather chaises in dim, multi-colored lighting. Is that the star of the latest blockbuster to hit theaters chatting up a leggy blond in the corner? I can't be sure before I'm already eyeing the next breathtaking figure.

It's a strange game of visual ping pong, and I feel dizzy when Dahlia finally sets her glass aside, her eyes on me.

"You had questions," she says, gently returning to the topic of this bizarre conversation.

I wring my fingers together, wrestling with what question to ask next. In the end, I blurt out a barrage of them. "What is this place? Who is Mr. Riley to Mr. Bellamy? Are you an escort?"

Dear god. I blush at that last inquiry though Dahlia laughs warmly, seemingly not insulted.

"I take it he didn't tell you much?" she asks before sipping her drink.

"No. Not that he should. I mean, we don't have that kind of working relationship," I admit.

In essence, I'm more or less a glorified babysitter. Still, I won't deny that the prospect of him hiding information from me stings. A lot.

"I used to work in corporate before I opened my own law practice," Dahlia says, fingering the rim of her glass. I can't deny I'm impressed. I'm guessing she was the McNair in the McNair and Associates law firm where Bellamy's initial meeting with Riley occurred.

"Is Mr. Riley your client?" I ask, stating the obvious.

She shrugs, her gaze distant. "I don't work for Adrian, per se, but being within his orbit has its... benefits—" Her voice dips in a sultry way, and I feel my cheeks flush. "So no, I am not an escort. You can consider me a member of the Red Room, like anyone else here."

Does that include Graeme Bellamy? I'm too chicken to ask. Besides, apart from her beauty, Dahlia isn't like "anyone else here." I can sense it in the way her eyes keep returning to the direction of Riley's office, as if she's more worried about what's transpiring in that room than I am.

To stop being nosy, I sample my drink. It's strong, instantly eating away at some of my nerves. Endowed with newfound courage, I blurt out, "So are you dating him? Mr. Riley?"

Dahlia laughs, her expression the picture of poise—minus the faint flush that barely starts to color her golden cheeks. "No. Merely *acquaintances*," she explains. But if I'm not mistaken, there was a wistful, almost disgruntled note in that last part.

"Did you know Mr. Bellamy before that meeting the other day," I ask, gently changing the subject while hoping to glean more information about the obvious connection between the two men.

Dahlia shakes her head. "From what I know, Adrian and Graeme were childhood friends," she says. "At least until a few years ago. Something happened to drive them apart— you know how men are. As for the club, it isn't as sordid as you think. It's more like a hive where some of the most elite minds in the world congregate to mingle and relax. It's all good fun. No orgies here, at least, that's what we tell the uninitiated."

She laughs again while I just gape.

"I didn't even know Mr. Bellamy owned a club."

Let alone that he even remotely understood the concept of fun.

"As for why *you* are here, I'll give you a warning." Dahlia sets her glass aside and leans in, her head cocked conspiratorially. "What's happening in that room right now isn't a business transaction as much as it is a game, and you, my dear, are at the center of the gameboard."

I clear my throat, intrigued by her tone. "I'm guessing that you don't mean in the business sense."

"Oh no, darling," she says, her lips upturned in an amused smirk. "Not even close."

Is that a hint of jealousy I detect? I can't tell for sure as I follow her pointed stare toward Riley's office. While we have no way of knowing what's going on between the two men, I can guess that Dahlia's picked up on the same bristling tension I have. "What does that mean?" I ask.

She winks. "It means, trust no one and keep your eyes peeled. Oh look, it seems as though their meeting went as well as can be expected," she mutters under her breath, as my arm is firmly gripped from behind. I nearly fall out of my seat, sloshing cognac onto my gown and instantly throwing at least two grand of Graeme Bellamy's money down the figurative drain. Good, after the position he's put me in, he deserves the added expense.

"We're leaving. Now." The hand encircling my arm becomes a manacle that yanks me to my feet and spins me around to face the man attached to it. He looks strange up this close... with the lighting so dim and more than a few sips of brandy in my system. His eyes seem brighter. His jaw stronger. His lips softer...

"Evelyn." He scowls at the glass clutched in my fist, and I scramble to set it on the counter.

"Thank you," I choke out to Dahlia, who merely watches the exchange, her cat-like eyes glimmering.

I don't know if she ever says a word in return before I find myself dragged through the thick of the club and shoved into an elevator. Bellamy's scowl alone deters anyone else from trying to squeeze in beside us, and he smashes nearly his entire fist against the button for the lobby.

As Dahlia surmised, the meeting apparently had gone as "well" as expected when you threw two powerful men into a room alone. My eyes trace Bellamy's jaw, searching for any hint of a bruise or scratch. I find nothing but flawless skin. Nothing but a face most women would die to have directed their way. Nothing but a man who ironically seems tailor-made for a place aptly named the Red Room. Physically, at least.

The cognac in my system makes me blurt out the words that should have stayed locked up. "I didn't know you were a gigolo." It's funny how disappointed I sound. In forty-eight hours, I went from knowing everything there was to know about Graeme Bellamy to working for a stranger who consorts with the owners of "gentleman's clubs" and apparently even owns one of his own.

"I know you aren't drunk, Evelyn," Bellamy warns.

But what if I am? Even a little. My scowling reflection faces me in the polished interior of the elevator before the doors open, splitting me right down the middle. A drunk Evie would be entitled to feel hurt, betrayed, uneasy...

Either he doesn't experience such emotions himself, or he doesn't care because Mr. Bellamy says nothing by way of support when he breezes past me and starts across the main lobby. Even scowling and sour—or perhaps because of that— the bastard still draws eyes wherever he goes. He can't help himself.

For once, I don't hurry after him. I take my time, balancing on each wicked heel as I scan Bellamy from head to toe, trying to discern what he might be thinking. He's watching me as well, with his head tilted as though he's trying to disguise that fact. Then he stops short without warning and turns around. My breath catches at the realization that I have his full attention. Slowly his eyes perform a march up my hips, then down. Up again.

A hot, uneasy feeling washes over me, making me squirm. Shiver. His jaw is clenched, his gaze narrowed. Almost as if he's...

Checking me out in a way no boss should view his subordinate.

"Evelyn." He spins abruptly and waits for me to catch up before storming onto the street. James is already standing beside the car, and the moment I climb in after Bellamy, he navigates us through the streets.

"Take me home first," Bellamy says. His hands are laced together over his lap, the knuckles stark white. James must have put our takeaway in the front seat because the rich smell of steak permeates the entire space. If I'm not mistaken, I can hear Bellamy's stomach growl.

Serves him right.

Trapped beside him, I feel alongside my hip before realizing what I'm searching for—my planner. My fingers are itching for my pen—there is so much new information to jot down. So many key points to bold and underline. The Red Room. Adrian Riley—philandering businessman extraordinaire. And Graeme Bellamy...?

When my hand finally settles over a firm surface, I know instantly that it's not my handy dandy guide. It's too warm, for one. Flesh encased in tailored cotton, coiled over firm muscle sculpted by regular exercise. Pulsing too, as if an indescribable wave of tension threatens to break free. I don't know why, but I look up, seeking out his face in the dark.

He's already staring back, his expression unreadable. Then it hits me that I'm touching him without permission, and I instantly pull back. My fingers tingle, and I rub them along the skirt of my dress to displace the feeling. It doesn't. This odd, growing sense of unease keeps building in my chest the longer the awkward silence between us goes on.

After nearly a minute, I can't resist prodding him, "You could have told me."

In response, Bellamy grinds his teeth together so fiercely the sound almost seems mechanical.

"Before we went in. I mean... most people have certain proclivities," I add. Especially those rich enough to afford prime real estate to advertise it.

"*Proclivities*, Evelyn?" Bellamy repeats, clipping the word.

I don't rehash the slew of information I've found out tonight —though hell, I suspect James already knew. Dahlia certainly did. I was the only one unfortunate enough not to have been clued in on the true mystery surrounding Bellamy and Riley.

Because one of those men had worked very hard to cut me out of said knowledge despite dragging me along with him and paying me a fixed salary that depended on my knowing everything about his life.

I don't like this feeling building in my chest. This prickling, creeping sensation that crawls over my skin. My eyes land on a stack of magazines tucked into the back pocket of the front seat, and I lunge for them. Business Journals and old copies of TIME. I shuffle through the covers, organizing them alphabetically in the darkness.

"You could have told me about your past history with Mr. Riley, for one. Rivalries happen all the time. I would have understood."

"Would you?" He turns to inspect me, but something in his gaze feels... off. Cold. Pointed. Sharp. "I'm sure there are things about your past that you could have told me. You didn't."

*Mayday, Evie.* A hot flush creeps over me, and I pinch myself discretely to fight back the panic. He couldn't possibly know about... Could he? *No.* I shake my head firmly. I made sure to have all traces of my past erased and expunged. He's just being his usual paranoid self.

Without a word, Bellamy snatches the magazines from my hands and shoves them back into the seat pocket, their covers askew and their order messier than before.

"It's late," he growls, as if the time alone combats the fact that he apparently is a shareholder in some kind of sex club. Seconds later, James pulls up before his building, and Bellamy reaches for the door handle. He pushes it open and places one foot on the curb before my hand lands on his shoulder.

"Wait." I rise out of my seat and reach for the bag of take-away. Then I shove it onto Bellamy's lap before he can argue.

His eyes are on my fingers, narrowed in suspicion. I can sense his body tense beneath my fingertips before he shrugs me off and steps onto the curb. When he marches toward the door-man, he's still holding the bag of food, however.

That's one small win for Evie King in a day of straight losses.

I'll take it.

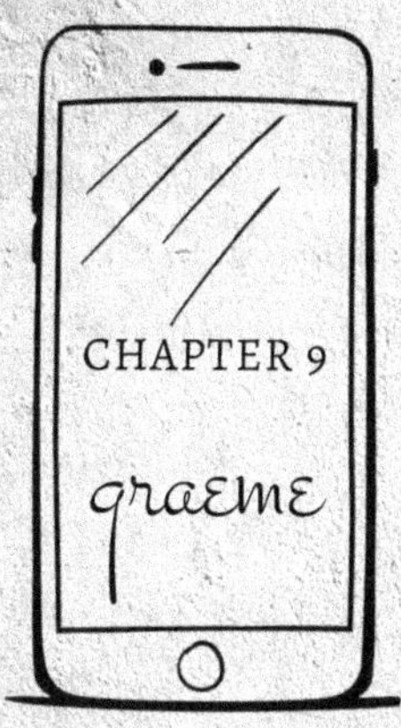



"Graeme." My bedmate's voice is a husky trickle against my ear. "You could have told me..."

Told her what exactly? She doesn't say. She doesn't mention being part of a high-profile kidnapping saga either. Or that her name isn't truly Evelyn King.

For the moment, none of that seems important. In fact, all conversation ceases to matter as her mouth travels south. She's small, her weight balanced on my chest, her narrow hips straddling mine. Her rose perfume clings to the inside of my nostrils, but I don't feel the need to shove her away.

Instead, I feel through the darkness, dig my fingers into the thick of her hair and yank to indicate where her mouth should move next. Her breath fans my throat as she laughs. "Patience, Mr. Bellamy."

Easy for her to say. I let my eyes open and take her in, roaming the thin torso barely covered by an ebony bra. One strap hangs down her shoulder, revealing a dangerous array of pale skin underneath. My fingers twitch, aching to pull the damn thing off entirely and take her in bare. Her hair messy, her lips swollen and parted, her body begging to be fucked as her hips grind rhythmically against mine. But those eyes...

Wait.

"Is something wrong?" She cocks her head, sending her hair cascading down one shoulder. "Mr. Bellamy?"

I don't answer. I just shove her off and jump from the damn bed.

Something is wrong, because if there is one woman who shouldn't be anywhere near my cock it is Evelyn, bloody King.

The damn nightmare jolts me awake at four in the morning. The day gets no better when I check my mobile and discover several missed calls from Gloria. Bloody hell, that woman can sense the most inopportune times to intrude into my life.

I entertain the thought of humoring her while I pull on a pair of fresh clothes. Then I regain my senses and head to the gym instead. Two hours of lifting weights do little to help relieve the exhaustion—and even worse, they don't distract from the ghastly memory—Evelyn King in *my* bed.

In three years, I've never dreamt of her. Until now, I would have assumed that any nightmare she *did* star in would involve her chasing me around with a banana while screaming about blasted hypoglycemia.

Not her in my bed... naked. And it definitely didn't make sense for me to wake up from said nightmare with a lot more than a frightful shock. Even dripping sweat and panting with exertion, the front of my shorts doesn't loosen. No matter how many damn barbells I curl or weights I lift, Evelyn King's face won't disappear. Ultimately, I settle for the lesser of two evils when I return to my loft and snatch my cell phone from the bedside table.

"What?" I growl, the moment Gloria sleepily answers the other end. I glance at the clock on the wall above my bed—it's six-fifteen. Even for her, it's an unusual time to be awake without a drink.

"Good morning, Graeme," she replies, her voice raspy before her morning sip of vodka. "Did you get my messages—"

"I did," I snarl without an ounce of remorse for the tone. "Now, what is it?"

"Well, perhaps we should discuss this over lunch, darling."

I feel myself frown. Gloria rarely retreats from any chance to exert her particular brand of mothering. "What. Is. It?"

She sighs and surrenders with a single statement. "Alexander is flying to America."

My jaw snaps shut, and I brace my palm against the wall to keep my fingers from curling. "What did you just say?"

"I tried to convince him to call you—"

My hand withdraws from the wall and meets it again—so harshly that Gloria hears the resounding thud on her end and gasps.

"Graeme—"

"When?"

"He got on the plane early this morning." Apparently, she meant morning in London, hence the four-a.m. phone call. I do the math, frowning with every blasted second that's passed.

"Where is he headed?" The question is merely a formality—I already know the answer.

"Here, of course. It's only for a month, darling. He just needs some time to get back on his feet. His last business venture failed, but he's already secured the capital for a new investment opportunity..."

A month. Which for Alexander meant nothing more than a span of time during which he would try every trick known to man to accomplish whatever asinine scheme he believes will make him rich this week.

"Fine. Goodbye." I hang up and toss the phone aside without bothering to see where it lands.

I pace the length of the bed while mentally tearing through my options—there aren't many. The doorman already has Alexander's profile with strict instructions not to let him in —not that it will be enough. I'm sure Gloria gave him the address out of spite. I'm sure he's already mapped out the quickest route to my office from the airport. He must have used the money she sent him to buy a ticket in the first place.

And I'm sure his sudden desire for travel can be traced back to none other than Adrian Riley.

That, if anything, should take precedence over whatever else transpired since last night. My main focus should be anticipating whatever move my so-called brother might make next.

Not a woman. Not this blasted feeling of discomfort that only grows whenever I so much as take a bloody step. There's only one damn way to get rid of this feeling. I enter the bathroom and turn on the walk-in shower to the coldest setting. When I strip my boxers and climb beneath the spray, I believe that it'll work.

Apparently not. Five minutes in, my teeth chatter while all the blood in my body seems determined to stay south. Damn it. I switch the water to warm and palm my cock in my fist, picturing the usual specimen I prefer to have in my bed—brunette, large tits, plenty of pedigree. Four strokes should do the trick. By the fifth, I'm shaking, my teeth gritted, my free hand pressed against the shower stall. The only damn way to end this seems to be to allow my brain to play the images it wants to—red silk, black lace... blond, messy hair that isn't quite straight, but it's not curly either. That face...

My breathing quickens as heat roils through my abdomen, and I sacrifice pride for comfort. The images come faster. *Those lips. Those eyes. Her hand on my shoulder, the nails clenching.*

My grip tightens as I rock on my heels, pumping into my fist.

I see an image of her half naked, and it's over. Any evidence is washed down the drain, and when I finally leave the bathroom, draped in a towel, I'm sure that the presence of Evelyn King in my dreams is a sign. A promising one.

Men like Adrian Riley go for the jugular when planning an attack. They strike exactly where they expect their victim to bleed the most. Once, his target was Alexander, and now, he seems to have set his sights on Evelyn. Can I blame him? Not really. After all, everyone has a weakness that can easily be exploited.

Everyone but me.

## CHAPTER 10

### EVIE

It's another one of those dreary mornings where my ringtone competes with the buzz of my alarm clock to snap me awake. When I sleepily scroll through my messages, I find that all three are from Branden, each one increasingly urgent.

*He's in the office early,* claims the first one. *He's already hunting for his dossier,* adds the second. The final message sends me lurching out of bed and staggering toward my dresser—*He's asking for you.*

I stub my toe on the edge of my end table but bite back the pain as I snatch the hanger containing my outfit for today— already picked out a week in advance—and dart into the bathroom. In ten minutes, I'm dressed and save time by throwing my hair into a bun without bothering to brush it. Breakfast for myself is a limp piece of bread, while Bellamy's is already prepared and waiting in the fridge. I count down the minutes as I toss everything I need for the day into my canvas bag, and scan the end table on my way out of the door. *Picture. Vase. Statue. Ficus.*

Perfect.

The next hour passes in a blur as I race to the subway station and the four blocks to the corporate offices. By the time I arrive on the top floor, I'm panting, my blouse is sticking to my body by a layer of sweat, and Mr. Bellamy is nowhere in sight.

"He's in the boardroom," I hear Ann call from her desk.

Strange. While it's not unusual for Bellamy to arrive at the office early, he typically sends me a terse email commanding that I also show up. I quickly check my messages but find nothing again. Odd.

My heart pounds as I exit the office and start down the short hallway. I find the infamous boardroom door wide open, and Graeme Bellamy already seated at the head of the long table, his eyes stern and focused.

A bad sign.

"Evelyn," he says, jerking his chin for me to enter the room. "Have a seat."

"When I asked to renegotiate my contract, I meant at the end of the day, of course. Here, you should eat." I step forward while digging through my bag for the lunch box containing his breakfast. "It's orange slices and toast today," I tell him. "I also made oatmeal, and if you'd like, I can get you some coffee from—"

"Have a seat." Something in his expression makes me stop dead in my tracks. He isn't wearing his usual early-morning scowl—no, this is so much worse. His face is blank, each carefully chiseled muscle arranged into an expressionless mask. Those eyes are a sizzling, electric blue, however. Apparently, his temper hasn't cooled overnight.

It's detonated.

"Is something wrong?" I croak.

He merely gestures toward a chair with a wave of his hand. "Sit."

I do, unintentionally taking the seat furthest from him in the process. I don't miss how his eyes scan me as I scoot further onto the hard-backed leather chair—they narrow over my blouse and follow the curve of my body to my modest-length black skirt. Is another impromptu shopping excursion on the horizon? God, I hope not.

"Mr. Bellamy." I turn to find Branden in the doorway. His eyes cut warily in my direction before he rushes forward and places a white envelope before Mr. Bellamy.

"Thank you," Bellamy says, prompting Branden to scurry out again—but something about the exchange seems all wrong. Unnatural, even. *I'm* the one who fetches his mail and scours it to filter out any missives from those he doesn't like. I'm the one he calls in to meet him at seven-thirty-five in the morning when he can't sleep—which he obviously hasn't, judging from the dark circles around both of his eyes.

"Is something wrong, Mr. Bellamy?" My stomach tightens into knots. I shove one hand into my canvas bag and search for the three pens I keep inside it. I identify them one by one through touch. A cheap BIC for quick note-taking. The finer, silver-tipped one that I use to write in my planner. The fuzzy purple pen that a roommate in college got me as a joke.

"Is something wrong?" I repeat, the million-dollar question, it seems, given the way Bellamy nearly rolls his eyes.

"You could say that, Evelyn," he retorts. "Here."

He slides the white envelope in my direction. My name is written on it. Even more alarming, my name is written in Sarah's handwriting. Human Resources Sarah, who spells my name with an I and always puts tiny spirals on the end of her Es.

My fingers shake as I open it. Inside is a check. My name is on the line indicating the recipient. The amount is more than twice what I make in a year. Given as the reason someone scribbled...

What? I blink, desperate for my eyes to adjust. I must still be half asleep. After a few seconds, however, those words never change. *Termination of employment.*

"I... I don't." I shake my head to clear it. "What?"

"Ann will help you gather your things," Mr. Bellamy says. "And James will escort you out."

My mouth opens wordlessly. On impulse, I bite my lip, but when the pain doesn't startle me awake, I pinch myself. I seize a chunk of flesh from my forearm, dig my nails in as hard as possible, and pinch myself. For all my effort, I break the skin, draw a bead of blood, and leave a ruby smear on the check when I lift it again, checking for authenticity. I don't find any hint of a joke tucked within the official wording. No camera crew rushes in, reassuring me that this is all staged.

I don't wake up.

"You're... you're firing me?"

"In explicit terms, I suppose that's what this is." Mr. Bellamy shrugs and runs a finger on the collar of his suit. I've never seen him wear it before—dove gray with a royal blue button-up shirt underneath. "I hope the severance pay is enough."

"You..." I shake my head, unsure of just what I'm objecting to. "But... why?"

He cocks his head and raises an eyebrow as if the answer is obvious. "I think it's best if we go our separate ways."

It's because of yesterday. The breakfast. For all I know, his sugar could have dropped during the night. He might have spent the early morning hours in the hospital being fed glucose intravenously through an IV. I hadn't done my job, all because of one stupid anomaly that I hadn't been able to prepare for—Adrian Riley.

"I'm sorry," I hear myself croak. "I can—"

"James will escort you from the premises." He stands and marches past me for the door. I only seem capable of watching him go, still trying to decipher whether or not any of this is real.

That painful clenching in my gut like I've been kicked? That feels real. The burning sensation behind my eyes which forces me to blink them rapidly, definitely seems real. And Graeme Bellamy, turning the corner without so much as a glance in my direction... *that* is the most corporeal occurrence of all.

Ann helps me pack my belongings into a single cardboard box. There isn't enough time to organize my notebooks by size and color or carefully arrange my pens. Everything is just unceremoniously shoved into an artless heap that I'm forced to hold in place with my chin as I creep into an elevator.

Once I reach the main lobby, my humiliation commences. This strange "living-death" effect comes over anyone seen leaving a workplace with their things in a box and an envelope sticking out of their bag. The unlucky souls they cross don't know whether to say goodbye or stare. I'm irritated to find that most people take the latter option. I can *feel* their pity, more jarring than the icy rain steadily falling outside.

Luckily, I don't have far to travel as James is there to meet me at the entrance of the building rather than beside the car. Without a word, he takes my cardboard box and tucks it under one arm while holding a black umbrella above my head with the other. Gratitude renders me speechless—I can't even muster up a proper thank-you, not that he seems to expect one. Once we make it to the Mercedes, he gently tucks my things onto the seat beside me and drives me across town to my apartment.

"Let me help you, Miss," he insists, withdrawing the key from the ignition once we're parked in front of my building.

"That's okay!" I shake my head and gather my box before he opens his door. "I've got it. Thank you..."

I race inside before he can even make it out onto the curb. It's funny how your body can move on autopilot while your brain self-destructs. Without any witnesses, I reassemble my consciousness in pieces during a sleepy ascent up three flights of stairs. All the while, my brain repeats the same statement on a loop, as if to help it sink in—*Graeme Bellamy fired me. I, Evelyn King, who rarely failed at anything, was fired by an ungrateful bastard like Graeme Bellamy...*

The thought trails off when I almost collide with a wall. I blink and find myself staring at a section of peeling paint in the hallway near my flat. Muffled shouts reach me from the tenants above, ten hours ahead of schedule. At least the fight serves as the perfect chaotic soundtrack when I pull my keys from my pocket and make three attempts to unlock my door. The moment I finally get it open, I set my box down and kick it over the threshold before closing the door. Out of habit, I scan the items on the end table as I close the door behind me. Picture. Vase. Ficus...

Wait. I blink and look closer. Picture... vase...

It takes me another five seconds to realize that Mom's statue is missing. Did I knock it over when I came in? I glance under the table and find nothing.

And then I smell it—heavy cologne like the cheap kind used by addicts to cover up the scent of smoke. It lingers over the doorway, too far in to have been left by someone passing by. My nostrils flare, picking up the acrid scent underneath. It's so familiar I can instantly put a name to the brand—Lucky Cigarettes.

Once I finally look up, it isn't hard to spot the source of the stench. I don't know how the hell I missed him before, lounging on my couch with his feet on my coffee table. He's aged about ten years in the three since I saw him last. His baby fat has melted, revealing the bone structure he inherited from Dad. They style their hair the same, but Dad was always clean-shaven, never approving of the scruffy look. Danny, apparently, didn't inherit that habit. I wonder if he's show-ered this week. It certainly doesn't smell like it. Red stains splatter the gray sweatshirt he wears over a ratty pair of jeans. Paint? Ketchup? Blood?

Who am I kidding? I'd stake my money on it being a mix of all three.

He must have been asleep when I came in because he startles upright, scrambling to get his muddy shoes off my furniture.

"Eves," he croaks out. "I... uh... long time no see."

Long time. I guess to him three years might seem like a decent reprieve since he last showed up unannounced on my doorstep. For me, it's too damn soon.

"How the hell did you get in here?" I scan the table again, focusing on the spot where Mom's stupid clown figurine should be. It isn't long before I locate it—tucked in his grip. "That's *mine.*"

"Whoa... Eves." He scrambles to his feet, holding the clown up for closer inspection. Judging from his blank expression, one might assume he's never seen the damn thing before. But if memory serves me well, he's had his eye on it since the age of ten when he first learned to attach a price to other people's property—not many kids his age tried selling their sister's Barbies on the playground for spending money. "I was just—"

"Fine, you can have it," I tell him, crossing my arms over my chest. "If that's what it will take to get you to leave before one of your drug-dealing buddies comes by, then take it and go. I'm sure you can get at least seventy bucks for it. Maybe a hundred. It's vintage."

He has the nerve to look ashamed—his cheeks flush red, his eyes downcast. "Eves... I—"

"Well, I see that you already made yourself comfortable." My eyes zero in on my bedroom door—it's hanging open.

I *never* leave it open. My throat feels tight as my brain pieces together the obvious reason it is now. I guess he's already turned over the mattress and found the cash I keep there. Go figure. I'd been stupid enough to assume that, after the last five apartment switches, I might have been able to finally let my guard down. As per usual, the joke's on me.

"That didn't take long. Keep the cash. I don't even want to hear your pathetic excuses this time," I tell him before he can speak. My hand flies out for the door, prying it open so hard it smashes against the wall. "Don't let me stand in the way of your *fun*—"

"Evie!" I hear him behind me as I stumble into the hallway clutching my bag. My heart is pounding when I reach the lobby and race onto the street.

Above the rush, I think I hear him call out. Maybe it's an apology. Maybe it's a request for my bank account information. With Danny, you never know.

our meetings in one damn day trap me in the boardroom for most of it. Usually, I'd navigate the schedule like clockwork, guided by a silent scribe who would take note of every detail and only pause in her duties to shove an apple into my mouth every blasted hour. Without her, it's all a bloody mess. By the fourth appointment, Ann has already been reduced to tears twice, and she cowers beside her desk as I leave the office three hours late. The delay turns out to be a blessing in disguise when I finally surface to find that Gloria left at least twelve messages for me. Rather than return them, I exit the building alone for the first time in three years without an ounce of remorse for the person who isn't by my side.

Firing her wasn't cruel, but an act of mercy. Without any ties to me, Adrian Riley will have no desire to pursue her. She'll be safe, a fair trade after three years of dutiful service. *Liar,* a part of me counters. Even a ruthless bastard like Riley could have an interest in Evelyn beyond revenge. Especially after he saw her in *that* dress.

My throat goes dry at the memory. No one could blame any man for gaping at her open-mouthed, practically drooling. But *they* hadn't glimpsed what lay beneath the material. I can still see the image of her flashing through my skull, and I grit my teeth to chase the thought away.

She could be with Riley right now. He could have followed her. Coaxed her back to that blasted club. Coaxed her into his bed.

But, knowing the bastard, he won't expose her past for his own benefit, and that's all that matters. Besides, I can always find a new assistant. In fact, the silence is rather refreshing, considering that no one is there to nag about hypoglycemia as I find James waiting out front. Once inside the car, however, my nostrils flare to catch a scent they shouldn't— the faint hint of rose perfume. I roll the nearest window down to disperse the smell and slam the door behind me without bothering to examine why. Nothing will ruin this night.

Not Adrian Riley.

Not my mother.

Certainly not Evelyn King.

To feel any guilt now would be counterproductive. With her termination pay, she could move to another city and live comfortably—and with her references, she will easily find another position. Adrian Riley could root through the rest of my employees' pasts all he damn well pleases. Once the question of a merger is firmly decided, I will more than happily return the favor via one of his employees. One could say I spared Evelyn the pain and humiliation of being collateral damage to whatever revenge plot he has in store.

Besides, hurt feelings and ruined egos are the brutal cost of doing business. Evelyn knows that better than anyone.

"Goodnight, Mr. Bellamy," James calls as he pulls up before my building, snapping me from the thought. If I'm not mistaken, his tone is crisper than usual. Blunt. "Sleep well."

"Thank you." I step out onto the curb without overthinking it and approach the building, but I find myself frowning as I enter the lobby.

That blasted scent must cling to me, because if anywhere in the world shouldn't remind me of Evelyn King, it's an exclusive high rise—regardless, I smell roses. Everywhere. The bloody fragrance even chases me into the restaurant on the ground floor, where I head straight to the bar. Two shots of whiskey don't clear my senses any. In fact, I'm sure the liquor has caused me to hallucinate when my mobile rings, and I withdraw it from my pocket to discover who the caller is.

"You know that I prefer for you to contact me only during business hours," I snap the second I answer.

A tinkling laugh greets me in reply, along with a distant murmur that resembles harmonic chanting. "Brother darling! How are you this fine evening?"

"Bloody hell, Stella!" I wince and hold the receiver from my ear. "Are you learning spiritual enlightenment wherever the hell you are or how to deafen a bloke?"

"Oh dear," she replies with a dramatically exaggerated sigh.

"What's that supposed to mean?"

"You're drinking," she replies. "That's the only time you're this snappish. Usually, you'd at least berate me about getting the designs for the spring collection ready on time before launching into your typical whining. What's wrong?"

"Nothing," I insist while forming a fist that I brace against the counter. "I've just had the day from bloody hell, and then you're calling me in the middle of the damn night, screaming like a blasted banshee, and I can't even unwind over a glass of whiskey without being shamed for it."

"Well, where is Evie? I called the office earlier and tried going through your skittish little secretary, but the poor thing sounded like she might burst into tears. I merely wanted to tell you that the designs will be delayed just a tad while I visit a goat monastery with this yogi named Renata I met at a hostel in Berlin—"

"I don't give a damn if you're visiting the pope of the bloody goats," I snarl through gritted teeth, "you'll get me those designs on time, Stella. And as for Evelyn..."

"If you have her personal mobile, Graeme darling, just hand it over. I'd much rather go through her."

"She is no longer employed with Atelier Noir. Ann will handle my correspondence from now on."

She laughs, and between her cackling and the blasted chanting, I feel like I'm in some surreal, alcohol-induced version of hell. "You don't have a humorous bone in your body, Graeme, but I will admit you gave me a laugh. Now, seriously, please just get me in contact with her and—"

"I fired her, Stella." The heat in my tone draws the eye of every blasted patron in the bar, and I gesture for the bartender to pour me another shot.

"Damn. Well, no wonder you sound so horrible. Dear lord, we'll have to increase our liability insurance with you running around unsupervised. What on earth made you fire her? Or did she quit? I certainly wouldn't blame her."

"She was terminated," I insist before snatching up a fresh drink the second it's poured. "It was for the best, and I won't be questioned about it."

"You and I know our arrangement only works because we keep to our respective talents. I am the creative mind, and you are the surly Neanderthal that haunts the boardroom to keep our shareholders in line. But, while I admit you have some skill in the business realm, I suggest you pull your head out of your ass and offer Evie whatever she requires to come back. You need her—hell, we all do! What on earth do you think would happen to the company if you threw a tantrum and insulted some distribution agent without her there to smooth it over? Or if you dropped dead of starvation because you forgot that despite being a cold-blooded capitalist, you still require human food occasionally?"

"Stella?" I hold the receiver from my mouth. "I can barely hear you. You're breaking up."

"Graeme, don't make me leave my quest for enlightenment all because of your blasted male ego! I swear I'll go through Mum. She's the only one you ever humor—"

I hang up and stand, leaving the bar, no less haunted by the memory of Evelyn King. I can still smell her. Her goddamn perfume forms a taunting trail all the way to my suite.

I make a mental note to track down the damn manufacturer and buy out the bloody company as I dig my key card from my pocket and swipe it through the reader affixed to my door. One step over the threshold, the aroma of roses intensifies, easily overpowering the stench of lemon-scented cleaner.

That isn't the only detail out of place. I slam the door behind me and enter the kitchen to find the coffee maker on, with a mug already waiting on the counter beside it. Suspicious, I open the fridge and feel my frown deepen. Maria isn't so obsessive as to color code the perishable items by date of expiration. Only one figure could be responsible for that level of organization.

Predictably, the damning trail of roses leads to my bedroom. I throw the door open to find my bed perfectly made with a sprig of lavender resting on the pillow—along with what appears to be my entire collection of Oxfords spread out over the floor. Amid the chaos, my ties form a carefully arranged rainbow with each color in its scientifically accurate place. I'd prefer either occurrence to the sight I settle on last, however

—exactly three bottles of the most expensive wine I own sit on the floor alongside a woman who seems determined to sample them all.

Bloody hell. She looks almost exactly how she did in that damn nightmare. Her hair is loose. The strap of her black camisole hangs off one shoulder. Her lips are swollen, though perhaps because she's in the process of biting them as she sets out the very last tie in a shade of black.

"Evelyn."

She doesn't look up. Instead, she raises her hands, lowering each finger one by one while counting out loud. "There are nine letters in *severance*," she declares as though fascinated by the fact. Her head falls back, and her eyes finally meet mine, wide and utterly devoid of fear. "You have exactly nine bottles of imported wine."

"Three bottles of imported wine," I tell her, taking a step toward the bottle of a rare Italian vintage she reaches for next. "The rest are champagne."

Without care for my presence, she wraps her lips around the bottle and throws her head back, exposing a throat sculpted as if by god for a man to sink his teeth into. She misjudged how much she could swallow at one time and jerks forward, sputtering priceless wine all over the cream carpet. Despite all appearances, I can tell at a glance that she hasn't drunk much from any bottle. Even so, her cheeks are already pink, but her grip is steady as she sets the bottle aside.

"If you leave now, I won't bother with alerting security," I tell her, but the words lack the conviction I'm used to. As if to bolster them, I dig through my pocket for my mobile. "I *will* call, Evelyn."

"I know," she replies, almost matter-of-factly. "But before you do, all I want is to ask you one question." Bracing herself on the palm of one hand, she slowly climbs to her feet. Once she's standing, she faces me directly, her chin jutting into the air. "Why?"

"Evelyn," I start as my finger hovers over the security contact number. "I suggest you save this discussion for when you're sober—"

"Bullshit!" She doesn't back down, and I would expect no less. "Why did you fire me?"

My eyes narrow. "Do you really need a reason?"

"Yes!" She flinches as though I've slapped her—which doesn't make any damn sense. Her hurt pride aside, I gave her more money than she would have seen by the end of the year, with extra for the hell of it.

"You've been more than adequately compensated," I point out. At the same time, I don't know what possesses me to snatch her opened bottle and take a sip right from the rim. Damn, I can taste her essence, lingering among the glass, sweeter than the liquor itself.

"Compensated?" Spittle flies from her mouth as she snatches the bottle back. "Are you kidding me? I've devoted three years of my life to working for you, and this is—"

"Ah," I say, nodding. "So that is what this is about." I reach into my breast pocket for a pen and snatch a monogrammed notepad from a drawer in my nightstand. "Name an amount, and I'll have Sarah adjust your check in the morning—"

"This isn't about money, you pompous ass." All at once, Evelyn King deflates before my eyes. Her shoulders slump. Her gaze drifts to the floor. She never lowers that stubborn tilt to her jaw, however. No matter how broken she is, she won't lose her damn propriety. "I just want to know why..."

*Why.* "Explanations are rarely required beyond a reason scribbled on a customary check, Evelyn. Frankly, I'm not quite sure what you want to hear."

That her dismissal had absolutely nothing to do with her work ethic and everything to do with...

"Is it about him?" she asks, a hopeful note creeping into her voice that I instantly dislike.

"Who?"

"Adrian Riley."

"No." I clench my hands. Unclench them. Then I snatch for the bottle again, though this time she relinquishes it freely. After a hefty swing, I choke out, "Why would you think that?"

"Why?" Either she's mastered her poker face, or that wine has made her oblivious to the warning in my tone. "Because I know my work ethic is above and beyond anything required of my position, and because you hate him *that* much. It's obvious. Or... or maybe this is about the club. Do you think that I can't handle it?"

She squares her shoulders, seemingly oblivious to the fallen strap of her camisole, which dips a dangerous fraction.

"Handle what?" I shove the bottle toward her, obscuring any bit of flesh potentially bared by her posture.

Rather than drink, she sets it aside, her eyes downcast. "Is that why you fired me? Because, for the record, I *can*. It makes perfect sense for Atelier Noir to have a side business that can help foster relations between prized clientele. I could even assist you in its operations."

"Could you, Evelyn?" Perhaps. Even Adrian Riley would have trouble manipulating someone like her—I can admit as much. Do I want to take that risk? No. Nothing is worth the potential loss. "Consider this your last warning. You have five minutes before I ring for security."

I turn my back on her and head for the hall. James should still be out front—he can take her home once she's escorted out.

"Wait."

That sharp tone alone makes me stop in my tracks. When I glance over my shoulder, she's swaying on her feet, her lips pulled back from her teeth.

"You—" She jabs her finger in my direction though her voice is too breathless to convey much of a threat. Instead, she sounds exhausted, and somehow that's more alarming than her anger. "You... you are a *mean* person, Graeme Bellamy."

"That's certainly an understatement," I blurt out in surprise. Regardless, something that could be shock makes my brow furrow. Evelyn King called me mean. Until now, she was one of the few people who never insulted me, at least not to my face.

"That's why people don't like to be around you," she adds softly. "And do you want to know the truth? I wasn't shocked that you were associated with a place like the Red Room because of the sex or debauchery."

"Oh really?"

"Yes... *really*."

"Then enlighten me." I take a step toward her. Dare I say it? I'm bloody curious. "Why was prim and proper Evelyn King so shocked, then?"

She inhales sharply and draws herself to her full height. Even then, she's still forced to crane her neck to look me in the eye. "Because... to be honest, you are the very last man *I* would ever want to meet if I belonged to one of those clubs."

It takes me nearly a full minute to discern what she means. *The very last man...*

I throw my head back and laugh. Long. Hard. I can't stop myself. When I finally fall silent, her cheeks match the color of the wine stains over the carpet.

"Oh, Evelyn, you have one thing correct—*you* are the very last woman that I would ever even agree to meet anywhere, let alone the Red Room."

She withstands the barb with only a slight wince to reveal how much it stings. "I'm not saying that you aren't handsome," she clarifies, leaving me even more unsure of her meaning. "That's what makes it worse, I think. But, you're selfish. You have 'one and done' written all over you." She steps closer, and her eyes dart to my hands as if the words were scribbled over my knuckles. "And I don't mean to say you're a player—" She takes another step. "I mean *one* thrust because you can't stand to be near anyone else for longer than that. *Done* because the only pleasure you concern yourself with is yours."

"Interesting observation," I tell her. She's close enough now that I can feel her breath fanning my throat. "Considering that, as far as I know, we've certainly never fucked."

In reality, at least.

She shrugs. "Your exes love to talk to the tabloids. It's not exactly an open secret that pleasing a woman during sex isn't your forte."

I should have rang security and left her there. A childish sparring match with Evelyn King is the last damn thing I need to cap off this day. Though, there's a bloody first time for everything.

"As if *you* are an expert on sex," I tell her. In three years, I've never seen her successfully return a flirtatious compliment, let alone accept the offer of a date.

"Go ahead. You can say it—I won't be offended," she says through gritted teeth. "I may be *single* but trust me, that makes me more of an expert on pleasing a woman than you. At least..."

"At least what?" Somehow my mouth is near her ear. I can sense every ragged inhale she takes. Smell every damn bit of rose perfume seeping from her pores.

She squares her jaw again and forces her gaze to meet mine without flinching. "At least I know how to get a woman off."

"Do you, now..." She's too damn close. A wise man would back away. Tell her to leave. Even I know that there's no point in taunting her further. But no one insults me. Not Gloria. Not Adrian Riley. Definitely not *her*. "Then I suppose it's a good thing for both of us that you are the last woman I would ever want to fuck."

An image of my nightmare flashes through my skull, as if my own subconscious is calling me a liar.

"Of course, I would be," she agrees, her nostrils flaring. "Because unlike Portia, or Catherine, or Penelope, or any of your other past lovers, your money and a few photo ops wouldn't satisfy me enough to make up for where you... lack." Her gaze drifts pointedly to the front of my slacks, and I don't even register reaching out until her chin is in my palm. I grip it tightly—not enough to hurt, but firmly enough that she can't look away. Not that she tries to. Eyes blazing, she holds my gaze with every inch I lean toward her.

"Is that a dare, Ms. King?"

"Of course not." Her tongue shoots out to dampen her lips, but she doesn't pull away—her mistake. No, true to form, Evelyn King must have the last word. "I'm not cruel enough to challenge someone who doesn't have a chance in hell of winning—"

She doesn't expect the moment my lips collide with hers. Hard. Her first instinct is to pull back—and had she been anyone else, and had that nightmare not been so fresh in my mind, I would have let her go. Instead, my fingers latch onto the back of her skull, tangling through her hair to hold her in place. My teeth seize her lower lip and tug hard enough to draw a gasp from her lips. Hard enough to end this game. I've made my damn point. I don't have to shove my tongue between her lips as well. I don't have to palm her ass, feeling the swell against my palm as I grind my pelvis against her. I consider each searing brush of friction a spoil of war.

*That* is all this is—battle.

She's panting when I pull away and swipe her taste from my mouth with the back of my hand. I'm more than ready to call security and have her hauled out right on her ass. The ass that's still in my palm. The ass that makes her entire body arch when I dig my nails in through the fabric of her skirt. Hard. *Harder.*

Without warning, her hand flies up, the palm colliding with my cheek. I grit my teeth, still reeling from the slap, when I feel her free hand press against my chest. Her fingers curl, snatching for my tie, yanking it from its nestled position in my jacket. Before I can retaliate, she tugs, turning it into a leash that gives her enough leverage to force my head lower, my mouth within her reach.

Our lips meet again. Harsher. Rougher. Teeth. Nails.

When her tongue unabashedly goads mine, it feels... in-bloody-describable. But it doesn't mean a damn thing. She was foolish enough to propose a challenge.

And I refuse to lose.

She's caught off guard when I shove her away, breaking the kiss. Clumsy, she staggers back and trips onto the bed. I expect the distance to knock some bloody sense into her, but her eyes just narrow, refusing to tear away from mine for even a second. I'm the one who breaks the contact to take the rest of her in, piece by piece.

Evelyn King doesn't seem so prim and proper now. Her camisole has ridden up over the flat of her stomach. Her skirt is askew. When I start forward, she bites her lip, her head tilting back against the duvet. Messy blond hair tangles around her shoulders. Like bloody silk. It parts for me when I fist my fingers in the thick of it, pinning her head flat while I seize her mouth and shove my tongue against hers. Deep. Deeper.

Only Evelyn fucking King can turn my every assumption on its head. She tastes like goddamn roses. Like coffee. Like honey. Like hell. Two. Three. Five fucking searching thrusts aren't enough to taste her fully. I have to wrench on her scalp, fusing our lips together, mounting her with my weight until she has no choice but to take me as far as she can. When I attempt to go even deeper, own her completely... her teeth clamp down over my tongue.

"Fuck!" Withdrawing from her is like surfacing from under-water—boiling water. My ears pop. Pain sears through my skull. I shake my head to clear it, but by then, she's writhing, trying to crawl out from under me.

As if it would be that fucking easy.

"Oh no, you don't." I hook my hand within the waistband of her skirt and drag her back before she can get far. "Dare or not, I accept your challenge."

My palm grazes her thigh, sliding between her legs. I go far enough for the tip of my thumb to brush a thatch of silk and lace. I let her own unsteady breathing count the passing seconds.

If she told me to stop, I would. She doesn't.

Her hips jerk. Her lips fly apart as she pants. Her eyes meet mine, and rather than flush and turn away, they shine with a dare. *Do it.*

So I nudge the panel of her underwear aside with my index finger and slid my thumb underneath. She's tight. Hot. Already quivering...

Her entire body quakes when I slide a single finger inside of her. Deep. I grit my teeth at the way she feels... every greedy, hungry clench. I draw my hand back. Thrust again.

She tightens.

Once more, and she moans. Harsher. Faster. *More.*

I slide her panties down enough to add a second finger, before flicking both apart to stretch her while my thumb assaults her clit. One pass. Two. Her knees rise up on either side, trapping my body between them. Her breath hitches when I increase the pace, but when I draw back on my knees and lower my head, she bucks.

"W-Wait—uh!"

Her argument dies as I plunge my tongue between her legs, and finally taste every inch of Evelyn King. Pure fucking sin. Hot. Raw. Wet. I can't resist flicking my tongue along the length of her, using my fingers to stroke whatever I can reach.

Vibrations run through her skin—but I don't hear her complaining. Just her hammering pulse. The damn sounds she makes. The way the mattress creaks when her back bows and she laces her fingers through my hair, tugging... pulling.

"Fuck," I growl the word when she finally convulses, her orgasm punctuated by one shrill gasp.

Her chest is still heaving when I pull back and dismount the mattress backward. I kick over the bottle of wine when I stagger into the bathroom. I barely get my pants down around my ankles before coming into my fist so hard I have to brace one hand against the counter. There's no way to hide the evidence this time. For the second time in one day, I came because of Evelyn King.

And I'm more than willing to make her pay.

W ine turns my brain into a merry-go-round. Usually, I prefer vodka instead, even though it makes me sick to my stomach. I'd take puking over waking up like this any day. Dizzy, sore, and...

"Oh shit." My eyes fly open to an unfamiliar ceiling—the first clue that something is horribly wrong. On second thought, the ceiling isn't so much unfamiliar as it is seen from an unusual angle. I'm not used to looking up at it from the bed, after all—the massive, king-sized bed that I've only ever made or turned down. Unsurprisingly it feels divine to lay on—the perfect support for my head as shame threatens to turn my pride into a pancake.

*Don't think about it, Evie,* I tell myself encouragingly. *Just get up. Get dressed. Go home.*

Where exactly home would be, considering that, thanks to Danny, I no longer have an apartment to run to? Well, I'll just have to figure that out later.

I close my eyes and then peel them open again, one by one. I can make out the huge floor-to-ceiling window without craning my neck any. Overcast daylight streams in—the curtains had been left open, meaning it is highly likely that I spent the night in this room alone. God, I hope so.

When I finally gather the nerve to lift my head from the mattress, I have a perfect visual of the mess I left on the floor. Every tie owned by Graeme Bellamy is spread out in what was once a neat row, now partially trampled by an expensive pair of leather loafers and two muddy ballet flats. My chest is already heaving at the horror of it—but that's not all. No, because three bottles of expensive wine joined the fray, along with every version of a designer Oxford known to man.

The only fact that makes this scenario even remotely more bearable is that Bellamy isn't anywhere in sight. I strain my ears above the rasp of my ragged breathing, but I don't hear the shower running or the thud of footsteps in the other room. Which means that I have an unknown amount of time to get the hell out before he comes back.

With only that goal in mind, I peel myself from the surface of the gray duvet and climb to my feet. My head pounds. One step forward, I realize that my underwear is halfway down my legs. I only find one of my shoes in the chaos, and I have no choice but to shove it into my bag and race from the penthouse barefoot. Scanning my phone, I find four messages from the same unfamiliar number. After reading the first, I have a good idea who sent them.

*We need to talk, Evs.*

*Please just hear me out.*

*I'm sorry for barging in on you.*

*I left your apartment. Let me know when we can talk.*

I can't think of Danny right now—my only focus is getting as far from this penthouse as physically possible. Thankfully, it's early enough that not even the doorman is by his post, and I sneak out of the building unnoticed. The first cab I hail mercifully stops, and the driver merely takes me in with a smirk before asking where I'm headed.

Which is a pretty good question, all things considered. Thanks to Danny's reappearance, my apartment is out of the question. I no longer have a job. With no other options in mind, I direct him to the self-storage unit I rent on the other side of town. Forty-five minutes and seventy bucks later, I find myself wandering through the maze of metal containers until I reach the one constant I've had over the past ten years —a ten-foot by ten-foot storage unit with a rusty door that doesn't close all the way. I still keep Dad's stuff here. Some days I even entertain the thought of emptying it out and moving everything into my current apartment like a normal person might.

But today isn't that day.

I switch on the flickering lightbulb hanging from the center of the unit and find the box where I keep my old shoes. I settle for a pair of sneakers and dig through one of the many packed suitcases for a fresh pair of jeans, underwear, and a sweater. I take the suitcase with me, along with the few things I salvaged from the last place. Then it's a cold, dreary march to Square One—which just so happens to be the name of a diner I stumble into a few blocks down.

Only once I'm served a steaming cup of coffee and two pieces of French toast can I begin to process what's transpired within the past twenty-four hours. Danny is back—and ironically, that's the easiest surprise to stomach. At least I know what to expect—he's obviously in trouble and probably needs money, my blood, or my liver. Either way, it's a crisis I can easily handle—by running to another part of the city until he tracks me down again.

Next on the list is the small fact of being fired from the longest job I've ever held—with a severance pay of more than twice what I made in a year. That event alone could justify a month spent in bed, eating ice cream out of a tub while contemplating the hollowness of my future.

But no. Evelyn King always has to go a step further and compound her own humiliation. This time I've royally outdone myself.

I went to his home.

More specifically, I broke in.

Then, I raided his liquor cabinet and stress-organized his closet.

But I just couldn't stop there, could I? No, *I* had to call Graeme Bellamy bad in the sack, and then...

*Oh god.* I chug my coffee, but the searing caffeine doesn't erase the memory—Graeme Bellamy's hand between my legs. His voice a husky growl in my ear. His mouth on mine. Why stop at being homeless *and* jobless? Pity, almost-sex with a man you hated was a perfect way to celebrate a descent to rock bottom.

The icing on the cake is that I hadn't even been able to keep my word about his lack of prowess. A man like Graeme Bellamy, who could barely return a handshake with a business associate, shouldn't have been so good with his hands. *Sinfully* good, I admit, before taking a scalding sip of coffee. I'd taunted him, and in the end, he'd had the last laugh. Literally.

I'm trembling when I finally set my coffee aside. The narrow café is nearly empty except for a man steadily typing away at his keyboard. He looks up at me and smiles, the picture of everything I would sell my soul to be again—a content human being.

When I pay my tab and head out onto the street, I have no solid course of direction and wind up on an aimless trek through the city. Despite my internal outlook, it's a beautiful day, with everything sparkling beneath a fresh coat of rain. Skyscrapers glisten as if speckled with diamonds. The rare bits of green sprinkled throughout serve as a reminder of spring.

Somehow I catch a bus and ride it to a familiar part of the city. The moment I step onto one of the worn paths of Central Park, it's like I can breathe again. The place had always been my one refuge during the old days when Dad would drag us back to the city after some excursion overseas or to another state. Our address may have been different, and Danny and I had grown older, but for some reason, this part of the city rarely seemed to change at all. There would always be the same old paths. The same old benches occupied by flirting couples or sleeping junkies. If you ventured far enough, the deafening sounds of the city would soften—almost like a distorted lullaby of honking horns and shouting voices. In those rare moments, I could feel truly, entirely alone...

"Evie?"

I whirl around, already digging into my shoulder bag for my pepper spray. If Danny followed me...

Though, on second thought, the voice sounded more like a woman's, probably belonging to the woman, waving frantically from a nearby bench. Even from a distance, I can tell she's striking with her perfectly-smoothed bun framing a beautiful, if familiar, face. "How weird that I run into you here! What a small world!"

*Small* is an understatement. Dahlia—*Adrian Riley's* Dahlia, to be exact—hadn't struck me as the type to go for early morning walks through the park during our previous interactions. Her outfit supports that theory—a cream skirt with a matching blazer. Only when I glance down at her six-inch heels do I notice the small dog padding around her feet. "Pouchie loves this route," she says, glancing down at the dog with a small smile. "Are you on your way to work?"

"Um..." I can't help it. I flinch, and my fingers tighten their grip over my rolling suitcase. "N-No."

Dahlia frowns and reaches down to scratch Pouchie's head. "Day off?"

I somehow manage to shake my head. Small talk has never been my forte, and I'm not sure how to navigate a normal conversation without cutting in to ensure that the other person ate meals at a reasonable time. I'm not sure if it's typical protocol to blurt out that you've been fired to a total stranger.

Before I can help it, some variation of that truth spills out anyway. "I took some... um, time off. Not by choice. I mean, I just... I'm taking a walk."

"Oh." Dahlia shrugs and rises from the bench. Pouchie falls into step behind her, and they create an impressive pair as they stroll toward me. "Same here. I decided to treat myself to a spa day, actually..." Her gaze roves down to my suitcase and the overly-stuffed canvas bag on my shoulder. "Are you traveling out of town?"

"Something like that," I croak. My palms are sweating. My heart is racing. I'm blinking too rapidly.

"Are you okay?"

I don't know how to respond to that question. For the first time in so long, I'm simply not prepared. There's no plan on the horizon. No neat list of tasks to complete. I'm virtually homeless, and yet I have more money in my account than I've ever seen at one time. The irony makes me burst out laughing, and Dahlia's concern only seems to grow.

"Evie?" She takes a step closer, preceded by a cloud of heavy perfume. Her fingers brush my shoulder, and the gesture feels oddly... reassuring? Like the friendly hugs I shared with my roommates, back when I had a normal social life. "Is everything alright?"

I tear my free hand through my hair, only to irritate a million sore spots I hadn't noticed before. Oh, that's right. Graeme Bellamy has a penchant for pulling hair, *in addition* to being a chauvinist pig with the ability to kiss like a mythical Roman god.

I bite my lip so hard I taste blood, as if the pain can erase the memory of him there. Then I shake my head. Nod. "I just need..."

"A spa day?" Dahlia guesses with a knowing grin. She tugs on her pink leash, sending her puppy skipping to her side. "Care to join us? Pouchie and I have room for one more. Perhaps I could even give you some tips on how to play my favorite game." Her pointed tone makes me recall our previous conversation. A game. That's how she described Riley and Bellamy's relationship.

With me smack dab in the middle of their twisted gameboard.

"Evelyn?" She raises an eyebrow as Pouchie tugs on his leash. "Perhaps you're too busy?"

As she gives in to Pouchie's silent commands to move, I follow her. "Wait..."

I'm smart enough to read between the lines as to what she's really after—a trade. Information on Bellamy, perhaps, in exchange for clarity about his relationship with Adrian Riley.

Any other day I'd refuse her offer on principle—Evelyn King didn't need pity from anyone. But any other day, I would have a job. Any other day, the last man to get into my pants wouldn't have indirectly paid for them through my salary. *And* any other day, I wouldn't be trolling central park with all my belongings shoved into a suitcase and no clue where to go next.

So, I nod and smile warily at the only person I've met within the past forty-eight hours who doesn't seem determined to fire or unnerve me.

"Sure," I say, alarmed to realize that I almost sound genuinely excited. "I'd love a spa day. And, a chance to learn this *game* of yours."

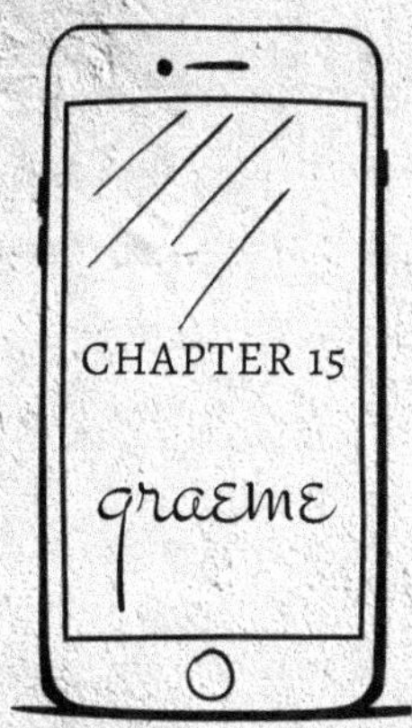


"I have your messages, Sir," Ann declares with a nervous swallow. She stands in the center of my office, trying her damn hardest to meet my gaze directly, but her eyes keep darting toward the same spot exactly two paces beside my desk, as if fascinated by what—or who—is missing. While Evelyn King has put up with me for three damn years, I doubt Ann could last three more minutes if today is a repeat of the last.

"Summarize them," I tell her, attempting to keep my tone as neutral as possible. The restraint is in vain—she flinches anyway and runs a trembling hand down the front of her skirt. I can't help the impatience in my voice. Riley may have won the last battle, but I intend to win the war—starting with tasking James with finding out anything he can about Evelyn King *or* Evelyn Browning. Normally, he could have an opposition file on my desk within hours.

It's been days.

"Okay. Three are from your m-mother," Ann stammers. "Two are from Andrew Perigrine. One is from the majority shareholder in that accounting firm you met with last week, and one is from Adrian Riley."

I sit forward, my eyes narrowing. "Say that name again."

Ann flinches, her cheeks flushing a delicate pink. "Um... Adrian Riley?"

I glance at my watch and note the time. It's barely nine a.m. Riley prefers to let his prospects stew, so either he changed his mode of operation overnight, or he's plotting something. "The last one," I snap at Ann, who stiffens on the spot. "What did it say?"

"Uh, he just wanted to know if you would like to join him for lunch."

Another alarming sign. Riley loves more than anything to dangle any newfound leverage over the head of his enemy—especially in a public setting. A meal was a symbolic representation that typically ended in him gaining the upper hand, our last disastrous meeting included. If I had any ounce of tact, I'd refuse this newer invitation without a second thought.

"Return the call," I tell Ann while lacing my fingers together so they can't curl into fists. "Tell him noon. I'll pick the place." Preferably, some loud, uncouth venue where they only serve beer on tap and cognac is mistaken for a last name.

"Um... Sir?" Ann wrings her hands nervously and refuses to meet my gaze.

"What is it?"

"*He* already mentioned a time and place."

"Oh, did he now?" My eyes narrow further. "Where?"

Ann turns three darker shades of red. "Somewhere called the Red Room?"

A bark of laughter breaks loose before I can help it. Well done, Riley. At least the bastard has tipped his hand already—he *definitely* found some form of leverage to justify being this bold. Which family secret will he exploit today? Given my mother's own warning, the answer is obvious. I can picture it now—Alexander waiting in the wings, ready to dump another mess onto my lap should I refuse Riley's offer.

Well, they both will be in for a rude awakening.

"Fine," I bark at Ann, who scurries out without another word.

Against my better judgment, I will play Riley's game. I'll even let him think he has the upper hand—harkening back to the only advice my father ever gave me. I think the context was in relation to him attempting to outsmart Gloria during their divorce proceedings by funneling as much of his assets as he could to his current mistress. *"To defeat thy enemy, you must become thy enemy."* Whether or not that meant him emulating Gloria's social life by buggering every socialite in her tea club remained to be seen.

Either way, the method had proved effective when Gloria put it into action by seducing his divorce lawyer and taking the bastard for all he was worth.

Regardless, the question of what Adrian Riley might be planning makes my jaw ache. I run my finger along it, only to remember the *real* reason for the slight sting. I can still feel the tiny nicks her nails left behind, too ragged to have been made by my razor. I can still feel her teeth along my lower lip as well. Her body on my fingers. My tongue.

I glance at my watch again. Nine-fifteen. Evelyn King is many things, but never late. Anyone else would have already paraded before my desk with their hands outstretched. Much like Adrian Riley, she now has her own leverage to hold against me, and yet she seems to be taking her sweet damn time using it.

I palm my mobile and open the email I sent her earlier, detailing the instructions needed to finalize her termination with human resources.

And said email, according to the receipt, has been unopened. Which was... unlike her, to say the least. I swipe to clear the screen and find myself composing a message directly to her mobile. *It is imperative that you respond to the email.*

Nearly ten minutes pass without a response.

Frowning, I try again. *Respond to the email. Now.* I wait a full twenty minutes before I give up written communication and call her. After only one ring, the call goes straight to voicemail. Gritting my teeth, I stand and cross over to the window where the signal is the strongest, full bars, and dial again.

*The number you are trying to reach is not available at this time...*

Cheeky woman. I should have had her escorted out by security last night rather than leave her there. I should have black-balled her name and rescinded all references. Evelyn King thought she had the last word?

She has another bloody thing coming.

I call her again. And again. Each time, the call switches over to voicemail. Either she's deliberately ignoring the attempts, or for the first time in her natural-born life, Evelyn King doesn't have her mobile physically glued to her hip. I don't know which potential scenario irritates me more.

Though, it's not like I give a damn. She could be on a plane headed out of New York by now—it wouldn't change a damn thing. As long as she was far from Adrian Riley's reach, any schemes he might have had in the works involving her are now irrelevant.

And when the bastard is fully over the idea of a merger, there isn't a place on the continent where Evelyn will be able to hide. And *when* I find her, she *will* give me an answer as to how well I fulfilled her little dare.

"Mr. Bellamy?" Ann peeks in from the doorway. "Your next appointment is here."

"Good."

She shows in the owner of an account I've been tracking for months. We're closer than ever to an agreement, but for some damn reason, my hand keeps drifting into the pocket of my trousers.

Finding my mobile. Checking for a response. Each time I discover nothing—she hasn't even opened either message. Could she still be asleep? Though if she is, it isn't in my bed. I know that she left the penthouse—and her mess behind—after a frantic early-morning ring from Maria, who'd worried I had been robbed.

"Mr. Bellamy?" The man across from me frowns and shuffles the documents of the presentation he seems to be in the middle of giving. "Is this a bad time?"

I shake my head and shove the phone back into my pocket. "Of course not."

Nothing gets in the way of business.

And *no one.*

James has kept the car running for the past twenty minutes that I've sat outside the Red Room. Riley requested we meet at noon, but I don't step out onto the curb until one. Something tells me that the bastard has been watching the entire time from some high-up window, however. Despite my best attempts, he'll still see the delay as a win in his book.

Not that I give a damn either way. My next meeting is at two. Adrian Riley has twenty damn minutes of my time, more than he deserves. When I enter the lobby, a blond waits for me, her suit crisp, her smile devilish.

"You must be Mr. Bellamy," she calls while slinking toward me in wickedly high heels. I take her outstretched hand and shake it once, surprised by the strength in her grip.

"I'm Giselle," she says, simpering as my gaze takes her in.

"Charmed." I turn my back on her and head for the elevator. "Is he in his office?"

"Not today." I hear the telltale click of her heels striking the marble in tandem as she struggles to catch up. "He's in his suite. I'll escort you."

"His suite?" I stop in my tracks, drawing eyes from the patrons occupying the lobby. "For *lunch*?"

"Yes, of course." Unperturbed, Giselle continues past me, her hips swaying with every step she takes. "He thought it was the perfect setting for an informal meeting between two old friends."

*Friends.* I grit my teeth at the word choice and reluctantly follow Giselle into an elevator. The floor we arrive at appears to be nothing more than a long hallway with a single door branching off the end.

"This way," Giselle calls before leading the way forward. Once we reach the door, she twists the doorknob and pushes it open. Feminine laughter spills out—the first contradiction to Riley's supposedly private lunch. I glance over Giselle's shoulder to find the spacious, empty entryway to what I assume is one enormous suite. The furniture is impeccable, the layout both elegant and casual. I don't find Riley after scanning the foyer, but the laughter grows, and I cock my head, attempting to decipher it. Two women. One voice is lighter than the other. Familiar...

"He's in here," Giselle says, indicating a hallway leading away from the giggling. I follow her warily, fully prepared to face a sneering Alexander standing in the middle of the office I find myself ushered inside.

Instead, Riley is waiting alone, but his knowing smirk isn't comforting in the slightest. "Bellamy," he says. "So nice of you to join me—"

"Let's cut this short," I interject, peering around at the corners of the room, hunting for the signs of whatever trap he's set. "If you're still asking about a merger, the answer is no—"

"I'm sorry to hear that," Riley replies with a shrug. He smooths out his collar before adjusting the ring on his left hand. Every motion is suave and nonchalant. My answer doesn't surprise him, but that's not what makes me instantly raise my guard. He's too calm. Too collected—much like an assassin poised to deliver a killing blow. "Please, do reconsider lunch, though, if you're hungry. I've had Dahlia order from her favorite café."

*Dahlia.* I instantly put a face to one of the giggling voices I'd heard in the foyer—the huskier tones definitely belonged to the dark-haired woman from dinner.

"I can't, I'm afraid," I reply to the invitation. "You've caught me at a bad time, Riley. I have another meeting in less than an hour."

"Oh." He nods understandingly and gestures to the doorway. "Allow me to see you out, at least."

The seemingly friendly gesture sets me further one edge, though the tension is momentarily shattered when the woman formerly introduced as Riley's legal counsel, now clad only in a colorful silk robe, races through the doorway.

"Excuse me," she calls with a giggle as she darts toward the desk. She pulls open a drawer and rummages through it, withdrawing a pair of scissors. Brandishing them in one hand, she hurries from the room, calling to someone who must be in another part of the suite. "Oh, come on! Don't you dare run! I'll get someone to help me hold you down. It'll be just a small trim!"

Another woman's exasperated sigh drifts from the hall in response. For some reason, the sound itches at the back of my mind like a puzzle whose missing piece lurks in plain sight.

"I won't keep you any further," Riley insists, reminding me of the task at hand. He strolls for the doorway but pauses right before crossing the threshold, his head cocked. "Is Evelyn on her own lunch break?"

I stiffen. To untrained ears, the casual tone would seem genuine, devoid of any dangerous note of inflection.

"Not that it's any of your business, but Evelyn King is no longer a part of my company. I took your *advice* to heart. A scandal is the last thing either of us wants to see happen. So..." My voice lowers as I meet his gaze directly. "You can cut her out of any schemes you may have in mind."

I gauge his reaction carefully, noting every nuanced shift of his expression. Is he surprised by the news? Intrigued? I can't tell if it's shock I find lurking behind his gaze or merely smug satisfaction.

"Is that so?" He nods seemingly to himself and continues into the foyer. "So that explains it..."

I'm on his heels. "That explains what?"

He takes his time turning to face me again, his head cocked slightly to the side, his expression mockingly innocent. "Why Dahlia ran into her alone, in the park earlier this morning."

His words act like some sick cue. From a nearby room, a single figure races out into the hall. She, too, wears a silk dressing gown, her blond hair hanging loose over her shoulders.

"Evie," Dahlia's amused voice calls after her. "Come back! It looks fine!"

Oblivious to anyone else, Evelyn King attempts to race down the hallway on her tiptoes, freshly painted a glaring shade of red. It's only when she's paces away that she finally looks up and sees Riley and me. Her glossy lips part in shock, and those blue eyes, now lined in kohl, widen as she scrambles to close her robe over a pink bra and panty set. "Oh my god—"

"Get back in here, you!" A smug Dahlia prances out and seizes Evelyn by the shoulders, steering her manually back to the room. "Your makeover is almost done. I promise." She glances back and casts a knowing wink. In my direction or Riley's?

It doesn't seem to matter either way.

Shock ricochets through my system. Followed by anger as every slight implication of what this means crosses my mind one after the other.

For starters, I've been outsmarted—as if a woman like Dahlia regularly went for morning strolls and just so happened to run into Evelyn King. Second, Riley had known. All along, he had *known* I would terminate her employment. He had someone follow her to ensure this damn lunchtime surprise. Did he know where she'd spent the night as well? The fact would only add another weapon to his arsenal.

I would have preferred to have found Alexander lounging in his knickers in the heart of this damn club. I expected as much. Not this.

As much as it fucking kills me to admit, Riley caught me off guard.

The bastard knows it.

"What a small world," he muses while fiddling with his ring. "It's a shame, really, that you couldn't join us for lunch…"

"Oh, it *is* fate, really," I counter.

Riley frowns. "Is that so?"

"Yes," I grit out. "Because my next meeting is already here."

My mind is already salvaging the shock in favor of retaliation. I start down the hallway and barge through an open doorway, startling the two women inside. One of whom is already blushing crimson and promptly turns three shades redder.

"Smart of you to meet me here, Evelyn," I tell her. "We can commence with our meeting sooner."

"Um..." She blinks while Dahlia runs her fingers through her hair. "Our... our what?"

"Get dressed, and we can go. Now."

All eyes are on the two of us. Watching. Waiting. Smirking.

After a moment's hesitation, Evelyn nods and scrambles to her feet. "Excuse me," she mutters before darting into what appears to be a bathroom adjacent to the room. Minutes later, she reappears wearing jeans and a plain green sweater. I've never seen her dressed in anything but a skirt. The lack of polish makes her seem like an entirely different person— some casual phantom merely wearing the face of Evelyn King.

"Here are your things," Dahlia says, crossing the room to where that infamous bag rests beside a rolling suitcase. She hands them both to Evelyn, who musters up what can only be described as an exhausted attempt at a smile.

"Thank you. Really," she gushes. "For everything. I needed this more than you know."

Dahlia nods and flashes a knowing grin. "Anytime."

Still smiling, Evelyn turns to face me, only to have her expression dramatically falter. A careful mask replaces it as she sizes me up, her eyes wary, her posture tense as if warding off a blow. "Mr. Bellamy—"

"Let's go." I turn my back on her and try to navigate the floor plan through memory. When I reach what I assume is the entrance, I can tell she's still on my heels, her breathing ragged and unsteady against the back of my neck.

"Evie, wait!"

I glance over my shoulder to see Dahlia approach, still shamelessly wearing only that robe. She extends her palm, revealing a cell phone about ten years outdated. "You nearly forgot this," she says. Her eyes dart to me, and she adds, "The main rule of a spa day—all connections to the outside world *must* be confiscated."

"Thank you." Evelyn tucks the phone into her pocket, oblivious to the way I glare at the device. At least the question of her dead silence is answered. I wonder who held onto her "confiscated" mobile all this time? Riley? Did he peer through every incoming message, smirking to himself?

The smile he wears now doesn't reveal a damn thing. He merely nods, displaying a row of straightened teeth. "Until next time, Bellamy. What a shame about lunch."

I say nothing when I turn to the door and wrench it open. Evelyn follows, dragging the suitcase behind her while wrestling her bag onto her shoulder. The bloody thing looks even heavier than usual. She struggles in my wake, and with a sigh, I reach back.

"Give it to me."

"No." She shakes her head, still attempting to maneuver the suitcase with her free hand. "I mean... It's okay. I've got it—"

I seize the handle of the rolling suitcase regardless and tug, easily ripping it from her grip.

When we reach the elevator, I gauge her reaction from the corner of my eye. Her cheeks are red, her chin jutting haughtily into the air. She doesn't say a damn word until we descend to the lobby and exit the building.

"I'll take that now, thank you." She hurries to stand in front of me and points toward the suitcase.

Without acknowledging her request, I push past her, toward James, who circles around to the boot of the car when I nod toward it. I toss the bag inside and slam the lid before she can reach for it.

"What are you doing?"

"Lunch," I tell her, stepping toward the back seat as James moves to open the door. "We have a meeting." The real appointment will be pushed back. After all, it won't take long to square away what few details I have left to discuss with Evelyn King. I replace James and grip the door by its handle, jerking my chin toward the opening. "Get in."

A freshly-plucked eyebrow rises into a fringe of blond hair. It's two inches shorter than before, courtesy of Dahlia, I suspect. The resulting length frames her face, barely brushing her shoulders. I frown. A bob doesn't suit her. Her hair should be longer—long enough to use as a leash to drag her to heel when she chooses not to listen.

"I don't think so, Mr. Bellamy." It takes all her professional, polite nature to tack my name onto the end of that sentence.

"Everything that needed to be said, we discussed last night." She inhales shakily and hikes her bag higher on her shoulder. "So, I'll be leaving. Now." She glances expectantly at the boot, but I make no move toward it.

"Is that so?"

She nods, but the way her cheeks redden warns me that she already suspects what my next line of attack will be.

"I think we left a lot of things *unsaid* last night."

"If you want to press trespassing charges, you know where to reach me."

I can't tell if she's deliberately avoiding any mention of what happened or if it really didn't stick out in what seems to be a string of moments spent half-dressed in the home of another man.

"And what if I wanted to press charges of sexual assault?"

She reddens even more and inhales as her mouth wordlessly opens and closes. "You... you can't be serious."

I jerk the door open wider. "Get in."

She doesn't move. Instead, her chin juts even higher, her hands clenching into fists. "No."

"No?" Before today, I've never heard that word come from her mouth, directed at me. No.

"Press charges," she tells me. "Do whatever you want. The least I can offer you is to have the carpet cleaned—"

"And the bedsheets?"

Within the span of a second, something snaps inside Evelyn King. Her eyes are brighter than I've ever seen them—blazing. She draws herself up to her full height and steps toward me, heedless of the scene we create. "Do you want me to admit it? Is that it?" she demands. "I got fired. I got drunk. I got *finger-fucked* by my egoistical ex-boss, and I thoroughly regret it. Are you happy now, Mr. Bellamy?"

Her little outburst draws attention from the patrons entering and leaving the club, and everyone within a one-block radius. Something tells me that we've caught the attention of a certain duo watching from the upper floor as well.

"Get in." I take my hand off the door handle and grab her arm instead. She doesn't expect the motion and can only gasp in shock when I shove her onto the back seat. I climb in after her before she can scramble back out. Her hand is already grasping for the handle of the opposite door, but I beat her to the punch by reaching past the front seat on my end and engaging the master lock.

"James," I start as I slam the door behind me. "The *Petit Manger* café—"

"No." Evelyn maneuvers her body as close to the door on her end as physically possible, her hand digging through her bag. A second later, she withdraws a small, nondescript bottle, the nozzle aimed at my face. "Let me out. Now."

For the second time in as many days, Evelyn King makes me laugh—really laugh. I throw my head back. My chest heaves with each sharp bark. When I finally trail off, I don't answer her directly, instead turning my attention to the front seat. "James."

"James?" Evelyn seconds, her voice a higher octave than usual. "Let me out."

It shouldn't take the man nearly a minute to make his choice. In the end, he squares his shoulders and silently steers the car into the thick of traffic. I can see his expression in the rearview mirror—furrowed brow and terse frown. I make a mental note to increase his next check before focusing my attention right back on Evelyn King.

She's glaring, a look similar to the kind she gave the bureaucrat that she verbally eviscerated in French. That snobbish, prudish sneer. In fact, I almost believe she just might use that pepper spray.

"I don't have anything to say to you. Mr. Bellamy," she adds at the last possible second, making the moniker seem more like an insult than anything else. *Mr. Bellamy.*

"Good," I tell her, glancing from the window as the buildings of midtown streak past. "I suppose you'll find it a relief that all you need to do is listen."

"To what?"

I mull over her question. Which of the many pieces of advice did she need to hear? How about the most helpful tip to begin with. "I'll keep it simple. Stay away from Adrian Riley."

"I'm sorry?" I glance at her from the corner of my eye just in time to see her eyebrow raise. "In case you weren't aware, firing someone typically means you don't get to micro-manage their social life."

I frown at that little quip. Maybe it's her tone that catches my attention. So bitter. So... hurt. The woman has no bloody clue. I did her a favor by removing any reason she had to be in the same vicinity of that bastard Riley. But no, trust Evelyn King to do the exact opposite of what would make her life even a fraction easier—she has to jump right into the frying pan and bathe herself in oil while she's at it.

"You were in his suite," I start. But no... my voice sounds too deep. Guttural. Less concerned and more... furious. "Half naked."

"Oh." Her cheeks redden further, but she does her best to sit haughtily in her seat, still aiming the can of pepper spray. "Once again, I fail to see how that's any of your business, Mr. Bellamy."

"Any of my business..." I'd heard those words once before, directed my way by someone else who'd fallen into the claws of Adrian Riley. It never did seem to be "my business" until the jaws of his trap snapped shut, and only I was left to clean up the mess. "Consider it a parting piece of advice," I tell her coldly. "Stay away from him."

"Parting," Evelyn echoes the word, her tone crisp. "Does that mean that I can go now?"

"No." We're around the corner from the café, but I'm starting to entertain the prospect that she might choose to bolt into the middle of the lunch rush crowding the side-walks. "Humor me just this once, and then you'll be free to frolic in the uptown suites of as many men as you please. James," I say before the man can pull up alongside the curb. "Change of plans. We'll have lunch at my place."

"No." Evelyn shakes her head, and her finger seems dangerously close to pressing down on the nozzle of the can she holds. "No lunch. Not there. Not anywhere."

"What are you afraid of?"

The question catches her off guard. She blinks. "I... I don't. What?"

I lean in and watch her throat contort around a hard swallow. "Are you afraid that being alone with me might lead to another incident wherein—as you so elegantly put it—you get drunk and finger-fucked by your... what was it? Selfish, egotistical, *ex*-boss—"

"At least I don't have to worry about being fired again," she interjects in a surprisingly deadpan tone.

"Yes." I find myself nodding. "There's always that."

"Fine." She stows her pepper spray back into her bag and shifts around to face forward. Her legs cross primly at the ankles, her hands folding neatly on her lap. "This shouldn't take long. I'm more than fine with the severance amount if that's your concern."

"Of course, though, I'll have to subtract for the cleaning of the carpet."

"And the sheets, too," she retorts without a hint of inflection. She's cold, professional, organized Evelyn King once again.

The only slip in her façade is the way she bites her lower lip when she thinks I'm not looking, tugging at the plump bit of flesh.

"Yes, the sheets," I agree. "Though perhaps I should deduct Maria's severance from the amount as well."

"You wouldn't." She faces me, her eyes wide, her lips pursed. "It was my fault. Don't fire Maria... Though, if you do," she adds quickly, raising her chin, "I will be more than happy to hire her. We have one reference in common, after all."

That's more like it. I'm used to hearing people boast about what they could buy with their payoff amount. The right number of zeros can cool any temper or sore ego. I only have to discover which sum will make Evelyn King merrily skip off into the sunset. "Don't forget your panache for deception and colluding," I tell her. "You and Maria seem to have that in common."

She says nothing, her gaze focused on her window. It's only when James pointedly clears his throat that I realize the car isn't moving. "Sir?"

We're parked outside of the Royal, and probably have been for at least the past ten minutes.

"I suppose we're already done," Evelyn says when I reach for the door on my end. Her relief is palpable—from the corner of my eye, I see her run a trembling hand through her hair, flicking aside the freshly-cut strands. "James, can you take me—"

"We haven't even begun," I tell her as I step onto the curb. I hold the door open pointedly and glance back to find her still seated. Her expression reminds me of a cat Gloria had once— some imported bastard from France that tried to decapitate anyone foolish enough to reach into its carrier and drag it out. Applying feral traits to someone like Evelyn King is a surreal scenario, but I know that any limb I stick into that car will be at her mercy. Teeth or nails? One look at her, and I know the answer. *Teeth*, definitely. I find myself gritting my own at the memory of her slap.

"If you have anything else we need to clear up, I would prefer an email," she says tersely.

"I *did* send you an email," I admit. "Frankly, you were too busy cavorting with Adrian Riley and his associates to pay it much attention."

She glances down at the pocket containing her mobile and promptly turns three shades redder. "Well... I can always—"

"Let's not make a scene, Evelyn. I do have another meeting to attend." One that I'm already running late for. If Ann is worth even a fraction of what I pay her, she has already found a way to stall. I have another hour to kill, at least. "Can we please get this over with, Ms. King?"

The impatient tone does her in. She frowns, but climbs from the car, and when I head for the entrance of the building, I know she's reluctantly fallen into step. There's a small bistro adjacent to the lobby, and I sense some of the tension in her posture loosen the moment she lays eyes on it.

"We'll talk here?"

"Of course," I reply, though I don't miss how relieved she seems in the presence of witnesses. "Did you think I would actually take you upstairs? Unlike Adrian Riley, I am not so unprofessional as to meet with a colleague in my private home."

If the language insults her, her expression doesn't reveal it. Instead, she sits at the nearest table and faces me from the other end. "Okay, Mr. Bellamy. What do we have to discuss?"

"Nothing too serious," I assure her. "I merely have one simple question to ask."

Her eyebrow arches once again. "Oh?"

"What will it take for you to stay away from Adrian Riley?"

She frowns, and I clear my throat.

"Perhaps I wasn't clear enough, Evelyn. How much damn money do I have to shove into your bank account for you to stay the hell away from him? Name a price, and it's yours."

1

My dad was a big proponent of the mantra "Never say die." No matter the stakes. No matter how high the odds might have been stacked against you... as far as he was concerned, you always went in with your head held high or not at all.

However, Graeme Bellamy might have tried even his patience. For someone so successful, he is too damn stubborn. Wasn't there some joke about the flexibility of business? The only thing flexible about Bellamy at the moment seems to be how many different ways he can frown and yet somehow *not* seem as petulant and childish as his words reveal him to be.

"Round figures," he prompts me when I gape at him, speechless. "Let's make this quick."

"Yes," I force myself to croak when the shock of his request wears off. "Lightning quick. I'll give you a round figure—zero. Just one," I add to clarify. Then I stand, keeping the bulk of my bag between us as if it can serve as a sufficient shield against the searing look he shoots my way. "Thank you for meeting with me, Mr. Bellamy. Sorry, to have kept you from your next appointment—"

"Sit down." He nods to the empty chair when I don't comply, his voice taking on that hard, guttural tone I loathe. Vibrations jolt down my spine, awakening every nerve before I can help it. "Please."

The dangerous hint of politeness makes me swallow my pride and join him at the table again. My heart flutters in my chest. I feel like I'm navigating a minefield blindfolded with no clue of which direction to head in. I was used to handling Bellamy's temper alone, but rarely did it spark to life in the first place because of me.

"Alright," I say softly. "What do you want?"

"A solid number." He reaches for the pen he always keeps in his breast pocket and snatches up a napkin from the center of the table.

Being that this is an expensive bistro that probably serves imported coffee from wherever coffee is born, the napkins aren't average napkins. They're crisp white, thick, with the bistro's logo embossed on the front. To make a good enough impression with the ink, Bellamy has to force the nib of the pen down—hard.

"Big enough to fit on the line of a check," he adds impatiently.

How typical. If there was ever a problem that Graeme Bellamy couldn't solve with his name or ruthless personality, he threw money at it. A *lot* of money. Like when he dumped his last girlfriend a week before her birthday and sent her to Acapulco with the tennis instructor she'd been cheating on him with, just to keep the mess out of the tabloids.

That kind of money. This was the same man who sent his mother a check on her birthday so he wouldn't have to be bothered to meet her for lunch if he didn't feel like humoring her. To him, placating an employee he'd fired after three dutiful years could easily be accomplished with a few zeros and a well-placed decimal point.

"I don't want your money," I insist, stressing every word. "So, if that's all you have to discuss, then we really are done here."

I make no move to stand, however. I watch him instead. His eyes narrow and turn a dangerous hue of blue. That sizzling, electric shade. I've only seen that color a handful of times. Once when he kicked a man out of his office after the bastard tried to grope me. Once again, when his mother mentioned any "family" gatherings. Oh, and again last night. When I pretty much called him selfish in the sack, and he...

I blink back the memory, but my body is slow to catch up. Heat prickles in my belly and travels lower. My clothes feel tighter. It's too hot in this damn place.

"I'm not playing coy, either," I add when Bellamy doesn't speak. In fact, he's too quiet—sitting there patiently like a wolf about to strike the moment its prey lets its guard down.

"Maybe before this mess, I would have accepted a raise, but I don't need your money—"

"Then what?" he demands. "Property? A high-rise apartment in LA? Name it. It's yours."

"That's not what I meant," I say.

"Then what?"

He seems more frustrated than he should be. As if, for all his worldly experience and success in trade, it's like Graeme Bellamy really can't fathom anything someone might want other than money or material things. Perhaps that cold, ruthless persona isn't all an act?

The poor man really has no fucking clue. Though maybe it took someone who couldn't risk forging an existence solely based on money or property to see that.

"I don't want or need anything from you," I try to reiterate.

"There must be something." His hands form fists over the table, and the pen he still holds jerks across its makeshift notepad, leaving a glaring black streak over the ivory. "Name it."

"Maybe..." I lick my lips and try a new line of attack. "Maybe the truth?"

His mouth tightens into a flat line. The pen falls from his grip and rolls across the table. I have to lunge for it before it can fly off the edge. "The truth?"

"Maybe if you told me *why* you don't think I should associate with Adrian Riley, rather than try to browbeat me with your checkbook... That might go over a tad better."

Though, it's not as if the answer isn't painfully obvious—he hates the man, and something tells me that Adrian Riley more than readily returns the sentiment. A mutual anger simmers between them—but the polished, suave kind that makes them provoke each other with veiled words and casual threats when any other man would have resorted to fists.

Like Danny, for instance. My brother has never met a problem he couldn't solve by beating it into a bloody pulp— or being beaten into a pulp. Whichever came first.

I jump, torn from the thought, as Mr. Bellamy stands. One of his hands tugs at his tie while his gaze sets the air between us figuratively on fire. "This isn't a conversation that I want to have—"

Oh, thank god. "Me either," I admit, bolting upright. "I'll leave—"

"In public," Mr. Bellamy continues over me. He turns and crosses the small dining room, drawing eyes with every step. Not even because he's fuming, his jaw clenched, eyes blazing. Most likely because, in spite of being furious, he looks damn handsome *while* fuming. For the first time, I notice the slight curl to his hair that usually isn't there. He must have washed it this morning and left without combing every single strand into place as per usual. I can't resist the part of me that pictures him in the shower, washing away every wayward germ that might have touched his skin. Washing *me* away.

The thought makes my breath hitch in my throat. I wonder if the water was cold...

"Ms. King?" He doesn't even bother to look back at me as he dominates the doorway, his posture rigid enough to rival that of a statue. I start forward, picking my way through tables, and he leads the way across the lobby, toward the elevators...

"No." I dig my heels into the polished marble, shaking my head. Only then do I realize where he might be headed. *This isn't a conversation that I want to have in public.* "We can talk in the car," I suggest while Bellamy casually strikes the button, indicating he plans to ascend to an upper level.

When the elevator finally does arrive, he glances back at me, and for the first time in so long... I can't read his expression.

"You named your price, Ms. King," he says in that raspy, warning tone. "I'm willing to pay it. Unless you've changed your mind and decided to accept my previous offer."

Standing there, the picture of poise, as he offers to take me up to his private suite and discuss what I assume is an inti-mate aspect of his personal life... Graeme Bellamy has never looked more intimidating. Or more dangerous. He could offer me a million dollars, and—as much as I might kick myself for it later—I could easily walk away. But if he instead promises to reveal even a sliver of information about himself that I hadn't learned on my own?

Well, it is a tempting proposition, to say the least.

"Ms. King?" He glances back before stepping into the eleva-tor. He braces one hand against the side, preventing the doors from closing, but his terse frown warns me that he won't wait forever.

"Fine." I start forward and enter the elevator, pressing my body against the corner as far away from him as the narrow space will allow. I hold my breath as the doors close, and the lift begins its ascent, and then I do the unthinkable and follow Graeme Bellamy right to the door of his penthouse suite.

He pulls his card key from his pocket and swipes it through the reader. When the door opens, I don't see any hint of Maria in the foyer. Did he really fire her? I glance at him, letting my eyes drift over the firm set of his shoulders. Despite everything that has transpired between us within the past twenty-four hours, I still don't believe he'd be that cruel. Firing me without warning was one thing, but even I could admit that, given our history and despite my dedication to the job, for all I knew, it could have been a long time coming.

As he slams the door behind him, I tally up all the reasons Graeme Bellamy could have amassed over the past three years to reach the decision to let me go. Our relationship wasn't exactly friendly, for one. I constantly nagged him about his meals, admittedly overstepping a few boundaries between concern and borderline obsession with his health. Not to mention, I'm the only one apart from Gloria who seems to have no trouble telling him to his face just what I think.

"You said something about a conversation," I say, prompting him when he doesn't speak. Ignoring me still, he moves to stand before the impressive view of the city revealed through a row of floor-to-ceiling windows that lines this side of the loft. It's turned into another dreary day with a storm hovering over the horizon, a fitting omen of my luck. "Perhaps we can reschedule," I add, when Bellamy still makes no attempts to speak. There are much more important ways I could be spending this day, such as tracking down a moving company to help clear my apartment before Danny makes himself too comfortable.

"Don't let him fool you," Bellamy says to me, and I promptly lose my train of thought—correction—the train flips the tracks and explodes in a fiery wreck. The look he gives me from over his shoulder... Intense would be one way to describe it. Maybe even vulnerable. Real emotion spills out, bubbling beneath the indigo crust of those two incredible eyes.

"Who... who fool me?" I pant once I find my breath. *Snap out of it, Evie.* I lace my hands together behind my back and pinch myself on the wrist, just once. The little bit of pain tethers me somewhat back to reality, but his gaze never loses that honest quality, even as he frowns.

"Adrian Riley," he says as though the answer were obvious. Though maybe it is. These past few days, everything seemed to lead back to that name one way or the other.

"Who is he?" I ask, taking a single step closer. To hear him better. The impulse has nothing at all to do with the way my fingers twitch as if aching to brush his shoulder. Because touching him would be a very stupid thing to do... Even if he looks seconds from sending his fist through one of the crowning centerpieces of his high rise. Okay, on second thought, preventing vandalism seems to be a damn good reason to shirk the rules. I reach out. Inhaling sharply, I brush the tips of my fingers along the side of his forearm, just hard enough that he flinches and glares at my hand. The gesture distracts him from the window, at least.

"Someone you do not want to entangle in your life, I can assure you that," he says while I take a quick step back and tuck the offending fingers into my pocket. They burn. A lot. Or maybe it's more like a... tingle. The same tingle I feel in a place where I haven't "tingled" without the aid of a battery-operated machine in so damn long.

Okay, maybe not that long. Since last night, when *his* fingers had made an impromptu stand-in. I can tell in the almost mirror-like reflection shining off the glass before us that he isn't looking at me. Thank god. I fight to school my own horrified expression into a blank mask and then take another two quick steps away from him. "It's not like I've gone out of my way to associate with him, so I think you don't have much to worry about—"

"You haven't," Bellamy interjects. "*He* has. Don't tell me you're really naive enough to think that Jezebel woman just randomly crossed your path—"

"Dahlia," I correct, irritated for reasons I can't explain. Perhaps it's the self-centered way that he assumes the one bit of human interaction I've had outside of him had to be all about... well, *him*. Granted, I didn't believe that Dahlia had been out on a casual stroll either, but the point was—that was the most amount of fun I've had in years. All three of the ones spent working for him included. I had needed that. So. Damn. Much. It's funny how I hadn't even realized it until

Dahlia had whipped out the first bottle of disgustingly pink nail polish while we waited for her masseuse to arrive. "And I can assure you that neither you, nor Adrian Riley, were mentioned once during our spa day."

Those two words draw an almost comical reaction from him —he wrinkles his nose like a boy caught staring at his mother's lingerie drying on the clothesline. "I can assure you that anything he or his associates do always has an ulterior motive lurking behind it."

"Well, maybe I did as well. Have you considered that?" I counter, crossing my arms over my chest. "After all, how else would I score a private meeting with a Swedish masseuse flown directly from Sweden—"

"This isn't a game, Evelyn," Mr. Bellamy says, his tone crisper and drier than usual. I glance up, following the rigid line of his jaw. I have sat in on enough of his anger management sessions to know that look, and I instantly feel a twinge of guilt in my stomach. I wasn't letting him speak. I wasn't letting him get out whatever it was that seemed to be making him so angry. As aggravating as his smug little insinuations are, now is not the time for banter, even I can admit that.

"Okay," I tell him, shuffling three steps closer so we stand side by side before the window with the perfect amount of professional distance between us. "I'm listening."

"We grew up together," he grits out. "Me. Riley. My brother..."

At first, I assume he was somehow referring to Stella— perhaps there were more secrets lurking within the Bellamy-

Ashton skeleton closet than even I could imagine? But no. It was all in the way he uttered that word. Brother. I have never heard him direct even a fraction of that malice toward his sister, considering that, next to him, she was the most valuable asset to the company as the head designer.

"You have a brother." I say the words carefully, still woefully unprepared for the moment he nods. We're still not facing each other directly, but I can almost picture his reaction even as I watch it play out over the glass in front of me like some bizarre psychic vision—he'll straighten his tie, run a hand through his hair, frown. To negate any bit of intimacy that this revelation might foster between us, he'll, of course, find some way to turn it all on me.

"Yes," he grunts. "Of course, don't blame yourself for not knowing that particular piece of information—I hid that fact on purpose."

I blink. The gruff, bitter tone, yes, that seems to be according to plan. But no insulting barb tacked onto the end of that statement? I don't know how to process that.

"Why?"

"Because considering the lengths you go through for Gloria, I didn't really desire to watch you extend the same courtesy to *him*," Bellamy admits. "He's spent his whole life taking advantage of the goodwill of others."

I have to take several deep breaths to keep my emotions in check. No... Could I be feeling sympathy for someone like Graeme Bellamy? His situation seems similar to mine. Go figure. Not that I would turn this venting session into an episode of tit for tat.

"I take it that you guys don't have the best relationship," I say cautiously, taking a stab in the dark. "Believe it or not, I can relate to that. If you'd tell me about him."

I expect him to refuse outright. Instead, he frowns, glaring at the view of the city before us. "He failed every preparatory on the continent. My mother eventually had to send him to school in America, where he proudly made a mockery out of our family name every chance he got."

I say nothing, marveling that he's speaking to me at all. The strangest part? I can relate to the hard, bitter note in his voice.

"At eighteen, he cut off all ties and disappeared in France for a year," he continues. "When he turned up again, he broke into the summer house in Nice with some trashy American tourist and ransacked the place without realizing that my mother had been there on holiday. The bastard damn near gave her a heart attack."

I wring my hands awkwardly and stare down at the polished wood floor. It's the first time that I've ever seen him display some hint of real concern for his mother.

"That's just the overview of every asinine thing he's done. More recently, it was entangling himself with Adrian Riley and making a bet that he lost. Spectacularly."

"And then what happened?" I despise the breathless quality my own voice has taken.

Like someone watching a scene from a tabloid spill out right before her eyes, and she can't fucking help the greedy desire to learn more. *More.* It's like this little itch inside me won't be satisfied until I do. And not about Adrian Riley, but Graeme Bellamy. How many times has he tried to help his brother and failed? Because I know that damn look—his anger stems more from frustration than true loathing.

God, I need to snap out of it. I shake myself and reach out to drag my fingers down the window glass' smooth surface. Poor Maria will have to use a bit of Windex to erase the fingerprints, but the icy surface seems to snap some sense into me. Enough that I can look at Graeme Bellamy again without feeling... what is it? Pity?

"Riley and I got into a disagreement. Out of spite, the bastard tricked Alexander into an investment opportunity," Bellamy admits. "He made it seem like prime real estate, but it was just some sleazy gentleman's club on the Lower side of London. He also ensured the tabloids discovered that fact so that my family's name got dragged through the mud. If you look hard enough, you can still find the articles I didn't manage to bury into obscurity." He laughs, the sound punctuated by the thud his palm makes when it connects with the window. Hard. Again. A third time.

I can't stop myself from reaching out, and this time I don't pull my hand away when he frowns down at it. I let it linger on his forearm—a testament to the insane thrill running through me like a lance. I'm touching Graeme Bellamy. On purpose. For a damn good reason—he stopped hitting the glass, at least.

"Is that the club in London he mentioned?" I ask carefully. Skirting an unfamiliar territory with him feels like playing Frisbee with a lit stick of dynamite. One wrong direction and boom.

"Yes." He shifts his stance and adjusts his collar as an excuse to rip his arm from my grasp. "Alexander had no choice but to sign the damn thing over to me. He wanted me to sell it, but I decided to make it an... example. If Riley thought to shame me, then I would turn the tables and embrace the challenge."

His tone is guttural, his expression fearless. This is the man who could move mountains and ruthlessly conquer any task or business he set his mind to.

"I took control of the club. Even managing it in *absentia,* I managed to turn it into an exclusive venue that the wealthy and elite clamored to join. I did it out of spite," he admits. "It was only later that I learned Riley had a similar club here in the States. I think he used the allure of it to convince Alexander that his own club would be a good investment. He named his establishment the Red Room. Naturally, I did the same." He shrugs, running a finger along his lapel. It strikes me then that money isn't just a magic cure or a Band-Aid to him. It's cathartic. He used it to fix his own problems, so of course, to him, it would suffice as a way to fix everyone else's. "Now, seven years later, the bastard wants to make a 'merger' official," he snarls. "As if I will just roll over and let him take back what I've made mine."

"That... gives me some perspective on the situation," I say carefully. More like a whole different frickin' outlook. I do my best to still appear professional, however. The man beside me may have fired me and been a total ass, but even I could admit that having someone from your past waltz back into your life and lay claim to things they had no right to could make for a crappy way to kick off the week.

"Alright," I say to my sullen reflection. Damn, Graeme Bellamy for making even pissing him off after he insulted me in just about every way imaginable seem cruel. "I'll stay away from Adrian Riley. Based solely upon my own judgment," I add hastily.

The last thing I needed in my life was another manipulative asshole. Both Mr. Bellamy and my own brother have that department covered.

"Good," Mr. Bellamy says, straightening his tie once again. The arrogant bastard has the nerve to clear his throat before stepping away from me as though to pointedly reinforce that any moment of confession is now over.

"Good," I echo. "And now I'll be leaving."

"Yes." Bellamy nods, still eyeing the view. "That will be all, Ms. King."

*That will be all.* The way he says those words resonates oddly in my brain. And then it hits me. Something insane. Something so selfish and impulsive that it should have come from a toddler and not a grown man. "Is that why?"

He frowns. "Why what?"

*Oh, no, you don't,* I think as I approach him. "Is *that* why you fired me? Adrian Riley?"

Bellamy laughs. Not a real laugh, per se. One of those obnoxious "oh hardy, har har, the riff-raff can be so delightfully amusing" rich person laughs. The kind I'd been subjected to my whole life as the poor girl on scholarship while her father traveled the world, and her delinquent brother scandalized every young, desperate girl within a ten-mile radius. One of those fucking laughs.

"I won't deny that he wouldn't hesitate to use you in some scheme should the idea strike him," he admits. "But seriously, Evelyn, your work wasn't exactly flawless."

My entire existence could be summed up with the need for tough skin. I can roll with the punches and handle any insult tossed my way. I was too short. Too skinny. Too chubby. Too blond. Too blue-eyed. Too this. Too that.

Whatever. The remark might sting in the moment, but I could shrug it off. Stiff upper lip, like Dad always said. Anyone could insult me all they liked—Evelyn King. But never my work. Especially not three fucking years of it.

I inhale sharply as everything flashes red. The view. Graeme Bellamy. My shaking hands. I do my best to wrestle the anger back down. Deep breaths. Deep breaths. Somewhere during the process, I wind up choking on it all.

"My work?" I repeat hoarsely.

"Yes," Bellamy nods along with his own warped logic even as it spews from his perfect mouth. "I won't deny that you were efficient, Evelyn, but you could be insubordinate. And lately, you've had a habit of leaving your tasks unfinished..."

My right eye twitches. Unfinished. "Like what?"

He turns on me. With one well-placed advance, he has me staggering back against the window. The beautiful view becomes a prison, pinning me in place for the single searching, fiery look he sends in my direction.

"Your *last* task, to be exact," he says with so much anger prickling from his tone that my entire body jolts beneath the sting. "When you seemed to be in the middle of demonstrating all of the multitudes of ways that I am a failure in bed."

My mind goes blank. Dead. Naked. Empty. "T-That... that..."

"Yes, that," Bellamy says with a nod. He fingers his tie again, entwining his forefinger around the gray silk. It's dangerous imagery. All those memories I've been fighting back since waking up this morning in this very penthouse threaten to descend.

"That was nothing—"

"Then we're of agreement," Bellamy says over me. "Which brings me to our final piece of business. Admit it, and I'll let you go." He sounds like a teacher, bestowing extra credit upon a bothersome student as long as she says please.

"Admit what?" I manage to croak. His eyes, god, his eyes... I don't like the way they scan my face, searching for any sign of weakness to exploit. I don't like the increasingly ruthless way he clenches his jaw. Or how his fingers tighten their grip on his tie so much the knuckles whiten.

He steps closer, towering over me amid the scent of designer cologne. The motion forces me to crane my neck back just to continue to hold his gaze. In an instant, I know with frightening certainty just where he'll attempt to steer this already dangerous conversation. "Admit that I made you—"

"Unemployed?" I supply, thinking fast. If I kick him in the right spot, I might be able to run past him and reach the elevators before he could stop me. I let my brain toy with the plan, but my body seems unwilling to set it into motion.

"Should I give you a reminder?" Bellamy wonders. He has no damn business looking so... menacing as he tears his hand from his tie as if displaying every sinful finger. "Something about my not being able to get a woman to—"

"I was drunk." I say the words as though they explain everything. To him. To myself. I was drunk—ergo, anything that happened afterward could be proudly blamed on the wine. Not his touch that raised goosebumps over my body whenever I let myself think about it. His fingers. His voice... every gritted, barely audible word being growled into my ear as he moved his hand between my legs. "Congratulations, Mr. Bellamy, you achieved what my hand operated dil—"

"Shall I give you a refresher?" He touches my chin, placing his thumb against my lower lip. I could bite him if I wanted —not that I'd give him any other reason to chase me down. "You said, and I quote, 'your money and a few photo ops wouldn't satisfy me enough to make up for where you lack.'"

The sudden rasp in his baritone does something strange to my heartbeat—it's surging. I can't seem to catch my breath.

My sanity. Anything. I can only feel his thumb against my lower lip and breathe him in—he smells like all things impossibly rich and impeccable. Designer cologne. Ink from a seven-hundred-dollar ink pen. Cognac.

If someone who was even half of what he represented flirted with me, I knew myself well enough to admit my guard would fall... and my panties would easily follow. But Graeme Bellamy does not flirt—he intimidates and overpowers to get his way.

"I think I achieved one goal to make you rethink your words," he tells me, his voice softer. Volatile. "Should I be blunter?" His mouth is by my ear, his body dangerously close —within reach of my frantically heaving chest.

"I think I should leave now, Mr. Bellamy." It's a struggle to even get the words out. I try to slip past him, but his hand meets the glass beside my head before I can move, trapping me.

"I think you should admit it, Ms. King," Bellamy says as though he's proposing the most natural thing in the world. We're discussing the weather—not this. Not... "Admit it, and I'll let you go. Our business will be concluded, and you'll have the highest recommendation to list in your references."

"And what should I admit, exactly?" He's too close. He knows how fast my heart is beating. He can see the sweat beading over my brow. His tongue shoots out along his lower lip as though tasting the panic I can't even attempt to hide.

Then he leans in even closer, dragging his thumb from my lip to my chin. "Admit... that I made you—"

"I need to leave." It's like the sane part of me takes control just to gasp out those words, but my body malfunctions. My nerves are frazzled by his heat. His words play a dangerous game along my spine. I know he's not serious. But that knowledge doesn't seem to resonate when my eyes meet his. *Lightning.* It's the only word that comes to mind to name the alarming jolt ricocheting through my body.

"Come," he growls against my earlobe. *That* growl. "Admit that I made you come. Climax. Orgasm. Whatever pretty term suits your fancy. Just say it out loud, Ms. King. I made you do it."

My head won't stop spinning. I'm having a stroke, obviously. Graeme Bellamy didn't really say those things. He really doesn't mean...

"I'm leaving," I choke out the words to the sliver of ceiling beyond his head. I mean them at that moment. I *do*. But whenever I try to take a step, he's right there. His lips graze my earlobe, and I can feel the moist heat of his tongue when he speaks.

"You *do* need a refresher," he grits out, irritation lacing his already gruff tone. "Fine. Let me paint the picture for you, Evelyn—" His hand leaves my chin and moves to my waist. I feel his palm graze my hip through my jeans, before bracing flat against the glass of the window near my head. "My fingers. Inside you. You were wet," he adds with a dangerous undertone, but his expression makes it worse. Shocked, as if he can't believe the words coming out of his mouth. "Tight. I only had to *touch* you for—"

"E-Enough." My hand flies out to collide with his arm—but I don't do the smart thing—push him back. My nails seek out the contours of the muscle underneath, plying the rigid coils. I remember... Even though I'd been riding fast and loose on the dizzying wine merry-go-round, I can still recall his touch. His body pooled between my legs. That orgasm—stronger and more violent than any before it. But I had been drunk—as had he.

So, it didn't count.

"I bet you're wet now," he tells me, his breath hitching in his throat. Even as the words spill from his mouth, he knows it's wrong. This is wrong. "I bet that little toy of yours you reference so much couldn't get you off the way I did. Did you have to use your fingers when I left you?" God... His voice gets raspier, each word broken and gritty. I've never heard him sound like this. His lips keep moving, and he just can't seem to stop. "Tell me."

I squeeze my eyes shut to hold in the truth—maybe I had... Maybe alone in his room and still too dizzy to climb to my feet and leave, I had needed some extra little help getting him out of my head. Off my tongue. Just enough to pass out. So, I'd imagined him. Just once. Twice. Again. Over and over until the bastard's face chased me into my dreams. And there, he didn't just end it with his mouth and fingers. No, Graeme Bellamy had ruined even my typically platonic nightmares.

I'd woken up shaken, swollen, and sore...

Because of him.

"You did," he suspects, smug with triumph. The warmth from his breath drifts from my ear and down my neck. "Look at me and admit it."

I was quite content to stare at the inside of my eyelids. If I ignored him long enough, maybe he'd go. As if to spite my own hope, my fingers clench the ridge of his shoulder just a *little* harder. My nails curl a *little* deeper. Graeme Bellamy shudders.

"Say it," he commands. "And we'll return downstairs. I'll have James drive you home. I'll let you keep that damn pride of yours—"

*Or?* My mind skips ahead before he even lays out the terms of his threat.

"Or..."

He's closer. I feel his chest brush mine when I breathe in... out. My nipples can't bear the contact. They stiffen against the padding of my bra. *Everything* stiffens. I feel like a rubber band being ruthlessly stretched taut. One wrong move, and I'll snap.

"I'll have to refresh your memory for you," he says, all but breathing the words into my skin. Into every damn pore. "With enough detail so that you can jot it down in that bloody planner of yours and never forget. So, take it back."

His words remind me of those playground taunts children play. Say a mean thing. Pull the bully's hair until they cry uncle, and apologize. I was the master of that sort of revenge

—usually on behalf of Danny. Now, it's only my own pride at stake, but I can't seem to say anything in my defense.

Graeme's breath fans across my lips. He's rippling beneath my touch. I can feel the pulse of every single nerve and bit of muscle as he fights to keep control. From doing what? I don't know. A part of me wants to find out. Damn, that part.

"Where did we begin last time?" he wonders, each word ripped from his throat. I stiffen even before his hand palms my waist again, inching toward the erogenous zone beneath my zipper. "I think it was when you mentioned something about me being a 'one-and-done' kind of man..."

He finds the circular clasp of my jeans, his thumb resting against the copper. My stomach roils with each lazy flick of his nail. He's not trying—not really—and my body knows it. Hates him for it. Needs it...

"Stop!" Trying to pull away from him is like attempting to surface from gallons of water—while a sea monster down below grabs my ankle and tries to drag me right back down. He finally flicks the clasp with purpose, and it springs open. The pad of his thumb finds the head of my zipper and pins it flat against my pelvis. The only way I can retaliate is to dig my nails into his shoulder—but the action backfires. He coils beneath my touch. Like a piston, readying to spring. A sound rips from his chest. Ragged. Grating.

He lowers his thumb, and I feel another finger join it, gripping the top of the zipper, pulling down...

"And there was something else," he adds near my ear. His breath reverberates off the window glass and leeches into my skin. He's breathing harshly. Fast. Panting. "Something about me being the last man—" He tugs on the zipper, and my heart drops along with my loosened jeans. I could stop them from falling if I tried—spread my legs out, anything. I can't seem to move either way, and then he's sliding more fingers underneath the waistband of my panties. A thumb. Forefinger. Everything. The whole damn hand.

My eyes fly open as I brace myself against the window with one hand. He either doesn't see my lips move, struggling to form words, or he doesn't care. Before I can gasp out anything intelligible, he cups me fully, groaning at the way I feel. My cheeks catch fire, knowing how he'll find me—embarrassingly, *painfully* wet.

"The very last man you would ever want to fuck," he says gruffly, even as he curves his hand, forcing my hips to arch, my body on tiptoe. "Something tells me that you were lying, Evelyn."

I snatch my hand from the window and bring it to his collar, reaching for his perfectly straight tie. He doesn't like that. His eyes narrow. His mouth opens, but I work my thumb into the thick of the cape knot before he can say a damn thing and tug. He breaks off when the tie tightens, and the brief moment of control snaps some damn sense back into me.

*Fight,* Evie. Every cell in my body urges me to turn tail and run. I start to shove him back, trying to wiggle my hips from his grasp, but the bastard recovers before I can make even an inch of progress. Two fingers rub me raw. Stroking. Teasing. Detonating. He's rougher than he was last night—cocky.

I don't have a chance to catch my breath before he slides a finger inside me and watches my body collapse in on itself. My head flies back, my body arching, hips jerking, knees shaking. He's the only thing holding me up, and my nails dig in, one at his neck the other at his shoulder.

When he picks up his speed, grinding out earth-shattering friction, I say things I don't mean. Words that have no business flying out of my mouth, directed at none other than Graeme Bellamy. To save myself, I block them out, but he counters every plea, growling his responses into my neck.

"Faster?" he grits out, flexing the finger he has inside me before adding another. "Harder... Like this?" He thrusts both, and my head spins, my body buzzing. "More?" He grinds his palm against my clitoris, and everything ceases to matter but the friction. He's ruthless. When he shifts the angle of pressure, I moan. Greedily. Breathlessly. Every groan rises in pitch the harder he strokes. I can't stop whatever he unleashes inside my body. When he shoves both fingers inside me at once and flicks them apart, I go deaf. Numb. With a speed not even my trusty battery-operated boyfriend, or B.O.B for short, can achieve, I promptly shatter into a million pieces, and none other than Graeme Bellamy himself is there to pick them up and crudely shove them all back together.

"It was something like that," he tells me while I shudder through the last throes. "But I remember you being louder. And mentioning something about god..."

"And I remember you being much quieter," I rasp out when I find my voice again. It takes everything I have to meet his gaze fully, but I don't like what I see there. Blazing hot heat. Hunger, even. Like he wants to swallow me up whole in a way that is totally unprofessional. He still has his hand between my legs, two fingers still inside me. He continues to move them, lazily slow, as if it's just that easy. "Much quieter," I continue. "Because your mouth was occupied, as I recall. Doing something useful for once."

His smug grin falls flat and becomes something else. Something deadly. "That it was..."

He's on his knees in the blink of an eye. Graeme Bellamy is kneeling before me, dragging my panties down my legs and off before wrenching the hem of my sweater over the ridge of my stomach. He licks the skin there first, right below my navel. Then he uses his teeth to plot a path downward...

Oh no. My head connects noisily with the glass as I squeeze my eyes shut. He paints a sensual trail I don't have to see to know where he's headed. Hot breath nuzzles my inner thigh, and then his fingers are back... *Shit.*

"Does this feel familiar?" This man doesn't even sound like Graeme Bellamy. Self-assured, arrogant Graeme Bellamy—he sounds feral. And then I feel him. Tongue. Teeth. Everything... all at once.

My knees buckle when he makes the first pass with his tongue, setting every nerve on fire. He uses his thumb to aid in the second sweep, and suddenly I'm not standing on my own anymore. Dizzy, I wonder how in the hell I'm not crashing to the floor—then I feel the answer, practically fucked into me with every searing jab of his tongue. "I've got you."

Those words... The way he says them. In this moment, he means them, every word. He has me for what feels like hours, but it can only be minutes. Minutes before he has me thrashing, shaking, climbing that peak faster than I ever have before. Too fast.

It hits me like a train. My spine curls. My nails fist in his hair, dragging him closer, deeper... anywhere he can reach. When I finally get there, I do so loudly. My ears pop with the force of it as my brain disconnects from my body and spirals out of control. I'm barely back inside my head when I hear him—growling. Still moving. Sucking. Lapping. Oh god...

It strikes me then—he's trying to kill me.

"Okay!" I gasp the word out in two strangled syllables. *O... kay.* He doesn't stop. My body is on fire. I see sparks when he parts me with his thumb and simulates an action that should be done with a much larger part of his body. I fist my fingers into his hair, desperate to find enough leverage to pull him back. As if to spite me, he latches his entire mouth over me, shoving my legs apart, demolishing any semblance of balance I may have had on my own. I suck in air and practically scream out a plea, "Okay, enough! Enough..."

He withdraws his mouth so suddenly my stomach lurches at the loss of sensation. I need it back... I'll shatter if he does go back. *Need it...*

"Enough, what?" He's regained some semblance of that old haughty arrogance in his tone. True to form, Graeme

Bellamy is determined to get his way. He wants my surrender, and I know damn well that if he doesn't stop now, he will get it.

"You..." I croak out the word, muscling every ounce of self-control I have left to spit out three more. "Your... your turn."

That makes him freeze, his mouth inches from my throbbing, needy flesh. I do my best to slam my thighs together as my eyes open one by one. God, the sight of him on his knees. It's breathtaking. It's insane. I brace my weight on the hand buried in his hair to find the leverage to stay upright. My free hand has a mind of its own when it drifts over to the knot of his tie. I yank the tail of it from the fold of his suit and tug until he grudgingly stands.

The shift in the atmosphere is palpable when I take a step forward, and he counters me by taking one back. Forward. Back. Back. Forward. We stumble in tandem that way until the back of his knees hit the nearest leather chaise, and he sits, his legs parting. There's a dare in his eyes as he gazes up at me. I know just what he's thinking—that there's no way in hell I'll follow through on my own unspoken threat.

But curiosity is a dangerous, terrible thing. I can't stop myself from stepping forward, right between his legs. My fingers dart for the fastening of his slacks, and he even arches his hip off the leather seat to give me better access. The moment I touch the gray button, my teeth snap together. He's straining against the front of his pants in a way that's totally obvious. Vulgar. He's aroused, and he doesn't give a damn who knows it—especially not me.

The corner of his mouth quirks into the semblance of a grin when I hesitate, my fingers hovering over the zipper. My nerves falter for all the wrong reasons—I shouldn't *want* to commit a vulgar act on Graeme Bellamy. I shouldn't *want* to see how he reacts to my touch. I shouldn't *want* to hear the sounds he'll make if I touch him in the right way. I shake my head to clear it, but the unwelcome thoughts persist.

In the end, I let his smug expression goad me on. I sink down to my knees. I bring both hands to the front of his pants and undo them swiftly with none of the teasing care he used on me. The moment I free him from his boxers, I curl one hand around the base of him and swipe my tongue along the helmet. With my head down, I don't have to hide the shock I feel. He's perfect. Beautiful. His taste explodes over my tongue—everything a man like him should taste like. I can't stop myself from wrapping my lips around the crown and bobbing my head just once.

To prove that I can, of course. That's all this is... A sick, sordid game that I refuse to lose. In all reality, I have no excuse. At the tender age of thirteen, a stripper named Peaches gave me a detailed play-by-play on how to give a blow job that will make a guy "pay you at least twice the usual rate." In her expertise, it was all in the way you took your time to savor, rather than just "jerk and leave." My mother, of course, hadn't appreciated the impromptu lesson, but I had tucked the words away for safekeeping regardless—a lot of good it did me. Though one boyfriend—as he listed out all his many reasons for dumping me—claimed while I may have been a controlling bitch, at least "you give good head." That's always a plus.

Usually, I don't get much enjoyment out of the act—but the moment my tongue swipes the silken surface, and I hear the ragged groan he releases... I hollow my cheeks and take him in. His hands tangle in my hair, dragging me forward until I'm balanced on my knees. I take him deeper. Deeper. It's still not enough.

His entire body ripples with every stroke of my tongue. To the point that his nails break the flesh of my scalp. Blood rushes through my ears, muting the backdrop of his grunts and the few words he manages to grit out. "Fuck... Fuck... bloody fuck."

There's a moment when he shoves himself in so deep that I gag, and I know he's at the point of no return. I probably only have seconds to get clear before he does, but my body doesn't want to budge. My fingers keep twisting...

"Enough!" He yanks on a handful of my hair, dragging me back and freeing him from my mouth. Any brief bit of triumph I might have felt is quickly melted away by the look in his eye as he stands, fisting his cock with his free hand. He shudders for a full second, holding himself, but it's not until nearly a minute passes that I realize just what he's doing—staving off his own orgasm. Why?

Maybe his intentions have something to do with the way he drags me up by my hair once he seems to regain enough control over himself. His eyes meet mine, and they are so dark that I can't even name the shade of blue swirling around the irises. Using his grip on me like a leash, he steers me backward while advancing with every forced step. From my hazy knowledge of the layout, I know we're heading toward the stairs. Which can only mean...

"Shall we bet?" Bellamy wonders, his voice nothing more than a growled snippet of words. "How many thrusts will it take before you are 'done,' Evelyn? I know. One."

My heart hammers against my ribcage. Intelligible conversation is a distant concept, but somehow I find a few words to fling in his direction. "Is... that... a... dare—"

He tugs my hair so hard I wince. The pain should snap some sense into me, but it seems to travel right past my brain and down between my legs. He lunges, and I feel out with my free hand to find the curve of the banister as my foot scrambles for the first step.

"Wrong answer," he tells me, before manually hauling me up another step. Another. "I won't... even make it inside you... before you scream."

The promise sets my blood on fire. I will never scream for him. I want to. "Won't," I choke out, fighting to hold onto my pride.

"Will." Three more steps, and we're in the hallway. Seven more take us into his bedroom. My scalp is on fire, my eyes welling up when he finally lets me go and shoves me backward. I hit the mattress hard, but he's already mounting me from the edge, his eyes focusing on mine as he knees my legs open.

In one fluid motion, he lunges across the bed for his nightstand and tugs open a drawer. He yanks it *out*. A few items within bounce across the bedspread—a silver pen, a notepad, a bottle of sleeping medication. He rummages through the remaining contents until he finds what he's after and promptly withdraws a small, square foil package. Rising on his knees, he tears the condom open with his teeth and rolls it onto his length.

Never. In my life. Have I seen something so... perfect. My body pulses. The ache between my legs turns painful. I need him. I need him *now*. I...

A shrill sound pierces the soundtrack of my heartbeat thundering in tune to his. I blink, distracted from the man in front of me. What in the hell?

"Bellamy." Within the blink of an eye, Mr. Bellamy has his phone to his ear. *Mr.* I make sure to drill that designation in while my chest heaves to suck in air. This man, for all his looks—and god, his touch—is *Graeme Bellamy*. World-famous C.E.O. My boss. Or at least he was...

"Ten minutes?" He glances down at his wristwatch and scowls at the priceless face formed of gold and crystal. "You can't stall any longer?"

Relief hits me so fiercely that my head falls back against the sheets. I can breathe again for a split second, and I use the newfound clarity to scoot away from him and draw my knees together. Saved by the bell. Nothing comes between Graeme Bellamy and his business. Not sex. Not me. *Nothing*.

"Cancel it—"

"What?" My outburst must mirror that of the person on the other end's. Bellamy's eyes narrow in the way they do whenever someone dares to disobey him.

"Cancel it." He hangs up the phone and tosses it aside. It bounces across the floor and crashes into the wall. By then, he's crawled toward me on his hands and knees. His fingers sink into my hair again, finding enough leverage to drag me toward him, pinning me down by my skull.

I don't expect the kiss. The *devouring*. He shoves his tongue into me. Breathes into me. Consumes me. Teeth. Nails. Whatever he can use, he does. I'm already liquid when he finally reaches down and guides himself into his palm. My legs spring apart. My teeth seize his lower lip, and the strip of flesh muffles my gasp as he enters me in a single hard thrust.

I've never had anyone like him. Never like this. So damn full. To the brim. I can only arch my back and savor the achingly tight fit. There's no air left in my chest to make a sound when he flexes his hips, pulling nearly all the way out, before ramming himself back in.

To his credit, it takes more than just one thrust. More like ten, each one intensified by his thumb against my clitoris and his breath in my ear. I feel like a windup toy with my spine as the turn-key. Twisting. Tightening. And then, all at once, the tension snaps, and I come undone.

It's almost as if he waits until I do. Right until my body clenches over him like a fist. Then he moves. Harsher. Faster. Rougher. Growling. Grunting. We cease to communicate in words—just motion. Every wicked thrust. Each lash of his tongue at the crook of my throat. My nails in his shoulders, raking down and straining the expensive fabric of his suit.

It's too much. I thrash. Whine.

And then, with one last thrust, he throws his head back, and the sight of him bellowing out his release is the most breathtaking thing I've ever seen.

Perfect.

If only the bastard didn't look so damn triumphant as my vision went hazy, and I quickly followed suit.

He is already bending to snatch his pants from the floor while I struggle to find meaning in my once-content existence. Every muscle in my body throbs beneath a layer of sweat. The silken sheets chafe—my skin is that damn sensitive.

Every pore is alight, every nerve stretched thin. And god, it all feels so damn delicious...

*Snap out of it, Evie.* Focus. I'm in the bed of the enemy. The enemy who certainly knew his way around said bed. I wish I could have had only one lapse of judgment to explain my presence here. But one had turned into...

I'd lost count.

"Where is your bag?" I glance up to find him fishing one of his oxfords from the floor. He frowns and tugs it on before hunting for the other and his phone. "Your bag, Evelyn," he snaps when nearly a minute passes and I don't answer. "Where is it?"

"I... downstairs?"

He straightens his tie before turning for the doorway. I scramble out after him, wearing only my sweat-soaked sweater and his sheets wrapped around my waist. I chase him down to the foyer, where he finds my canvas bag on the floor, snatches it, and promptly digs through it.

"What the hell are you doing?" I'm too breathless to put much indignation into my voice. He doesn't seem to hear me anyway. Instead, he withdraws what I recognize as my wallet from the depths of my bag. Then my planner. He then tucks both under his arm before marching for the door.

"Stay here," he tells me from over his shoulder. "You will receive these when I return."

*When I return...* He's already in the hallway when I realize he's taking my personal belongings hostage.

"Wait!" I stagger to the doorway before common decency keeps me from crossing the threshold. I can only watch in horror as Graeme Bellamy turns the corner up ahead, my money, identification, and virtual life in his hands.

I don't know how long I stand there, gaping before I turn and kick the wall with my bare foot. Pain shoots through the toes, but it's not enough to counter the ache that still lingers.

Damn him. *Damn,* Graeme Bellamy.

If he thinks that one (more) small lapse in judgment gives him the right to control my life, once again, he has another damn thing coming.

233

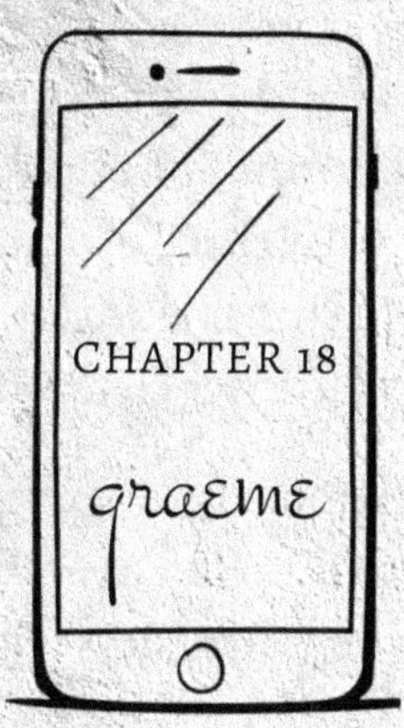


The piercing dial tone cuts the silence. It drones on three times before a gruff voice finally picks up from the other end. "Riley."

"The terms of your merger," I start, foregoing any niceties. "I trust you already have them drawn up?"

I don't receive an answer, but I know he's listening. I can almost hear the gears of his brain turning at the prospect of how far he can expand his business connections with my club in his hands.

"Good," I say, taking his silence as my answer. "Bring them by my office later. The longer you delay, the more likely I'll change my mind."

I hang up, clenching the damn phone in my fist, wishing I could smash it into a million pieces, and Adrian Riley right along with it. If it wasn't the property of the hotel I've taken refuge in, I would. Instead, I toss the handset on the base resting on a nightstand and grit my teeth at the prospect of meeting Riley in my territory for once. The last thing I want is to negotiate a deal with that bastard—but business is the only thing in the world that makes sense. A man's greed and the flexibility of his wallet never changed.

Some constants, as bloody infuriating as they were, were much more preferable to the unknown. Evelyn King, if that even is her real name, represents everything unknown at the moment. I can't decide if I want to peel her down to the innermost layer or cut her loose the way a smart man cut any other loss.

*Peel,* the part of my brain controlled by my cock demands. Starting with whatever modest blouse she has on, and then the knickers underneath. My breath catches at the thought. Damn, I can still taste her. Feel her.

But what if she has more tricks up her sleeve should I return and attempt this examination in person?

I glance over at the clock on the nightstand and frown—it's barely six a.m. I haven't slept, and despite the pounding ache behind my temples, I damn well don't need to. I sit up and shift so I'm at the edge of the mattress and feel along the nightstand for the remote that operates the blinds. Within seconds, garish light streams in, illuminating the economic suite.

Almost as if on cue, there's a knock at the door. I open it to find a man dressed in the hotel's uniform standing on the other end, a silver tray of coffee in his hands. "You requested a wake-up call, Sir." He glances questioningly at my starched suit and the oxfords on my feet.

"That I did," I grunt before snatching a mug of coffee from the tray and closing the door. I take a sip and nearly spit it out while I reach for my mobile again. I take my time dialing the next number. Not because I'm anxious—merely curious. When I finally bring the receiver to my ear, the person on the other end has already picked up.

"Have you found anything?" I demand.

"Only the article you referenced," James replies, referring to the paper Riley brandished regarding Evelyn's past. "I contacted some associates to find more. I'm waiting to hear back."

"Good. And... No distress from our guest, I hope?"

"She's gone, Sir," James replies.

"When?" My tone is harder than it should be. *Damn, Evelyn.*

"Late last night, Sir. Not long after you left."

I glance at the table near the entrance where I've kept her wallet and that precious book she cherishes so much. I think I laugh before I hang up the phone and throw it so hard it ricochets off the wall and leaves a dent in the gray paint. I know without even bothering to check that the screen is cracked. I'll have to buy a bloody new one. If only it were as easy to find a new goddamn assistant as well. I could snap my fingers and hire a new yes-man with a stack of bloody credentials longer than my damn office building was tall to do my bidding.

But not one who could fuck me like a hellcat, all while claiming to not enjoy a single damn bit of it. *Cat,* being the operative word. I had to venture into my office and find a high-collared shirt from the stash I keep there to disguise the marks Evelyn King left on my shoulders. My neck. She'd bitten my lip, too, and the slight swelling is harder to ignore. I rub my thumb over the tender flesh and can almost feel her gnashing there. Touché. The woman knew how to work that mouth when she wasn't nagging with it. Even I could give her that much.

Apparently, there was more to Evelyn King than following men around with granola and micromanaging her life down to the last detail.

Unless she'd already found a new man to pester.

According to James, she left not long after I had. Where could she have gone without her bank cards or I.D.? I tried not to give a damn. Instead, I crossed over to my mobile. The damn thing still works, and James again picks up on the first ring when I call.

"Sir?"

I glance at the nightstand, reading off the hotel's name from the glossy brochure propped against the body of a silver lamp. "The Hilton suites. Come and get me—"

"I'm already outside, Sir," James says smoothly over me. "But there is something else we should discuss. I think it might be best to do so in person."

I raise an eyebrow at that. James isn't one for cryptic preludes. In fact, the only other time I remember him sounding that concerned was when a rival company stole our winter collection, and Stella had to draft up new designs in a fortnight. The memory makes my jaw clench. Has Riley done something similar? I'd been waiting for the other shoe to drop where the bastard is concerned. Before leaving the suite, I pause only to grab Evelyn's belongings from the dresser, the mug of coffee still steaming on the nightstand.

Out front, James is waiting, as promised, ready to usher me into the vehicle. One look at his face, and I know that whatever has concerned him is far more than some damn designs.

"What is it?" I ask as I settle into the back seat. After closing the door on my end, he says nothing until he claims the driver's seat. Even then, his only form of communication is to reach back and drop a stack of documents onto the seat beside me.

One glance at the topmost page, and I see red. Evelyn King is staring at me, barely clothed, the dressing room of Atelier Noir visible behind her. The page itself is a printout of a website page, with a glaring black headline—BELLAMY REPORTED TO EXTORT EMPLOYEES FOR PERSONAL GAIN.

Apparently, the writer meant to aim this as a hit piece against my reputation, but the only images he chose to use are of her. Evelyn King vulnerable and exposed—and every one she'd sent only to me. *Fuck.* I can't think straight. My hands are in fists, and I have to force myself to grit out, "What the bloody hell is this?"

"I found that on a tabloid website an hour ago," James replies, all while effortlessly steering the car into the early morning traffic. "I had it taken down, of course. The publisher of the website refused to name their source, but with some mild persuasion, I was able to learn a location from which the photos were emailed."

He's playing coy on purpose, too tactful to insult my intelligence by stating plainly what I already fucking know. Damn it. I scowl at the memory of that Riley woman prancing after Evelyn with her "innocently" misplaced mobile. One might think the action too childish for Adrian Riley, but I know the bastard.

And I know the only logical solution to solve this problem.

"I'm going to kill the son of a bitch."

"All traces of the images have been removed," James replies, his tone level. "The publisher has given me his word that he will not share them again. Still, I have alerted the legal department. Shall I inform Ms. King?"

"No! No…" I slam a fist into the leather upholstery of the car, but the pain lancing through my knuckles does little to snap some sense back into me. If Evelyn knew, she'd be furious, liable to remove Adrian Riley of his balls. I'd have every right to make her eat crow and admit that I've been telling her the truth about the blasted git all along.

And in the process, she'd be humiliated.

"Sir?" James prods. "I could have the legal department reach out to her should you not want to get involved—"

"I'll handle it," I insist with a sigh. "Just get me to the office before I have you contact a hitman."

"As you wish, Sir."

Twenty minutes later, he lets me off before the Atelier Noir headquarters, where Evelyn King and her damn scent are nothing but a distant memory.

"Good morning, Mr. Bellamy," Ann calls once I ascend to the top floor and pass her desk. I don't even have the sense to return the greeting before entering my office. A janitor must have snuck in early and tidied it. One could never tell, despite the odd angle of the leather chair behind my desk, that I had spent most of the night in this room before pride dragged me to that damn hotel, picked at random.

She wouldn't make me sleep in my office two damn nights in a row.

I toss her things onto the desk and approach the closet where I keep a set of spare suits. I switch the gray tie for a black one and straighten the collar. In the mirror affixed to the inside of the door, the swollen lip is more noticeable. Fuck me—she drew blood. I'll make her pay for that. I seal the promise by dragging my thumb over the pinprick mark her teeth left behind, smearing the pinkish remains of blood.

"Mr. Bellamy?" I turn to find Ann in the doorway, her expression... puzzled. "You have a phone call," she says carefully.

The confusion in her tone instantly sets me on edge. My mother. Alex. Adrian Riley, ready to gloat over his failed publicity stunt. The potential suspects form an unwelcome Russian roulette as I approach my desk. "Forward it to my cell," I tell Ann. Inhaling sharply, I snatch up the mobile the second it rings and snarl into the receiver, "Bellamy."

"I want my things back," a woman demands, her tone still haughty despite the exhaustion racking it. I take some solace in her obvious annoyance. If she'd learned about the photos, she wouldn't sound this damn haughty.

Perhaps I feel a small shred of smug pride that I wasn't the only one who'd had a rough night, apparently. Evelyn King sounds like hell. Restless, raspy, husky hell. "Now," she adds when I say nothing in response. "This could be considered theft. Return my things to me immediately, and maybe I won't go to the police."

"Most people would need an appointment to contact me directly," I remark. Ann's hesitation suddenly makes sense. "In what way did you harass my secretary?"

"I simply told her it was urgent," Evelyn counters, her voice rising the way it does when she's in danger of... Well, in danger of telling men to go fuck themselves in French. "Which it is. I'll give you the directions of a P.O. box where you can drop off my stuff by the end of today, and maybe I won't press charges."

"Is that so?" I take a seat and find myself reaching for the wallet resting beside a stack of proposals Ann must have left on my desk. It's patent leather. Beige. Elegant. Simple but no less eye-catching than a flashier design. Evelyn King, in a nutshell. My thumb flicks the silver clasp to spring it open, and I'm presented with a neat array of credit cards and money that could only be described as... organized. By color and by size, to be exact. Her driver's license is front and center. I grasp it between my thumb and forefinger, scanning her full name before observing the picture of her pasted to it. Her smile seems strained, every hair neatly in place. "Is that so?" I echo when the only reply is the sound of her breathing. "Evelyn Rose King."

Her sharp inhale reverberates through the line. "Are you going through my personal belongings?"

I set her license down and snatch up a credit card. "I can neither confirm nor deny."

"This... this is a violation," she declares, and I can't help the gruff laugh I bark out in response.

"My fingers inside your *wallet* is a violation..."

She goes silent. So silent, in fact, that I almost believe she's hung up before I hear her release another harsh sigh.

"Return my belongings—"

"What about *your* fingers?" I ask her. Through the doorway, I spot Ann at her desk, absorbed by whatever is on her laptop's screen. "Did they violate any of your personal 'belongings' last night? When I left," I clarify in a gruff undertone that makes her clench her teeth so tightly I hear the resounding snap.

"You're an ass," she says. Her proper tone makes it seem more like a rightful designation than an insult.

"An ass," I repeat, feeling the corner of my mouth quirk. "Is that what they call it these days? When a man thoroughly raids a woman's... wallet. Being an *ass*?"

"If you must know, my fingers were busy... violating, this morning," she says. Fuck. My cock jerks at the ragged way she clips every single word. "Being left high and dry will drive a woman to find any sort of relief."

I laugh again. Louder. Harsher. "I may have left you many things last night," I tell her coldly, "but I know for a fact that *dry* was not one of them."

I can still taste her. Still feel her. Still hear her. Breathless. Panting, almost like she is now. "Is that so, Mr. Bellamy?"

Her voice dips on the edge of a dare. I don't take my eyes off Ann, who's still studiously typing away. "Do I need to refresh your memory once again, Ms. King?" I tell her softly. "Of our *meeting*?"

"You may have to," she says casually. "My memory is a little fuzzy as some parts were rather... lacking."

My free hand curls into a fist. "Interesting," I grit out. "You didn't seem to think so while I was thrusting my... credentials into your *wallet*."

"You're bigger than I'd thought you be," she admits, almost as if the thought genuinely surprised her.

If only she could see me now, stiffening like a bloody teenager.

"If only you weren't so..."

"So what?" My tone catches Ann's attention this time. She stiffens in her seat and glances at my office before turning away again when the phone rings. The faint sound of her voice, cheerily wishing the caller a good morning, is an almost innocent backdrop for what Evelyn King says next.

"So quick."

The little tart. She's teasing now. It's fucking working. I have to unclench my fingers one by one to get the blood flowing through them. Then I curl them again, imagining every nail sinking into her flesh, pinning her flat. "Funny. I recall that you were the first one to..." I glance at Ann again. "Merge all over my hand."

Her haughty laugh trickles through the receiver. "You wish, Mr. Bellamy."

"Tell me where you are, and I'll show you how *quick* I can be."

She stops laughing. "That wouldn't be very wise, Mr. Bellamy," she says softly. "A man's ego can only take so much."

Minx. I stand and cross over to the door to my office. Ignoring the way Ann looks at me questioningly, I palm the door's handle and slam it shut.

"And yet you seemed more than capable of taking *so much*, Evelyn." My knuckles whiten over the receiver. My throat feels dry, and every word comes out harsh and grated. "All of me. Every inch. But I bet you can take me even deeper..."

"Stop."

Like bloody hell, I will. "Put the phone down," I tell her. "Near your ear, where you can hear me."

There's no indication from her end whether she's obeyed or not. Just silence. And then her own harsh intake of air. That damn sound affects me instantly, making it harder to sit still. For the third time in as many days, I'm hard because of Evelyn King. She'll more than suffer for that.

"Take your hand. Slide it down your belly." Smooth, pale, flat. "Now go lower..."

Grazing her narrow hips and then that thatch of golden curls.

"Now touch yourself." Bloody hell, I can see it. Her fingers parting the thatch of hair before drifting lower. The tease... she'd drag a finger over herself, just once to prove she could. The second would be an accident. And the third... "You remember what it felt like. Me inside you. You were so fucking tight."

I have to brace one hand against the wall. I hear a faint sound come from the other end. She hasn't hung up yet.

"Slide a finger inside if you need a reminder—"

She gasps—I know she's obeyed, too damn stubborn to back down.

"You're wet already," I tell her, my throat going even drier. "You're already aching, and I've barely touched you. *I'm* the one touching you—"

*Fuck,* that softer, breathier sound. It's a moan. My hand leaves the wall. Heads to my slacks…

"I'm the one touching you," I grate into her ear. An image of her in those lacy knickers from the unreleased collection flashes through my brain, and I can't ignore the possessive impulse that rises within me. Should Riley dare to exploit even a pixel of those photos, I'll kill him. Every one is mine. She is mine. "Me," I breathe out, "Harder. Faster. The way you like… no *need* it. But it's not enough, is it, Evelyn? I need to add another finger—"

The second needy moan sets my blood on fire. "It's still not enough. Even when I drag my thumb against your clit—" another throaty groan, louder this time. Undeniable. "It's not enough. Not hard enough. Thick enough. Deep enough. You need… me. Say it."

She doesn't. But I swear I hear the mattress creak with the shifting weight of her body—her head thrashing, toes curling, fingers fighting for the right amount of leverage.

"Admit it. You need me." My fingers land on the fastenings of the slacks. I get the clasp undone and tug at the zipper. "Tell me where you are."

I hear her breathing raggedly. In and out. I'm sure she'll hang up without an answer. "I… I'm at—"

"Mr. Bellamy?"

I hear the door open, followed by the delicate sound of Ann's footsteps, trailed by a heavier, slower set. "Your next meeting is here."

Shit. I fasten my trousers one-handed. Evelyn's still in my ear, the words slurred, barely intelligible. "I'm at four… six… street—" I hang up the phone and shove the damned thing into my pocket.

Adrian Riley stands in the doorway to my office when Ann retreats to her desk. The bastard's smiling. "I hope I didn't interrupt something important. It appears you might have been—" He cuts his gaze down to the front of my trousers, despite the barrier between us. "Preoccupied."

The git.

"You have some damn nerve coming here." I ignore his outstretched hand and turn to my desk. My fingers curl, my teeth gritted, every nerve on fire. Evelyn should be my sole concern, not him. It's only as I brace my hands against the desk's surface that I realize I didn't hear the whole address she'd started to moan. Bloody hell. Four. Six. Street. I'll have James drive around the entire damn city to find her if I have to.

But first things first.

"I should beat your face in," I bite out before glancing up to find Riley standing in the center of the room, wearing that bloody amused expression. "I'll have you know that your little game didn't work, foiled out of the gate. By the way, I suggest you destroy any trace of those photos your accomplice squirreled away. Otherwise, I'll bury you in enough litigation to leave your children's children in bankruptcy."

His smile only widens. "I take it you changed your mind about the merger?" he questions, cocking his head slightly. Did my reveal surprise him? Good.

Anger washes through me as my fingers clench. God, I want to punch the bastard. So damn much. But if Evelyn were here, I know exactly what she'd bloody say—*Don't give him the satisfaction. Use your brain, Mr. Bellamy.*

"I've changed my mind about hearing your *plans* for the merger," I clarify. When I sit behind my desk, he follows suit, claiming one of the chairs in front of it. We're on an even playing field for all intents and purposes, but I get that bloody suspicious itch crawling up the back of my neck. Like the bastard knows something I don't. *Four. Six. Street.* At least none of those words have anything in common with the address of his club.

Riley reaches for his briefcase and flicks the clasps to open it. "Even though you've had a *change* of heart, you may find these worth a look," he says, sliding a stack of documents onto my desk.

At first glance, they seem to be brochures sporting the club paraphernalia—an embossed logo, R.R.

"We could announce it at the next annual meeting," he says, while I flip open the topmost booklet and scan the details printed on the first few pages. They're blueprints, transfixed over the existing building in London, expanding the layout. "The general terms we can decide now. More... pertinent details, such as leadership, can be decided later."

I glance up to find the bastard still smirking, but there's a colder look in his eye that I don't like. "Is that typical of your mergers?" It damn sure wasn't for any corporate merger I had overseen. When one business swallowed the other, one associate always took the lion's share.

"To be fair, Bellamy, this isn't the typical situation."

Fair enough. I flip through the brochure again, familiarizing myself with every nuanced term and phrase, searching for a trap lurking within the polished presentation. "In name only?" I repeat, when I come up surprisingly blank.

Riley nods. "For now. Considering your club already shares the same name, it shouldn't be too jarring a change."

I let the veiled insult pass without challenge. "I assume this means that your connections become mine as well?"

He nods. "And vice versa."

Again, a fair enough trade, though I'm not naive enough to assume that is where this game will end. He's waiting for me to name yet one more term. I know the fucker's salivating for it.

"And one more thing—You stay away from Evelyn King," I demand. "If you so much as breathe in the same air as her, the deal is off."

His eyes narrow, and I feel a small shred of triumph. I caught him off guard, dangling the very thing he wants before him.

How badly does he want to claim ownership over this blasted club? Badly enough, it seems. "I must admit, I didn't think you gave a damn about anyone but yourself." He stands, and I can't get a read on his expression. No longer is he smirking, however.

"I suppose that's all, then." With that, he leans over the desk, extending his hand once again. This time, I reach across the desk to take it. We shake once—a single, jerking motion of our arms, our grips bruising. I release him first, and he starts for the door, twirling his ring around his right pinky finger. "Oh, and Bellamy? The next time you're in the area, do visit the club again. Our clients desire to experience firsthand what your... outside perspective might bring to the table."

There's an insinuation lurking within those words. An insult. If my mind wasn't still replaying the earlier phone conversation—on a bloody, sordid loop—I might have cared enough to decipher it.

"It will be interesting to see how you run things, here in America," I say, leaving it at that.

Riley chuckles, but he doesn't look back before stepping over the threshold of the office, and I can't picture what his expression might be. Not that I'd give a damn to.

My mind's eye seems capable of only displaying one image at the moment. One face—swollen pink lips, blue eyes upturned mockingly, blond hair wild from fucking.

I can still hear her voice, huskily whispered into my ear, on the verge of a climax...

Only then, as Adrian Riley approaches Ann, who eagerly offers to show him to the lobby, does the bitter reality sink in.

I had Evelyn King breathless and panting for me. She told me where she was.

And like a fool, I didn't demand she repeat the blasted address.

400
300
01

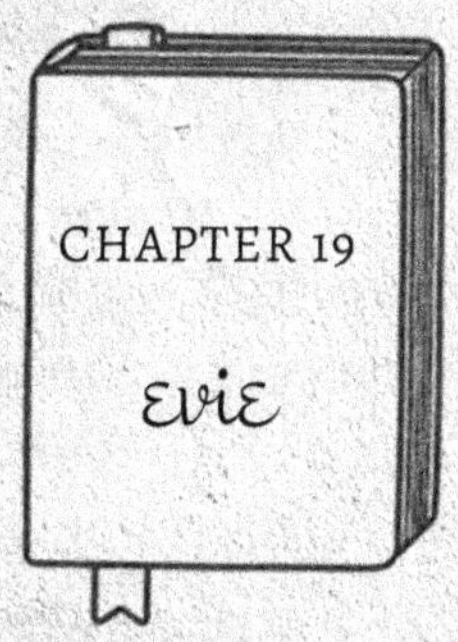

## CHAPTER 19

### EVIE

Someone, I assume is the housekeeper, ignores the "Do not disturb" notice tacked onto my door and knocks anyway. Though, to be fair, I *am* in a motel, and those signs seemed to be a dime a dozen when I scurried down the hall at midnight, right after checking in.

A rush of anger displaces any sense of embarrassment I might feel, however. Graeme Bellamy did this to me—sending me on a nomadic trip through Lower Manhattan. I can only remember a few bits and pieces, like the daze experienced right after waking from a nightmare. What will my life look like without adhering to the rigid daily schedule of Graeme Bellamy?

I have no idea. In a sick twist of irony, my severance package frees me from having to worry about finding a new flat. With the amount written on my parting check, I could go anywhere in the world. Though, in the interim, there isn't much I can do without access to my bank account, credit cards, or any identification. Poor me. Bellamy probably expected me to show up at the Royal, begging for my belongings back.

*Yeah, right.*

I knew which part of the city wouldn't give a damn about keeping things one hundred percent legal and rented a room using the hundred-dollar bill I kept at the bottom of my shoe. That left me with only about twenty bucks for food and transportation, but also led to step three of my foolproof plan. It took all the courage found in a ten-dollar bottle of whiskey before I gathered up the nerve to call him. His office seemed like neutral territory, and nothing... risqué could happen at seven in the morning via a phone call.

Boy, had I been wrong. With a few crass words, Graeme Bellamy had me breathless. Panting. Surrendered.

All without my having to leave the lumpy mattress or with him being even in the same room. Which brought me to my next point—how much of my location had the bastard discerned before hanging up? It wasn't like I was going to stick around and find out.

"Please come back later," I call at the door when the handle is tried for the tenth time during the tense moments after my disastrous phone call. The housekeeper says nothing before retreating down the hallway, and I finally gather the nerve to crawl from the thin mattress to pick up my jeans, and my dignity from the floor.

It feels strange wearing the same clothes as yesterday. I do my best to wash up using the complimentary toiletries supplied by the motel—a sample size of shampoo and toothpaste. My fingers attempt to comb through the tangle of my hair, but the moment they touch my scalp, it throbs. Oh, that's right. Graeme Bellamy nearly ripped it out yesterday.

I fight back the memory by grabbing my canvas bag, shoving my feet into my shoes, and leaving the room. The housekeeper is nowhere in sight when I enter the hallway. The only witness to my escape is a man leaning against the wall a few yards down, his hands stuffed into the pockets of his jeans.

Thus, day two of my life of unemployment begins, and Graeme Bellamy can eat his heart out. I don't think of him. At all. Not once. Not with every step, which triggers an aching throb between my thighs. Or the hours I spend in the internet café, killing time while plotting the retrieval of my personal belongings. I don't know what makes me peek at my email account. Boredom? Or perhaps a prescient suspicion that I'll find a message lurking there from my past employer—three of them, to be exact. The first must have come before our meeting yesterday—a rather pointed reminder to negotiate the severance. The second summarized the termination of my employment. And the third...

The title alone makes me choke on a sip of coffee—*In reference to our fucking.* I blink. Rub my eyes. Click out of my browser and open the window again. The message never disappears, and the wording never changes. When I finally gather the nerve to open it, its contents are relatively mild. *Ms. King,* the bastard had written. *To retrieve your belongings, come to my office before the end of the day. That is all.*

I delete it and then promptly escape back to the motel. With ten dollars to my name, I can't afford to stay another night, not that it matters. Even sleeping under a bridge is preferable to begging Graeme Bellamy for anything. I even let myself consider the satisfaction of filing a police report as I head up to my room, intending to wait out the final moments before I'm forced to check out.

It's a seedy place, overall. Peeling gray wallpaper lines the hallway, and the faded green carpet must have had some life to it at one point before being beaten almost flat by a constant parade of footsteps. It feels emptier now than during the early hour I checked in—go figure. Apparently, a place like this makes most of its business at night, from people who don't plan on exactly sleeping.

God, I can only hope that Bellamy hung up before deciphering my location. Thankfully, he's not in the hallway, lurking outside my door when I mount the stairs. There's no sign of the housekeeper either, when I open the door to my room and spot the bed, still unmade. You get what you pay for, I guess.

"Hey."

I glance over my shoulder to find that the man leaning against the wall hasn't budged. He nods in my direction, his eyes dark, his beard scruffy. "Your name Evelyn?"

*Shit.* Alarm shoots down my spine, awakening old instincts. My right hand plunges into my bag, the fingers clenching around my can of pepper spray. I have the door open, but I'm unsure how quickly I can get inside and shut it before he can reach me.

"Never heard of her," I say in the man's general direction, fighting to keep my voice emotionless.

"You look like him, you know?" I hear rather than see him pull away from the wall, his hands still tucked within his pockets.

Shit. Shit. I scramble over the threshold and try to slam the door behind me. At the last second, it stops inches from the doorjamb as an unfamiliar hand curls around the edge, holding it open.

"You've got the same eyes," a gruff voice says against my ear. The stench of stale cigarettes wafts from the man's general direction—the typical scent of most people Danny likes to associate with. "That boy owes me a lot of money."

He shoves on the door when I try to slam it shut in his face. A harsh chuckle warns me exactly what he expects me to do.

Scream. Cry. Cower while he spits out some threat for Danny's benefit and hits me up for the cash supposedly owed to him. Unluckily for him, he's about four years too late for that reaction.

Some things you never forget, like riding a bicycle.

I don't even process turning on my heel and jabbing the nozzle of my pepper spray into the bastard's face until he jerks back, his eyes narrowing. "You wouldn't dare, you little—"

Two sprays are all it takes to have him howling, shouting expletives as he swipes at his eyes with both hands.

"Forget my name," I say over him. "And maybe I'll forget your face, asshole. If Danny owes you money, you talk to him. Not me."

I push past him and reach the stairwell. Two steps. Three. Four. I nearly trip down them all in my rush to enter the lobby first, and I race through the entrance without looking back.

Damn it. I don't even have the time, or the desire to figure out how the shady bastard could have found me. That means Danny probably has as well, along with any other little "friends" who might get the idea to come after me to settle a score. All in all, this was shaping up to be the typical sibling bonding festivities where Danny was concerned. The chances are he's already raided my apartment. I can't even call the landlord to be sure because my phone is dead, and the charger is in my suitcase—the suitcase still locked in the trunk of Bellamy's Mercedes. Not that I would chase the bastard down to get it back.

I flag down a cab solely out of the desire to get far and fast in the opposite direction instead. It doesn't matter that I have only a few dollars to my name and no way of accessing my bank information without an I.D.

I'll figure out a plan in the end. I am my mother's daughter, after all, and Danny inherited his knack for trouble from somewhere.

1

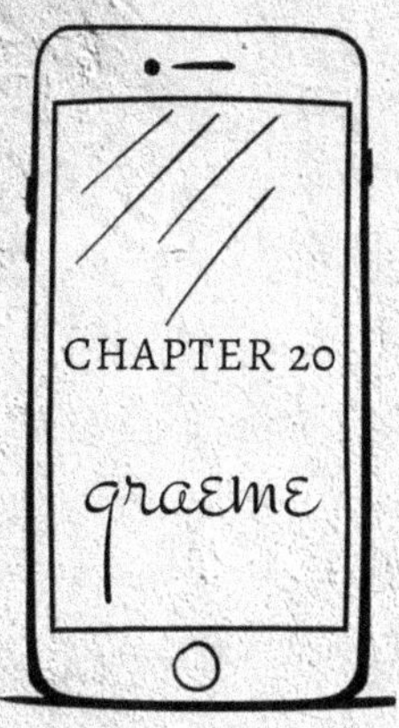


Adrian Riley has outdone himself trying to bring dignity to a profession that most men wouldn't touch with a ten-foot pole. At least not with their legal, Christian name and assets on the line.

He's made more than just a name for himself here, carving out a slice of esteem built solely upon the art of seduction and all the secrets that skill could glean from those with information to exploit. Had he been anyone else, I might have admired the bastard.

As it stands, I don't trust him or his supposed "in name only" plans for a merger farther than I can throw him. Admittedly, it seems simple on the surface—but nothing ever is in Riley's playbook.

I scan the stack of brochures he left behind for the tenth time, scouring the paragraphs of print for any hint of duplicity. The man certainly knew how to cover his tracks well. He framed a venue expansion in terms that resonated with the business side of me. He cited figures and potential statistics I couldn't ignore. The man even had connections I might deem beneficial if the thought didn't make me want to put a fist through the wall.

Rather than decide on an answer, I shove the documents into my desk and call for James instead. I don't head for the Royal at first. I dine at one of the most exclusive restaurants in Manhattan. I sample wine worth the equivalent of a certain woman's salary. I eat bread out of spite.

Two hours later, I find myself standing in the middle of my suite, thoroughly checking the emails on my mobile. There were quarterly reports, reminders from Ann, and even the odd missive from Gloria.

But nothing from Evelyn King.

From the moment she first set foot in my office and met my gaze without flinching, I knew the woman was stubborn. But never this stubborn. How the hell she managed to survive twenty-four hours in the city without her damned planner—let alone her wallet—I would never understand. It wasn't the recklessness of the matter as much as it was the sheer insanity that had me scowling out at the view of the city, picturing her scurrying from awning to awning to avoid the rain.

Though, there was always the possibility that she had another man's apartment to seek refuge in. Until ten hours ago, I hadn't even known the woman's full name. Only god knew what else there was to discover about her.

She likes pink, apparently. Or so I discerned from the freight in her suitcase after I dragged the damn thing from the foyer

—where James had left it—and unzipped the middle to reveal its contents. She likes lace as well, despite her haughty indignation at wearing the undergarments I picked out for her.

*Minx.* I spot exactly three pairs of knickers. Three matching bras. Her wardrobe is a sensible mixture of pale blouses, modest skirts, and the odd sundress. I find not one shred of lingerie or the hint of anything to contradict her polished persona. Evelyn King is a bloody, open book—the thick, archaic kind that recounted some obscure historical lesson one might be forced to read in school.

Her wallet is equally as dull to peruse. There are no pictures hidden within the pockets. No receipts for whips and chains tucked within the change purse. On the surface, it's like she transformed into a mouthy tease overnight.

It's not the surprisingly sexual nature to her that has me curious. Or so I decide after the third glass of wine taken from the restaurant. It's her fucking cheek. No one is this clean. This sensible. This bloody unpredictable.

I fist one of her knickers as if it might hold the answer. It smells like her—damn roses. I drag my thumb along the strip of fabric meant to go in between her legs. Once. Again. For purely valid reasons. I can discern that the cotton, while of decent quality, isn't silk or something overtly expensive. She's frugal as well as practical.

*And* sensitive. My stupid fucking cock presents that point before I can brush it aside. The sex meant nothing to her, apparently. It damn well meant nothing to me. *She* meant nothing...

"Sir?" The voice proceeds the rapt on my door. It's familiar—the doorman's. An ominous feeling clenches in my gut, and I kick the suitcase closed with my foot before entering the foyer. Sure enough, William is waiting on the other end, his face more serious than usual—which means that someone is dead, or something has happened pressing enough for him to break what seems to be an unspoken rule by approaching me directly.

"Sir, you are needed in the lobby," he says, standing straight with his posture erect. "There is a... disturbance."

"Call the police," I tell him. Alex must have lost all tact to attempt to enter the building directly. "His identity should be on file. He shouldn't—"

"She seemed quite insistent, Sir," William says over me.

The anger surging through my blood promptly becomes confusion. "She?"

I'm already pushing my way past him before William can clarify. I take the stairs rather than the elevator and arrive in the lobby just in time to witness Evelyn King tell a man where and how he could go fuck himself. In English.

"I told you," she adds, her typically posh voice strained and tense. "If you just let me go, I'll get my wallet and—"

"You owe me, lady," the man, a towering bloke with a beer gut and a goatee, snarls. "If you don't pay, I'm calling the cops—"

"I don't think that's necessary." I step forward, clenching my jaw, my hand already in a fist. The anger coursing through my veins comes as a shock. Would I bludgeon some poor git just for raising his voice at a former employee? *Yes,* a primal part of me warns.

Especially when Evelyn bites her lip, beyond exasperated. "Look, if you would just let me get my damn wallet—"

"Here." I insinuate myself between both figures, dig into my breast pocket for my wallet, and shove a handful of bills into the man's hand. He blinks down at the money before licking his fingers and pointedly counting each note. Judging from Evelyn's mortified expression, it's more than enough to settle whatever score they have between them.

"Fine," the man grunts, shoving the money into his pocket. "But you're blacklisted, lady—" He jabs a finger in her direction. "She had me drive her around the city for two fucking hours, and then claimed that she just needed to get her wallet. As if I'd fall for that shit."

He storms out of the entrance, much to William's relief.

"Give me my wallet, now," Evelyn says without glancing at me. "I'll write you a check."

She looks like hell. Her eyes are bloodshot, her hair a mess. She's wearing the same bloody sweater from yesterday, and I suspect the same jeans. The fact that she's here is enough proof to warn me that Evelyn King isn't in the mood to be prodded—which makes it all the more fun to goad her anyway.

"You're late," I tell her, turning on my heel and heading for the elevators. "My home is not a storage for your belongings, Ms. King."

I'm eager to witness what reaction the words draw from her. I can imagine it well enough—that furious expression, her cheeks red, her eyes blazing. The "real" Evelyn King, a woman I'm starting to realize I enjoy verbally jousting with.

Rather than reply with a biting comment, she sighs. "I'll wait here," she says. I can almost hear the rubbery squeak of her attempting to dig her heels into the marble floor.

"Then I'll see you in the morning," I say without looking back. "Good night, Ms. King—"

Light footsteps chase me into an arriving elevator car. She pushes herself into the farthest possible corner from where I stand, her arms crossed over her chest, clutching that damn bag of hers. "Do you think this is some kind of game?"

I frown at the genuine dismay in her tone. The elevator doors close, and the car lurches upright by the time I settle on a fitting response. "It would be cruel to play a game, as you put it, with someone who has no chance in hell of winning, Ms. King."

There's an audible crunching sound like that of her teeth grinding together, and I can't ignore the rush of excitement I feel. How much longer until the claws come out? For the time being, she doesn't say a word until we reach the topmost floor. Rather than follow me out into the hallway, she positions herself in the doorway of the elevator with her hand preventing it from closing. "I'll wait here," she tells me.

I don't even attempt to hide the way my mouth quirks. "In that case, I'll see you in the morning."

There's no reason for her to come inside. Frankly, I should have sent her things with William rather than even bother to meet her in the first place. Hindsight.

Needling her in person is merely her punishment. I know she received my email. I know she ignored it. No one's ever kept me waiting.

"You can just bring them to the doorway then," Evelyn pitches hopefully, once again following reluctantly in my shadow.

I could... But I won't. "I am not your servant, Ms. King."

That draws a scoff from her as I withdraw my card key from my pocket and swipe it to open the door. The first thing she sees is her suitcase lying in the middle of the foyer, still partially open.

"You went through my stuff." Her tone is flat, but the expression in her gaze when I look at her from over my shoulder is anything but.

I shrug, well aware of how the action only irritates her further. She marches past me, her chin darting into the air, and does her best to repack her belongings. I know to her that every second spent in this suite is one too many, but she can't seem to bloody help herself. When she sees the state of the clothing, she sighs and sinks down on her knees to carefully re-fold every garment and arrange them neatly in the case. She's methodical. Efficient. I'm almost impressed by how quickly she creates order from chaos.

"Something is missing." She shakes her head and runs her fingers through every garment. "A pair of…"

Her eyes drift to mine, horror burgeoning in them before I even reach into my pocket.

"Oh. Here." I curl my fingers around the bit of lace, allowing the garment to dangle from my fingers.

She stares at my hand for a full five minutes before swallowing hard and slamming the lid of her suitcase closed without reaching for the knickers. "Keep them. Obviously, we have the same taste."

"Not quite." I raise the underwear to my eye level, observing the plain cut and texture. "Black doesn't suit you—" She clenches her jaw. "I much prefer the red."

"I'm sure you do." She stands, hefting her suitcase as she does. Spotting her wallet and planner on a nearby end table, she proceeds to snatch those up as well, tucking them both beneath her arm. "Well, I hope they fit, Mr. Bellamy," she says before heading for the door. "Enjoy."

I clear my throat before she can even reach for the doorknob. "I believe you are forgetting something…"

"Oh." She digs through her wallet for a checkbook and balances it against the back of the door while juggling a pen in her free hand. "How much did you give him? I'll make out the check for the exact amount—"

"So that the check can bounce, and you disappear again? I think not, Evelyn."

She sighs, her shoulders stiffening. "Unlike you, I strive to keep my word—"

"Unlike me?" She shrugs off the warning in my tone, still waiting for a figure to jot down.

"You aren't exactly reliable, Mr. Bellamy, and I've had one hell of a day already. I really don't—"

"*You've* had a hell of a day?" I've moved toward her without realizing it. She flinches but doesn't budge an inch from her position by the door.

"Yes," she snaps. "So, if you just tell me a damn amount, I can—"

"Funny. I've had one hell of a day myself," I admit, picturing that bastard Adrian Riley, and my mother's persistent hounding. Not to mention the rather eventful morning. "A very long, very *hard* day."

Her breath hitches in her throat. The next second, she shoves her checkbook into her bag and fumbles for the door handle. "I'll send you the cash in the morning—"

"I don't think so, Evelyn." I smell roses when I come up behind her and place my hand on the door near hers, keeping it shut.

She scrambles out of my reach, even if the action takes her farther from the exit. Given the haunted look in her eye, I wouldn't be surprised if she considers jumping out of the window a viable option.

"You're an ass," she declares, her tone laced with steel.

I frown. "I thought we had already established this. During our conversation this morning," I add, in case she forgot.

Her cheeks redden. Her lips part. She hasn't forgotten. "That was..." She apparently doesn't find the right words to describe it. She grits her teeth together instead and rolls her eyes as if anything before this moment was beneath her to discuss.

"Unfinished," I state when she says nothing else in return. "I never did hear that last part—"

"Stop it."

"When you seemed to be in the middle of begging me to... Well, I think my memory's a little fuzzy on what, Ms. King."

"I gave you the address to a gay bar," she admits. "At least there, you'd have no fear of rejection."

Only she could deliver a compliment wrapped up neatly within an insult and uttered with a deadpan expression. I don't know which insinuation I find more amusing. The blatant questioning of my sexuality? Or her own denial? "I think it's been more than sufficiently established which sex I prefer," I state. "Though, I would be more than willing to give you a demonstration..."

She nearly runs to the opposite corner of the room when I advance. Her chest heaves, her pulse surging—I can almost hear the damn sound. "Take one more step, and I'll contact every tabloid I know with an exclusive on a sexual assault in the penthouse suite of Graeme Bellamy."

I advance another step. "As long as you have them explicitly mention that you enjoyed every minute of said assault."

"Did I?" She challenges me in every way she can. Her posture. Her defiant glare. The taunting set of her chin. "I think that could be subject to some interpretation, Mr. Bellamy."

I stop paces from her, just close enough to make her stiffen. "As I mentioned, I would be more than happy to give you a demonstration."

She sighs, and then all at once, Evelyn King deflates. Her shoulders slump. That defensive posture slouches. Her pursed lips part. "I'm exhausted," she admits. "I've been out all day. All I want to do is leave, find a new hotel, and sleep."

I blink. Can it be? Evelyn King actually pleading for something? I shake my head. No bloody way. "Another hotel," I repeat, glancing down at her suitcase. Suddenly the damned thing takes on a new meaning. It's too soon for her to have been evicted from her apartment due to an inability to cover the rent—unless she refused to cash the severance check. I hadn't checked with Sarah to know a definitive answer. "Is something wrong with your apartment?"

She draws herself to her full height. "That's none of your business."

She's hiding something. I can tell just from the look in her eye. "Well, don't let me stop you," I say.

"Good." She nearly races past me for the door. I let her get halfway before I reach out and snag the handle of her suitcase, ripping it from her grip.

"I'll even save you the trouble of finding a hotel in the city at the height of tourist season." In case she doesn't catch my meaning, I nod to the stairs. "You can sleep here."

"*Le salaud.*" She drags a hand through her hair and tries to snatch her suitcase back. "This isn't a game. Some of us can't afford to turn everything into a power play."

*A power play,* she says. I drag her suitcase to the stairs and mount them. A part of me doesn't expect her to follow, but when I open the first door on the upper floor and toss her suitcase inside it, she's there, watching me from the mouth of the staircase.

"I don't remember joking, Ms. King. You can stay here. Just as long as you abide by the rules, I expect any guest to follow."

"Oh really? And what might those be? Only wear my panties? Screw you on demand? Bow in the presence of your majesty?"

I counter her glare with a shrug. "Stay out of my way."

"You can't honestly be serious."

I glance at the bedroom. It's one of three in the suite, and the only time any of them has been used was when Gloria had been too drunk after lunch to make it to her own suite without an escort. "If you would prefer to rent a penthouse suite at a hotel, I wouldn't mind giving you a recommendation. I'm sure a few days' stay would only require half of your severance pay. And that's if I give you the economic options."

"Give me my stuff—"

"Unless you really don't believe you can remain professional for one night, Ms. King."

Her entire body tenses at the veiled insinuation. She blinks. Sputters. When she finally seems to regain control of her voice, her head rears back, allowing her piercing gaze to clash with my own. "I can't be professional? Says the man who hasn't stopped spewing innuendo from the moment I walked in."

"Innuendo?" I raise an eyebrow. "Frankly, I have no idea what you mean."

"Really?" She places a hand on her hip.

"I generally prefer *tight*, concise conversation, Ms. King."

"Like hell, I'm staying here."

"Perhaps it's for the best." I turn my back on her, heading for my own room. "After all, I wouldn't want you to spend the night uncomfortable, Ms. King—"

"On second thought. I'll take you up on your offer." The sound of a clasp being undone catches my attention. I turn to find her with her hands on the front of her jeans. When she's sure I'm watching, she wrenches on the zipper and drags them down her hips, revealing another pair of black panties.

"What are you doing?" My voice is too hoarse. She smiles, the picture of innocence, and then fingers the hem of her sweater. She raises it up over the ridge of her stomach. Higher... I can make out her nipples through the lacy padding of her bra—and then it hits me. She's wearing *that* set of underwear. The pair from the picture.

"I'm getting ready for bed, Mr. Bellamy," she says sweetly. "By changing into my pajamas. *Professionally.*"

I don't know who moves first, but she's already in the guest bedroom, slamming the door shut before I can even take a step. "Goodnight, Mr. Bellamy," she croons from behind the door. A second later, I hear a telltale *click.*

"Locked doors, Evelyn?" I try the knob to reinforce the suspicion—the door won't budge. "You really don't trust yourself..."

"Trust *myself*?" She sounds close. I imagine her on the other side, her back braced against the door, fighting to keep her voice from losing its polished cadence. "Frankly, Mr. Bellamy, the only person in this equation I do not trust is you."

I laugh, but the sound echoes back harsher than expected. "Perhaps it's better if you lock yourself in," I admit. "Because I wouldn't want to..." I shake my head and start for my bedroom. "Never mind."

I'm halfway down the hallway when I hear the door open. I find her standing in the doorway, still only in the bra and panties, her chin high in the air. "You what? Because you wouldn't want to what?"

I shrug, forcing myself to meet her gaze. I don't know if it's because she's breathing faster, her chest heaving with indignation, but the entire bloody hallway smells like roses. "Because I wouldn't trust myself *not* to call for security if you creep into my bed again tonight. Frankly, Ms. King, a lack of employment has left you unsure of boundaries."

Her mouth falls open. Her eyes widen. One might think I'd slapped her before her expression transforms within a second. She goes from furious to smiling. Speechless to simpering.

"Oh really?"

I've never heard such a pleasant tone come from her lips. I'm on guard before she starts toward me, her eyes blazing. She pushes past me, trailing that floral scent, and marches right to my bedroom and over the threshold.

"I wouldn't want to affect your sleep," she says while lifting the edge of the duvet. "So why don't I just take your bed? I'm sure you don't mind—"

"I do mind." She nearly jumps out of her skin when I advance another step, approaching the bed. "One non-negotiable fixture of my bed is *me.* I'm sure you prefer the safety of a locked door anyway."

"Are you sure you want to risk it?" She lifts one leg and braces the knee against the mattress as if readying to slip beneath the covers. "What if I can't keep my *creeping* hands to myself during the night?"

"I suppose you'll just have to keep the consequences in mind," I say, invoking my previous threat to call security.

"And what about you?" She braces more of her weight onto her knee. "Are you sure you can keep *your* hands to yourself, Mr. Bellamy?"

I turn to the dresser and undo my tie before shrugging off my suit jacket. "Trust me, Evelyn. I will have no damn problem in that department."

I hear her inhale sharply and then exhale. "Good," she says. "Because I sleep in the nude."

*Bloody hell.* My jaw tightens. I undo my shirt and kick off my oxfords, but leave the slacks on. When I turn to the bed, I find her sitting on the edge with her back to me... and her bra in her hands.

"That's fine with me." My damn voice sounds too rough. She stiffens but reaches back to drag a corner of the duvet closer and over her shoulders.

"Fine." She slides her body onto the mattress, each movement slow and deliberate to keep every inch of her shielded by the blanket. She gazes up at me, her eyes daring with the duvet drawn to her chin. "Goodnight, Mr. Bellamy."

I approach the bed from the other end and wrench the linens back. I position myself with my back facing her. "Goodnight, Ms. King."

I wake up in Graeme Bellamy's bed—naked—for the... No matter the number, this latest occurrence marks too many damn times. I wish I'd spent the night tossing and turning—as one might while sleeping beside a man who, for all intents and purposes, seems to thrive on my discomfort. Not to mention the mess with Danny and whoever might be after him potentially tracking me here.

I should have been a nervous wreck all night.

But no, my limp, languid muscles say it all. I've slept better than I have in... Way too long. Ever, even? I blame the mattress. It feels like heaven in comparison to the lumpy monstrosity from the motel. My body is liquid, every muscle rejuvenated and soothed—and the fact has *nothing* at all to do with the faint heat ghosting my skin or the scent in my nostrils. How in the hell is it possible for someone to smell so damn good? I bury my nose into the sheets and inhale before I can stop myself. Spice. Musk. Cologne. Graeme Bellamy is a drug unto himself, and I hate myself for the warmth that spreads throughout my belly as I breathe him in.

I can tell without even opening my eyes that it's already morning. Warm sunlight grazes the part of my shoulder not covered by the blanket. I don't know if he's awake, though I assume it's nearing the time he should arrive at the office. As if my thoughts are the cue, I feel the mattress shift beneath the weight of another moving body.

"Four times." He sounds husky in the morning, and my damn toes curl within the sheets, the traitors. "I counted," he adds.

I take my time responding, arching my back to stretch out my body as though I've just woken up. "Four, what?"

"Four times that you touched me during the night."

I drag myself upright, clutching the top sheet to my chest. I crane my neck to look down at him and instantly regret it. Polished, the man is handsome. Rugged, with tousled bed-head and heavy-lidded eyes, the bastard is a god. My heart skips a beat when I take him in—several beats, in fact.

"I counted," he reiterates tiredly while my brain struggles to overpower the hormones that demand I rake my fingers through his hair.

"You... you mean you hallucinated four times," I stammer once his accusation actually sinks in. There is no way in hell I'd so much as stray past the bed's midline during the night. Had I?

"Eleven-forty-five p.m.," he recites, indicating toward his foot with a wave of his hand. "Your ankle brushed mine."

I follow his gaze to find that he slept in his slacks and socks. I'm not sure if he spent the night without blankets either or had just recently kicked them off.

"I didn't," I snap, but I tug my feet beneath me, resting my body on my knees.

"One-twenty-three a.m.," he continues, lifting his left shoulder from the mattress. "The tip of your left forefinger brushed my arm."

"Did not," I counter, but the denial falls flat. God, he slept without his shirt. Rippling muscle—I'd forgotten the bastard spent nearly every other night in the gym. A master craftsman couldn't have chiseled a more perfect specimen from stone. My eyes trace him greedily, drifting all the way down to the trail of dark hair leading beneath the waistband of his pants.

"Four and five a.m., respectively," he says, reaching up to drag his hand through his hair, swiping a wayward fringe out of his eyes. "Your hip brushed mine. However, I won't bother with ringing security. This time."

"Well, how benevolent of you." I shove the thicker duvet aside and wrap the top sheet around me before dismounting the mattress. My bare feet hit the floor, curling within the plush carpet, and I know without having to look that he followed suit.

"Don't let me chase you from bed, Evelyn," he says. "Enjoy the time to yourself."

I don't know if he intends the double meaning or if his implied innuendo is an accident this time. My cheeks catch fire, regardless. "Maybe I will."

I sit back on the mattress, glancing at him over my shoulder. I deliberately shift until I'm in the center of the bed and spread my legs out, claiming part of the space where he'd slept during the night.

"Hmph." He turns his back on me and heads for his closet. "Take *all* the time you need," he says, though once again, I can't help feeling like there's a double meaning tucked within the words. "Frankly, I'm just surprised you aren't nagging me about breakfast."

Bastard. "I've been fired, remember," I retort, though I can't see his face as he enters his walk-in closet. I hear him rummaging through the drawers, and I can't help but wonder which outfit he'll pick. The blue? The black? The gray? Not that I give a damn either way. "You can make your own damn breakfast."

He says nothing, and a moment later, he exits the closet wearing a steel-colored suit with a gray undershirt and matching tie. I would have suggested a blue one, but the bastard still looks impeccable, regardless. Without a word to me, he crosses the room and enters the bathroom. I hear the water running, followed by the scrub of a toothbrush against his teeth. He renters the bedroom a few minutes later while dragging a comb through his hair, slicking back every dark strand into his signature coif. I don't mean to stare, but I can't tear my eyes away until he sets the comb on a nearby dresser and enters the hallway, as casually as if I'm not lying naked on his bed.

I wait ten minutes before crawling off the mattress and creeping into the guest bedroom for my clothes. I get dressed in a simple blue sundress that doesn't require ironing, and I wet my hair in the guest bathroom, leaving it to dry naturally rather than attempt to detangle the mess with my fingers.

I take my time to re-organize my suitcase while picturing Bellamy sprawled in the back seat of the Mercedes, on his way to the office. He'll arrive an hour early, like always, and set to work scouring through his email. Typically, I would review his itinerary before force-feeding him at least a banana before his first meeting. Today, for all I care, he could go into a hypoglycemic coma before lunchtime.

When I finally gather my belongings and make my way downstairs, I fully expect to embark on the walk of shame down to the lobby without an audience. I'll write the bastard a check before I leave, of course, and maybe tape it to his door. The thought doesn't even finish forming in my mind before I lock eyes with the figure standing at the foot of the staircase, a frying pan in hand.

"Taste this," he demands, offering a bit of what appears to be eggs on a fork while I promptly trip down the next step and lose my grip on my suitcase. It clatters to the bottom, not that Graeme Bellamy spares it a passing glance. His eyes hold a challenge, and his hand never lowers the pan or the fork.

I must be hallucinating. For one, I didn't know that Graeme Bellamy was capable of finding his way into a kitchen, let alone operating the appliances. I sniff and only inhale the spicy tang of garlic—not smoke. A glance at the doorway to the kitchen doesn't reveal flames shooting from the stainless-steel stovetop, either.

"Any day, Ms. King..."

Drawn forward by curiosity, I'm already standing in front of him before I realize it, just one step above. He casually raises his fork, and my mouth opens against my better judgment. One small bite and my eyes widen. "You can cook," I blurt out after swallowing.

"Yes..." Shooting me a puzzled look, he steps back, stirring the substance in his pan—scrambled eggs, I think. "I can. My own damn breakfast, to be exact."

You'd think the bastard showed off his culinary skills every day. But the fact is that I tasted more than just the typical salt and pepper I was known to cook with—maybe olive oil if I wanted to get fancy. Clove. Garlic. Fresh rosemary.

Were those things even in his fridge?

"Leaving so soon?" Bellamy calls from the kitchen.

"Y-Yes." I scramble down the final step and rush to pick up my suitcase from the floor.

"Oh. You're welcome to stay until you find another hotel." His tone is way too cold to seem genuine. Besides, like hell I would stay another night in the same mile radius as him.

"No, thank you." I do my best to heft my bag higher on my shoulder before heading for the door. I get it open one-handed, balancing the handle of my suitcase against my hip.

"You're not eating?" His voice reaches me before I step over the threshold. Surprise, surprise, it contains yet another dare. Another challenge that I should smartly refuse. "You should," he adds. "After all, I wouldn't want your blood sugar levels to drop."

Damn him. I stagger back into the foyer and slam the door behind me. When I join him in the kitchen, he's innocently ladling eggs onto two plates, complete with perfectly-browned toast. "Coffee?" he asks, gesturing to the coffee maker that I would have never assumed he even knew how to operate.

I frown. It could be poisoned, yet resisting him lately seems much more perilous. "Fine."

I take a seat at the center island, left with nothing to do but watch him. As insane as it feels to admit, even to myself, the man knows his way around a kitchen. There is a polished ease with which he scrapes the pan clean before tossing it into the sink. It's almost enough to negate the poised image I've always had of him as a child with a silver spoon literally rammed down his throat.

I'm not sure if I like this new image of him. It's too strange. Too... normal.

"Butter, Evelyn?" He holds a dish of the condiment in question in one hand, his head tilted questioningly. It's not the word itself that sets me on edge but merely how he looks saying it. *Butter, Evelyn. Will you take the bait, Evelyn? This is a trap, Evelyn.*

"N-No, thank you." A moment later, he serves me—a porcelain plate that seems like it had been meant to spend its existence locked within a display case rather than used, sporting exactly two pieces of toast and a heap of eggs. He pours a measured amount of coffee into a mug and slides it across the counter in my direction.

His eyes don't leave me until I snatch up a fork and reluctantly take a bite. The first taste wasn't a fluke. The bastard somehow has learned to combine flavors despite the past three years of my not knowing him to be capable of even opening a wrapper on an energy bar without being forced to. One bite quickly becomes a ravenous rush to devour the entire plate. I'm on my last bit of toast when I find him leaning against the opposite counter, still watching me. "You're not eating?"

"No," he says in a soft, dangerous tone that instantly puts me on guard. "Watching you eat your words is fulfilling enough."

Bastard. I lean across the counter, snatch a piece of toast from the second plate, and thrust it in his direction before I can stop myself. "Eat."

The fleeting smile that shapes his mouth for a second inspires butterflies that explode inside my stomach. He takes his sweet time crossing the kitchen and accepts the toast, taking one giant bite.

"Shouldn't you be on your way to work?" Damn it. I want the words to come out less curious and more taunting, but a good night of sleep seems to make the irritation he inspires in me harder to stick.

"I'm going in late today," he says, leaving it at that.

A late morning. For the first time in as long as I've known him. "Another meeting?"

He frowns and bites off another piece of toast.

Ah, so he's being secretive again. Which is a good thing, of course—I don't need to know another damn thing about him. I'll finish my breakfast—out of spite—and then leave without a backward glance and a single thought devoted to where he might be spending this "late morning." It's like my eyes have other plans, though. They scan the room and land on a stack of brochures resting on the other end of the counter. A prickling sensation on the side of my neck makes me glance up to find that he's noticed them as well.

He stiffens. I lunge. By virtue of being closer, I manage to grab them first. It's hard to make the motion seem casual as I tuck them under my arm and maneuver my stool out of his reach. "How thoughtful," I tell him without looking up, striving to make my voice as sweet as possible. "A bit of morning reading."

Not quite. Every brochure in some way, shape, or form pertains to the Red Room. A business manifesto. Building design. There even appears to be a brief history of the club's origins—they apparently strive to... I snort.

"Have you found something amusing, Evelyn?" Bellamy sounds even more sour than usual.

I shake my head and continue to flip through the pages. "It's just..."

I hear the thud of his Oxfords against the floor—one cautious step in my direction. "Just what?"

I inhale sharply and gather the nerve to look up. Despite everything that transpired between us within the past few days, he doesn't scare me. Not even when he looks like... *that*. Blazing blue eyes and a chiseled, guarded expression. "It's just that... you don't seem the type to belong to a club that claims to—" I clear my throat and read right from a crisp block of text. "Worship feminism and sexuality."

I hear the telltale thud of another step, and a shadow falls over my lap, obscuring part of the booklet I have open. "And why is that?"

I face forward, biting my lip. "You don't exactly seem... suave." As soon as the word leaves my mouth, I know it's not quite what I mean. Graeme Bellamy oozes poise and charm from every damn pore.

"Oh really." I flinch as his hand falls over my shoulder, the fingers curling to pin me in place. His breath lashes at my earlobe, ominous and searing. "Does that mean *you* just have very low standards?"

I suck in a steadying breath and turn to face him directly. He's smiling, of all things, rather than insulted. That fact alone is more than enough warning that, once again, we're dipping into dangerous territory. "No. I mean that *you* aren't the kind of man who I could see sweet-talking his way into a woman's bed."

"Oh?" He smiles again, but it doesn't reach his eyes. His storming, very blue, electric damn eyes. "Do go on."

"You're not a Casanova."

He laughs. In my face, and his breath somehow manages to smell intoxicating despite the lingering hint of garlic. "Is that so?"

"You're too..." I fish around for the right word, but only one comes to mind. "Arrogant."

"Arrogance." He swallows hard as if trying not to choke on the descriptor. "Is that what it takes to make a woman hop into your bed not one, not two, but three times—"

"Not everyone is like me," I snap, before I realize how self-disparaging that sounds. "I mean... you don't exactly woo."

"Woo." He strokes his chin with his thumb, and I hate the prickle of heat that shoots down my spine at the sight. "And how exactly would a man go about wooing a woman like you?"

*Like me?* I deliberately ignore the mocking edge in his tone. "Well, not be an ass, for one."

He frowns. "Oh?"

"And be suave. Sweet talk. Your idea of being charming seems to be throwing a check in someone's face—"

"And do you have an example of this so-called, charming, suave Casanova in mind?"

Uh-oh. I can taste the danger in his tone, hidden beneath the rosemary. But what the hell—I crane my neck back to meet his gaze fully and blurt out the answer. "Well, someone like... Adrian Riley."

His eyebrow quirks a fraction of an inch higher—the only hint of emotion revealed on his face. "And why is that?"

"Well, he's handsome," I admit. "He seems well educated. Interesting. Charismatic—"

"Oh?" Suddenly, he's closer, his body, whether intentionally or not, positioned slightly over mine. "In what way?"

"He wouldn't make it feel like a game." Why in the hell do those words come out so... serious? This *is* a game. A series of mistakes. There is no way in hell that something real could ever come out of this twisted "thing" between us now. I know it. He knows it.

So why is he frowning? And why the hell did something in my belly lurch once I said it out loud?

Desperate to salvage the moment, I clear my throat and say, "I should go..."

Just like that, he steps away and circles the counter, reaching for his mug of coffee. My fingers shake as I set the brochures down and rise to my feet. I start for the foyer again, only for his voice to reach me the moment I stoop for my suitcase.

"Stay," he tells me. The gruff baritone isn't the typical octave, but it's not that ominous growl, either. "I'll have William find you another hotel, and I'll deduct it from your severance amount."

"You don't have to do that—"

"Funny. I don't remember asking." He strolls through the doorway a second later, a piece of toast in hand. Aware of me watching, he takes a deliberate bite before walking past me for the door. "On second thought," he adds as he palms the door handle. "I wouldn't want you to feel that I'm being too arrogant in assisting your search, so do what you will. Enjoy your morning, Ms. King."

Just like that, the bastard leaves, and the scent of fresh herbs lingers on the air along with a feeling of... could it be guilt? Whatever it is, settles in my stomach no matter how hard I try to ignore it.

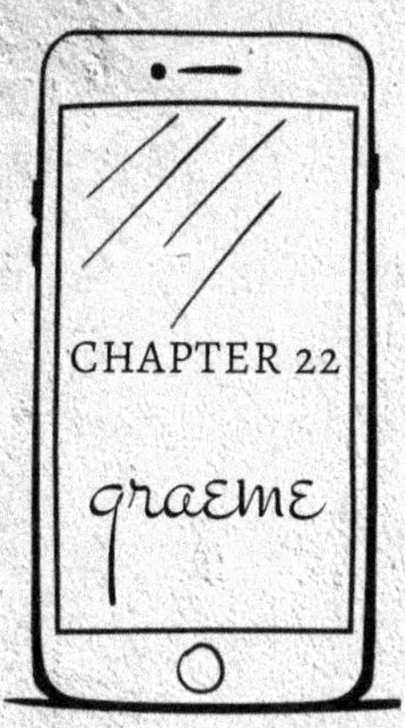


Riley himself is there to greet me in the lobby of the club. Dressed in a plain black suit, it seems as if he's dropped the pretentious act for once. His expression is nothing but the cold, stripped mask of a businessman.

"Bellamy." I take the hand he offers and shake it once. "I say we've passed the time for preliminary games," he says once the nicety is out of the way. "Let us jump directly into business."

It's about bloody time. I say nothing as he leads me to the elevator and up to his office. There, with the door closed, I finally lay out my terms.

"My solution is this—you can have *some* input in the London club," I start, standing while he circles around to the opposite end of his desk. "But I will require an equal say in yours. *And,*" I add, before an arrogant smirk can even begin to shape his mouth. "We maintain full leadership over our respective entities. No crossover."

"Always the cautious poker player, Bellamy," Riley says with a cold laugh. "You never had any of Alexander's, shall we say, flair for the dramatic. I take it you aren't a gambling man—"

"Not when it comes to business." A fact that I have no damn shame in.

Riley shrugs. "I will say that I'm disappointed. I expected you to march in here with a list of demands before you'd ever consider making a deal."

"Oh, that might be because I haven't begun yet." I brace one hand against a leather chair positioned before his desk and meet his gaze directly. "I know the signs of your meddling. Your methods leave a certain... stench. If you want my club, you come after *me*. Only me. Leave anyone else out of it."

The bastard smirks. "Interesting. Did you have anyone in particular in mind?"

"My mother, for one. My brother. My sister. Keep them out of any schemes you may have in mind. It's not a request."

I choose to omit the fact that Alexander was a willing accomplice in his latest plot. At least until he came to the same realization I had long ago—Adrian Riley cares for no one but Adrian Riley.

"Ah..." Riley nods and runs a thumb along his chin. "And Evelyn King? Are even past employees protected under this umbrella of yours?"

Confirming or denying her firing wouldn't make any damn bit of difference. So, I say nothing.

Riley smirks regardless, but he seems to leave that line of attack alone—for now. "I suppose this is when I lay out my own demands..." He opens a drawer and withdraws a leather-bound book which he places down between us. "For starters, two forms of leadership is simply not feasible—"

"And I assume you have the perfect solution," I interject.

"As a matter of fact, I do." He flips open the book, revealing a list of what seems to be names. "One of the prized features of the club that we promote is unity. Few decisions are made without the input of both our members *and* clients."

Apparently, the book is some sort of membership manifesto. "And?"

"I don't see why this matter should be handled any differently."

I frown, glancing over the ledger. "Explain."

"Why not let those who make up the club decide the direction of leadership? The membership bodies of both clubs will be consulted. Then we put it to a vote as to who should head both. Of course, the minor managing duties will belong to each respective owner, but—"

"Only one man can sit at the head of the table." It's what my father used to say before he and my mother divorced. *You put two bulls in a pen, only one will truly be able to call it home.*

"Something like that," Riley says carefully.

It's obviously a trap, designed to put into play one trait that Adrian Riley utilized to his benefit at every opportunity. Even Evelyn has mentioned as much, whether intentionally or not. He is a charming git, able to manipulate men and women alike to suit his own gain.

"And I am to believe that in a month, I can turn your loyal members to my side and win their votes?"

Riley laughs. "Therein lies the *challenging* aspect of a challenge, Bellamy. They are, of course, more familiar with Alexander, but I'm sure you can turn on the old Bellamy charm. After all, you seem willing to go to any lengths to protect that precious family name."

"Is that what this is about," I say with a forced scoff. "Your lingering jealousy. My god, man. One would think that with your success, you'd get over a childish slight from two decades ago—"

"A slight?" Riley laughs, but there's no mirth in it. His eyes narrow as the corners of his lips upturn, revealing a hint of perfectly-whitened teeth. Ah, there he is. The callous bastard I know and loathe. Gone is his perfect, charming mask. This is the true Adrian Riley, vengeful to his very core. "Is that what you call it when you, a pampered heir, born with a silver spoon in your mouth, withdraw all contact from your supposed friend without warning. A slight?"

"When that friend resorts to spreading vicious, nasty rumors, you can call it whatever you damn well please."

"Rumors." He laughs, his head tilted thoughtfully to the side. "About your father, you mean? Or should I say *our* father—"

"You can call yourself a bastard of whoever you like," I say coldly. "Leave my family out of it."

"Whatever you wish, Graeme," Riley counters. "If you want sole ownership of the club, then those are my terms—"

"Deal." I draw back from the desk without bothering to see his reaction. Smug satisfaction? Shock? Confusion? "But on one condition. You leave anyone not directly tied to the club out of it, meaning none of your usual tricks. No blackmail. No silly mind games. No extortion. That goes for my business, my family, my—"

"The spouses and other immediate family members of clients and patrons alike are off limits. Your business has no bearing on our negations over the club either. However..."

I glance over my shoulder to meet his gaze directly, finding nothing in his eyes but sheer amusement. "However, what?"

"However, anyone else, not *currently* associated with either your family or your corporation is, as they say, fair game." He makes a show of cracking his knuckles before steepling them before him. "For instance, if an old employee of yours were to join another company, or drunkenly converse about the quirks of her former boss in public... that would be quite the scandal, wouldn't it? You've worked so hard to rehabilitate your family's reputation, after all. I'd hate to see that effort amount to nothing."

"Is that so?" My hands form into fists. The bloody, arrogant git.

"Of course." He nods. "Though, when it comes to the club, I'll gladly accept your challenge, Bellamy." He even has the nerve to tilt his chin in my direction like a gesture of war. "I hope to see you there tonight."

My teeth are gritted, my reply curt, "You can bet on it."

I leave the bastard grinning beside his desk and head for the exit the moment I reach the lobby. It's raining out, the icy droplets splattering everything within their reach. I can't help but feel it's an omen—even bloody nature is reinforcing Evelyn King's own harsh assessment. Each drop of rain seems to hammer in that point—*You don't have a chance in hell.*

But I've staked my existence on proving everyone else wrong before.

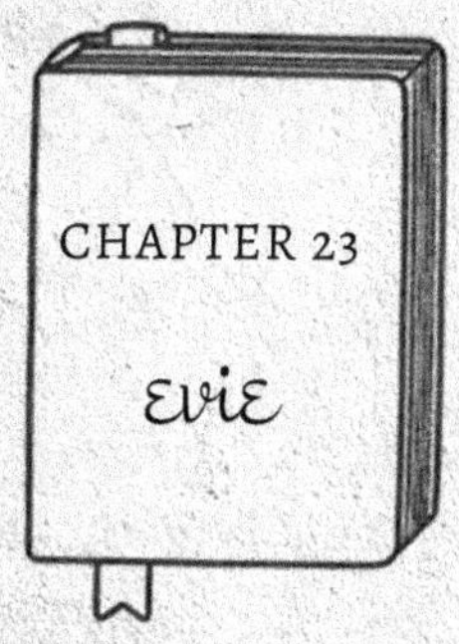



I am not hiding from *him*. I have to say it twice, under my breath, as I duck beneath the awning of the Royal and linger beside the entrance.

Of course, I wasn't going to go in. I was merely in the area—taking a walk to ponder my current life circumstances. When the self-pitying got too much, I switched topics. Perhaps rather than use my severance pay to galivant off to the tropics, I could pay off Danny and buy at least a year of peace. He seemed worried the last time I saw him—more than usual. How many thugs had he pissed off this time? How many of them knew my face? How many promises had he made using my money and belongings as collateral?

I refused to let him shape how I lived my life long ago. I still do.

But there is something instinctively attractive about a place that I know he won't have a chance of sneaking into. Even I catch weird looks when I enter the lobby on the days that the usual doorman isn't at his post. I need just a hint of that. A minute of feeling one-hundred percent safe and secure. A second, even...

"You're on time for once."

I jump as the deep voice ricochets down my spine. It's familiar—not Danny's, thank god. Though I'm not sure if this figure is a more welcome nuisance, to be honest. He still smells like garlic, his breath ghosting my ear.

I turn around and am forced to nearly stand on tiptoe to meet his gaze. "What the hell are you doing here?" Too late do I remember that *he*, between the two of us, just so happens to live here.

Rather than rush to snidely remark on that point, Graeme Bellamy just watches me shrewdly before inclining his head toward the building's entrance. "I was on my way to get lunch," he says—something I'm sure is a damn lie. "Care to join me?"

He starts forward before I can sputter out a response, and for some reason, I find myself following in his wake. I'll write it up to shock. Even with drops of rain rolling off his hair and onto the shoulders of his priceless suit, the man still somehow manages to seem impeccable. His life must resemble walking down one perpetual runway, all eyes turned in his direction, the audience watching his every move with bated breath.

He leads me toward the bistro and takes up a table near the corner of the dining room. When a smiling waitress appears to take our order, he asks for coffee before they both turn in my direction.

"I'm not having lunch with you."

The waitress blinks in confusion while Mr. Bellamy merely smiles. "Suit yourself," he says, sending the waitress on her way. "Though, I will mention that it's customary to sit at least."

I raise an eyebrow at the word choice. "Customary for what?"

"For when someone is about to offer you a job."

I throw my head back and laugh—I can't help it. Okay, maybe more like snort. Loudly. Rudely. Crassly. We catch eyes from all over—a woman draped in pearls sipping tea near the window shoots me a dirty look as if to exclaim, "Ugh, the riffraff."

When I finally regain control of myself, Bellamy is still smiling, the arrogant son of a bitch. "What in the hell makes you think that you could fire me, and three days later just hire me back? That I would ever want to be hired back?"

"Well then, I suppose it's good for both of us that I'm not planning to hire you back as my *assistant*. This is a different offer."

Damn him. Damn him. I'm curious, against my better judgment. Well aware of the mind games he likes to play, I'm also terrified. I know I should turn on my heel and leave him and whatever he has to say behind.

But I don't. I can't. Smirking, he knows it.

"What kind of job?" My voice catches in my throat. I swallow hard to relieve some of the pressure.

He nods to the chair across from him. "Sit."

I do. Mainly for my own benefit. From this level, I have better access to the pitcher of water that rests on the table between us—all the better to throw the damn thing in his face when he says something that will no doubt be designed to humiliate me further.

"I'm sitting. What?"

"You claim to be an expert on the tactics of a true Casanova," he starts.

Oh god.

"...So *advise* me."

I lurch to my feet. My hand reaches for the handle of the pitcher. "I'll leave you to your right hand, Mr. Bellamy," I snarl. "And you can consider this a head start to a cold shower—"

"I'm serious."

My grip loosens on the pitcher, and its base thuds back onto the table's surface. My fingertips shake. I wish I could say because of rage, but something else surges through my system and leaves me unsteady. Fear. Graeme Bellamy looks not only serious... My god, he seems *earnest.*

If I wanted to get really crazy with the adjectives, I might even say that he appears... vulnerable.

My mind goes blank. I can only stand there. Unsure of whether to slap him or run. I think I might do both.

"What the hell are you talking about?"

"You." He cocks his head and narrows his eyes as if trying to home in on what exactly about me he's singling out. "You claim that you know what it takes for a man to successfully 'woo' a woman, as you put it. Teach me how. I'll be willing to pay a retainer."

My head spins, and I collapse on the nearest chair, bracing one hand against my forehead. "Why? It's not like your current method keeps you from scoring sex."

Myself included. The man may have been a cocky son of a bitch, but... with *cocky* being the operative word.

"This isn't about sex."

"Oh?" My heart picks up speed, though I'm unsure why. Maybe it's the cold, hard gleam in his eye? I've only seen him look that way recently, when one man, in particular, happened to be the subject of the conversation. "Is this about the club?"

"No. That is a private matter I would prefer to discuss only with someone under contract." He reaches into his breast pocket and withdraws, of all things, a slip of paper—the very contract in question. He unfolds it and slides it across the table toward me, followed quickly by a silver pen. "I trust you find it the typical agreement."

I take my time scanning the block of text printed on the page. There's no job description or duties listed within the three paragraphs. Instead, I find a bunch of legal jargon that forms the basis of a confidentiality agreement.

"What's the job?" I ask, glancing up to find him watching me with a look I can't decipher. "Or is that the job? Keeping my mouth shut? Particularly around Adrian Riley—"

"How is this amount as your retainer?" He slides a check across the table, and I pinch myself to keep from gaping. Too. Many. Zeros. "That will be per week," he adds. "I'm open to negotiation if you require a larger sum."

A larger sum. This, paired with my severance amount, would ensure that I wouldn't have to work for a very, very long time. I could get a decent apartment in a nicer part of the city—a place with a doorman, even. Not to mention I'd have enough left over to bribe Danny into disappearing again while I attempted to re-piece my life together.

It sounds too damn good to be true.

"Does the offer seem tempting enough to you?" he asks.

*Tempting,* isn't a strong enough word to describe it. "I... I— you." My mouth opens and closes several times while I struggle to find the right words. In the end, I come up with three. "What's the job?"

The corner of his mouth quirks into a dangerous smile as he leans back, lacing his fingers together behind his head. "You teach me how to 'woo.'"

*Sex.* He wants me kept on a retainer for sex. My cheeks heat up. My stomach tightens... "You can't actually be serious—"

"I'm interested in wooing, not fucking, Evelyn," he says as if reading my mind, heedless of any other patrons around us. "As you yourself pointed out, I don't need any help in the latter department."

"Then what do you mean?"

He sits forward, bracing both of his hands, palms down, against the table's surface. "Wooing. Particularly, charming a clientele of lonely old socialites into doing my bidding."

His bidding? "Are you running for prom king?"

I expect a laugh or some other snide response. Instead, he shrugs. "Something to that effect."

Damn it, I'm curious. "I take it this has something to do with the Red Room?"

He frowns and nods toward the contract. "That is classified information, Ms. King."

Without breaking his gaze, I pick up the damn pen. My hand shakes involuntarily as I bring the nib to the pristine section of paper right above the dotted line. It feels like ages before I gather the nerve to pen a single E. "What would I have to do?"

I hear him sigh, and a fringe of my hair flutters. He must have leaned closer, bracing his weight against the table. "You seem to have a knack for getting yourself out of trouble. Winning people over to your side—"

"Making my way through life without brandishing my checkbook," I interject.

He chuckles. It's not a very happy sound. More guttural, and something in my skin quivers. "I keep you on retainer for your advice. When we are in public, you act as though you are enamored by me, as one would be in a genuine relationship. I will pay you when and only when you prove that you take this assignment seriously. In a month, you can go on your merry way, and we never have to associate with one another ever again."

He makes it sound so fucking tempting. I chew on my lower lip, mulling it over. *No amount of money is ever worth your pride*, Dad used to say. But Dad, thankfully, had never seen just how far Danny had fallen. Money seemed to be the only carrot tempting enough to throw far in the opposite direction to get him to leave me alone. For a little while, at least.

It's sad. It's pathetic. But there it is.

"Fine." I finish signing my first name. Then the last. It physically hurts when I finally set the pen aside. Like I've ripped away some innermost part of myself and slapped it right onto Graeme Bellamy's palm. Smiling, he gleefully takes that piece of me. He crushes it.

"Good. We can continue this discussion in my suite. On the way, I'll have William cancel your hotel search."

"What? Why?"

The look he shoots me from over his shoulder makes the air hitch in my chest. I'm choking even before he declares, "Because you'll be staying in my penthouse. With me."

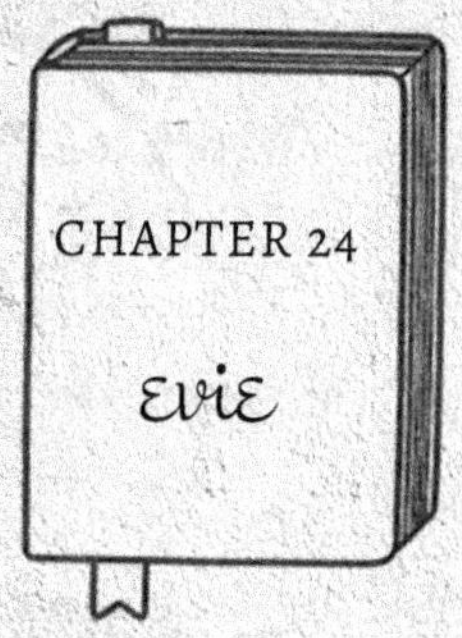


I have to catch myself on a nearby table, ruffling the neat pile of napkins arranged on top of it. "Like hell I—"

"You will be kept on *retainer*, Ms. King," Bellamy says, still marching for the exit and leaving me no choice but to scramble to keep up. "That means that I may have use for your skill at *any* hour. We've already established that you are unreliable with other forms of communication..." Apparently, he's referring to all those missed emails and text messages.

I shake my head. "No—"

"Yes."

I blink. Try again. "No."

"Yes. That particular detail is non-negotiable." The way he says it... The words don't sound sleazy, dripping with innuendo, but crisp. Cold.

He's hiding something. Even more alarming—the look in his eye warns me not to ask what.

So, I follow him. Past a stern-faced William, taking up his post near the entrance, and into an elevator. It's a tense, silent ride up to the top floor. When we finally enter the penthouse, I'm shaking. My lungs are desperate to find more air, and I think I even wheeze.

And it's all his damn fault. But what does Graeme Bellamy have to show for setting my world into turmoil for the umpteenth time this week? The bastard glances down at my hands and frowns.

"Where is your satchel?"

I blink and stagger a step away from him, keeping my body nearest to the exit. "At the reception desk," I admit. I'd convinced myself that it was better than leaving so much as a damn hair inside his actual suite while I went out. Now I'm not too sure. I should have gone back to my storage unit. I should have packed up whatever I could fit onto a plane and taken the next flight far from New York.

Anything to avoid being alone with this man once again.

"I'll have it sent up," he says as if it's a piece of wayward mail he's referring to, and not my personal belongings.

"I'm not staying here." I feel the need to punctuate the statement by slamming my foot against the floor, hard enough to make it sink in. Mainly into my own brain. No more Graeme Bellamy. No more indescribable, priceless bed. No more sex. With him, at least.

"That's rather discouraging, Evelyn," he states while turning to face me. "Quitting a job only after minutes of being rehired."

"This—" I gesture toward the massive suite. "Wasn't a part of the deal."

"Oh, wasn't it?" The smile he flashes for my benefit is nothing but sinful. "Look again, Evelyn. Always read the fine print."

I inhale. Exhale. Still can't seem to breathe. "You. Are. An—"

"Ass?" he supplies, his eyes narrowing. "I do believe we've already established that fact more than once."

We're at an impasse. A lethal, jagged one, and I'm not sure who has the upper hand. Me? Him?

It feels like an eternity before either one of us makes the first move—he steps toward me. Again. Faster. Herding me into the corner by the door. Blocking me in with his sheer size until I'm forced to stand on tiptoe, my neck craned to face him.

"On second thought, perhaps you are right, Evelyn," he says. "After all, are your skills even worth keeping on retainer?" He shrugs.

I scowl. "You can go to hell—"

"Woo me."

"W-What?"

"Convince me that you staying here is a terrible decision, and I'll—"

My right hand meets his jaw. Twice. Each resounding thwack reverberates through my palm, but it isn't until I feel the resulting sting that it actually sinks in what I've done. I've slapped Graeme Bellamy, owner of the proverbial goddamn universe.

And it felt damn good.

"That's not quite what I had in mind..." He rubs his jaw and then uses that same hand to seize my wrist. I'm prepared for anger. Maybe even a bit of manhandling from a man who doesn't seem capable of hearing the word "no" from anyone. But not gentleness.

I could easily break his grip if I wanted to. I *should* want to. Instead, I only stare as he drags my arm above my head and pins it against the wall.

"Let's try this again." He's closer. I hold my breath to keep my chest from brushing his. To keep from breathing him in. "If I were a man who pretended to subscribe to the philosophies of someone like Adrian Riley, how might I go about convincing you to stay?"

My poor heart gives up. It pounds like mad. It slows to a crawl. I should be blacking out at any moment. Any minute I'll wake up, and this entire week will have been some crazy dream. Any minute...

"Or maybe this could never work," he says, and the bastard almost sounds... disappointed. Frustrated, even? "Rip up the contract, Ms. King—"

"Listen," I croak, and he stops in his tracks, still keeping his grip on my arm.

"I am," he prompts when I don't say anything else.

It's a struggle to find the right words and remember how to convert them into verbal sounds. "You could try *listening*, first," I manage to rasp. "Actually hearing the words that come out of another person's mouth. And then trying to find the right words to say in response."

He frowns. "Such as?"

"I don't want to stay here."

Irritation flickers through his gaze as he processes those words, but to his credit, he blinks, and the emotion disappears. "Why?"

I flinch. He seems to be taking my advice. "Because... because it just isn't..."

"Professional?" He toys with the word, dragging his tongue to stress each syllable.

I jerk my head just once. "Yes."

"I'm listening," he says. "But frankly, I don't give a damn what you consider professional or not. How is that?"

I try to snatch my wrist away, but his grip tightens. Suddenly, it feels like he's even closer. "You get an F," I counter.

He drags his tongue along his lower lip. "An F for…"

Oh god. "Let me go—"

"It's your turn to listen," he says over me. "If your concern is because of the sex—"

I cringe, fighting back the memories that threaten to descend. Him. Me. The window. The bed. Parts of me have been exposed to areas of this penthouse that they were never in a million years ever meant to. "That's not—"

"Don't be," he says. "To be honest, Evelyn, you are the last woman on earth I would want to fuck. Now. Tonight. Ever."

"Ex… Excuse me?"

He has the nerve to smile once again. "I suggest you take your own advice, Evelyn. And listen."

I fight to keep from rolling my eyes. "So, there's nothing remotely sexual about you wanting me to stay here? For weeks on end?" Especially considering all that has happened within the past few days alone.

He shrugs, but the motion only seems to draw him closer to me, his face inches from mine. "No. Not a thing. I can't understand why you find that so hard to believe. Especially considering that *I* wasn't the one who touched *you* last night—"

"So, Mr. Bellamy, if I stripped right now, down to my underwear which you seemed so fascinated by, you wouldn't want to touch me?" My cheeks catch fire as the words leave my mouth, but I don't dare tear my gaze from his.

He glances me over and raises a single eyebrow. "I can't say that I would. The first few times were against my better judgment. After all, it's not every day that a hapless man is seduced by his former assistant."

Oh fuck. Him. "That's the way to woo a girl," I tell him, trying to ignore the pang in my chest. That isn't... embarrassment, is it? "Insult her sexually. You certainly know your way around sweet talk."

"That I do." His smile widens. "You have small tits."

Anger flares before I can stop it. Ignites. Explodes. "And you have a small co—"

"Oh?" He leans into me, pressing me back against the wall. His hips jar my belly, along with a hard, firm, unmistakable bulge, and I promptly lose my train of thought.

"I think you yourself commented on the size of my cock," he murmurs into my ear. "*Small* wasn't quite the word you used, though I would love to refresh your memory..."

My pride smarts beneath his well-placed jabs. My skin is on fire. It's a cruel war he's waged within my body. I try to push him off, but he doesn't budge. I hear him inhale instead, when every struggle forces me to move against him.

"I didn't want to hurt your feelings before," I rasp, struggling to find a way past him. His body is a wall, his heat consuming. I bat against his forearm with my hand, but I know it's as ineffective as trying to swat open a bolted door. "Sorry to say it, but you're small—"

"I said you have small tits." The voice reverberates through my ear drum. Damn, it's *that* growl. My head falls back against the wall for leverage. My eyes squeeze shut. This isn't happening. Graeme Bellamy isn't pulsing against me, hard, hungry. My traitorous body isn't answering that instinctive urge. I'm not panting. "I never said I hadn't enjoyed playing with said tits." He's even closer, crushing me to the wall, his lips brushing the shell of my ear with every word. "Touching. Squeezing. Biting..." His palm meets the wall beside my head before I can even think to shimmy in that direction. "Something tells me that you enjoyed playing with my small cock —" He grinds his pelvis into mine for emphasis. Fire. Heat. I squeeze my thighs together.

"D-Don't flatter yourself." I manage to get one of my hands on his shoulder, and I dig my nails in to shove him back, using the wall behind me for leverage. "Get away from—"

"If I spread you over the counter. Drape your *small* thighs over my shoulders. Show you just how much I enjoy your tits... would you consider that wooing?"

I shake my head to clear it. Blink. Dig my nails in just to hear him groan in the hopes that it snaps some sense into me. It doesn't. My senses shatter. My knees weaken. My brain starts to consider just how easy it would be for him to carry out every bit of his threat.

"Or if I strip you here... against the wall. Bring out my minuscule cock. Would that—"

"S-Shut up." My brain has the right idea. My body isn't convinced. *Don't.*

"As you wish…" His lips find my shoulder, nudging aside the strap of my sundress. While I stiffen in shock, he traces out a path with his tongue and his teeth…

I bite my lip to trap any sound I might make. The sinful sting of his bite travels all the way down, down, down, resonating right between my legs. It's electric. I need to shove him off. Scream. Kick the bastard right in his so-called *small* cock.

My head tilts instead, giving him better access, and he doesn't hesitate to nip a trail across my collarbone. One of his hands cups my waist, pinning me in place as he licks… bites again.

A gasp rips from my throat and escapes my pursed lips.

"Listening," he rasps against my skin. "Step one. Let me hear you…"

Both of his hands seize my dress. The next second it's being wrenched over my head. My arms rise to assist him, and then his hands are there, following his promise to the T. Kneading. Pinching. My body feels like putty in his fingers. My nipples stiffen, and he eagerly takes advantage. My eyes are somewhere on the ceiling when he decides to make good on his second threat.

I stiffen as he palms my waist and lifts me, cupping his palms beneath my ass.

"W-What are you doing—"

"Shhh." There's nothing comforting in the gruff sound he muffles into my shoulder. When he doesn't put me down, I have no choice but to wrap my legs around him, painfully aware of every inch. He staggers back. Into the kitchen, I see once I force my gaze to focus on our surroundings. He carries me right over to the counter. Drops me down onto the granite surface.

Oh god. He sinks to his knees, his head disappearing beneath the ridge of my stomach. I lift my head to track his descent, but he's too low, beneath the counter. I can only make out the top of his head, and then his hands are on my thighs, lifting... spreading them apart.

He doesn't bother to tease me this time. He slides a thumb beneath the panel of my panties, sweeping it aside to make way for his tongue. One searching thrust, and my brain goes blank. My pride tucks itself away into some distant part of my brain. My nerve endings explode.

"T-This... this doesn't count," I manage to croak out before he tastes me again. Deeper. Harder.

My moan clashes with the words he growls into me, punctuating each one with a jab of his tongue. "Count?" He uses the hardness of his thumb to spread me open wider. Licks again. "As you wish. *One.*"

My hips jerk, my knees instinctively trying to clamp together, but his head is between them, his shoulders relentless. Like a goddamn piston.

"Two," he growls, still ramming. "Three... eight... sixteen..."

God, god, god. My hips writhe. My hand flies out, grasping for leverage, and finds his hair, tangling within the strands.

"Twenty... twenty-seven. *Fuck.*"

The gritty, broken curse sets off a chain reaction. My back arches. A cry tears from my throat, rising in pitch with every stroke. Every suck.

"Fuck," I hear myself croak. "Shit."

"I'm listening." He makes me feel every inch his lips move. I don't just hear the words. He fucks them into me. *"So let me hear you."*

"Harder!" My nails clench, guiding him lower, deeper. "Lower..."

"I'm listening."

Like hell he is. My spine curls. My heels press into his back. I can't breathe. I arch against him, feeling every muscle in my body tighten. Clench. When he swipes his tongue against my clit, they come undone.

My head swims with the intensity of the rush that takes me high. Higher than the ceiling. Higher than I've ever been. He ruthlessly forces me even higher, shoving himself into me. Adding first one finger. Then another.

"G-Graeme." I've never called him by his first name before, and I don't realize it until he stiffens. Every muscle in his body turns to stone beneath my fingertips, and I can only interpret a rush of vibration to decipher the word he snarls against me next.

"Again—"

"Graeme." I shouldn't. I need to. Anything to keep him from stopping. I'll die if he stops. "P-Please..."

One of his hands slides beneath my ass and drags me to the edge of the counter—nearly off it. He's supporting most of my weight, and I let him. I take him. He inhales me.

The second orgasm hits faster. Harder. Ruthless.

I don't have time to catch my breath before he's already readying me for the third. The fourth. The cool air hits me like a slap when he finally draws back, his gaze meeting mine, his eyes on fire. "It is customary... for a teacher to reward her student when he completes an assignment," he tells me, his voice a guttural rasp.

And there's number five.

He groans when he feels me convulse around his fingers and waits until the final throes rack my body, and I go limp. Then he sets me down. He steps back. Licks his lips. Smiles.

"I'd say your expertise is well worth the retainer."

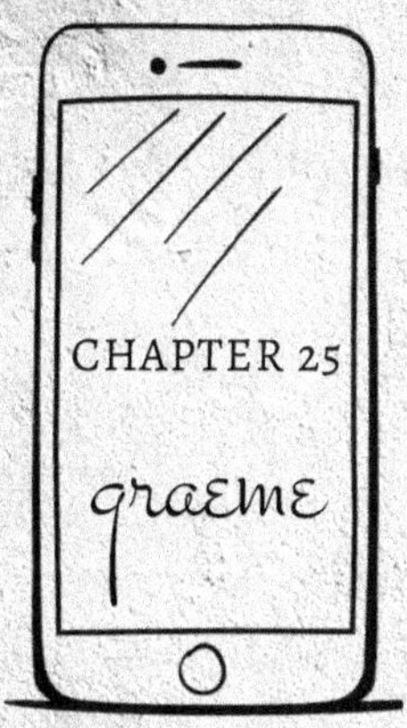

# CHAPTER 25

## GRAEME

The water pelting me from the shower head is ice-cold. My cock is on bloody fire. Her taste is on my tongue.

All things considered, it shouldn't be that hard to rub one off. She's in the next room. Her bloody juices still slick my fingers. I can hear her moans in my ear. God, her taste...

I lick my lips, but the action only seems to make my cock harder, the greedy fucking thing. My hand isn't enough to satisfy it. It wants the real deal. Her. Evelyn. Right here against the wall, dragging my name from her stubborn lips. Making her scream it.

*There.* I rock back on my heels, my hand pumping, my shaft twitching, and finally, I come into the shower spray, watching the evidence race down the drain. That should be enough, but when I finally step out into a towel, I'm still semi-hard. I can still fucking taste her. I can still see the scenario unfold bit by bit in my mind—Evelyn King spread out over my countertop like a buffet. Her body at my mercy. My name on her tongue.

She hadn't been playing fair by using that bloody trick. It certainly makes it harder to focus on the task at hand—beating Adrian Riley at his own game. I swipe my hand against the mirror, erasing the steam wafting from the sink. Glaring at the bastard staring back at me, I shove my hands beneath the spray and scrub my fingers clean of every bit of her. I rinse my mouth out twice. I pull on a suit and fasten the tie as if it's a noose, threatening to tighten the moment I so much think of shagging.

It's dark when I finally enter the bedroom and select a pair of oxfords from my closet, pulling them on without bothering to see if they match. Then I return to the living room. Focused. Collected.

I find her, lying on the couch, her dress dragged up over her hips, her hair a tangle, her knees tucked beneath her chin. Those blue eyes drift in my direction, and she stiffens. Much like my cock.

There are many ways to navigate this current situation—give up. Come clean. Let her leave. I draw myself to my full height instead and straighten my tie using the reflection of a nearby window as a guide.

"Get dressed," I tell her.

She follows my cue—ignoring the past hour. "For what?" She shifts sideways and places her bare feet against the floor.

She doesn't bother to smooth the skirt of her dress, however. It's wrinkled. Bunched. Clinging to her sweat-dampened thighs.

"Your second assignment," I tell her after a hard swallow. I wrench on the tie and tuck in the tail. When I face her again, she's watching me warily, her head cocked to the side. The motion only displays the ravaged flesh of her throat. I may have bitten her harder than I meant to. Either that, or she bruises easily. Bloody hell. "You are to accompany me. Tonight." I don't say to what, and surprisingly she doesn't ask.

Instead, she rises to her feet, though I notice that her thighs seem closer together than they normally would be—clenched. "Do I have to wear a dress?" There's only the slightest tremor in her voice. She runs a hand through her hair, smoothing the wild strands as she resumes her prissy posture.

"Yes," I say. Only when she's already halfway up the staircase do I add, "Not one of yours. Look in the bedroom closet and pick something from there."

Her footsteps slow for a second before resuming their regular pace. I'm left to merely imagine her reaction. What is that saying about foresight? I can't remember the exact wording. Something about being always prepared.

Truthfully, when I'd had James bring over the order from Atelier Noir, I didn't expect her to accept my offer. I certainly didn't expect her to stay. Maybe the move was my own callous way of imitating Adrian Riley's method—stack the cards against your victim. Maneuver them like a piece across a chessboard. Watch them willingly step into your trap.

Only, Evelyn King wasn't some unwitting pawn. She was the strongest piece on the board—the bloody fucking queen. One moment it might seem like I had her pinned, but the next, she was hopping to the other side of the goddamn grid.

I sense her creep toward the guest bedroom, and I don't hear another sound for what feels like an eternity. However, it can only be roughly fifteen minutes later before she appears at the head of the stairs. Her cold, icy expression ironically complements the floor-length black gown, the most modest of the selection I'd picked out. Somehow I'd known she'd settle for it.

I couldn't have anticipated how bloody well she fit it.

"I would assume you do more in your spare time than run Atelier Noir. However, nothing seems to be in *your* size," she says, promptly insinuating that I may be a crossdresser.

She stops before descending the final step, and I take her in. The dress hugs her from her breasts to her waist before flaring out at her hips. It's a simple cut—no doubt Adrian Riley will have women hanging off his arm clothed in a more eye-catching style. But none of them will have her class. Even with her hair pulled back to reveal the angry red, bitten flesh of her neck.

I step forward and beckon her closer with a wave of my hand. "Come here."

Her eyes flash with a challenge. That infamous bloody chin jerks just a fraction of an inch higher into the air, but she descends the remainder of the staircase and approaches me, stopping just outside my reach. I can smell that damn perfume wafting from her skin.

"What do you want?"

Her breath hitches when I step closer, invading her personal space. She's showered. Her skin is damp, smelling faintly of soap. Just how hard did she have to scrub to wash me away?

"Hold still." I raise my hand and curl a fist around the neat bun she somehow managed to form out of the tangled state I left her hair in. She flinches when my fingertips graze her scalp and find the bobbin holding the waves together. I tug it loose, letting her damp hair fall, covering the marks I left behind.

Something tells me that making sure I saw them was her only damn motive in the first place.

"Is this another condition," she demands while reaching to bat my hand away. Her fingers methodically comb through the displaced strands, smoothing them into place. "Dressing me. Styling me—"

"Until you develop your own style, then yes," I tell her before heading toward the foyer. "Come on."

To my utter shock, she does—without one snide remark or comment. In fact, she's silent during the entire descent to the lobby and even through the main doors. I see her frown when she spots James, already waiting beside the car. The accusatory glance she shoots me conveys what she doesn't say out loud—*You planned this.*

Maybe I had, but I don't feel like examining my motives as I follow her into the car. It feels like barely a few minutes have passed before James pulls up before the club, and Evelyn promptly stiffens.

"You were serious," I hear her croak. One of her hands runs over the skirt of her dress. She starts to reach for her hair.

"Deadly serious." My excitement mirrors hers. I just want this night over with. I want this whole damn debacle over with. I want Adrian Riley to eat his words and thoroughly regret ever raising the stakes of this challenge. "Come on."

She follows when I exit the car, remaining in my shadow when I enter the lobby. Riley hasn't sent one of his "associates" to greet us tonight, it seems. Instead, the man himself is there, surprisingly without a woman on his arm or an entourage.

"Bellamy," he greets before turning his attention to Evelyn. He doesn't seem surprised to find her beside me, and my suspicion only grows. "Ms. King. Allow me to introduce you to the members of the club."

He takes us on a "tour" that seems more like the parade of a captured enemy through the streets of the victor's city state. He shows us the club on the lower level, packed to the brim with socialites, clients, and the like. I recognize too many faces from either television or tabloid pages. If Evelyn's starstruck appearance is any indicator, she does as well.

They eye us warily before focusing the brunt of their attention on Riley. He laps up the accolades, basting in the glow of the spotlight. The power.

I know the bastard thinks he has the upper hand when he sets me loose, to "mingle." Perhaps, if I had been alone, he would have. But therein lies the infuriating talent of Evelyn King. By my side, she's quiet, admittedly unassuming—but I see her. I watch her. She takes in every detail of the venue. Every patron. Every glance we catch and muttered whisper. Then, somehow she manages to use the information to her benefit. My benefit.

It seems like an accident at first, when she starts to drift through the crowd, knowing I'd follow. The act brings me to a man I recognize instantly—a fellow who just so happens to own one of the largest banks in the city, let alone the country. Introductions are made, and then I am introduced to a woman whose husband is running for the senate.

And so, it continues. She's a subtle chess master, but no less skilled than Riley, able to manage my schedule flawlessly for three years while nagging me every step of the way. Naturally charismatic, she draws people to our corner effortlessly and, in only a few seconds, can strategize how best to get her victim to drop his or her guard. It's almost frightening how easily she spins a web that the most distinguished patrons can't seem to resist.

Even Adrian Riley.

He apparently intended for this meeting to be a quick one. We've only made it about halfway across the room before the man appears by my side. "There will be another gathering tomorrow night. I hope to see you there."

I smile without giving a damn as to how it might come across. "I wouldn't miss it."

Ten minutes later, we're back in the car, Evelyn slumped on the seat beside me, her face upturned to the window. "So, are you going to admit it now?" she asks as James pulls away from the curb.

"Admit what?"

She twists around to face me, her lips pursed in a thoughtful frown. "That you just wanted arm candy. It's not like you needed much help in the 'wooing' department. At least not professionally."

I choke out a laugh. I can't help it. It's gruff. Grudging. She has no damn clue. I decide to keep it that way. "I think you underestimate your own allure, Ms. King. Especially when you spent most of the night tugging your hair. I'm sure you caught a few eyes in your direction."

She's doing it now. Stroking her fingers along her neck, trying to avoid the ravaged flesh underneath... I angle myself away from her, but the front of my slacks tighten regardless.

Her hand falls to her lap. "And there he is, ladies and gentlemen. The real Graeme Bellamy."

I frown. "What makes you feel that you could, or ever would, know the so-called real me?"

She shrugs, her expression smug, those eyes alight. "I know the real you," she says, matter of factly. "I've even seen him with his pants off." James is in the front seat—a fact that she either ignores or doesn't seem aware of. "He isn't much to behold, to be honest..."

I flash a smile to hide just how much those damn words sting. "I've seen the real you, as well." I cut my gaze down to her breasts, and I can tell, even in the darkness bathing the car's interior, that she flushes red.

"The real you is also an ass."

We don't say anything else by the time James pulls up before the Royal. It's an equally silent trip up to my suite. Only after the door closes behind us do I realize the implications of what her standing beside me, her lips stretched around a yawn, means. She doesn't seem to understand until she starts for the stairs and cranes her head back to see if I follow. Then she falters over the first step, and I can almost see the reality hit her like a punch to the chest.

*Oh.*

"Why Evelyn, I have to admit that I find it refreshing when you don't argue, for once," I tell her as I start forward, eventually pushing past her to mount the stairs. "I take it that you've decided to accept my offer."

"N-No, I—"

I deliberately yawn, cutting her off. By the time I enter the hallway, she's still on my heels. Near the guest bedroom, she pauses, her hand reaching for the doorknob, but I seize her wrist, dragging her forward.

"I trust you'll keep your hands to yourself, tonight." She digs her heels into the floor and grasps the doorway before allowing herself to be hauled over the threshold.

"I'm not—"

"Oh, but we already discussed the fact that you feel more comfortable in my bed." I tug on her arm, and she has no choice but to follow, staggering into my chest. I don't mean to take the teasing any further, but with her eyes on me, her jaw set defiantly, I can't stop myself from hooking a hand around her waist and finding the zipper to her dress. "I believe we also established your preference for sleeping in the nude."

I don't intend to undress her myself. At least not until she lifts her arms, her expression daring. "I guess we have."

I tug on the zipper. The gown loosens. Slides. I barely make out the flesh underneath before her hands palm my chest, seeking out the buttons of my shirt. "And you sleep without your shirt." She's deliberately clumsy as she undoes the first clasp. Then another. Her eyes don't leave mine once, even as her breathing quickens, the shadows of her breasts heaving at the edge of my vision. Irritation flares. My cock stiffens. She knows damn well how to swirl a reaction within me and stroke it to her advantage.

She toys with the third button, biting her lip in concentration. I yank on the skirt of her gown, and it falls in a heap at her feet. Her first instinct is to flinch and cover herself. I can see one of her hands twitch toward her, aching to shield the dusky nipples I don't even attempt to pull my gaze from. She's blushing. Stiff. Flushing. Mine.

The fingerprints ground into her hips say so. I shake my head to clear the bothersome thought. It's still bloody there, lingering as she undoes the last few buttons and peels off my suit jacket before following with the shirt itself. The tease, she digs her nails in as she drags the sleeves down each shoulder.

We stand there at an impasse, her clothed only in underwear, her scent hanging in the air. She moves first, stepping back coyly to find the edge of the mattress and climb onto it. I follow her, taking up my side, watching her every move this time.

She lays back, and I don't take my eyes off her. She doesn't take her eyes off me. I can see the ridges and valleys of her body spread out beside mine. It's almost as tempting as it had been to have her breathless and writhing on the counter, my name on her lips, her taste on my tongue.

"G-Goodnight, Mr. Bellamy," she says sweetly. The minx.

"Retiring so soon, Evelyn?" I spread out and prop one of my hands beneath my head, giving me enough leverage to look down on her, claiming the pillow beside mine. "I thought now would have been the perfect time for you to deliver the next stage in your advice. I think I more than mastered *listening*."

She stiffens but, to her credit, doesn't look away. "What about watching?" she tosses back. "Seeing how your words are affecting people."

My mouth twitches. "I'm not sure what you mean. I think I watched you react to me plenty—"

"You only see what you want to see," she says over me. "That's how people like you operate." She flexes her hip, simultaneously turning her body on its side. A view of her plump breast becomes hindered behind the slope of her shoulder.

"People like me." I eye the ceiling, sensing the thinly-veiled insult in her tone. "I'm assuming you don't mean expert listeners..."

"The rest of us peons are invisible to you," she tells the wall. "At least until you need us for something. Then you are relentless. You never really listen to the words coming from someone else's mouth. You never really see how you affect them—"

"So, try me."

Her jaws snap shut.

"Something tells me that you just don't like talking," I say. "You can't blame anyone for not hearing you if you choose not to speak—"

"I loved my job." I don't expect that line of attack. She senses it and turns to face me over her shoulder, lifting her head from the pillow. "I. Loved. My. Job." She aims every word like a missile, straight in my direction. "And you just fired me. Without any warning. Without any explanation—"

"I have my reasons."

She rolls her eyes. "You have *one* reason—Adrian Riley."

"I'm starting to believe that maybe I'm not the one who has trouble seeing clearly."

She raises an eyebrow and turns to face me fully, heedless of how her breasts sway with every deliberate movement. "You're afraid of him," she tells me, her gaze boring deep, that mouth set in that haughty, prissy line.

"Now I know you're blind—"

"Not in the typical way," she adds, tilting her head back to size me up in a single, unamused glance. "He knows how to manipulate people into doing his bidding. Even worse—" She leans forward, wafting the scent of roses from every damn pore. "He manipulates people, and they *like* it. They flock to him in spite of it. His power over people scares you."

"Is that so?" Somehow she managed to manipulate herself so that she's resting on her knees, her hands braced on either side of her. The position reminds me of some bloody girl scout, gathered around the campfire to gossip about whatever bastard she can't stand. I glance at her navel and the ridge of her stomach visible above the waistband of her panties. In a porno, perhaps.

"So," she declares with a nod. "If I were in *his* bed..."

My mind instantly conjures up an image to accompany the suggestion—her, twisted and panting beneath the sheets. Adrian Riley sneering down at her as he mentally processed every way he could use their tryst to his own damn benefit. My jaw clenches, and something in my expression makes her frown.

"I'd probably be naked," she says, and something in my chest catches fire. Ignites. A sound rips from my throat that I don't recognize—was that a goddamn growl? "But he'd make it seem like my idea. It wouldn't feel like a game with him. Though maybe that's a point in your column," she softly admits. "At least with you, I know that *this*—" she waves her hand toward my side of the bed. "Will never become anything more serious."

She sounds so damn matter-of-fact. Though, it is the truth.

"In your rush to praise Adrian Riley, you seem to be over-looking that you *are* naked. In my bed. Right now."

She flicks a strand of hair over her shoulder as if the current reality is nothing more than a minor detail. "You didn't seduce me," she says. "You goaded me. There is a difference."

I raise an eyebrow and allow my gaze to drift. Her thighs. The curve of her ass. "Regardless of the method, I've gotten you naked."

"I've gotten a little something out of it, myself," she says, her eyes roving down to my hands. I flex each finger, and she blushes. She's more than just a cock-tease, full of a million little contradictions. Crass one minute. Playing innocent, the next.

"That you have." I run my thumb along my jaw. Bring it to my mouth. Graze the tip with my tongue.

I can practically see her throat jerk as she swallows before haughtily turning away. "And this is what I mean," she says. "It's all just a game—"

"If I were to attempt to woo you, then how would I go about it?" I ask, surprisingly curious.

She casts a suspicious glance in my direction. "Well, for starters, you might at least pretend to give a damn about me. As a person. Rather than my breasts."

I tilt my head in her direction and take my time observing every dusky surface. "They are beautiful breasts—"

She slaps her right hand over one. "You might also ask me a question about *myself* for once."

That is one suggestion I simply don't understand. "I would," I say cautiously. "If I didn't already know everything about you, that is... necessary."

She raises an eyebrow. "Necessary?"

"You were born in New York. You lived with your father. He traveled. You went to school in both France and Maine. An exclusive boarding school in both cases," I add, in case she decides to play the "You're un-relatable because I am but a poor pauper," card. "You got top marks nearly every year. You graduated at the top of your class in business management. You spent the majority of your college years working in cafés. You like the color pink."

God, it's like reciting a bloody manual. I glance up to see how well I've scored on the test of all things Evelyn King. Rather than impressed, she's expressionless.

So, I decide to take a page from Riley's playbook. "And," I add, watching her, "your name is not really Evelyn King. Is it?"

She stiffens, and I regret opening my bloody mouth at all. My hand grasps for her before I can help myself, gripping the fingers she has fisted around a handful of bedsheets. Her eyes drift downward, but she doesn't pull away.

*Damn.* Her heat is infectious, leeching a tortuous path through my right arm, straight toward my blasted cock. I barely hear her speak—her voice is so soft.

"My mother was a grifter," she says. "A hustler. A scammer. Con artist. Whatever term tickles your fancy. We lived with her and my dad until I was seven, and my brother was twelve. By then, my dad decided that our unconventional upbringing of being dragged with her to strip clubs and being groomed on how to look 'pitiful' enough to score cash from strangers wasn't ideal. They shared custody for a while, until one day, my mom showed up at school and decided to take my brother and me on a 'vacation.' Something as minor as a court order and charges of kidnapping didn't faze her back then."

She tilts her head, frowning at the memories, though, for the first time, her body loses some of that tense, proper posture.

"We spent two months bouncing around Atlantic City. We lived out of a different motel every night. 'School' was learning how many different ways to count cards on the rare times she managed to dress me up so that I looked old enough for her to sneak me into the casino. At night when she 'worked,' Danny and I would troll the strip and guilt trip people into buying us newspapers and magazines so that we could have our own 'social studies' class in the parking lot."

She shrugs as if the thought of it doesn't bother her. She blinks. Her breathing hitches and her eyes dart toward our joined hands as if she's questioning whether to pull away. I can't suppress an impulse I have to grip her hand tighter the second she tenses up. To my shock, she doesn't move.

"Whenever I wondered why we couldn't just go home, she'd claim, 'we're on an adventure, Eves.' I don't know if she just stopped making any money or if it all went up her nose, but one day the money dried up. The motels became shelters. She'd disappear for longer stretches, and I wore the bottoms of my sneakers out, circling every block, looking for her. It got so bad that one time I had to stop Danny from fishing someone's half-eaten McDonald's out of the trash. That's when I broke down, stole a tip jar from a gas station, and spent an hour on the payphone going through information to find my dad."

She falls silent, her eyes on the ceiling, and I don't say a damn thing. Not a word.

She wanted me to watch, so I do. I feel the way her fingers clench as if physically grappling for the control she craves. I see the way she bites her lower lip. How her entire body shudders when she inhales raggedly. "My dad came and got us. To say he was furious would be putting it mildly. He'd gone to the police. There was a warrant out on my mom for child endangerment. Kidnapping. Fun fact—we had to change our last name because our faces had been all over the news and missing posters. King was my grandmother's maiden name, by the way. Luckily Dad had a rich uncle who gave him enough money to put my brother and me in a 'good' school. France for two years while he was stationed there. The rest of the time, in the States. I think it was his way of trying to undo whatever our time with her had done to us. Either way, it didn't work much on Danny. The only thing he ever excelled in was getting himself expelled and following right in my mother's footsteps—"

She breaks off and looks at me. The expression that crosses her face can only be described as puzzled. Slowly, she pulls her hand away from mine. I barely blink and she's the composed, unshakeable Evelyn King once more. "What? No rude insinuations or cutting remarks? I'm not used to talking without you interrupting."

"I'm listening."

If anything, her frown deepens. I've caught her off guard, rattling her stoic mask. She bites her bottom lip before admitting, "Suffice it to say that... I don't like being taken advantage of. I don't like being lied to. It's not that I can't handle it. It's that I can *always* see it coming. Like a freight train in my direction. I prefer it when someone at least pretends..." She glances up at me through her lashes. A simple bloody look. My cock jumps. The reaction is impossible to hide, not that she seems to notice. "Pretends like they just don't want to screw me over."

"I've never lied to you," I point out, my throat dry, teeth clenched.

She shoots me a curious look. "Oh really? First, the mysterious Adrian Riley, whom I had never heard of in three years. And then there's the mysterious brother, Alex. Not to mention the fact that you own a gentleman's club—"

"Not lies," I interject. "Merely carefully concealed truths. Had you asked me directly about any of it—do you have a brother? Do you own a gentleman's club?—I wouldn't have denied it." Irritation prickles my chest at the realization that it's the damn truth. I could never lie to her. "After all, there were a few things in your past that you happened to leave off your resume."

She flicks a piece of lint from the sheets with her thumb. "Frankly, Mr. Bellamy. You never really seem interested in anyone but yourself. Apart from those you want to exploit or dominate, of course."

"Is that the next stage of wooing?" She blinks in shock when my knee grazes hers as I shift on my side to face her fully. I expect her to shimmy back, but she holds her ground. Touché, Evelyn.

"What is?"

"Allowing myself to be insulted?"

Her eyes narrow. "Close. How about opening up? You listened to me. I listen to you."

She makes it sound harmless, like it's just another game—but I know her. I see the way she sits straighter, fully at attention, her fingers flexing as if aching for that damn pen to jot down every word I say. She's not eager for secrets to sell, and that's the worst part. She's merely curious.

"You mentioned your mother," I state, gauging her reaction to the topic.

"Yes." She frowns questioningly. "And as much as you seem irritated by Gloria, your mother isn't anything like mine."

Because her mother plunged her into a kidnapping scandal, it seems, and forced her to live under an assumed name. It kills me that Adrian knew that part of her past, and I didn't. It means, for once, I'm not the one in charge of our dynamic.

I can't demand her trust. I have to earn it.

"Fathers then." Before she can interject, I pull myself upright and position myself across from her—but rather than tuck my knees beneath myself, I spread both legs on either side of her, trapping her body between them. "Mine is an American oil tycoon. He met my mother on a trip to Nice—with his first wife. By the time she became pregnant with me, they were in a torrid affair, and her family back in London was scandalized. You see, my grandfather meddled in politics," I add as an afterthought.

"Fast forward five years and three children later, and my father was well at work on his third wife, leaving my mother to 'raise three children alone, the shame of it,' as she tells it. And by 'shame,' she meant the embarrassment of moving back onto her family's estate and raising us under their rules. All the while, my father sought to extend his goodwill by sending us a private nanny as well as enough money to support her expenses and that of my siblings at least. We were sent to the finest preparatory schools for training in decorum. My sister and I were exposed to the highest of society from the time we could walk. My brother, on the other hand, preferred to spend his time bending 'society' over in the broom cupboard."

I wait, expecting that usual pinch of irritation that flares whenever I mention Alexander. Maybe the avid look of interest on her face makes me feel like I'm reciting an engrossing novel rather than my own life, but I don't feel it.

"Your father's American?" The question comes when nearly a full minute passes, and I don't say anything. She's cautious, trying to obey her own rules.

"American enough," I say. "My siblings chose to keep the hyphenated version of his last name. I dropped the Ashton in favor of my mother's, if only to keep her from skinning me alive when I took over her family's business. Atelier Noir was founded by my great-great-grandfather to supply trousers during the mining boom of the early twentieth century."

"An area not far from lingerie," she snipes.

"Over the passing decades, we've tried our hand at various enterprises. When I took over the company, it was a floundering, dying brand with no hopes of surviving in today's market."

"You changed that."

Damn her. The admiration in her voice sounds so genuine— and my cock hardens at the prospect.

"I did what I needed to do to keep my mother, sister, and even Alexander from having to beg my father for a payout," I explain. "He would have lorded any assistance over my mother for years. She seems silly and frivolous, but I know she sold her heirloom pearls to give me the starting capital to get a foothold over our previous shareholders."

"You love her, Gloria." She makes it sound like a fact she's only just now discovered. I can't tell if it surprises her or not.

"That's a strange observation to make."

She shakes her head. "I only mean it as... Sometimes you act like she's such a nuisance. Like you can't be bothered."

"She is." I bend one of my legs, and she leans against the knee without seeming to realize it. Her warmth is a delicate brush of heat that resonates directly through my cock. Still, I manage to keep talking. "And I can't. Keeping her comfortable comes with its own particular set of rules."

"Like?"

I frown. There's no reason to bring up a juvenile spat from years ago. Would she even understand my reasoning? Perhaps I'm curious, and that's why I finally say, "Like the fact that my nanny's son, whom my father insisted travel along with her, later claimed to be his bastard."

She sucks in a breath, her eyes comically wide. "You don't mean..."

"I think this would be a good place to end our lesson for today, Ms. King." I pull away and lie back, staring up at the ceiling.

She doesn't say anything as she copies my splayed position. Though, as I close my eyes, I swear I hear a grunted, "Good-night, Mr. Bellamy."

I smell garlic. He's made breakfast again, and shock snaps me awake. I'm so distracted by the prospect of him toiling over a hot stove that I almost forget the glaring tidbit of information he let slip last night.

Almost.

"It's about damn time, Ms. King," a voice sardonically announces the moment I stir, peeling one eye open. The sunlight streaming in through the windows threatens to blind me. My throat is dry. My body is... humming.

To say I slept soundly in his bed for a second night in a row would be an understatement. The first time had been a fluke —and not in a way that made me feel any better. Apart from the bastard lying like a log beside me, I have never experienced a deeper, more fulfilling sleep.

If only my awakening could have been just as tranquil.

He's standing at the foot of the bed—I see once I gather the strength to glance over my shoulder. There's another frying pan in his hand, and a plate placed directly onto the mattress beside my outstretched foot. I take advantage of the moment to inspect him from head to toe. Gosh, I don't know how I missed it before. The slight resemblance right *there*, in how they both hold themselves with the same mixture of cocky swagger and natural grace.

They aren't literal doppelgangers, but the similarities are striking. They most definitely could be brothers.

Not that Graeme seems willing to admit that out loud.

"I wouldn't want you to think I was a poor host by not attending to the blood sugar of my guest," he says, explaining away his impromptu breakfast. The sheer mocking in his tone negates any ounce of concern the gesture might have contained. "Eat." He jerks his chin at the plate, and I warily skim the offering—toast, eggs, and, of all things, a single banana.

I do my best to tuck the corner of the bedsheet beneath me as I haul myself upright. "What if I said I wasn't hungry?"

His eyes narrow and flash that breathtaking shade of blue. "Then I would assume that you were insulting my attempt at wooing and rethink your retainer."

*Ass.* I reach out and swipe the plate closer. Scowling, I snatch up a piece of toast and fully intend to remain frowning as I chew a hesitant bite. But he slathered honey on it. Rich, sweet, expensive honey. By the time I start on the eggs, I'm a broken woman. He flavored them differently this time—basil and olive oil with a hint of goat cheese sprinkled on top. I shovel in my next mouthful and happen to glance up, only to find him watching me.

"The look on your face makes it all worth it." His voice is gruff, resonating in my stomach and making every muscle clench.

"W-What?"

"Proving you wrong." He reaches forward before I can react and snatches my second piece of toast from the plate. His eyes home in on mine as he takes a ravenous bite, chews, and then deliberately swallows.

Ass.

I drop the fork and set the plate aside, but it's too late. I'm already blushing as he turns for the door and strolls into the hallway.

"Get dressed," he tells me. "You've made us late."

"For what?" He heads for the stairs without bothering to answer. That's not a very good omen. My heart pounds as I climb off the mattress and stagger into the guest room.

"Pick something from the closet," comes a demand from downstairs.

The closet. The closet he conveniently managed to stock with what appears to be the entire spring collection of Atelier Noir. I'm tempted to ignore him and wear something from my suitcase. I've only taken a step toward my luggage when a sharp grunt comes from below. "*Evelyn.*"

I roll my eyes, primarily for my own benefit, as I turn on my heel and approach the damn walk-in. Sometime during the trip over the threshold, my frown softens. I have never been one for material things, always preferring quality over quantity or a flashy designer name. It's aggravating to realize that the bastard seems to be of the same mind. I'd be lying if I didn't say that at least some of the clothes are... decent.

There are fashionable yet practical shoes. Sensible skirts. Blouses that I might have even picked out for myself had I suddenly had thousands of excess dollars to spend on the finest materials. It isn't hard to settle for a floral-print sundress and a pair of black sandals. The flirty length keeps it from appearing professional. Which is a good thing, considering I don't work for the bastard, no matter what godman retainer he throws my way.

"Evelyn—"

"Coming," I bite out before I enter the bathroom and take stock of my appearance in the mirror. I decide to risk his wrath in favor of a quick shower. I take another few minutes to run my fingers through my damp hair and settle it in the semblance of a style. Then I brush my teeth with a toothbrush fished from my bag, and by the time I dismount the final step, I'm faced with a furious Graeme Bellamy.

Well, furious for all five seconds that pass before he takes me in with a single sweep of his gaze. His eyes settle over the modest neckline, and suddenly the thin fabric feels... thinner. Tighter.

I know him too well—namely, that possessive, gleaming look in his eye. It's the same way he likes to survey the city from his office window, taking stock of his empire. In this case, it's every reddish bite mark on my neck that he seems to smugly take stock of. My face heats, and I nearly choke in my rush to blurt out, "Is something wrong?"

"No," he growls, clipping the word between his teeth. "It's just nice to see that you can take your own advice into account. Listening."

He's on edge. I can see it even before he tugs at his tie, sliding it around his collar. At first, I assume it's because of last night. Given that I was setting my own feelings aside to process later, I could admit that the thought that I had spilled my proverbial soul out—even a fraction—to someone like Graeme Bellamy was...

A bit like jumping headfirst into water infested with piranha while bathed in the juices of a thousand pigs.

It isn't my fault—the bastard got inside my head. First, by claiming he wanted to listen, and then by actually... *listening*. I don't know how to process that. Moody, disgruntled Graeme Bellamy is my area of expertise.

Thankfully, he seems to be back to his old self. Noticing my staring, he frowns. "Did you hear me, Evelyn?"

I blink. "Huh?"

"We're late." With one last yank on his tie, he heads for the door, and I follow him. When I reach for my canvas bag, which I find resting on the end table near the foyer, he shakes his head.

"You won't be needing that."

I reach for it anyway. "You can't be serious. Let me at least grab my phone—"

"Leave it." He turns to face me, his gaze honed sharp, and he doesn't move an inch until I step away from the table.

"Why?"

He flicks his collar, smoothing every wayward edge down flat. "Because today, we will be trying out a different variation of your wooing method."

My stomach bunches ominously. "How so?"

He's guarded again, his expression unreadable. "Today, you rely solely on me. Whatever you need, I will provide. Consider it my way of imitating the generosity of Adrian Riley you lauded earlier."

"I didn't mean that as an insult," I point out with what I hope passes for a gentle tone. Especially now that I have a better idea as to the root of their animosity.

Graeme scoffs. "You didn't?"

Battered ego. Sour expression. I recognize this side of him. On the surface, his bad mood could have entirely been caused by the tumult of emotions we recklessly engaged in last night —*after* the almost sex, even. But as much as it pains me to admit, I know him. Too damn well, to be exact. We went to bed tense but oddly... neutral? Something must have happened between then and breakfast.

"What do you mean?" I try to phrase the question as sternly as I can. When he frowns, I go for the jugular. "Keep in mind that you said you'd never lie to me."

Whether he truly meant that remains to be seen.

He frowns as if mulling over the promise. Then he cocks his head, his blue eyes flashing. "I can show you better than I can tell you. Come."

He turns for the door again, and I seem to have no choice but to follow him or stand there dumbstruck. The moment I draw even with him, he reaches out for my arm to pull me along—only his grip continues to slide downward until...

I stiffen. Graeme Bellamy isn't holding my wrist. No, he's holding my *hand*.

"W-What are you doing?" I can't even begin to hide the panic that creeps into my voice.

"Demonstrating." He yanks me closer when I attempt to dig my heels in and closes the door behind us.

With every step we travel from his suite, I am more aware of the reaction we garner. Curiosity. Intrigue. For all intents and purposes, he's a powerful figure, and I'm the slightly damp woman at his side. My cheeks heat up at the thought of the assumptions they might make. By the time we reach the lobby, I do everything I can to try and wrench my hand away —but the bastard thwarts my every attempt.

"T-This isn't professional," I croak out as he manually steers me toward the main entrance.

He seems unconcerned by the odd look we catch from a woman walking her poodle across the marble entryway. She smiles fondly and then quickly glances away. "That's the idea."

My mind goes blank. "B-But... but you know what this looks like."

He glances down at my hand, the fingers red from how tightly he had to make his grip to maintain the contact. "That's the idea," he echoes in a deadpan tone.

Obviously, I didn't hear him right. My mind is still spinning as he leads me to the car James has parked outside. Once we're both on the back seat, and only then, does he finally let go of my hand.

"First on the agenda," he says while running his hand along his thigh as if to erase my touch from his skin. "Lunch, with my mother."

There are so many things wrong with that one statement alone. Glancing at the clock, I decide to begin with the most obvious one. "It's ten a.m.," I tell him.

He shrugs, nonplussed. "Brunch, then."

Which, of course, brings up another question. "Shouldn't you be at work?"

His eyes narrow as he stares through the windshield at the remarkably light traffic for this time of day. "I took the morning off."

I have to brace one hand against the nearest door to keep from pitching forward and falling off the seat. Another "morning off." According to memory, Graeme Bellamy tended to handle his "off" days the way... well, the same way I had handled mine.

"Lunch, with Gloria," I carefully reiterate, rather than pick apart the larger questions looming behind his current sour mood. "And you need me there because...?"

I look at him expectantly, but he shrugs his shoulder as if brushing me off.

"You fired me as your assistant," I remind him. "Which typically means that I am not required to accompany you on ventures such as to a café to have lunch with your mother—"

"Ah, but you are on *retainer*," he says over me. "To assist me in cultivating the art of, as you so put it, 'wooing.' Think of this moment as another lesson opportunity."

"Oh?" I'm cautious even before he gets that look in his eye— the one that warns he's in imminent danger of throwing something into something else—typically his phone through a wall. "What kind of lesson?"

He raises both hands to his collar and flicks the edges. "A lesson in how *not* to cause a goddamn scene in a bloody café during 'brunch' with your mother."

I swallow hard. He's already well on his way to growling, and it isn't even noon yet—another bad sign in my experience with Graeme Bellamy.

"Is this lunch—brunch—about anything in particular?" It seems the least dangerous route to take to fish for information.

He frowns, his eyes narrowed into slits. "I received an email from the hotel my mother is staying at. In a suite that I pay for," he adds. "It seems that the other night there was some kind of... disturbance. The email contained a bill for damage that had been done to the hotel's property." His right hand drifts to the cufflink on the wrist of the left, fiddling with the round bit of silver. "One badly damaged wall. A cracked window. Broken furniture. An estimate for the amount required to clean the carpets of wine stains. Not to mention a noise complaint allegedly coming from every room within a floor of Gloria's sometime after midnight."

I can only blink. His mother may have had her vices, but I wouldn't have expected "wild partier" to be one of them. "Wow... that's—"

"After her nightly wine and brandy, my mother is always dead to the world by nine," Bellamy says, his tone icy. "Unless she truly is possessed, as those rumors like to claim, then someone who just so happens to be dwelling in the suite with her is responsible for this mess."

"Ah..." I nod, catching on. "Your brother. Alexander."

He doesn't react to the term. I might as well have suggested "your pet rat." Instead, he turns to glare out of the window, and it's only when we reach the block right before the one where the café his mother prefers sits that he finally says anything. "He'll be there."

The words sound like an omen. I don't know what to say in response, so I say nothing and, instead, dutifully follow him out onto the curb. For the first time, I notice that the once beautifully blue sky is now covered by a layer of gray overcast. Darker clouds loom over the horizon, readying to descend on cue. Even before we enter the café and are shown to the dining room, I can sense that Gloria is already here, seated at a table near the back corner. Beside her is a man I've never seen before, at least in theory.

I have to tell myself that more than once as my head swivels in Bellamy's direction—the one standing beside me, at least. The man seated at the table isn't wearing a designer suit, but a gray shirt and a pair of dark-wash jeans, which sets him apart. His black hair is longer and slightly more tousled than the Bellamy I know. His eyes are green. I have to make a mental note of every little difference, because other than that... everything from his height to his flawless bone struc-ture is nearly identical to Graeme Bellamy's.

"Graemy bear," he says, his voice an octave deeper than his brother's, his accent a tad crisper. "The prodigal son makes his appearance."

"Mother." Bellamy—or, in this case, *Graeme*—stares dead ahead, forcing Gloria to meet his gaze. She looks about ten shades paler than usual and is fiddling with her pearls, a bad sign. The last time I saw her so frazzled, it was the year she'd booked a "family" trip to Ibiza for the holidays, and

Bellamy... *Graeme* acted as though she'd asked him if we would like to willingly hop into a guillotine for a week. Though, now I suppose I know why.

"Wow, Graemy," the Bellamy-clone declares sardonically. "This is a much better reunion than I could have ever hoped for."

"Alexander," Gloria scolds, still clutching her pearls. She glances at the man beside me imploringly and musters up what I think is meant to be a hopeful smile. "Graeme. Please... can you *please* just sit down, at least?"

I'm impressed when he approaches the table without giving in to any impulse to flip it over as his posture suggests. He yanks out an elegant wooden chair instead and jerks his chin curtly. "Evelyn."

So he's reverted to ordering me around like a dog. I try to ignore the slight in favor of being supportive. Why I would want to support a man who seemed to entertain himself lately by firing, rehiring, and sexually harassing me? I'll figure that out later.

"Evelyn..." Alexander shoots me a surprisingly friendly smile. Seeing a face so similar to Graeme's contort into such a... genuine expression is strange. Frankly, it's unnatural. "You must be the assistant I've heard so much about. According to mother, Graemy wouldn't even know which knickers to wear for the day without you."

Gloria coughs delicately into her palm. "I didn't put it quite that way, darling..."

"Let us drop the pretense, shall we?"

My heart stops. Up until five seconds ago, I would have thought that I had seen Graeme Bellamy at his very worst. I knew how deep and guttural his voice could go. I knew the look in his eye he got whenever he was in the mood to send something hurtling across the room. I knew every facet of the man's worst shades of rage.

Or so I thought. His voice straddles a gruff baritone I've never heard before. If a wolf could talk and somehow managed to shove itself into a designer suite and forced itself to attend a makeshift family luncheon, it would probably make that sound. Every word is gritted. Oddly crisp. And then the bomb drops. "Let's talk about the fact that it took a very generous donation to keep the Palace Suites from terminating your stay prematurely."

Gloria shrinks beneath the intensity of his gaze. Alexander just smiles.

"These Americans sure know how to party," he says.

Graeme smiles as well, and every cell in my body goes on red alert. "Mother," he grunts without glancing in Gloria's direction. "*Please* pass me the kettle."

"I've got it!" I intercept, snatching for the handle before Gloria can so much as detangle her fingers from her pearls. I reach for the nearest teacup and pour the least dangerous amount of liquid into it before placing it before the man beside me. I pour myself a slightly larger amount before offering a cup to Gloria.

"Now, Graeme," Gloria starts cautiously, even though her notoriously strong-armed son now has scalding ammunition to throw. "I'm sure this is all one big misunderstanding—"

"Ten thousand dollars," Graeme says over her. "That's just the base fee the hotel required to overlook this incident. Let's not even mention the surmounting cost of the *actual* damage, including the hush money paid to the two women found strolling the hallway at two in the morning who both were, as the manager put it, 'completely sauced.'"

A funny thing happens when he talks like this—everyone within a mile radius seems to stop and stare. He's captivating in his anger. Like a supernova, growing brighter and brighter before the inevitable boom.

"Now darling, that was just a misunderstanding," Gloria rushes to say. It's the wrong thing.

"A misunderstanding?" Graeme's eyes shoot that cold, endless shade of dark blue as he runs his palm along the strip of white tablecloth in front of him. "Is that so?"

I'm not naive enough to take his whole trumped-up position as his "wooing" expert seriously. Obviously, he has another motive in mind for keeping me close. Out of my own desire for self-preservation, I'll humor it. But some part of me still can't help but remember his initial "assignment" given to me before this brunch—a lesson in how not to cause a goddamn scene in a bloody café during "brunch" with his mother. So far, I'm failing, big time.

"I'm sure it is," I blurt out, glancing warily at Gloria. "Just... a big misunderstanding."

Graeme turns the brunt of his gaze on me. "How so?" I have to inhale sharply to steal myself. From across the room, I spot a beaming waitress innocently approaching our table with a basket of bread. I beckon her over, take the basket, beg for "five extra minutes," and while she skips off, I rip a biscuit in half and place it down on the plate beside me.

At the same time, I add, "Well, no matter the cause of the damage—"

"Oh?" Alexander insinuates a darkly rich laugh.

"You made a donation to the hotel. If you double it, they might slap your name somewhere in the lobby. It's good branding for Atelier Noir." I reach for a tray of butter next and swipe off a hefty amount with a butter knife fished from the neat bundle of silverware near my place setting. I slather a chunk of bread, dab away the excess with my thumb, and then place the offering on Graeme's plate.

He's still scowling, but he surprisingly doesn't object before taking a single bite.

And it's like everyone can breathe again. While he chews, the waitress returns, and I skim the menu, ordering the richest, most satisfying foods I can within a healthy glycemic index. It's only when I trail off, and the waitress still stands there, waiting expectantly, that I realize I've only ordered enough for one person.

"Eggs," Graeme says gruffly as he reaches over to slam my menu shut himself. "Over easy, with two pieces of toast. Tea. Four sugars and cream."

It's the same meal I typically order during meals with Gloria. I don't know whether to write off his accuracy as a fluke or consider the impossible—Graeme Bellamy is actually capable of paying attention to something other than himself.

Thankfully, Gloria speaks up to order her own meal—a martini, stiff, on the rocks—and a smiling Alexander requests, "Whatever you recommend, love."

Blushing, our waitress scampers off, and I'm left with only seconds to steer the conversation toward safer waters. Changing the subject altogether wouldn't do much— Graeme could be like a dog with a bone when it came to a topic he'd sunk his teeth into. The best method would be to just approach the tension head-on. The trick is to find the right angle of attack.

My gaze falls over Alexander, who I find is watching me as well, his familiar lips quirked into a smirk. Inhaling deeply, I ignore Graeme stiffening beside me and bite the bullet.

"So... Alexander, will you be in the country long?"

Gloria makes an alarmed sound that she tries to smother beneath her palm, but Alexander merely flashes a winning smile. "Blunt and to the point," he says, glancing at Graeme. "I like her already."

Okay, so that attempt goes down in flames. I square my shoulders and try again before Graeme can interject. "I've heard a lot about you, from your brother."

Alexander laughs again, more deeply this time. "Beautiful as well as a charming liar. I bet you pay her handsomely, Graemy."

It's strange. Coming from his brother, the words would have been an insult. However, paired with Alexander's good-natured laugh and flashing grin, I can't tell. He seems more joking than sinister. I blink twice just to make sure I'm seeing things correctly. I would have never guessed that face was even capable of displaying anything other than a scowl or glare.

"I've handled this mess for you, this time," Graeme tells his mother without even glancing at his brother. "If it happens again, you'll have to call upon my father to bail you out." He starts to stand, and I don't know whether to copy him or scan the table for any potential weapon within his reach. "We'll have our meals as takeaway," he tells the waitress, who scurries in our direction.

Five minutes later, we're in the car while James tucks our freshly-packed meals into the trunk. My head is spinning. If I still worked as his assistant, I would probably send Gloria a card in his name to smooth over any sore feelings. As for his brother?

For once, I'm not sure which gesture fits the circumstances. Though, it's not like I don't have more pressing issues to worry about. The moment he slams the door to the back seat, I'm already tense, waiting for him to unleash the temper tantrum I know him to be capable of.

He reaches for his tie and gives it a brutal tug. Then he smooths both hands over his thighs, flexing every finger. "That... that went well." He actually sounds surprised by that fact.

So am I.

"W-Well?"

He glances at me and frowns. "Better than expected, actually." He leans back, resting his head against the top of the leather seat. "I'd say you've earned yourself another chance to prove your worth."

Prove my worth? It's a jarring change of topic from the volatile family gathering, but I'm desperate enough to take it without question. "How exactly would I go about that?"

He reaches into his breast pocket and withdraws his wallet— or, perhaps, what any normal man might deem a mere wallet. In Graeme Bellamy's universe, it is his heart. His soul. His one and only course of action for solving any problem to dare get in his way.

"When a man generally woos a woman, there is typically some level of trust involved..."

My heart skips a beat. Several. It stops. "I... What?"

The similarities to his brother are even more apparent when he smirks. It's not quite as charming or effortless, but my stomach clenches anyway. "I saw the look on your face. I know what you're thinking. That what happened back there —" He jerks his chin toward the now-distant café. "Was just about money. That it's all that matters to me."

I don't say anything. It's eerie how the bastard seems to read my mind. Could it be that someone as self-absorbed as Graeme Bellamy might have paid me actual attention over the last three years? More attention than a boss should extend to a mere employee...

"However, I hear that women find something alluring in generosity for whatever reason, so..." He opens his wallet and withdraws a credit card—one of those triple platinum, exclusive cards of legend that you needed a few billion dollars, a castle in France, and a sacrifice to the money gods to own. I can only stare as he offers it to me, his name gleaming on the surface in silver print. "Take it. Spend what you wish on whatever you wish. You have twenty-four hours."

I suppose this is the part where I blush in gratitude and automatically change my opinion of Graeme Bellamy for the better. Instead, I frown. "You don't think I'll really use it. Do you?"

He raises a black eyebrow. "I'm not sure how you got that out my offering you *exclusive* use of it—"

"No." I shake my head, trying to find the right words. "That's not what I mean. I mean..." My eyes narrow when something in his jaw clenches. "You don't think I have the balls."

He blinks. "After a quite thorough examination, I'm fairly certain you *don't* have balls, Evelyn."

"No, I mean that you think I'm too nice. Proper Evelyn wouldn't dare take advantage of her poor ex-boss by racking up a huge credit card bill should he happen to trust her with one. Did you think I'd clutch my heart and swoon over how gracious you are?"

"No." He blinks again and dribbles his next words slowly, as if to ensure I don't miss his meaning. "I thought that you'd take me at my word. Spend."

"Oh, I will." I hold out my hand. "I'll think of it as market research. Perhaps we'll discover how Atelier Noir's range stacks up among its competitors?"

Its equally-as-expensive competitors.

He tightens his grip on the card, inadvertently raising it higher, out of my reach. "I'll take you up on that," he says, the edge of a dare sharpening his words. "Let us see what the sensible Evelyn King might spend a man's money on."

"You're on." I lunge forward and snatch the card from his grip. It feels strange between my fingertips—the virtual keys to Graeme Bellamy's kingdom. I know that he has others, but for now, I have a direct line to the fortune he seems to value above all else. "What's the spending limit?" I ask as I curl my fingers around the Amex in a desperate attempt to mask how they shake.

He shrugs. "There isn't one."

I swallow hard. Grit my teeth. Meet his gaze.

Game on.

"Allow me to take you to your first stop. What will it be?" That arrogant smirk has returned, tilting his lower lip.

"Bristol's," I say, naming one of Atelier Noir's contemporaries that primarily specializes in evening wear. Their dresses alone are worth more than a year of my college tuition.

He snorts—or as close as someone as polished as him can come to the action. "*Bristol's?* I thought you wanted to spend *money*, Evelyn, not pocket change."

I brush off the jab. "Then where do you suggest?"

That smirk becomes a devastatingly colder imitation of Alexander's grin. "James, the boutique on Madison, if you please. I'm sure you know the one."

I don't argue, even though I have a vague idea that the prices in said boutique will put even Atelier Noir's to shame. I clutch his credit card instead, sensing every nick and groove in the slick surface of it.

"Am I limited to just one store?" I ask, fighting to keep my voice under control.

Bellamy's eyes take on that dangerous gleam that typically heralds the moment something mobile will go crashing into a solid surface. "Evelyn, have your run of the goddamn city." To drive the point home, he adds, "That is a dare."

*Have your run of the city, Evelyn.* By now, she's charged enough to build her own, complete with a solid gold effigy of herself in the bloody center of it. The moment I step from the elevator, my mobile chimes to herald the news of yet another purchase—a five-thousand-dollar one from Atelier Noir's primary competitor.

"Morning, Mr. Bellamy," a smiling Ann greets from her desk as I pass. I'm not sure if I manage to greet her in return by the time I bring my mobile to my ear and the recipient of the call picks up on the first ring.

"Good morning. Thank you for calling Bristol's flagship boutique. My name is Stephanie—how can I help you—"

"My card was just used there. Bellamy."

"Ah, yes." Her tone trembles with alarm. "Are you calling to report a fraudulent—"

"No. I merely want to know a summary of what items were purchased."

"Unfortunately, Mr. Bellamy, we only carry custom designs; each item is tagged with a code. I can't tell you offhand exactly what she bought, but..."

I grit my teeth as the woman pauses as though glancing over her shoulder for listening ears.

"I can say that I helped her personally. Your wife?" I don't answer, and the woman continues after a moment's silence. "I'm sure you'll be a very happy man."

I hang up without bothering to reply. When I toss the phone aside, I aim for the desk, but I overshoot, and it lands on the floor near the window, instead. What little strength remained in the screen promptly breaks, and the damn thing shatters. I'm down to my last working spare, fished from the depths of my drawer.

By the time I've waved Ann off—who rushed into the office, drawn by the noise—and gone through whatever business I had waiting for me on my desk, the day is already over. In theory. I have proposals to peruse. Executives to call. Board members to placate. Such tasks would keep me in the office until midnight on a typical day.

However, most men might find it difficult to concentrate while hemorrhaging investment dollars. Ten minutes later, I'm in the lobby, exiting the building just as the janitor begins to close up. For the first time in years, James isn't waiting for me like usual. I have to call him, interrupting what I assume was a smoke break. "On my way," he rasps.

Nightfall has barely graced the horizon by the time I enter the lobby of the Royal. My phone has been silent for nearly two hours now, but I know, even before I set foot inside the suite, that she's there. I smell roses in the foyer as my eyes fall over the mound of shopping bags placed strategically in the center of the floor. Given that Evelyn had barely updated her wardrobe in the three years I've known her, it's an impressive array. At the same time, it seems nowhere near enough to equal her tab. At a glance, I know that at least one purchase is missing—the one from Bristol's.

"Did you have a nice, calming, stress-free day?" The words are crooned from the kitchen. I follow them and find her there, braced against the counter with one hand. The other clutches her forehead, and a glass of water rests beside her.

"I know I did, as you can tell." She waves her hand toward the pile of bags at her feet.

Oh, I can tell. She cringes even as she tries her best to muster up a mocking expression that does little to mask the horror on her face. As much as I may have loathed the thought of having my bank account drained on her frivolity, it seems as though it pained her even worse. I can almost see the disgust written across her face that she doesn't dare voice out loud. What a waste. In one day, I've turned her into a woman no better than Gloria.

A moment ago, I would have gloated over that fact. I might have paired the observation with a few well-placed insults. After all, what could a woman who barely spent money on proper heels find in a department store worth five-thousand dollars?

But one look at her, and I can't say a damn thing. Her hair is sleek, her skin glowing—thus explaining away the two-thousand-dollar charge to a salon. She wears a gray dress I know damn well she's never worn before. It hugs her hips. It hugs her breasts.

When she notices my staring, her cheeks flush. "I thought I'd live a little and wear one of my new outfits from Bristol's," she says with a weak laugh. "Do you like it? The dress alone cost two thousand—" She seems to choke on the amount.

"Let me see the rest." My eyes fall to the bag sporting the name Bristol's. The salesgirl's words echo in my mind. "That one." I point to the bag, and Evelyn King promptly turns three shades redder.

"No." She kicks the bag with her foot, nudging it behind her. "I was under the impression that I would be shopping for *myself*."

"Let me see."

She jumps when I step closer, her hand flying out as if to ward me off. "No. It's nothing."

"Embarrassed, Evelyn?" I shrug and turn for the doorway. "So ashamed of your extravagant purchases that you can't even show them off—"

"Fine." I glance over my shoulder to watch her stoop for the bag and snatch a slender white box from the depths of it. She tosses the package onto the counter and lifts the lid. Her fingers shake as she fishes the garment inside and holds it up against her chest. "Do you like, Mr. Bellamy? It only cost seven-hundred dollars of *your* money."

The garment in question is a black, lace negligee. I can see more of her dress through the sheer fabric than its actual shape. Two thin straps hold the piece together, and a single strip of black ribbon circles where I assume her waist is meant to be.

My mind conjures her into the damn thing before I can help it. Her tits, barely visible through the layer of silk and lace. Her legs bared beneath the tiny hem. Every inch of her ripe for the taking underneath.

She bought the bloody thing purely out of spite—she never meant to wear it. Knowing that, doesn't stop me from issuing a challenge anyway. "Try it on."

She laughs and tosses the negligee back into the box. "Nice try, Mr. Bellamy, but I think you've had enough strip teases in one week—"

"Are you afraid?"

She blinks. "What?"

"Afraid that if you do give me another 'strip tease,' you won't be able to control yourself?"

"Yes. Physical assault is a crime, Mr. Bellamy. I would rather not give you a reason to press charges against me."

"Is that all?"

She lifts the lid of the box and slams it into place. "Yes."

"Good." I turn on my heel and head for the foyer.

"Though if I were to put it on..."

I stop dead in my tracks. "If?"

"It would only be fair for you to try something on as well?"

"Like what?" Her tone alone should give me pause—nothing good ever followed when Evelyn King simpered so sweetly.

"Like..." She hums, pretending to mull it over, though I suspect she knows damn well what she wants to say. "Do you still have those panties of mine you admired so much?"

I grit my teeth. Said knickers are upstairs, in a drawer, kept merely for the hell of it. "And if I do?"

"Try those on, and I'll try on mine."

Bloody hell. My jaw clenches. My cock twitches. The words spill out before I can even process them. "You have yourself a deal."

She gasps as I cross over the threshold of the kitchen. "W-What?"

I head for the stairs, fighting for the control needed not to mount every fucking step before she can get a word in edgewise. "You've set down the terms of your wager, and I've accepted." I glance over my shoulder to find her scurrying in my wake. "Unless you want to forfeit?"

She falters a step, but the next second, her chin is in the air, her eyes honed and sharp. "Shall you change first?"

I mount the stairs in earnest. "We change together. Aren't you forgetting something?" I glance back and nod toward the kitchen. "Your ensemble, Madame."

Her eyes widen. "You can't be serious…"

"Very. Unless you made a wager that you had no intention of following through on. If that's the case, I suggest you rethink your business practices—"

"Fine." She turns on her heel, her chin still high in the air while she marches toward the kitchen. Seconds later, her voice drifts back to me, markedly softer. "I'm changing in here."

In the kitchen. The same kitchen where I bent her over the counter and sampled more of the damn breakfast she liked to push on me so much. "Fine." The word sounds too guttural, my voice too thick. It feels like a race to enter the damn bedroom and find that pair of lace panties, tucked in the back of a drawer.

In theory, the idea of trying them on merely to see Evelyn King strip is laughable. But my fingers curl around the damn things before I can even begin to change my mind.

Lately, I seem to be in a joking mood.

And I intend to have the last laugh.

It's freezing in this optimally-ventilated penthouse. That is why my nipples stiffen, grazing uncomfortably against a thin layer of lace and silk. Said reaction has nothing at all to do with the man upstairs, who may or may not have been attempting to squeeze a part of his body into a pair of *my* underwear. On a dare, of course, and not because he actually wanted to see me nearly naked in racy lingerie that damn badly.

I tell myself that, over and over, as I fold my dress and tuck it carefully into a shopping bag. I sigh as my gaze takes in the rest of my purchases, and I bite my lip to ignore the nagging sense of guilt. There's about three cars' worth of clothing here. The money spent could have been used to feed a small village. Or perhaps to buy the man upstairs a brand-new personality.

What a damn waste. Rather than beat myself up over it, I swallow my pride and march into the foyer. The fact that I'm wearing two car payments sinks in once I catch sight of myself in one of the floor-to-ceiling windows near the staircase. How a panel of lace can cost so damn much—considering just how little it actually covers—I will never understand.

"Evelyn."

My breath catches at his tone as it reaches me from the upper level. He doesn't sound angry or disgruntled. Merely impatient. Impatient to see me? Impatient to remove whatever undergarments he's chosen to wear?

My heart picks up speed. A tingle begins in my stomach and spreads, setting every nerve on fire. Purely out of spite, I take my time, mounting each step with a second's pause in between. I know he can hear me. Maybe that makes it better. Maybe it makes it worse.

"How do I know if you've kept your end of the deal?" I call up to him. For all I knew, he could be waiting there fully dressed, merely to gawk and gloat over the fact that he could trick me so easily.

"After three years, I would think that by now, you are well aware of the fact that I never back down from a challenge."

Even I could admit there was some truth to that.

"Fine." I mount another step. Another. I can make out the shadow of his doorway now. Judging from how low his voice sounds, I suspect he's just a few paces inside... near the bed.

"And how do I know that you've upheld your end of our wager?"

"Well, I'm cold, for one."

I'm at the mouth of the hallway now. I can make out a sliver of carpet beyond the doorway and the base of the mattress, but no Graeme in sight.

"Oh really?" I don't miss how his voice dips an octave. The resulting grumble dances along my skin, raising goosebumps. "How cold?"

"Very." I do my best to make the statement sound as un-sexy as possible. Because, this whole scenario, despite involving the removal of clothing, is not about sex in the slightest. It's about power. Control. And I intend to have the upper hand.

"So cold I'll be able to tell the moment I look at you?"

I suck in a breath, and my proverbial hand starts to slip. "Is that the excuse you'll use to explain away your own appearance?"

Even I can admit it's a low blow, attacking his manhood. But I feel the need to use any weapon in my arsenal to keep him from turning the tables. I'm close enough to the doorway that I can make out his silhouette against the wall. Tall. Formidable. I think he's sitting, facing the opposite wall.

"I can assure you that the temperature isn't affecting my 'appearance' one damn bit."

My breath catches. The bodice of the nightie feels way too tight. His low, gruff tone warns that entering that room alone with him is a very bad idea. For some reason, I can't seem to turn back.

"You're not talking to me in falsetto, so I assume the panties fit okay?" I risk voicing the taunt right before my toes brush the threshold. Without craning my neck to take in the room fully, I can make out one bare foot, attached to a muscular leg graced with a pelt of dark hair that somehow seems perfect rather than scruffy. At least I know he took his pants off, though that realization doesn't feel very comforting considering that the only part of me with any real coverage is the bit of my waist covered by a strip of black ribbon.

"Why don't you see for yourself?"

I pause only for a steadying inhale before marching into the bedroom. I don't stop or look up until I'm in the center of the room, facing the bed. Then, I laugh. Or at least I think I do. My body processes so many damn emotions at once that I can't decide which reaction is caused by what occurrence.

The laugh, I think, is caused by the fact that in the process of "wearing" my panties, Graeme Bellamy has only managed to get one leg into the garment and could only pull it up to his right knee. Give the man points for trying, however, because he had stripped down. Completely. Bare. Naked. His smug expression reveals that he doesn't give a single damn as my gaze takes him in.

And I can't *help* but take him in. My eyes drift over his face first, skimming down to his chest and following the strip of dark hair leading downward. By then, I can only interpret him in snatches as my pulse quickens and my palms grow slick. Nestled among a thatch of dark hair, he is perfect— even more so than when I first had my up-close-and-personal glimpse the other night. There was just something primal about seeing him fully raw. No fancy silk slacks to tame him. No custom-tailored briefs.

Just pure perfection.

I'm vaguely aware that I try to turn my attention to other parts of him—his thick thighs, curling legs, even his feet hold some allure—they seem sculpted. But somehow, I find myself always coming back to his cock.

"I take it you're satisfied with the fit, Ms. King?" He leans back, propping his elbows behind him and inadvertently giving me an even better view. I lick my lips, alarmed that they've suddenly gone dry.

"I..." In a desperate attempt to regain my bearings, I look up and find him watching me. Not only that. His eyes skim, slowly... unashamedly. He scours every inch of me, from my visible nipples down to the rest of me. His eyes are so damn blue, his jaw a chiseled line. If he were acting or mocking, I would know how to handle him. Handle this.

But I forget the words I meant to say. His mouth opens once, only to close.

It's too damn hot. Too cold. Too everything. The desire to run away and change draws me to take a step back , and he bolts upright before I can so much as turn away.

"Come here." His tone is commanding, matching the authoritative way he jerks his chin to beckon me closer. "I want to see how well it fits. For that amount of money, it better *cling* to you."

My heart pounds so hard that it hurts, ramming itself against the inside of my rib cage. "H-How does that saying go? You can look, but you can't touch—"

"For what it cost, it damn well better be real silk." He sits forward, hunched over, his legs splayed, his gaze homing in on mine. "Unless, you don't have faith in your abilities to select true quality."

I take a step toward him before I can stop myself. "And if it is? What do I win?"

He drags his thumb along his jaw and licks his lower lip once. "I'll let you see how well *my* ensemble fits."

I nearly choke at the blatant sexual innuendo. My gaze darts to his right thigh, where the mangled remains of my panties seem in danger of cutting off his circulation.

"The quality is decent," he says. "But the strength in the design is questionable."

I take another step, turning my attention to his hands. They remain flat at his sides, braced against the surface of the mattress. "Look if you must," I tell him, stopping just outside his reach. "But I'm sure that I don't have to remind you not to touch—"

"The stitching seems fine. But is it sturdy enough?" His hand flies out before I can react and seizes the end of the ribbon. One tug and the knot holding the entire thing together loosens. "Note," he adds before I can even choke out a protest, "I'm not touching you, but the garment itself."

*Ass.* Technically he's correct, but my brain doesn't seem to give a damn about the logistics. I can feel the heat from his fingers—from his gaze. One more yank on the ribbon, and he forces me to stagger a step closer, our knees barely an inch apart.

"The fit seems well enough," he says, continuing his observation. "And the fabric seems to be of a high caliber." He fingers the hem with his free hand, lifting the lace away from my skin. "Apparently, you have quite the eye for lingerie, Ms. King."

I grow dizzy, watching his fingers toy with the satin between them. Either he's stronger than he knows, or he's using more force than necessary on purpose. The shoulder straps strain. The section of fabric he holds captive slowly inches higher and higher.

"So do you, apparently," I croak, attempting to bat his fingers away. He lets me, and I write off the pang in my stomach as relief. "Though I think I've won this little wager. You technically aren't *wearing* anything."

The corner of his mouth quirks up, and every nerve I possess prickles in warning. "Well, if you say it, it must be true." He slides his palm down his thigh, seizing the panties, and drags them down to his ankle before kicking them off.

I inhale sharply. "So does that mean you forfeit—"

"Let's add another layer to this wager," he says over me. His hands are on my waist, steering me closer before I can resist. "Just how practical is this garment? It barely seems capable of withstanding any... activity."

I fight for air and bring my hand to his shoulder to brush him off. "Well, I guess it's a good thing that I don't plan on putting it to the test with you—"

"Is that so?" His fingers flex, the nails digging in. "I guess that's understandable. I wouldn't want to ruin my own investment."

"As if you could."

The corner of his mouth twitches, but the expression is all wrong. The amusement drains from his features and becomes something else. "Is that a dare, Ms. King?"

He braces his thumbs on either side of my stomach, and I know he can feel every nuance of my posture. Every shiver as his other fingers fan out along my spine, wrinkling the negligee and causing the dangerously-short hem to creep even higher.

"It's not a dare," I force myself to rasp while meeting his gaze —though I can't seem to break his grip or pull away. My legs won't obey the frantic commands my brain issues to them. "It's not a dare if your opponent has no chance in hell of proving you wrong."

It's the wrong thing to say. He tugs me closer, his fingers finding the knot of the ribbon. One artful stroke, and it comes undone. I don't even have time to gasp before he pulls the edges apart, revealing everything underneath. Everything.

I try to kick him, but his knees clamp together over my leg like a trap. Robbed of my balance, I trip forward and brace both hands against his shoulders. I smell the musky hint of his cologne and feel his heat, even as my lips spring apart. I intend to utter some statement about how he is an asshole, and how I wouldn't react to him if he was the last man in the world.

But then he grabs my thigh. His fingers creep higher before I can form enough words to make him stop. One brush of his thumb against my skin... a second... and I come undone. "Undone" is the polite term to describe the sound that escapes my mouth and somehow gets uttered directly into his ear. How my nails dig in shamelessly while his free hand finds my ass beneath the flimsy fabric and squeezes. Then he slaps it.

I flinch in shock and feel his lips against my neck. "Merely an experiment to test how well this garment can withstand stress, Ms. King," he grumbles against the skin there while the offending hand slides down to the back of my thigh and nudges my legs further apart. "This is merely research..."

*Research.* The slap I intend to give him is merely out of scientific curiosity as well—but he catches my hand before I can and uses it as a leash to yank me even closer. Just like that, I'm straddling Graeme Bellamy against the edge of his bed. My breasts are in his face. My only form of protection is a sheer strip of lace and satin that doesn't seem to be holding up to the "stress" very well. Already, the straps are sliding down my arms. My shoulders shrug to make their descent easier...

Kissing him is merely an accident. His lips find mine and tease my lower lip. I open my mouth wider, intending to bite him, and he takes advantage of the potential assault by sliding his tongue against mine.

It's *just* a kiss at first. A wild, brutal, biting "kiss" that makes my senses melt and my body go haywire. I don't mean to fist my hands in his hair, straddling him in earnest. The bastard falls back, positioning his hands on my waist so I follow, my body pressed against his. The damn negligee pools at my hips, and I only have enough mind to pull back and gasp, "This won't go any further."

The look in his eye is more curious than mocking. "Is that a dare, Ms. King?"

I drag my tongue along my lower lip. It already feels swollen. "Yes. I mean no—I mean..."

His fingers inch upward, toward my ribcage, stroking as they go, and I promptly lose my train of thought. It's unfair how damn dexterous he is with those fingers. Considering that he was born with a silver spoon shoved down his throat, one might think he'd be so used to being catered to, he'd have no idea how to work with his hands. Or his mouth.

Said orifice nudges my throat, and I instinctively arch my throat in the opposite direction. Before I regain my senses, his breath fans along that exposed flesh, so damn warm I have to swallow a groan. Beneath me, I feel his chest flex, almost as if he just caught his breath, equally as overwhelmed by this moment as I am.

I've been alone for too damn long. Even the close proximity of a beautiful man goes straight to my head, and I do a dangerous thing. I lean forward and press my lips to his collarbone. One swipe of my tongue and I steal a taste of him —heady, masculine, musk. I've barely finished savoring him when he does the same to me—only with his teeth. I can't even tell if the pressure borders on painful or not. All I feel is a jolt of electricity that arcs straight down to my clit. Mindless, I rock against the only firm surface in reach capable of soothing the ache—a firm, masculine thigh, the owner of which doesn't seem to approve of the substitute.

He growls, seizing my hips between his palms. One firm yank brings my lower half in direct proximity with a part of him that provides much more relief than his limbs alone could. I'm already reaching down to swipe the flimsy fabric clinging to me aside just as he captures himself in a fist while snatching a condom from the nightstand with his free hand. Once sheathed, he guides me onto him, forcing eye contact with every sinful inch I take.

We go slow this time. So slow, the tension is incredible, and I bite my lip so hard I taste blood just to keep from crying out. White-knuckled, I brace myself against his shoulders, moving my hips in time to match his unhurried thrusts. Before I realize it, our eyes meet, and the man beneath me doesn't even resemble the callous, sometimes unfeeling bastard I've become accustomed to.

His eyes glow, fixated only on me. He doesn't bother to remain silent, grunting with every thrust, his teeth clenched, throat cording. For once, he's... vulnerable, too far gone to care about maintaining his suave persona.

This is a man I could get used to having taunt me into bed every night, and the thought scares the hell out of me. Luckily, before it can fully take hold, my ever-building orgasm reaches a tipping point. My head goes back as I feel him grip me tighter, coming undone at the exact same moment.

He doesn't voice a single word, but somehow, I swear I hear his voice echoing in my skull, smug and satisfied—dare accepted.

And I just lost, and I don't regret it one damn bit.

One of us broke the rules last night—*apart* from the sex. I wake up to find his thigh flush against mine. One of my palms is braced against his chest, and one of his hands is still in my hair—tangled in it.

The bastard has a thing for hair, apparently. Pulling it. Running his fingers through it. My entire scalp is sore, but in that strange aching way, that isn't really painful. Just sensitive.

Everything about me feels sensitive, balanced on this luxurious mattress. Namely my pride. Graeme Bellamy liked to manhandle that too.

"It held up well enough."

I shiver as the raspy tone races down my spine. He knows I'm awake, but I take my time before opening my eyes to find him staring. Judging from the faint gray light that filters in through the windows, it's painfully early. Even still, the man somehow manages to look perfect, bedhead, heavy-lidded eyes, and all. He nods down to my waist, and the crumbled wad of lace and silk still somehow draped around it.

"I'm surprised the damn thing didn't tear," he declares, followed by a satisfied sigh. "I'd say it's definitely worth the price. Do you agree?"

My cheeks heat up, and I turn away before he can see the reaction. Bad idea. Now I'm faced with the sad, lifeless remains of my stolen panties lying on the floor a few feet away. More than anything, that sight drills in the implications of just what happened within a few hazy hours.

More sex.

More confusing tidbits of information to process about Graeme Bellamy—such as the fact that he likes to use his hands. He *really* likes to use his tongue. His favorite position seems to be missionary, allowing him to stare directly into his partner's eyes as she comes, reinforcing the knowledge that it was because of *him*.

Either Portia, Penelope, and that girl related to some duke or duchess he dated once had all experienced something different, or they had bold-faced lied to the tabloids. Not that it mattered either way, because this certainly wouldn't happen again.

"Where are you going?" He tightens his grip on my hair when I attempt to sit up, forcing me to lie back down. He's closer than before—his heat bastes my back, and his breath fans the side of my throat. He doesn't even sound alarmed, merely curious as though we spent every morning like this, and it was completely natural for him to give a damn.

"Do I require your permission to use the bathroom now, Mr. *Bellamy*?" Either the title or my snarky tone makes him let go. I glance over my shoulder to find him smirking, though, unperturbed in the slightest.

"I like it better when you call me Graeme," he admits. "By then, you're so breathless that I can barely hear you."

"You're an ass." I draw myself upright and do my best to untangle the negligee from around my hips. I'm annoyed to find that the bastard was right—the damn thing held up despite being dragged across the bed during half the night and subjected to tugging, groping hands.

"Am I truly in this situation?" Graeme's expression is genuinely curious as he sweeps his gaze along my bare shoulders and then to the matted tangle of my hair. "After all, I've brought you breakfast in bed twice, yet you don't seem inclined to return the favor."

I choke out a sound that's more like a cross between a laugh and a snort. "I'm not making you breakfast in bed." *Because you fired me,* is the part I hold back. When I was under his employ, I had been more than willing to bring him food wherever and however he wanted it, just so long as he'd eat. But now, his well-being is no longer any of my concern.

It isn't.

"Considering that you weren't the one doing the lion's share of the work last night, it's understandable that you wouldn't feel as ravenous as I do."

My cheeks catch fire as memories flood my brain. Every kiss. Every touch. Everything else that happened in between.

"What are you doing?" I can't ignore the note of panic that leeches into my tone as I scramble to the edge of the bed. It's still there, though, building in my stomach as I brace my feet flat on the floor and look back at him over my shoulder.

He still looks half-asleep. Still damn near perfect. "What do you mean?" I flinch at the rougher octave his voice dips too.

"This—" I wave my hand around the room, indicating the bed and my discarded panties. "You keep treating this like it's all just a game."

Even before the words finish leaving my mouth, I know they're the wrong ones to say. I'm not sure why, but I don't miss how his jaw clenches, and his eyes touch on that cold, distant shade of blue I typically saw only in a boardroom when he was at his most calculating. "Maybe I don't see it as a game," he says. "Or maybe I find it all simply entertaining."

I don't know how to process that. Not this latest tryst or the fact that he doesn't seem to be throwing this last lapse of judgment in my face merely to be a prick. Rather than focus on the emotions wreaking havoc on my system, I stand and wrench on the ribbons of my nightie, tying it closed. For added security, I enter the bathroom and grab his robe. Dear God. It smells like him, deliciously musky—a fact I struggle to ignore as I return to find him watching me, unmoved from his position.

His eyes light up with recognition at the sight of what I'm wearing, but he doesn't seem to disapprove. Sputtering, I attempt to steer his focus back to what matters. "I still have use of your credit card," I remind him. "I'm going to order *me* room service."

Twenty minutes later, I've momentarily lost my mind long enough to order the most expensive items from the bistro menu that I find clipped to the front of the fridge. The tab alone costs more than a month's rent, but it's all for a good cause.

Getting Graeme Bellamy to eat his smug words.

By the time the food arrives, I'm convinced that this stunt alone will revert the scales of control. I almost smile as I mount the stairs with the steaming bag in tow. Or maybe it's a snarl. Regardless the expression quickly becomes one that features my mouth hanging open when I find him still unashamedly naked, lying on his bed with his head propped on one of his hands.

Not one to be outdone, I strip his robe and toss it aside before mounting the edge of the mattress, as far from him as possible. I place the bag between us and lay out the extravagant selection—a lobster and caviar frittata, with crème puffs drizzled in Belgian chocolate.

I don't attempt to offer him any, but he maneuvers himself closer anyway, snatches up a fork, and we eat in silence from the same containers. An awkward, tense silence that at the same time somehow manages to seem... easy?

Too easy. I'm still wearing that damn negligee—something I don't realize until I spill a bit of egg down my front, and a thick finger is there to brush it away, electrifying my skin through the layer of satin. I could cringe and make a bigger issue of the contact, but I don't... and whether because of that or merely by coincidence, he's closer. We're halfway into a mound of caviar when I feel his hand on my waist, nudging me sideways so that he can swing himself onto his stomach, his bare ass visible.

"See something that you like?" I drag my gaze downward to find him watching me watch him while chewing on a buttered scone.

I ignore him in favor of another massive bite of caviar, and we stay that way until nearly every morsel is gone. Then he stands and pads to the center of the room without bothering to so much as wrap a sheet around his waist.

And I simply can't be blamed for not turning away.

"Get dressed," he tells me while I clean up the empty containers.

"Why? For another 'lesson'?"

He doesn't deny it outright, and when I glance up, I can't read the look that crosses his face. "You probably want to shower alone rather than with me," he says, ignoring my question completely. He crosses over to his dresser and rummages through a drawer, withdrawing a fresh pair of briefs—masculine ones this time. "You have ten minutes," he calls back before heading to the bathroom adjacent to his room.

It's funny how a week ago, the commanding tone wouldn't have made me blink twice. I would have hopped to action—and not only because he paid me, but now...

"What makes you think that I can't shower with you?" The words are out before I can take them back. Strangely, a part of me doesn't want to. It's incredibly satisfying to tilt my chin into the air and march past him toward the walk-in shower, knowing he's watching me.

But then he reaches over me and yanks the water on, sending it cascading down, and I have no choice but to strip out of my nightie completely and step inside. I back myself into a corner, and he follows me in, holding my gaze as he snatches a bar of soap from a metal shelf built into the wall. He lathers up while I snag a washcloth and copy him.

All in all, the experience is rather... platonic at first. He washes himself methodically while I wet my hair beneath the spray and attempt to comb out the mess he left behind. The monotony lulls me into a false sense of security. I've almost begun to relax when I feel his thigh press against my ass.

Oops. The professional thing to do would be to excuse myself and make a break for it. Instead, I remain there, sandwiched between his heavy body and the frosted glass of the shower's wall.

"You missed a spot, Ms. King."

Holy crap. His voice is sinful, dipping several octaves lower, and my entire body buzzes with residual vibrations. Then the bastard steps closer and runs his fingers along my forearm before seizing my washcloth mid-swipe.

"Allow me to assist," he murmurs before pressing against me fully from behind.

My eyes drift shut as I register the feel of him. All six feet, whatever inches of hardened muscle and British charm soaking wet and at my mercy. The effect he has on me is so unfair. As his breath fans my shoulder in a slow, heady rhythm, I find myself leaning into him.

Before I can stop myself, my shoulders are pressed firmly against his chest, and another part of his anatomy is straining against my lower back. Despite his obvious discomfort, he still seems utterly in control as he reaches around me brushing his palm over my stomach before heading downward.

He isn't even using the guise of "washing" me this time. The rag is in his other hand, and all I feel are the warm, rugged surfaces of his fingers, slipping along my clit in teasing swipes. Once. Again. I'm panting with every brush, hating how quickly he has my brain turning to lust-addled mush.

"Do you approve?" he asks. To my relief, he sounds just as breathless, as if he feels every jolting bit of pleasure shooting through me.

I can't even form a coherent reply. I just rock on my heels, letting his touch work its magic. My knees buckle when the pleasure finally spills over, and Graeme stumbles in his rush to hold me upright.

"You're right," he says as I catch my breath. "I think we can shower together in relative harmony, Ms. King."

Bastard.

Minutes later, he steps out into a towel and tosses one back at me.

"The foyer. Five minutes," he commands before heading once again for his closet.

Five minutes. I spend three of them wrestling with the decision before I finally creep into the guest bedroom and grab one of his outfits from the closet—a beige sundress paired with leather sandals. One benefit to the ensemble is that the dress has a pocket the perfect size for my phone to fit in.

When I descend the staircase, he's already waiting by the door, dressed in a gray suit, black tie. I wonder if he dressed that way on purpose. Without a word, we enter the hallway, only before I even step over the threshold, his hand captures mine.

"You're on retainer," he reminds me, and my mind spins for the millionth time that morning alone.

One minute he's enforcing boundaries. The next, we're eating caviar in his bed. He fires me without warning, yet re-hires me, and demands we hold hands in public.

Maybe all his rapidly fluctuating sugar levels have affected his brain? I haven't figured out a suitable answer by the time I follow him out front and into the waiting Mercedes. He must have communicated with James beforehand because the driver takes off without any direction from Graeme, forcing me to ask myself.

"Where are we going?"

"To the club," he says, answering me directly for once. Whatever ease he'd had in his penthouse is gone, replaced by the icy scowl that transforms his face whenever Adrian Riley seems to be the topic of conversation. "I have some business to attend to."

I can't tell if it's merely a statement...

Or a threat.

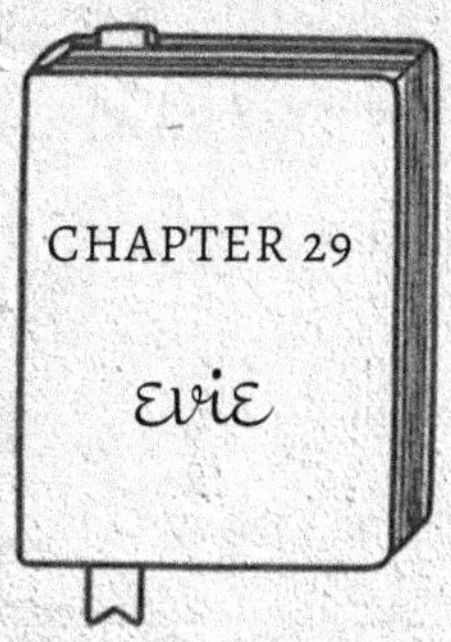



I t's almost like I'm his assistant again as I follow dutifully in his shadow the moment we pull up before the club, and Bellamy steps out onto the curb. It's a short trip through the lobby, where Dahlia is waiting by the elevator. "Nice to see you again, Evie."

She winks at me, and I can't stop myself from reaching up to finger my hair. In the end, she was right about it needing a trim. Still, I can't deny that this moment feels awkward as hell after our spa day was so rudely interrupted. Rather than show us to Adrian Riley's office or private suite, she takes us to another level, where women and men alike wander an elegant series of halls.

"Bellamy," Riley greets, appearing in a nearby doorway in an almost perfectly timed arrival. "And Ms. King." He glances at me with a curious expression that I don't have time to decipher before he leads us down an adjacent hallway and into a spacious lounge, decorated in accents of black and gold. "Have a seat."

Bellamy sits first, taking up a leather chaise on the opposite side of the room. I follow him, and I've barely settled down when a trickle of people enters the room after us.

"I thought I would introduce you to our core members," Riley casually suggests.

Bellamy's frown deepens as he takes stock of the men who crowd the room, filling whatever seats are still available. They're all well-dressed, handsome, and seem to have the same polished charm as Adrian, complete with dashing smiles and vague expressions.

Sitting there feels a bit like being inside a warped funhouse mirror, with a million variations of the same reflection staring back at me from every angle. If anything, Bellamy handles the "meeting" in style. Even I'm enthralled by the confident way he carries himself as he makes introductions with every club member. Tucked by his side, I go mostly unnoticed—until Riley singles me out by talking to me directly.

"Evelyn. There's no reason for you to waste your afternoon away in boredom." He jerks his chin, and a man steps forward as if on cue. "Allow me to have you escorted on a proper tour this time. You'll have your run of the club—"

"She doesn't mind staying here." And there it is again, that infamous Bellamy drawl. His voice is just an octave higher than that foreboding growl, but at the moment, I'm not sure which is worse—the tone, or the cold gleam in his eye that warns me not to move a single muscle. "Do you, Evelyn?"

My mouth opens, but before I can get a single word out, Riley cuts over me, "I think it would be best if we conducted our business in *private*, Bellamy."

I don't even look at Graeme to see how he processes that statement. Instead, I stand, and force myself to smile at the man beside Adrian, who holds out his hand.

"Michael here will give you the grand tour," Riley says.

His smile is positively dashing, but I don't even have to look to picture the glower of the man behind me. For three years, I've dutifully stood by Graeme Bellamy's side, risking life, limb, and injury should he feel the urge to hurtle something across a room.

But even I know when a risk is too great to take, and the tension between him and Adrian Riley isn't even worth my curiosity to withstand.

Taking Michael's hand, I eagerly leave, keeping my ears peeled for any signs of violence.

Though, it's not like I could intervene should the two men come to blows.

The club sure is grand—not that I see much of it. With little fanfare, Michael brings me to a large seating area bathed in shadow where women dressed in skin-tight gowns flit around with trays of champagne.

I don't know if it's the intimate setting, or the fact that I swear I can feel Graeme Bellamy's gaze boring through the back of my head from several rooms over. My skin feels hot, and the air seems to thicken with every breath I take. As Michael babbles about his professional credentials, something in me snaps.

I need to breathe. I need to think. I need to get organized. Suddenly, as if answering my prayers, I spot a familiar face mingling with a pair of handsome men in ebony suits near the back of the room. With a hasty apology muttered to my companion, I nearly bolt across the room in my rush to head her off.

"Evie?" Dahlia beams when she sees me and seems genuinely happy. "Couldn't stay away?"

"Something like that," I reply, glancing back for my companion. "Would it be too much for our burgeoning friendship if I asked for a rescue mission? I just need some fresh air."

Her smile widens. "Of course." Boldly, she hooks her arm through mine and pivots, guiding me across the room and through a doorway. A moment later, we're entering an office that looks remarkably like Bellamy's.

"This is Adrian's private business suite," Dahlia explains.

I glance around, impressed by the simple yet elegant surroundings. In contrast to Graeme's sleek, modern preference when it comes to style, Adrian Riley seems to prefer bold tones and polished wood.

His desk is tidy enough, with only a laptop and a few file folders neatly placed on top of it. Thankfully, the room is quiet, and I can parse through my thoughts in peace. In all the mess with my current employment status, I haven't had time to think about Danny. With Graeme Bellamy breathing down my neck, I'd be a fool to try and message him. But here, I can finally review his messages and try to devise a game plan.

"Feel free to relax," Dahlia says as if reading my mind. "No one will bother you."

A part of me stiffens at the suggestion. Perhaps Bellamy's paranoia is rubbing off on me, but I doubt Adrian Riley would be above spying on his rival's subordinates if the mood struck him. Still, despite everything he's put me through, I'm worried about my brother. Considering the size of the goon who tried to corner me, he's pissed off the wrong people this time.

Taking Dahlia up on her offer, I sit at the desk and pull out my phone to review my messages. I find three texts from the same unknown number as earlier. The first is a simple, heartfelt plea that I "hear him out." By the third missive, he cuts right to the chase.

*Please, Eves. I know a place we can meet. Come whenever you want. Just hear me out.*

But I can read between the lines. Hear him out before he tracks me down, perhaps right to Graeme Bellamy's front door.

*Fine,* I reply. *But on my terms.*

When I finish, I find Dahlia watching me intently.

"Thank you," I say awkwardly.

"Of course. And frankly, I shouldn't gossip, but I'm surprised you have another man in your life, given how your boss seems so possessive of you." She has her head cocked, her smile mischievous.

I nearly choke on my own spit in my rush to say, "Oh, no, he isn't my... Wait, is *that* why Mr. Riley had me tour the club with Michael?"

To make Graeme Bellamy's head explode.

Dahlia beams. "According to him, Bellamy has you on his arm for a reason. He bet me a few grand that he couldn't last an hour without hunting you down."

"Can I get in on that bet?" I ask. At least then, I'd have something to give Danny to placate him for a while. Not to mention the added benefit of watching Graeme squirm in a dilemma of his own making.

Dahlia laughs. "What is your wager?"

"From the time the bastard finds out where I am, I give him ten minutes," I say. "You can time him if you'd like."

"By all means," Dahlia murmurs, extending her hand. "You're on."

The bastard makes a game of stalling. Wasting my time. Parading me through his damn club as though I'm one of the drooling gits in his thrall. The entire while, he dangles the reality of Evelyn alone with one of his pawns as if this is all one bloody session of chess.

But, unlike our childhood years when I retreated from his attempts at bluster, I refuse to let him declare checkmate.

"I will admit your establishment is impressive, Riley," I say, without a shred of genuine admiration. After the bastard showed his true colors once again, and disclosed his intentions for my club, he's lucky I'm still standing here. The git likely realized with Evelyn on my arm, his guaranteed win wasn't so guaranteed anymore. "But I don't see the point of a tour when you've apparently changed your mind about the so-called importance of member input. You want me to either sell or fold. I don't plan on doing either, so where does that leave us?"

Physically, we're in the lobby, hours after he's droned on about membership and the rules that are enforced. Figuratively, we're at an impasse, though I suspect he's deliberately drawing out this little session, withholding the real topic at hand until the last damn minute.

"Well, I suppose I've held you up long enough for today," he tells me without answering my question. Smirking, he heads toward the entrance where a sheet of darkness broken by the brilliant lights of the city waits beyond.

"Though—" he checks his watch and feigns what I assume he thinks passes for a shocked expression. "It's later than I thought. Ah, there is Dahlia. *Without* dear Evelyn, it seems."

The simpering woman in question appears near the mouth of a doorway in a display that I can only deem rehearsed. The bastard sure knows how to put on a show.

"Michael decided to take Evelyn to dinner, Sir," she explains. "I hope that was okay."

From his sly smirk, Riley seems practically giddy at the turn of events. "Shall we join them, Bellamy?"

Something inside me simmers at the words. The implication. The unspoken challenge. "Fine."

Rather than lead me deeper into the club, Riley heads through the entrance and onto the street. The club's peak hours must be later in the evening, for there's barely a trickle of traffic leading toward the building. About half a block down is a restaurant tucked into a small corner of the street. It's an intimate venue that smells as though it serves Italian.

Hidden away in a smooth booth is Evelyn and one of the members of the club. He might as well be a part of the background, utterly bland.

But her...

My eyes are drawn to her like a goddamn magnet, and I grind my teeth at every detail I note in her appearance. She's laughing, for one, her head thrown back, her eyes squinted, her throat on display. I bristle at the sound. It's *real* rather than the hollow giggles I've known her to issue under the guise of amusement. The moment she sees me, her smile falls flat, however, and the proper posture returns in full force.

"Oh." Riley glances down at his watch. "I've let the time get away from me, I'm afraid. I hope to see you tomorrow at the club, Bellamy. Ms. King." He nods at the table and exits the restaurant without a backward glance, the git.

"You've let the time get away from you too, I'm afraid." My eyes are on the bastard across from her. Some bloke whose name I don't bother to remember. He stiffens in his seat and then stands.

"It was nice meeting you," he says to Evelyn, extending his hand across the table. She takes it and smiles in return.

When he leaves, she folds her hands primly in front of her. "That was rude."

I take the now-vacated seat across from her and bat the bastard's glass away. "Was it now?"

She raises an eyebrow, and her expression becomes unreadable. "His name is Michael. He's from Pennsylvania." She reaches for a glass of water beside her and takes a sip. "We talked about hockey."

"Is that *all* you talked about?"

She shrugs, tossing a fringe of blond hair over her shoulder. "I'm not sure what you mean, Mr. Bellamy—"

"Are you done?" I reach into my breast pocket for my wallet and drop a bill onto the table. "Let's go."

Surprisingly, she follows me out. I call James and wait for him to meet us while she lingers a few paces away. The distance is purposeful. Her eyes keep darting to my hands, and when I approach her, she deliberately curls her own into fists. I reach out, and she tucks her hands behind her. "I-I don't think..."

"Retainer, Evelyn." Her exasperated sigh makes the damn gesture worth it when I pry her hand loose and tuck it within mine. She's shaking. If I didn't know her better, I'd say she was emotionally distressed—but I do. Evelyn King only gets this animated when she's just finished organizing something alphabetically or...

When she's gloating. The moment the car arrives, she nearly races into the back seat, but I force the contact even once we're seated. Out of sheer spite, I make her wait until we reach the Royal before I let her go. While she grouses on the curb, I approach James, ensuring she's out of earshot.

"I want you to watch her," I say. "If she so much as glances out the window, I want to know about it."

Or if she plans to meet with Adrian Riley and one of his pawns without my knowing.

"Of course, Sir."

When I rejoin Evelyn in the lobby, I expect some half-hearted argument before she follows me up to the suite, but she's silent. Once inside, she prances past her shopping bags—still piled in the center of the foyer—and up the stairs.

I'm cautious as I take my time to mount the staircase after her. The door to the guest room is closed, but when I reach my own bedroom, she's already there, stripping down...

Aware of me watching, she crawls beneath the sheets, allowing me to glimpse bare, naked flesh before she's covered. The look she shoots me from over the blankets is the definition of smug. "Good night, Mr. Bellamy," she croons. "I hope you have a nice, long, hard slumber."

Bloody hell. Judging from how my cock twitches, I'll honor her little request.

With painful repercussions.

CHAPTER 31

EVIE

Graeme Bellamy is trying to drive me insane. I wake up—in his bed—with every boundary we set utterly demolished.

He's lying beneath me, while I straddle him, still half asleep and woefully at the mercy of his voice. It's so husky when he's just woken up. His heavy-lidded eyes work their magic twofold, and it's like the bastard has cast some spell that strips away my common sense.

"You've had your fun. No more. I want to know what happened last night," he murmurs.

*Oh, that.* After leaving the club last night, I decided it would be best to keep the terms of my wager with Dahlia private. Apparently, Graeme is still dwelling on that little display with Michael. One of his hands snakes up my inner thigh to settle over my waist. My breath catches, and I barely hear him add, "Between you two."

"Who?" I ask innocently.

He shifts his hand to palm my ass. "Don't play coy."

Fine. Biting my lip, I mull over the risk-reward analysis. Come clean—that our conversation lasted all of five minutes before he came barreling in—or... Fudge the truth a little. After all, Dahlia's advice seems rather poignant at the moment. If this is all some twisted game, I refuse to let Graeme Bellamy think he can just push me around the board at his leisure.

Meeting his gaze, I run my fingers along his chest, settling near his unfairly-beautiful navel. "What do you think happened?" I toss back, keeping my voice as level as possible.

The truth is, I'm curious. Did he stew in irritation all night, wondering if a few words from another handsome man had been enough to "woo" me, as he put it?

His eyes narrow, and I can't get a read on what exactly he might be feeling. "Because a woman as dutiful as you claim to be wouldn't violate her new agreement so soon. Would she?"

Despite everything, I still laugh. "I'm sure Michael could pay for my company if you fire me." I intend to sound playfully wistful.

From the dangerous sound rumbling from his chest next, he, however, thinks I'm serious.

"Your relationship progressed that much over dinner, did it?"

I hold my breath. *Damn him.* He makes a harmless conversation sound so much worse. Perhaps because our current conversation is transpiring with us both naked.

"And if it did?" I try to sound nonchalant. Judging from his snarl, I succeed. "What's between us is merely a business arrangement, remember?"

Again, I've said the wrong thing. He removes his hand from its erogenous position, only to cup my inner thigh instead.

"I've had firsthand experience with where your business arrangements lead," he explains, his voice gruff. "I hope Michael didn't achieve the same level of success."

*Double damn him.*

"And if he did?" I counter with a shrug. "You don't own me. I'm merely 'on retainer.' Remember?" As I mimic his tone, I almost snicker.

The joke doesn't land. His expression takes on a stern quality that instantly sets me on guard. His eyes darken to that stormy, alarming shade of blue they touch on right before he starts throwing things. In the office, at least. Here in the arena of his bedroom, he seems prone to another impulsive form of action.

Touching me. I barely feel his fingers at first, ghosting along the flesh of my thigh again. Higher. Then, with mind-melting accuracy, they barely brush my outer folds, and I lurch, nearly pitching sideways.

"I think you weren't lying, Evelyn," he murmurs as I right myself, his voice barely audible. "I can tell that no one, especially not a bumbling buffoon, has been inside you recently."

"Thank you for that assessment," I choke out, arching my hips to escape his reach. It's a halfhearted attempt, and he takes advantage of my hesitation by withdrawing his touch to a barely-there caress.

Damn him. I hesitate, right on the tips of his fingers. Before I can move, his other hand comes from nowhere to cup my hip without applying force. The warmth seeping from his palm lulls me into a false sense of security, and I relax at the exact moment he invades me with the tip of a thick finger.

"You're welcome," he replies, though I barely hear him above my startled gasp. "In fact, I would like to offer a remedy to your predicament, if you'd like."

*Mayday, Evie,* a cautious voice in my head warns. We're on dangerous ground—again. I can't risk another lapse in judgment where Graeme Bellamy is concerned.

Again.

Before I can formulate a reply, he bucks his hips, forcing my gaze downward, directly into his.

"Me," he grates. "Would you be amicable to that resolution?"

The greedy, whorish part of me, newly awakened by his touch, whines a clear affirmative. Thankfully, the logical Evelyn is still very much in charge.

"You're going to be late," I gasp out, glancing at the clock. "I'm sure your first meeting is scheduled for nine, and—"

He extends that probing finger, and my entire body clenches in response. I'm reminded that the bastard is good with his hands. Too damn good.

"You are my first meeting of the day," he replies, his tone serious. "I refuse to leave until we come to a viable agreement. Any professional relationship must follow that rule."

Damn.

I can't stop myself from writhing, letting his fingers contact the flesh aching for him the most. A moan rips from me as he strokes me inside and out.

"I'll take that as your consent to continue this 'meeting,'" Graeme remarks. "So perhaps we should cut to the chase?"

He rolls over, pinning me beneath him. The shock robs the air from my lungs, and any remaining is promptly expelled as he presses his mouth to mine.

The kiss is feral. His teeth nip at my lower lip, and I promptly return the favor. Then, something strange happens.

His tongue brushes mine in a motion that can only be described as a caress. One of his hands palms the side of my face, and our eyes meet again. Only, we linger. Stare.

Then he enters me—slowly—all while maintaining eye contact. I can't stop a tortured sound from escaping my throat. An answering growl rumbles from him, and then he moves, sinking into me with a groan.

As the devious friction overtakes me, I forget everything but the need to experience him. All of him.

"Damn," he breathes out against my ear. "You feel... You're damn perfection. Tell me when you're close."

My eyes are already fluttering shut, but I still find the presence of mind to choke out, "What?"

"When you come," he grunts out against my ear. "That clench... Need to feel it. Tell me when..."

He's barely coherent, but the bastard still has the power to make my toes curl with just those four freaking words. I hate how earnest he sounds. Like he means it. Then he rocks into me with renewed vigor, and I forget why orgasming around him would be a bad thing.

Intent on his goal, he does whatever he can to hasten the inevitable. His hand slips between us, and he uses his thumb to stroke me right above where we're joined. It's electric. I can't silence a gasp, and his answering groan is smug with triumph. Writhing, I try to stave off the pleasure building like a freight train in every nerve and muscle.

It's no use.

The telltale signs of ecstasy seize my body in a vice grip. I'm a slave to his movements, rocking against him with mindless need. There's no real obligation to honor his request.

But I do, anyway. Voice shaking, I barely recognize myself as I croak, "Graeme, I'm—"

"Yes." He slams home, and I feel his release at the same critical second that freight train orgasm hits me at full speed.

We wind up breathless, entangled in the sheets, and he is most definitely late.

But I can't escape the feeling that something between us has changed in a way neither of us is ready to acknowledge. At least until I shift and come to a horrifying realization at the same moment that he hoarsely croaks, "Fuck. I didn't use a rubber."

He rakes a hand through his hair and shifts to face me, his expression contorted in genuine horror. "I'm sorry. I'm a bastard. I didn't even—"

"It's okay," I blurt out. Though is it? The Evelyn from a few days ago would have been thrown into a panic at the thought of unprotected sex, even with the presence of a backup plan. "I have an implant," I admit, and Graeme collapses beside me with a groan.

"Thank God," he says.

I don't know why his obvious relief makes me feel so... strange. Without thinking, I say, "Worried I'd take your ass to the cleaners in child support?"

"No." His genuine laugh startles me, and some of that uneasy feeling leeches away. Without warning, he tilts his head, letting his eyes meet mine. Gosh. Their endless blue makes me catch my breath. Usually, they're narrowed, honed with the razor-sharp focus of a perpetual businessman, but now... It could be how the light hits them, but they seem to sparkle, displaying a softness that catches me off guard. I'm staring, and a muscle in his jaw twitches as if the scrutiny unnerves him. Then it hits me—he isn't used to this level of intimacy. "I was worried you'd rightfully tan my hide for being so damn inconsiderate," he murmurs, his voice so husky my freaking toes curl. "I am sorry. I just got..."

"Carried away," I finish for him. Didn't I know the feeling?

Together, we just lie there, staring up at the ceiling, listening to each other's ragged breathing. I'm sure the same thought was on both of our minds—What the hell have we done?

When Graeme finally leaves for the office, I decide I've had enough roleplaying as his perfect little assistant turned damsel-in-distress. It's time to take charge of my life. I'm not the type of woman to hide in a billionaire's penthouse while the world goes on around her.

I'll confront my demons head-on the way I always have, starting with Danny. His meeting looms overhead like a doomsday clock. First things first—I still need to check that he hasn't already pawned the contents of my entire apartment.

The idea seems good, in theory, but as I shower and get dressed in a pair of gray slacks and a blouse, dread starts to seep in. While I can handle my brother, his new friends might be another story. Before leaving, I take one of Graeme's heavy black coats, and cover my hair with a wool cap that smells suspiciously like him. Rather than alert James, I call a cab and ask him to let me off at least three blocks away.

About an hour before noon, I approach my apartment from an alleyway. Danny had the decency to close the door after him, at least. At a glance, nothing appears stolen. Mom's figurine is on the coffee table, beside a folded note.

*I need you, Eves,* it reads, mirroring the short, snappy phrasing in his texts. *I'm sorry. I'm in too deep this time. I need your help, even if I don't deserve it. Please meet me.*

I crumble it up and toss it in the trash, but my chest feels heavy the entire trip back to the Royal. I'm so lost inside myself, that I don't realize someone is speaking to me until they reach for my hand. By that point, I'm mere paces from the elevator.

"Evie?"

I blink, startled to find Dahlia beaming at me, dressed to the nines in a yellow sundress and killer heels.

"You left this at the club last night." She offers a beautiful silver bracelet way too extravagant to have been owned by me.

"It's not mine—"

"Well, you can keep it. Consider it your winnings." She tucks it firmly against my palm with a knowing wink. "I take it last night turned out in your favor?"

Oh, that. My cheeks are on fire, and I can't stop a wry smile from shaping my lips. "Perhaps."

Dahlia raises an eyebrow. As experienced in innuendo as she seems to be, I'm sure she sees right through me. "Good." To my surprise, she leans in with a conspiratorial tilt of her head. "Want another chance to turn the tables?"

I can't stop myself from glancing around the few visitors in the lobby as if I expect to find Graeme Bellamy hiding behind a potted plant in the corner. When the coast seems clear enough, I meet Dahlia's probing gaze. "What did you have in mind?"

She smirks. "Let me see your closet. We'll find you the perfect suit of armor to wear."

"To what?"

Laughing, she throws her arm over my shoulder and steers me toward the elevators. "A party at the Red Room, of course."

1

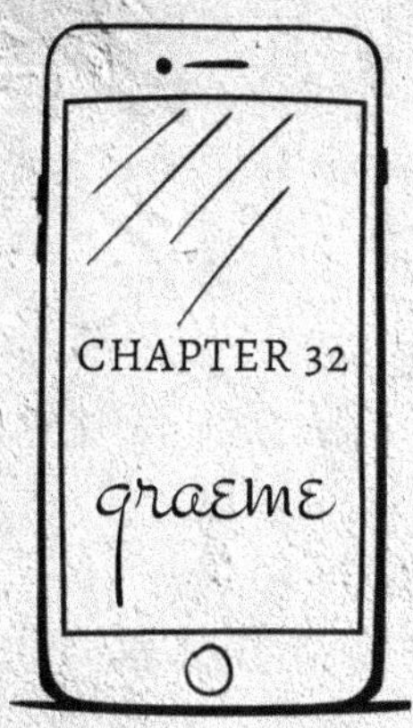



Riley has run roughshod over my entire week, playing his little game, but I'm sure he's not done yet.

The bastard's planning something. I can sense his deceit, lingering in the air. I feel no closer to forging a merger with the man than I do to jumping headfirst into the river, and the moment I step inside the Royal after a day of meetings, I sense something is wrong.

I'm not sure what until I exit the elevator and find a woman leaving my suite. Her black hair catches the light, marking her as one of Adrian's women. She smiles when she sees me and offers up a wave.

"Goodnight, Mr. Bellamy!"

In silence, I watch her enter the vacated elevator. Only when I'm sure she's gone do I march forward, and wrench open the front door. Evelyn's standing over by the windows, her eyes on her mobile. Whatever she sees has her biting her bottom lip, but the second she notes my approach, she lowers it, angling the screen away.

"I didn't invite her," she says before I can get a damn word out. "Not that I wouldn't." She angles her head, ready for any confrontation I might initiate. The motion merely highlights the line of her throat and draws attention to the fact that the dress she wears is one of mine—one she bought on my tab. Elegant. Tailored to flare out at her waist while clinging to her breasts. Like magnets, my eyes are drawn to a sliver of bared cleavage, and I barely hear her add, "She came on her own, to invite me..."

She shifts to contort her torso away from me. Like bloody magic, I can think clearly again.

"To what?" I snap as she trails off. Shaking my head, I force my gaze upward, settling over her wary expression. She's doing her best to hide her nerves, but her teeth keep seizing her bottom lip.

When she lifts her shoulder in a casual shrug, I can sense the unease lurking beneath the gesture. "To a party at the club."

"Riley." He happened to mention the same "party" earlier, one stocked with executives from the London club. Coincidentally he hadn't said a word about extending an invitation to anyone else. "And you turned her down, I hope."

She runs her hands down the front of her dress, ruffling the loose skirt. "Why would I do that?"

"Oh, I don't know." I take a step closer, watching her throat work to swallow. "Perhaps because we agreed you would stay away from Adrian Riley."

"But *he* didn't invite me—"

"The hell he didn't."

"Maybe it hasn't crossed your mind, Mr. Bellamy." She takes her own step forward, bringing herself within my reach, her neck craned to meet my gaze directly. "But you just throwing money in my direction doesn't mean you own me in the slightest."

"I don't want to own you." The words come from fucking nowhere, and I write them off. "I just want..." I inhale and shake my head to clear it. "Stay away from him. He's a lying bastard and won't hesitate to take advantage of any trust you extend his way."

"Are you saying that because of what happened with Alexander," she counters, her chin in the air. "Or because of you."

I grind my teeth so hard I feel my jaw ache. Damn her for throwing a reckless bit of pillow talk back in my face. "Fine. It's your well-being at stake. Who am I to care?"

I turn on my heel, ready to leave the damn building entirely.

"Graeme, Wait." I've barely gone a step when I feel her hand on my shoulder. "It's funny how you didn't ask me whether or not I had any intention of going before jumping to conclusions and issuing orders." She's frowning when I face her, both hands on her hips. "Though maybe I will go now—"

"No."

She's closer. Either I stepped forward, or she did, but I breathe in roses. I can make out the scar slicing through her left eyebrow and the stubborn gleam in her eye that I grudgingly admire. My hand moves, seemingly of its own accord, brushing along her cheek. Her eyes widen and a part of me tenses, expecting her to pull back. She doesn't. If anything, I swear I feel her lean in, letting my palm fully connect with her skin. "You will have to respectfully decline, Ms. King. And that is not a suggestion."

She does pull back her eyes narrowing. "And why is that, Mr. Bellamy?"

"You have a previous engagement."

That throws her off. She blinks and struggles to hide her confusion by pursing her lips. "I wasn't aware of any—"

"Another chance to earn your retainer," I say, cutting over her.

"Like how? And shouldn't *you* go to the party? Aren't you trying to—"

"This is more important." Nothing trumped out-maneuvering Adrian Riley. Nothing. If he plans on setting her up with another man to needle me, he has another damn thing coming.

"You will meet me in the lobby tomorrow at six p.m. sharp," I tell her, turning on my heel. It's a stupid plan. It's a foolish plan. It's the only one guaranteed to keep her out of Riley's crosshairs. He won't dare toy with her life then. "I'll sleep at the office tonight."

"And what if I decide to leave?" she counters.

I snap my jaw shut. Given that here she has safety, security, and access to luxury, I can't think of why she might want to go elsewhere. Except, of course, to cavort with Adrian Riley or one of his pawns in secret.

"I'm asking you to stay," I finally choke out. "Can you give me that much? Just hear me out."

She releases a haughty sigh, but I can feel her guard lower. "Ok. I'll be ready at six p.m."

"Good." She doesn't say anything when I leave, which makes matters worse because I can practically feel the questions ripe to explode from her.

After all, when I lay out the details of this next "plan," I know that the most formidable opponent in my way will be none other than Evelyn King herself.

But I intend to earn her agreement, no matter the cost.

Or the risk involved.

In the quiet seclusion of my office, reality sets in. If I intend to shelter Evelyn King from Riley's machinations, there are several hurdles to clear first. Gloria will need to be notified, of course, as for the only other Bellamy whose opinion matters...

Luckily, despite it being the middle of the night here, I'm sure it's early morning wherever the hell she's traveled to now. As I fish out my mobile, I'm prepared to spend at least an hour tracking her down. To my utter shock, she picks up on the first ring within forty-five minutes—after I've gone through about three of her personal assistants for the right number.

"Hello?"

"Stella, it's Graeme. I need your opinion on something."

"Brother, darling!" She sighs, and I swear I hear goats bleating in the background. Given how distant her voice sounds, I suspect she isn't even holding the damn cell to her ear. "Perhaps Mum forgot to tell you, but I'm a bit busy on a trip of self-enlightenment. If it's about the spring collection, just forward your concerns to my personal assistant—"

"No," I snap. "This is about something else."

Amid a crackle of static, I hear her reply, "About the company?"

"You could say that... What would you say if I told you I was thinking of marriage?"

More static obscures the connection. Even so, I can hear her raucous, cackling laughter as if she were right here in the bloody office. "You? Married? To who? One of those mindless twats that you like to chat up?"

"No. Evelyn King."

The silence that comes from her end is notable. It isn't like her to be speechless. Then, "Please tell me you don't have her locked in a cell somewhere. Have you finally snapped after all these years?"

"You're hilarious, sister. A true comedian."

"In all seriousness, Graeme, I doubt that Evelyn would want to congregate with you outside of the office, let alone marry you."

"Weren't you the one that said I needed to pull my head out of my ass and offer her whatever it takes to get her back?"

"Well, I suppose..."

"Be honest." I shift in my seat, glowering at the night sky beyond the windows. "Are you saying that you don't approve of her?"

"Of course not!" Suddenly, the static dissipates as if she finally brought the receiver of her mobile to her bloody mouth. "Evie is wonderful! In fact, without her acting as a liaison between us, I suspect we would have killed each other the first day we took over Atelier Noir. But I wanted her to work for you, *not* be tethered to you in matrimony. You know that the very concept of marriage goes against my holistic principles, and I would never want to see Evie hurt."

The earnest belief in her tone makes me grit my teeth. "So, you're saying I'm not good enough for her."

"You're damn right you aren't! You're a right git and an awful partner in business or otherwise. You have a terrible temper, can't stand constructive criticism, and the only person in the world whose company you can bear to tolerate—apart from Evie, of course—is Mum. Those aren't exactly prized qualities in a husband. That's not even mentioning the fact that you aren't the romantic sort. What is this really about?"

"What is that supposed to mean?" I demand, avoiding her last question. "I'd say my exes—especially the one I bought that twelve-carat diamond bracelet for—would say I can be very damn romantic."

"Money isn't love, Graeme," Stella replies brusquely. "Though you always were like Father, so damn stubborn and arrogant. Oh, wait! Don't tell me this is about *him*?"

"Father?" I grit out, feeling my upper lip curl. "Hell no."

"You know who I mean. Him. Adrian. You're a raging prick on a good day, but no one can bring out your worst, most childish impulses like Riley can. Even when we were children, he knew exactly how to get under your skin."

I scoff. "Why ever would you mention him?" Though, while Stella may be flighty, she isn't oblivious. For all her inclinations to wander in the wilderness, I know that she keeps an eye on the goings-on at the office, no matter what country she's traipsing through.

"I know he's in the city," she says. "And I know that you can't get over your childish feud, and that you blame him for Father leaving even though he spent less time with the man than we did."

My eyes narrow at the insinuation. "It isn't like you to be so damn sentimental, Stell. Though I will admit that you seem to have a good view as to what that git might be thinking. Almost as if... you still talk to him."

A burst of air implies that she's set aside her mobile again. "Of course, I do, Graeme! Whether you want to admit it or not, he is family. I won't hold the past against him, and I suggest you don't either."

"The past. Like when one of his blokes got you drunk, and Alexander nearly caught an attempted murder charge after beating him into a pulp?"

She sighs, and a high-pitched yowl confirms my earlier suspicion about the presence of goats. "Look, brother dear. I have to go. It's time for the morning repast, but if you were serious about Evelyn... I hope that you really do care for her, and that this isn't just some silly pissing match between you and Adrian. She isn't the type to put up with your nonsense for long. Ciao!"

The line goes dead, and all I can do is dwell on her parting words. They eerily echo what Evelyn herself said, *And what if I decide to leave?* The question haunts me as I stand to pace the darkened office. To be fair, she'd have every right to venture from the Royal, even if it's to join another man. Could I blame her? No. I reckon I'm the only red-blooded fool in existence eager to flee the woman taking residence in his bed. For now. At least until I'm sure where her allegiance lies.

Until then, my only course of action is to remain one step ahead. Focused. A task nearly impossible to accomplish with Evelyn King lounging around my goddamn penthouse. When my mobile rings, and I see that James is the caller, I have a grim suspicion as to the topic of conversation.

"You asked me to alert you if Ms. King left, Sir?"

"Has she?" I glance at the clock on the mobile's display. It's only just seven a.m., well before any legitimate business hours.

"Yes."

My eyes narrow as her preoccupation with her mobile last night takes on a new meaning. "Follow her," I snap, rising to my feet. "I'll meet you there."

A smile shapes my lips as I stand and race from the building. If Evelyn King seeks to betray me, I'll ensure she suffers.

LOREM IPSUM

I've put it off long enough, but I still can't ignore the dread I feel at the thought of seeing Danny again. Before heading to his meeting spot, I take the same precautions I did the last time I snuck out of the Royal, but when I arrive, free of Graeme Bellamy, I'm not any calmer.

God, the jerk isn't just determined to barge into my personal life—he's in my head. Our time together, good and bad, is starting to trick me into forgetting our healthiest dynamic— as boss and employee. I'm questioning things I haven't in all the years I've spent alone—like that, maybe it wouldn't be a *bad* thing to wake up to being served breakfast in bed by a surly British bastard with dangerous blue eyes every day...

It could be that I'm falling for Graeme Bellamy's perhaps not-so-nonexistent charms, or I'm so damn high-strung these days that my logical brain can't cope. If it's not occupied with mindless lust, then paranoia takes over.

Even now, I feel like I'm being watched everywhere I go. While I made sure not to alert James when I left the Royal, it seems as though every dark, fancy car in existence happens to appear behind my cab on the trip across town.

By the time I finally step out onto the curb, I'm ready to just toss Danny the bracelet and run. Unsurprisingly, when I enter the small café he indicated, tucked in between a laundromat and a liquor store, it's devoid of anyone but a waitress who smiles warmly.

Go figure. Danny was never known for his punctuality—and if he's truly in the amount of danger he thinks, maybe he won't show at all.

For a fleeting second, I regret not asking Graeme to loan me his security detail or telling him about this meeting. He would refuse to let me come outright, I suspect, given his outdated misogyny. Or, god forbid, he'd insist on calling the police first. Danger aside, I can handle my big brother, no matter what trouble he's gotten into.

And I can definitely handle a spoiled billionaire without taking advantage of his misplaced jealousy.

I bet he hasn't even realized I've left. In fact, he's probably galivanting around the office, scheming ways to get one over on Adrian Riley. Whatever happened between them in the past has reduced both to little more than preening school children trying to steal each other's toys. Though, am I any better? With a sigh, I pull out Dahlia's bracelet and slip into a booth at the back of the café. Gosh, the elegant piece of jewelry looks even more priceless in the flickering, fluorescent light above. Hopefully, it will be enough to buy Danny off for a few weeks.

Before he gets himself into yet another mess.

Resigned to the task at hand, I alternate between staring out of the window forlornly and watching the clock hanging on the wall above a battered linoleum counter sporting an array of pies for sale. When the waitress comes by, I order a coffee and prepare to wait for however long it takes for Danny to show up. Before she's returned with my drink, the bell above the main entrance chimes as someone new enters.

"Eves... You came."

I look up at the figure approaching my table. God, he looks so tired. I almost feel guilty for blowing him off the other night.

"You have five minutes," I croak as he sits down. "What do you want?"

"Can't we just talk?" He snaps his fingers to flag down the lone waitress as she reappears with a steaming cup of coffee. "I'll have a coffee too, and anything she wants is on me—"

"No thanks," I snap. As she flits off, I meet Danny's gaze directly. He has a black eye and, judging from the purple bruises under both, he hasn't slept in days. The no-nonsense attitude I brought in with me starts to waver. I fight to keep my voice steady as I say, "Four minutes."

"Alright, Eves." He scoffs and rakes a hand through his already disheveled hair. He used to do that when we were kids, utilizing his natural charm to talk his way out of trouble. Twenty years later, he's still utilizing the same old tricks, but hardened criminals are harder to schmooze than a disappointed teacher, parent, or sister, I suspect. "I wanted to ease into things, but like always, you just have to jump right to the chase."

"That's not fair," I point out. "I'm not the one who dragged you out to the middle of nowhere. Just tell me what it is you want now."

"Eves…" He shoots me a sheepish look, and I'm reminded of the many, many times we've been in this position before. "I know I've put you through a lot of shit lately. But I mean it. Once I settle a few things, I'll get my life back on track."

Color me skeptical. To be polite, I sip from my coffee to hide my scoff. Still, I can't resist asking, "What is this, the tenth time you've made that promise?"

"You know what, I don't know why I even came here." He jumps to his feet, and the bruising on his face looks even worse in the faint sunlight coming in through the window. "If you'd rather hate me than help, fine—"

"How much?" I demand, lacing my fingers together. Dahlia's bracelet is back in the pocket of my borrowed coat, but I don't reach for it yet. "I want the dollar amount, Danny. No more games."

Slowly, he lowers himself back down. "Fifty," he says.

"Fifty dollars?" My brows furrow in confusion. That can't be right. Knowing Danny, he could have easily scammed that amount out of a stranger walking by—he's *that* damn good of a bullshitter.

"No, Eves…" His heavy sigh tells me that my suspicion was correct. "Fifty grand."

My eyes bulge, and I nearly fall off my chair. "You think I can come up with that kind of money on a personal assistant's salary?"

Because there's no way in hell that I would ever take out a loan for that much or, god forbid, ask Graeme Bellamy.

"No," he admits. "But maybe you can get a loan from your company or something."

"Of course," I snarl. "Because it's that damn easy. I can just waltz into the office and ask for fifty grand. Maybe a hundred for good measure—"

"Look, Eves…" He has the decency to wince. "I'm in deep, deep shit. The people I owe money to, they won't just take an IOU. They mean business."

"So do I, Danny." I push back from the table, my heart in my throat.

"Wait. Wait! Alright, do you want to know the truth?"

"That you have a gambling addiction? I could have guessed."

"No. The real reason why my name got dragged into debt in the first place," he says. "I never wanted to tell you. I knew you'd be pissed. I tried so fucking long to handle it on my own, but I can't anymore. I'm tired, Evie. I need your help."

I take a step toward the exit. "Danny, I'm *tired* of hearing your excuses—"

"It's Mom, Eves. This is *her* debt I'm trying to clean up."

Just like that, I sit back down. "Explain," I demand.

Rather than meet his gaze, I turn my attention anywhere else. This part of the city is practically vacant this time of day, and only a few cars dot this lonely stretch of road.

"I guess she's gambling again, but she's been using my name to square her debt. I tried to keep you out of it—I fucking tried. But I can't handle this alone."

"Danny..." I fixate on one black vehicle in particular while I gather the courage to deliver what my father—when he was alive—deemed as "tough love." "I'm sorry, but this isn't my fight. I can't always clean up her messes. Yours either!"

"I know," I hear him say, but he might as well be miles away. Bitter nostalgia snaps me back to the past, when Danny would handle Mom's binges with a stone-faced clarity that no child should ever have to put on. "But I don't have a choice. I'm tired of dealing with this alone."

I'm still watching the car that's been idling across the street for the past few minutes—a black Mercedes. On second thought, a model that expensive seems out of place in this part of town. Not to mention, the sleek paint job seems eerily familiar. It looks just like...

"Damn it," Danny hisses. When I turn back to him, he's already standing, motioning for me to do the same. "We gotta go."

I copy him, my heart racing. Dear god. We definitely do need to leave because, for some reason, Graeme Bellamy's car is here. Though, I'm not sure why that would send my brother scurrying. Before I can question, he snatches my wrist, pulling me out of the booth entirely.

After eyeing the front door, he hisses in alarm. "Shit, do you have a back entrance?" he shouts at the waitress.

Wide-eyed, she points to a narrow hallway that he practically shoves me down. Within seconds, we're stumbling into an alleyway reeking of garbage, and my brother looks pale enough to have seen a ghost.

"Danny?" I try to tug my hand out of his grasp to no avail. He's not even looking at me, scanning our surroundings instead. "What's going on?"

"They tracked me. Fuck! We have to go. Now—"

"Who tracked you?" For a split second, I entertain a scenario equally as amusing as it is horrifying—that Graeme Bellamy somehow doubles as a criminal loan shark in his spare time. Then I spot the three shady men storming down the opposite end of the alley, and it all clicks.

Big, burly, and covered in tattoos, they look like men one would not want to owe fifty-thousand dollars to.

"Shit," I croak as Danny shifts to stand in front of me.

"We should split up," he says over his shoulder. "I'll head them off and—"

"What's the rush, Daniel?" One of the men moves to block the mouth of the alley. Menacingly he cracks his knuckles, and I vaguely recognize him as the same asshole who tried to pin me down in my apartment building. He smiles when he sees me, revealing a blackened front tooth.

"Look," Danny says. "I can get you your money, but I need more time—"

"That's what you said before you ran, you little punk. Hiding behind this broad's skirt won't help you this time."

"No one's hiding behind me," I snap, stepping forward. Admittedly, there isn't much I can do against three most-likely-armed men, but I scour them all and form a plan of action anyway. Maybe I can kick the one in the middle between the legs and make a break for it with Danny. Then I can kick *him* for dragging me into this mess.

"Back off, Evie," Danny warns near my ear. "Just let me handle it. Remember how you used to help me take down those bullies who'd bother you on the playground?"

I do—and the memory stings, a brutal reminder of how close we used to be. Back then, he was the one always saving *me*.

"Let's do that now," he adds, nudging me forward. "Three... Two... One!" He lunges for the largest of the three men while I take advantage of the shock to dart between them. Back in our playground days, I would run to get an adult at this point. This time, I fumble through the pockets of my borrowed coat for my cell phone, aiming to call 911. I'm so intent on my escape that I nearly run into an unfortunate bystander walking by.

"Sorry!" I try to push past him, turning back to see Danny.

"Evelyn?" Suddenly, the "bystander" grabs my wrist, and I note the distinct British accent in how he said my name.

*Shit.* I spin around and take in the height of the figure accosting me. Sure enough, my ex-boss turned lover is the one holding me captive, his blue eyes blazing.

"I think I can see now why you were so damn confident of my lacking skills," he murmurs. "Considering you had a whole hoard of other men on the side."

My cheeks flame. I don't even know which of his insinuations to address first. That I would sneak away to mingle with a bunch of creepy strangers? Or that I care that he would make that assumption. Stammering, I try to form a reply. Then I hear Danny grunt in agony, and adrenaline takes over. Gripping Graeme Bellamy by the lapel, I shove him back.

"We need to go. Now!"

Rather than escape the building danger, the bastard just snatches for my arm again. "You need to come with me," he counters. "I don't know what the hell you're up to, but—"

"Fuck! Evie, watch out!" The sheer panic in Danny's voice makes my heart sink.

As I turn around, the next few seconds unfold in painfully slow motion. I see one of the men accosting Danny brandish something I can't make out clearly. It's small, and black, and its vaguely triangular shape triggers a primal fear that shoots through me like an electric bolt. In the same instance, Danny lunges for him, and Graeme Bellamy—bless him—finally realizes this isn't some secretive orgy at his expense.

His blue eyes widen with alarm, and then he does the unthinkable.

"Evelyn!" He rushes toward me, his arms outstretched in a protective barrier. A heartbeat later, a monstrous crack rips through my eardrums, and all the air is knocked from my lungs. Breathless, I wind up on the road, pinned beneath a heavy body that smells like priceless cologne and masculine musk.

"Graeme?"

His eyes are closed, and when I touch his shoulder, my fingers come away red. Utter panic sweeps through me, unlike anything I've ever felt.

"Oh my god!"

Suddenly, the world explodes into chaos as the sound of sirens fills the air. Someone crouches beside me, Danny, his expression serious.

"I called the police. Eves... I'm sorry."

But for once, this isn't his fault. It's mine.

All I know is that if Graeme Bellamy dies on my watch, I'll never forgive myself.

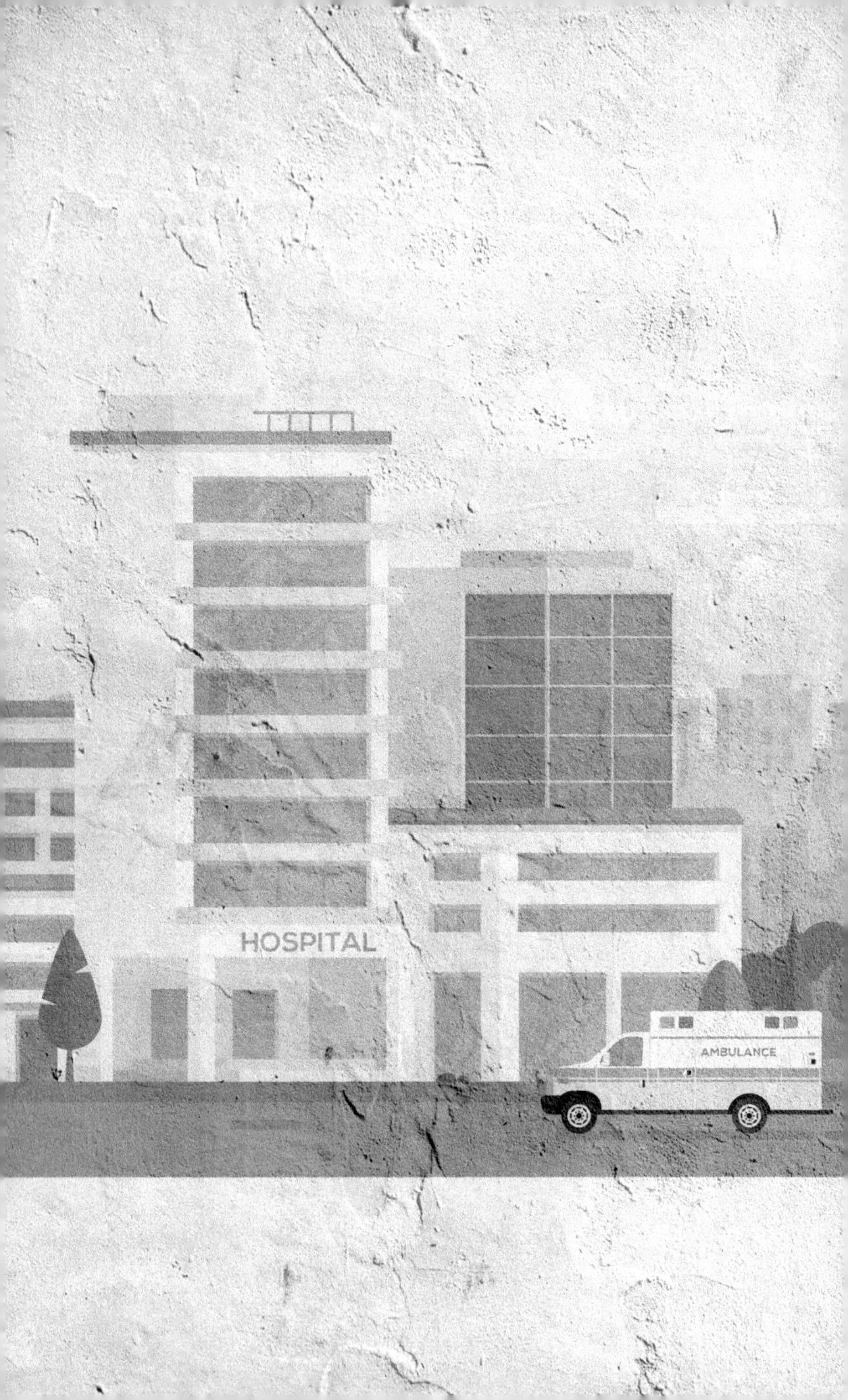

HOSPITAL
AMBULANCE

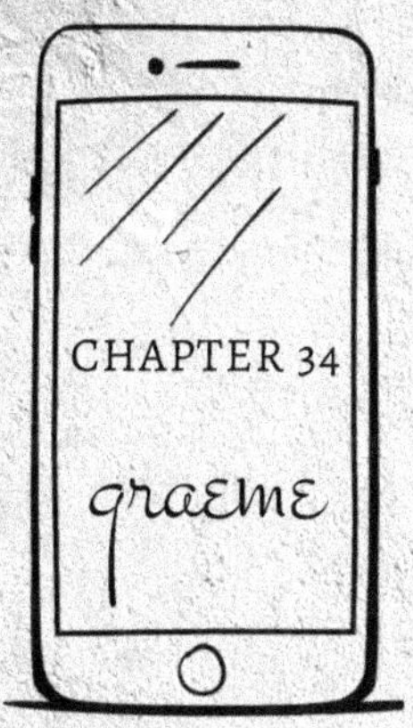


"You shouldn't be smiling at a time like this," Evelyn scolds while fluffing the pillows beneath my head for the umpteenth time. She sounds so bloody serious, so intent on me that she hasn't stopped to take her own appearance into account. Her hair is a tousled mess, and with her bottom lip trapped between her teeth, she looks damn near... *vulnerable.*

Any anger I may have felt at her for putting herself so blatantly in danger vanishes. I know now that even if she had been secretly cavorting with Adrian Riley, it wouldn't matter. She's mine. I can feel it. Hell, I could taste the evidence of it on our last moment together.

But time is running out for me to make that claim in a way that the whole world knows it.

"And why not?" I counter, reaching for her hand. A tremor runs through her, that I feel an irrational impulse to stop. My thumb strokes the inside of her wrist until some of the tension leaves her mouth. At least she's no longer in danger of severing that beautiful lip. "Frankly, Evelyn, having you playacting as my nursemaid seems like the perfect moment to be smiling—"

"Don't joke!" She pulls her hand away, and while aggressively plumping her next pillow, she hesitates as if wrestling with the thought of hitting me with it. Then her expression crumbles, and she sits on the edge of the narrow hospital bed. "I'm so sorry, Graeme."

Bloody hell, the way she says my name... Even when lowered, her voice easily overwhelms the beeping of the machinery attached to me. For all the fuss, one might think that I have a grievous bodily injury. A glance downward reveals that my only battle wound is a scratch covered by an unnecessarily large square bandage. The shirt I was wearing—now folded in a plastic bag supplied by a nurse—barely has a bloodstain to show for the trouble.

"Honestly, Evelyn, I don't get what the fuss is about."

"Graeme." She draws back, her eyes comically wide. "You were shot. And now you'll have to spend god knows how long answering questions from the police and dodging any nosey reporters. It's a miracle that James intervened and managed to keep your name out of the press."

"I was *grazed*," I correct. That doesn't mean the abrasion doesn't bloody smart. A grimace contorts my mouth, and I hold up a hand just to keep her from lunging for me. "The doctors claim it's little more than a scratch. They aren't even keeping me overnight—"

"That's not the point," she snaps. "You were shot because of *me* and my stupid family drama. Graeme, I'm so sorry." She reaches for my hand, and I watch her delicate fingers against mine. When she isn't following me around, clutching a bloody pen, it's easier to note how slender this part of her is. How delicate.

"If a small, inconvenient scratch earns this kind of reaction, Evelyn, I would have taken a bullet for you sooner."

"Seriously?" She blinks and looks in danger of passing out. "How can you be so calm about this?"

"Because..." I capture her hand and bring it to my cheek. She's shivering, her concern genuine. Good. It better be. "Your guilt will make it far easier to convince you to go along with my next plan."

"Of course." Her eyes narrow. "Only someone like you would see this as a business opportunity." She snatches her hand away.

I yank it back. "Only someone like you would choose to fight with a man grievously injured on your behalf." Her wince lets me know that my barb hit the bullseye. "Which brings me to my first stipulation. Who the hell were those men, and why were they after you?"

She looks away, biting her lip in that infernal way. "I'll stay until you're discharged, of course," she says, changing the subject. "I'll take care of everything and make sure Ann clears your schedule for the week. You need to rest, and you need someone to help you with your bandage. The doctor clearly stated that you need to change it on a set schedule to prevent any infection." She eyes the small square of gauze in question. Damn her. I'm the one who's been bloody shot, but I feel like she's hurting far more than I am. I need to know why.

"Tell me the truth," I insist, "and I'll let you change my bandage after I'm discharged."

"Twice a day," she blurts, shifting her attention to the tangled cords coming off my chest. "On a set schedule. No fussing. And I get to make sure you eat regularly. No complaints."

"As you wish," I reply.

"I'm not used to you being this agreeable." With a sigh, she turns to me and runs her finger along the edge of said bandage. "The truth is... My big brother has a gambling problem and needs me to bail him out again. Fifty thousand dollars' worth of trouble. I didn't tell you because it's my cross to bear—not yours."

She looks like she might be ill. I tell myself that concern of that outcome is the only reason I reach for her chin, tilting her face within my view. Her skin is pale, making her eyes seem massive, swollen with fear.

"Let me guess—he thinks you are responsible for paying off his debt?" That I can relate to. Alexander seems to subscribe to the same school of thought. In the case of Evelyn's brother, I'm willing to extend a bit more understanding. Were I in his position, perhaps I'd be content to let her fix all my messes as well. It's not every sister who would take a bullet for her sibling.

She shrugs, evading my grasp. "That's what family is for, right? But honestly, I haven't been that good of a sister to him, either. When our dad died, I cut and run after he landed himself in jail for a third time in a row. Maybe I should have tried harder to help him. The past ten years have been a game of cat and mouse between me, Danny, and his many criminal creditors."

"You've dealt with those men alone?" It's a struggle to keep my voice steady. Given how they reacted to me, I can only imagine the hell she's put up with. All while maintaining a stellar performance record without a day off. "In three years, you never asked for assistance."

She scoffs. "From a pampered billionaire who has no concept of a credit score? I think not."

"I would have helped you," I insist, more affected by her doubt than I suspect I should be. Danger aside, I mean every word. Especially if she looked then as she does now. Wistful. Thoughtful. Defenseless. Vulnerable. "Even without Adrian Riley holding your secret over my head."

"What?" Her eyes threaten to fall from her head. "You mean... You knew?"

"Not the full truth," I clarify. "Just the kidnapping, and your full name. And... There's something else."

Her face falls as she traps her lower lip between her teeth. "Let me guess—he threatened to expose my past merely to humiliate you?"

"Worse. He somehow got ahold of the images you sent me. You remember the ones. He attempted to have them published—"

"Oh, my god." Her eyes widen, and I feel a sense of relief for not telling her in the moment. I'm pretty sure my original guess as to her reaction would have been proven correct, and Adrian Riley would have been manually castrated.

"I handled it," I add before she can worry. "He won't bother you anymore."

"The merger," she says, her eyes on my face. Damn. It's like she can read my bloody mind. "That's why you agreed to it. No wonder you were so pissed. What a bastard! I'll give him something to exploit..." Her voice cracks, and those eyes take on a familiar, fiery gleam.

As much as I'd enjoy watching her lay into Adrian Riley, he is my cross to bear. "It isn't personal, if that makes it any better. Riley would stop at nothing to undermine me, no matter the collateral damage."

She frowns, processing the realization. "No wonder you can't stand the man, disputed paternity aside."

"He doesn't matter—" My hand moves without prompting. When I smooth a lock of hair from her face, she sighs in a way that almost makes me wish I'd actually taken a bullet for her. It would make her far more appeasable toward the plan I have in store.

"Any other truths we need to share?" she asks with a shallow laugh.

"Perhaps one... I hate your cooking."

"Really?" If anything, she looks more shocked by this revelation than by Riley's machinations. Shifting to face me, she cocks her head. "But you love my oatmeal."

"I endure it," I clarify. "You'd nag me otherwise."

*And I didn't want to hurt you,* is the part I hold back.

Oblivious to the more personal sentiment, she releases another wistful sigh. "I guess this means that I'm indebted to you twice over, then."

"Exactly. Now you have no choice but to accept my assistance. For one, you will no longer slink off on your own without alerting myself or James as to your whereabouts." I feel callous enough to add, "I was worried."

She rolls her eyes. "I did not slink off. Why were you following me in the first place?"

I consider stretching the truth. Then she frowns as if reading my damn mind, and I change tact. "Given your recent preoccupation with your mobile, I thought you were seeing another man."

She laughs. "Seriously? You're that damn paranoid I'd conspire against you."

"Conspire," I echo. "Or congregate."

Or wind up in someone else's bed, tangled in their sheets. The mere image sends a sound rumbling from my throat, making her cheeks redden.

"Wait..." A blond eyebrow goes up. "You were jealous. You weren't just worried that I was with another man, but with Adrian Riley."

I bristle at the word choice. "Bloody hell, of course not! Maybe you should go get that doctor. I feel a headache coming on."

"Oh really? Let me find a nurse!" She nearly bolts to her feet, and I grab the sleeve of her blouse to keep her seated.

"I'm fine," I insist. "Just don't repeat that infernal name."

"What really went on between the two of you?" she asks softly. She sits back down, close enough that her hip nudges mine. "Besides the whole questioned paternity thing."

I frown at the subject. Frankly, it's one I haven't pondered myself very often. Why does the mere thought of being in the same room with the git make me want to strangle myself with my own blasted tie? Perhaps because...

"He always made it a point to needle me," I say, fumbling over the words. "To prove that he was always faster, stronger, more capable. That he was the better son. He used to make a game of wooing people to his side. Alexander. My sister Stella. Everyone always chose him, in the end."

"Why bring me around him then?" she asks. "Was I just some kind of bait?"

She's angry—I can hear it in her voice, though in this instance, she doesn't need to be.

"No." I hesitate. Sentimentality was never my forte, but one look at her makes me rethink my stubborn adherence to stoicism. "I took you to meet with him because I knew you, of all people, wouldn't fall for his games," I admit. "You're logical. Levelheaded. My view is already colored when it comes to him, but I knew you could be neutral, without being fooled by his charms. You are loyal to a fault. But I did anticipate that he might use you against me."

Like by exposing intimate photos that were meant only for me.

She conceals her anger well, but those eyes flash with her trademark irritation. "That's why you were so damn irritable."

"And why I fired you, with a hefty severance, I might add. All to make you a less compelling target. I thought I was protecting you."

From her expression, it's clear she doesn't feel the same. "So now I owe you for something else. Great. And I am sure that you fully intend to collect."

"Well," I take her hand again, observing the pale flesh of her palm. "I do have a few stipulations while you're still feeling wholly responsible for my predicament."

Ever the dutiful employee, she crosses her legs primly at the ankle. "I'm listening."

"No more gallivanting off on your own."

Her fingers twitch in my grasp, but she doesn't pull away. "Fine."

"And," I add before she can argue, "you let me handle this predicament with your brother. I'll make some calls and track down the original debt. If he's telling the truth, I'll give him whatever tools he requires to clear his name."

"I can't ask you to do that." She sighs, biting her lower lip again. Damn. I swear the heart monitor speeds up, pinging a mile a minute.

"Are you okay?" Evelyn asks with a worried glance at the blasted machine.

"Fine. It must be malfunctioning."

"Paying Danny off won't fix anything," she grouses. "If he's lying about everything, he'll just be back in a month, asking for a hundred thousand the next time."

"And you'll let me handle that as well." If I spent years fending off monetary requests from Alexander and Gloria, one more debt added to the pile wouldn't hurt a damn thing.

"And what else?" She looks so skeptical. "You're building up to something, I can tell."

"You owe me a favor," I say cryptically. "One you can't refuse outright."

If gentle extortion is what it takes to ensure that neither Adrian Riley nor anyone else can harm her, I'll do it.

"What?" She tilts her head, her expression thoughtful. "That I run away from the city and never speak to Adrian Riley or his cohorts again?"

My upper lip quirks at the suggestion. "Something like that."

"I'm not a piece of property, Graeme." She sounds so damn convinced of that—as if Adrian Riley didn't mark her as *mine* from the second he saw her. "Besides, I like Dahlia. She doesn't seem so bad when you or Riley aren't around."

"Then, at least promise you'll hear me out first."

She bites her lip for the umpteenth time. Then her eyes flit toward my chest, and she nods with a sigh of defeat. "Deal."

When I'm discharged, she does all but try to sling me over her shoulder and carry me out. Upon reaching the Royal, I manage to escape her grasp.

"I need to see Gloria."

"I called her," Evelyn admits to the shock of no one. "She sounded worried, but I assured her you'd be discharged today. I can arrange for her to visit you—"

"No, I'll go see her personally," I say, thinking ahead. Her guilt will make her more amiable to the conversation I have in store.

She wrings her fingers. "Maybe I should come."

"No."

"Graeme, you were just released from the hospital."

I grab her hand and press her slim fingers to my mouth. "I'll be back tonight."

She's so startled by the action that she's rendered utterly silent—a moment of shock that I take advantage of by locking my door and signaling James to drive on before she can react.

Gloria's reaction to my miraculous brush with death is to dab at her dry eyes with a handkerchief when I enter her private suite in an exclusive hotel as far from the Royal as her standards would allow. "Darling." She sniffles into her napkin. "Thank heavens. Evie called and told me about that horrid incident. Are you in pain—"

"Enough of that," I snap before taking the chair opposite her. The wound does smart like hell, but I'd rather suffer in silence than have her fuss over me. Evelyn, on the other hand...

She'd be frantic were she here, biting her lip in that infernal way while blathering on about the dangers of infection. My upper lip quirks at the mental image. She'd be too distracted then to put up much resistance if I fingered the hem of her modest sweater and lifted it, revealing the taut line of her stomach. She'd shiver in that goddamn delectable way, and her eyes would meet mine. After she paused to mutter some half-hearted reason why we shouldn't fuck, we would.

And, Evelyn being Evelyn, she'd endeavor to make sure the ridiculous bandage stayed intact while riding me like a hellcat.

"Oh, my darling!" Gloria reaches for my arm, tugging at the sleeve of my suit jacket as if she expects the damn thing to be dripping with blood. "You don't look shot. Oh, I've been in bits all morning—"

"I know that those tears are really for the fact that my survival denies you the chance to dig out my will," I say tiredly. That damn mental image of Evelyn King in the throes of ecstasy won't leave my mind. Then and there, I endeavor to make that fantasy a reality.

"Must you be so difficult?" Gloria tosses her handkerchief aside with an exasperated sigh. "Oh, Graeme."

"Spare me the lecture, Mum. I didn't come here for your dramatics. I want... Your opinion."

"Really?" She sits forward, her despair entirely forgotten. "Regarding what?"

A dilemma I've been wrestling with since Adrian-bloody-Riley made his return into my life. Ironically, the sole solution has been obvious all along. Smug, I lay out my plans for Evelyn, but Gloria reacts to my proposal with none of her usual fanfare. All she does is gape.

"Graeme. Are you serious?"

"I'm surprised you aren't jumping for joy, or however it is, you express your happiness these days. With two glasses of brandy instead of one?"

"Darling, don't joke," she says, unnervingly sober for once. "Is this what Evie wants?"

"Of course, it is," I snap. "She will have security, protection—"

"You make it sound so... business-like, Graeme," Gloria remarks. "What about romance? I'm sure Evie isn't the sort to be trapped in a loveless marriage."

"And why not? You were."

She sighs. "Darling..."

"I'm late. I thought I should at least let you know."

"Just ask yourself one question. If, to make Evie happy, you had to let her go. Would you?"

"I don't see the point of a hypothetical scenario, Mum."

"Just ask yourself. Think about it carefully, and think about Evie. I am happy for you, darling. More than you will ever know. I just don't want you to sabotage your own happiness the way you tend to."

"Thank you for the kind words, Mother. I'm still decreasing your monthly allowance," I tell her, rising to my feet. Only then do I make out her panicked expression as her gaze flits to something beyond me.

Or someone.

"Graeme." Alexander stands in the doorway. I shouldn't be so damn surprised. Of course, he would be hiding behind Gloria's skirts.

"I'll go put some tea on," Gloria says before darting off. As if she's ever touched a kettle in her life.

In her absence, Alexander steps forward, eyeing me from head to toe. "I heard you were shot."

I stand straighter, making damn sure not to so much as wince. "I heard you were conspiring with Riley to stab me in the back."

He chuckles and steps closer, feigning interest in a row of porcelain cats Gloria has on display nearby. With his gaze narrowed in concentration, he fingers a grinning tabby. I make a mental note to warn Gloria to count them later. "Not everything is about you, Graemy," he says. "I came back to earn your favor. Work my way in. Adrian was merely my means to get you to talk."

I raise an eyebrow. "To force us to be business partners?"

"No." He turns to face me fully and shrugs. "To force us to talk. It's that thing humans sometimes engage in to exchange ideas with one another. Have you heard of it?"

"Talk," I echo. "About what?"

"You. For once." He crosses his arms. Then uncrosses them. My curiosity is piqued by the display—rarely is Alexander Bellamy ever flustered.

"Go on, then. Speak."

"I am not our father, Graeme." He delivers that line with so much sincerity one might think I've spent the past thirty damn years calling him Louis Ashton. "Neither is Adrian—"

"That's bloody clear."

He holds up his hand. "*And* I think we'd both prefer it if you stopped treating us like it. Father's a dick. He hurt our mother, and for that, you've always wanted to hold him accountable."

"Gloria seems to be in perfect health to me."

He wrinkles his mouth, an eyebrow raised. "Do you even know what the proper rules of a conversation are?"

I do, thanks to none other than Evelyn King. Listening. Being vulnerable. Two attributes I have no damn intention of embodying here.

*Why is that?* She would ask were she beside me. *You have a wall up without giving him a chance to say his peace.*

Who asked her?

"You know, our mother was the one who convinced me to come here and try to talk to you like a civilized creature, but if you'd rather communicate like our bastard of a sire, then so be it. I'll be on a plane back to London as soon as I can—"

"Wait."

He makes a show of spinning on his heel, but he lingers near the foyer, his posture rigid.

"I'm... listening," I grit through clenched teeth.

"You're a git," he declares, spinning around. "You're an insufferable prick, and you waltz around as if you're the only one who ever knows best. For bloody sake, you don't know how damn hard it's been having to be in perfect Graeme's shadow."

"So you conspire with Adrian Riley?"

"Adrian was the only one willing to give me a chance, Graeme. Yeah, I blew it, but can you blame me? I just wanted something of my own."

"And then you promptly burned it to the ground."

"Out of ignorance," he says. "But now I can see that constantly making messes for you to clean up only served to make you look even more perfect. The prodigal son. I want to take care of my own mess. So, give me the club. I want it back, and I'll repay you in installments. Then you'll be free and clear of it, and I can run it as I see fit."

On its face, it's a logical proposal. Perhaps too logical. "Why now? Riley wanted me to sell. Not gift the club to you."

"Leave him to me. He thinks I can butter you up to guarantee a sale, but he doesn't know you. The last thing he'd want to do is be forced to work with me. I think that's revenge enough."

"And what do you get out of it?"

He smirks. "I get to show that my perfect brother isn't the only one capable of success, of course. And... Maybe then, we'll finally make amends."

He turns to leave, passing a wide-eyed Gloria who reappears, sans any cup of tea.

"I hope you two can get along one of these days," she remarks, reclaiming her chair. "For my sake, at least."

I don't know if it's because I'm free to wander the entire penthouse for once, but no amount of organizing stray ties or making up the king-sized bed seems to ease the uneasy dread I feel like a constant itch. *However*, I refuse to believe the discomfort has anything to do with the fact that I spent the past few hours worrying about the man who wasn't here to whine about my "micromanaging."

Guilt for getting him shot is understandable, but *missing* him would be absurd.

To banish the mere idea of it, I strip the bed for the third time, re-making it with fresh sheets from the linen closet. I spend the rest of the morning putting away that disgustingly expensive wardrobe—which Maria, I suspect, had moved into the guest bedroom—and it was only as I shoved a folded shawl into a dresser drawer that I realized that this action could technically be seen as giving in. And for all I care, the bastard could choke on his seven-hundred-dollar lingerie.

It's still early by the time I find myself creeping back into his bedroom. For research, I tell myself. I go through the drawers of his nightstand, organizing what little items I find. It's entirely by accident that I stumble into his closet, and once I see the severe state of his clothing—ties left lying beside each other in no particular order, for chrissakes—I simply can't help myself.

By the time five-thirty rolls around, I've finished organizing his briefs by shape and color, and only then do I have time to process the strange feeling building in my stomach. That couldn't be... unease, now could it? Nothing good ever seemed to arise from one of Bellamy's mysterious "wooing lessons." "Good," as in, I always seem to wind up with my panties off and his hands on my body in erogenous places.

I won't let that happen this time, even as my thighs tighten and my stomach bunches into knots at the prospect. Tonight, all my clothing will remain on—Graeme Bellamy won't get inside my head *again*.

With that thought in mind, I head down to the lobby to meet him when the time nears six. I find William the doorman standing at attention, but no Bellamy in sight. When I glance through the main entrance, I don't see the Mercedes out front.

Strange. I have never known the man to be late, though these days, he seems determined to prove everything that I've learned about him over the past three years wrong.

I wind up waiting in the corner of the lobby, perched on a cream chaise. I've barely sat down when a familiar figure makes his entrance. The moment his eyes find me, he jerks his chin for me to follow before grabbing my wrist anyway, pulling me along.

My heart picks up speed when I follow him—even before I see his expression. Blank. Composed. Unreadable.

Where Graeme Bellamy is concerned, the lack of a smug grin heralds alarm.

"Where are we going?" I ask as I climb onto the seat beside him and allow James to close the door after me. "Shouldn't you be resting?"

I pointedly eye his arm and the bandage I know lurks beneath, but he doesn't respond, still holding my wrist despite my feeble attempts to pull away. He feels so warm, and his fingers—whether by accident or intentionally—stroke the inside of my wrist with breathtaking care. Instead, it's a nearly silent twenty-minute trip through the heart of the city. When James brings the car to a stop, I glance out of the window and frown. We're in front of his law offices—the firm that handles the bulk of the negotiations for Atelier Noir.

"Are you adding litigation to my record, in addition to being fired?" My heart skips a beat as the words leave my mouth. They sound less joking and more... worried.

Rather than answer, Bellamy wrenches open the door on his side and steps out onto the curb. I take my time before following, fully convinced that if the bastard plans to humiliate me further, I won't hesitate to leave him a parting gift right over one of his beautiful eyes.

I've barely taken a step in his direction before he turns on me and grabs one of my hands from my side.

"Name your price," he tells me, his tone gruff, his eyes an icy shade of blue. "Any number."

"F-For what?" I don't like how serious he sounds. How stern he looks. This past week I've grown accustomed to the mocking, shameless side of him. I'd almost forgotten just how intimidating he could seem.

"You," he gruffly replies. Before I can take offense, he adds, "I have a proposal to keep you out of Adrian Riley's crosshairs. Will you accept it?"

I attempt to disentangle his hand from mine. "Well, it depends on what it is—"

"An agreement," he says, releasing his grip. He turns on his heel and approaches the entrance to the law offices. One of his hands tugs at his collar while the other pushes open the main door. "One that admittedly benefits us both."

I instantly don't like the sound of that. "How so?"

He nods toward the entryway of the office, beckoning me inside—but I don't move a single muscle. Graeme Bellamy, in all the time I've known him, rarely acted like this. Secretive. Vague. Evasive. Those traits, in fact, have only appeared more recently.

Right after the first time we had sex, in fact.

"What exactly does this 'arrangement' consist of?" I gather up the nerve to ask.

It feels like an eternity that he holds my gaze, his mouth set in that stern frown that would send many of his business partners scurrying for cover. Finally, he sighs and attempts to close the door, forcing me to step inside or be caught in the doorway. "I'm making you an offer that you can't refuse," he says without turning to face me. "One that solves both of our familial problems."

"Like what?" Be re-hired as his assistant? Help him infiltrate Adrian Riley's club so that he can set it on fire? Pay off Danny's debt and send him to a secluded island where he can't get into trouble.

He turns then, and my heart lurches to the back of my throat. The look in his eye catches me off guard—raw, piercing emotion that I've never seen in him. Or maybe I've only seen glimpses up until now. This vulnerable part of him that seems somewhat... human.

His jaw is clenching again. He's no longer staring at me directly, but at the wall behind my head—ruthlessly, as if he'd like nothing more than for it to crumble into pieces. "I see only one solution. Family members and wives are off-limits according to his silly rules—"

I frown. "So... are you replacing me with Gloria?"

"Bloody hell no." He grimaces. "My solution is simpler than that—I'll keep ownership of the club but let Alexander take charge. Then, to keep you out of Riley's crosshairs... I want you to marry me."

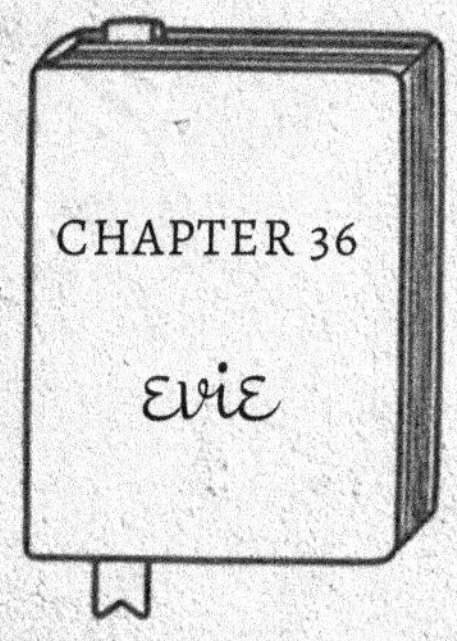



I think I faint—or whatever it's called when you lose your balance and need to cling to the nearest solid surface to keep from falling face forward. It doesn't help that that "surface" happens to be Graeme Bellamy's arm. I promptly shove him off, only to find myself staggering back against the nearest wall instead and using it for support.

"You're insane." I'm surprised by just how much genuine pity leeches into my voice. Poor Graeme Bellamy. The man may be a total ass, but no one deserves to damage their mental health before the age of forty. "You really are actually *insane—*"

"What's so insane about it?" he snaps. His eyes touch onto that molten hue of indigo, and he adjusts his tie with a brutal twitch of his wrist. "You've spent three years by my side. It should be only a formality to marry me. You'll have access to my money, of course, to settle your brother's debts—"

"You're serious." My throat goes dry as my brain scrambles to comprehend his logic. Too much. More than enough. It's disgusting how easy it is for him to throw dollar bills at his problems in the hopes they disappear. "What if I don't want your money?"

He blinks. Then he throws his head back and laughs, long and beautifully. The sound takes on a dangerous edge as it trails off, however. Like the sound a car's engine makes right before it stalls out. "What else could you possibly want?"

It's a good question, considering that a part of me is wondering that same thing. "Well... peace, for one. Being around you hasn't exactly brought me much of that."

But it has brought me a sense of purpose that I can't deny. Fighting with him in a luxurious penthouse has, admittedly, been way more fun than scurrying from apartment to apartment, outrunning my past.

"Peace." He scoffs. "With the amount I'm offering, you can buy a bloody island and live in peace."

Something inside me shrivels into a ball when I realize he's probably right. "I don't..." Trying to find the right words, I shake my head. In the end, all I come up with is, "There are things in the world more important than money."

"I know that." The look that transforms his features catches me off guard. Is this actual sincerity? "Use whatever excuse you will, Evelyn, but admit the obvious. Your real hang-up is that you couldn't last one day as my wife."

My brain short-circuits as the insult clashes with my common sense. In reality, no, I wouldn't make a good wife to Graeme Bellamy—very few women would. Without winding up in prison by the second day, at least. Though, at the moment, that fact seems to be beside the point. "And why is that?" My voice sounds too soft—my equivalent of his growl.

He raises a dark eyebrow. The expression, paired with a dazzling grin, makes my heart flutter. At least until he murmurs, "You can't handle me without the excuse of a paycheck. You can barely stand to be seen in public with me, and you know that I need you more than you need me."

Wait... What? My brain short-circuits, and the bastard takes advantage of my bafflement to step in. Warm, his breath hits me full in the face as he adds, "Just admit that you don't have what it takes to be the wife of a man like me, even for a month."

Technically the bastard is right—though, if we substituted "what it takes" for "the lack of brains." Apart from the convoluted logistics of his proposal, the man is flat-out self-ish, egotistical, rude, and arrogant. Not to mention irra-tional. And... Thoughtful enough to notice my favorite color without me consciously ever saying so. Selfless enough to take a bullet for me. So damn infuriating that he makes me want to strangle him one minute and kiss him the next...

My head is swimming with all those conflicting sentiments, and in the end, I just blurt out, "You're too arrogant to ever share the spotlight with anyone, let alone a wife."

"Well, you're a woman who can't even admit to herself that she more than willingly *fucked* this arrogant—"

"The answer is no. We barely know each other, and we hardly get along." I should mark this moment by turning on my heel and marching dramatically for the door. Slapping him. *Anything.*

I just stand there. He just stares, and neither of us can seem to walk away—which sums up the cause of our recent... problems.

"Just... listen to me... please," he grits out, and my heart damn near stops. I can't tell if it's a dangerous please or a genuine one—which seems even more alarming than the former. His gaze is intense, boring into my own. I can't even begin to describe the hue of blue his eyes touch on—something light and dark at the same time that makes me cross my arms over my chest and back away until the edge of what seems to be a framed photo bites into my shoulder.

"Ok," I croak. "I am."

He inhales sharply and exhales the breath all at once. "This arrangement will keep you... safe."

We both frown at that notion.

"Me safe or just your business?" I can't help how defensive I sound. Just a week ago, this man seemed unable to tell me apart from the background scenery in his office, and now...

He's demanding I marry him on a whim.

As if sensing my train of thought, he frowns. "Does that matter?"

I choose to avoid the question. "And what would I have to do?" I counter instead. "Just... marry you in name only? Flash a ring for Adrian Riley's benefit?"

He rubs his chin, his gaze thoughtful. "Not nearly quite that simple," he says. "Riley may toe his own boundaries, but it would require some effort on your part to make it believable. You would be expected to play the role."

"Of your wife?" That word sounds so very dangerous, coming out of my mouth. It contains too many variables to consider all at once—the public persona alone of being Graeme Bellamy's wife.

It's unnerving how easily he can write off what, for most people, is a life-altering experience. Something they dream about their entire lives. I had never been that girl to make-believe a grand wedding with her Barbie dolls, but whenever I *did* picture the prospect of settling down, it definitely wasn't with a man like him.

"Is this just your way of trying to score more sex out of me?" I do my best to seem indifferent, but my throat is dry, my heart racing. I can't quite get my tone just right. I sound more breathless than anything. "I mean, it was good, Mr. Bellamy, but not *that* good—"

"And you are a damn liar," he interjects with a harsh laugh. "Seriously—" his voice dips an octave, his eyes abnormally stern. "What do you require to make you say yes?"

I run my tongue over my lips, overwhelmed by the ask. He's serious—I can tell. Does he want me merely to orchestrate a checkmate against Adrian Riley or...

For himself.

"Make it real," I blurt out, leveling the challenge, though even I'm not exactly sure what it entails. "You want the world to believe it? So make *me* believe it. I could certainly use the entertainment. You can start by proposing to me properly. No games. No lies. No bribery. I want an honest explanation as to why you think this would even work between us."

He blinks, taking on the cool, calculating persona of a businessman. "I would rather get your agreement in writing before I do a damn thing—"

"Then my answer is no," I declare, conveniently holding back the part where my answer would be no anyway. "You want my signature? Then propose to me. For real. Make me believe it, Mr. Bellamy. Or..."

"Or what?" The growl reverberates across the space between us, but to my credit, I don't flinch.

"Or are you simply not man enough?"

That resonates with him. He draws his shoulders up, rising to his full height, and meets my gaze directly. In two steps, he's standing before me, merely a toe outside of entering my personal space. I brace one hand against the wall as I crane my neck back to look at him.

"Ms. King..." He trails his thumb along my cheek, and it takes everything I have in me not to bite the offending finger.

"I don't remember saying anything about touching—"

"Ms. King," he repeats. "Frankly, what has happened between us these past few days has made me realize one very important observation..." His hand cups my chin fully, his voice a low sensual rasp... his facial expression like the blank one someone being lobotomized might wear. "I cannot go on another minute... without ensuring that you *aren't* used as a pawn in some scheme to circumvent me. So out of your own sense of self-preservation, will you do me the very real inconvenience of marrying me?"

I feel a cramp in my lips—they purse so hard. "Lovely. How very romantic." Am I actually disappointed? The man can't even pretend for five seconds to convey sincere emotion. Despite all that harping about "wooing," he can barely let go of his checkbook for long enough to even try. Or... maybe the heart of the matter was that, despite being very capable of expressing himself physically, the man can't even feign genuine human emotion. "The answer is no."

I attempt to step away from him, but his body becomes a wall, pinning me in. His breath is on my neck before I even feel his teeth there, grazing the outer shell of my ear. "Shut up," he tells me, and I swear I feel his teeth, nipping just once. "You know how good it can be between us. A *deep*, satisfying connection."

My breath catches, and I force my eyes to roll toward the ceiling. Of course, he'd reference sex.

"I don't—"

"Forget the money. Forget the titles. Forget the whole bloody lot of it. Just simply picture me and you—there's more there. You feel it. I feel it…" His voice takes on a gruffer baritone, more alarming than the growl. The same one I've only heard in his bed, or in some compromising position in another part of his suite, gritted into my ear or murmured into my skin. "You know no one understands you better than I do. That no one will ever understand me any better than you do."

My mind struggles to find the obvious flaws in his façade—his broken, unsteady breaths, the way his fingers flex against the wall. How he swallows hard, his Adam's apple flexing. I'm not used to this side of him. A man without his cocky, confident swagger to hide behind.

He's being honest, and the realization scares the hell out of me. Even so, I can't stop listening, a slave to every word.

"You feel it, every time I touch you." He slides one of his hands down to my waist as if to reinforce that assertion. In response, my stomach tightens. My skin grows warm. Hot. "Every time I'm near you. Do you want to know why I didn't want to get you a ring at first?" His thumb hooks beneath the waistband of my skirt, hauling it down before I can choke out a protest and slipping underneath. "This is all I need…" His fingers find my panties and pry the panel aside just enough for him to force one through the gap in the fabric and circle me. Once. Twice.

My entire body melts beneath the friction. The rough way he touches me. The sound he growls into my ear at the feel of me. "This," he grates. "You at my fingertips. There's no other proof I need to know you're mine, Evelyn… Are you?"

His nearness does something to me—addles my brain to make the impossible seem... desirable. Graeme Bellamy all mine, to strangle—or more—at will?

When his lips graze my cheek, I can't stop myself from choking out, "Yes."

"Good."

My mind spins as he draws back, withdrawing his hand from my skirt and wrenching the waistband up. His gaze is unreadable as he pops the offending thumb onto his tongue and slowly licks the pad clean. "Marry me," he demands gruffly before letting that hand fall back to his side.

I can't speak, but he's already turning on his heel, storming off. I don't even realize I've taken a step toward him until he pauses near the threshold of a doorway and glances back at me. "Before I forget..." He reaches into his pocket and withdraws a small black box that he tosses in my direction. "Here. The choice is yours, but you know where I stand."

A part of me suspects what it is before I even open it—as he would say, a *bloody fucking* ring.

ONE WEEK LATER...

If I envisioned myself getting married, it certainly didn't involve a billionaire still sporting a healing gunshot wound who paid off my brother's debts with thousands of dollars of his own money.

And even if I'd had a fantasy—or perhaps a weird vivid dream—that entailed as much, I certainly wouldn't imagine that I could actually care for the bastard. It's ironic, in a way. My father used to say that my mother put the "moan" in matrimony, the few times he did talk about her. He definitely didn't mean in the sexual sense, either.

No, he meant *misery*, and I always swore to never willingly put myself in that position. My terrible relationship track record aside, I was well on my way to achieving that goal before this moment. It was one of the few promises I made to myself, right after the little one claiming I would never let Graeme Bellamy get the better of me.

Breaking *both* of those vows at once proceeds a bit like how I imagine signing your soul away to the devil might—though albeit with less pomp and circumstance, and a little bit of excitement. In lieu of a fiery pit, I'm led into an office commandeered by a man wearing a suit who appraises us from behind wire-rimmed glasses.

"The judge," Bellamy mutters to me. Somehow I'd managed to convince him to boil down our ceremony to a hasty exchange, but I suspect that Gloria is already planning something far more extravagant.

Given that Bellamy still has ownership of the club to work out with Adrian Riley and Alexander, only god knows what he might be talked into by her while distracted. For now, a courthouse wedding in relative privacy will have to do.

Once we take adjacent seats in front of the desk before him, the "ceremony" commences.

Foregoing any pretense, our vows apparently consist of a few lines of legal-sounding jargon.

"Do you solemnly swear to uphold this union?" the judge asks once the terms are set.

"I do," Bellamy agrees before glancing pointedly at me.

A part of me wants to stomp my foot beneath the scrutiny. Make him wait. Pout, even. But something tells me that whatever tantrum I could throw, he would be willing to create an even bigger scene. I've never seen him like this. Only one word comes to mind to describe the tension gripping his body from head to toe. *Desperation?*

So, damn it, I give in, under complete duress. "Yes."

"Then please sign on the dotted line."

Confidently, Bellamy signs first, and I follow. Just like that... we're married. I suppose. The judge stands and prompts Bellamy and me to shake hands. And that's that. I've experienced more hassle while opening a bank account, but in little under ten minutes, I've married a man I used to work for with little pomp and circumstance.

Oh, apart from the ring.

As I'm herded out of the office, I flip open the box and glance at it again. At first, the shape seems relatively simple—a circle formed of rose-colored gold. On second appraisal, however... *Damn.* I can tell that it's finely crafted—definitely *expensive.* Even for a man richer than god, the gesture seems extravagant for what, in theory, should be a simple token. I glance at him from the corner of my eye as he tucks the legal documents into his breast pocket. The smirk he shoots me in return offers no answers, the bastard.

Either way, I close the box without putting it on and follow him to the car. He's already holding the door open for me as I approach. A strange enough occurrence that I wind up just standing there, watching him. I may or may not be open-mouthed as well.

"Evelyn," Bellamy starts, his tone an ominous warning. "See something you like, Luv?"

*Luv.* That choice of word sets my entire body on edge. Bellamy *never* casually dished out cliché British colloquiums.

Well, *almost* never. Such a phrase typically marked the stage of his temper just beyond "murderously polite." It was a level of rage that I'd only seen him reach once before, when his blood sugar levels nearly bottomed out after a day of skipped meals, and a business rival had the gall to insult him, in public, along with all of Atelier Noir for good measure. "Thanks for enlightening me, chap," Bellamy had hissed, right before he threw his fist into the bastard's face. It was a hush-hush scandal that took bribing nearly every major news outlet in the city to keep under wraps. In the end, Bellamy wound up paying for the man's medical bills—one broken nose and several stitches—but I don't think it fazed him one damn bit.

For him to switch from Evelyn to "Luv" in ten minutes... somewhere during our hasty marriage ceremony, I had done something to piss him off. Royally. I rack my brain to figure out what.

Those eyes reveal nothing, however. The only other clue to his souring mood is how tightly he clenches his jaw, causing his cheekbones to stand out in even starker contrast. "You should get in the car, darling," he all but growls. "Please."

*Oh, hell no.* I back up a step. "I don't remember you mentioning that my marrying you involved you ordering me around—"

"Liar," he says with a harsh shrug of his shoulder. "Your marriage duties do not negate your current retained services. They will overlap."

Overlap? I struggle to hide my confusion with an indignant laugh. *Ha!* "Once again, I don't remember anything in my 'retained' duties about—"

"As I told you before, read the fine print, Evelyn." He snaps his fingers and jerks his chin toward the awaiting back seat. "Get in. Please."

Oh, dear god. That *please* sends my heart into overdrive as I grapple with the reality of the precipice I find myself balancing on. Refusing him could send him into an even more volatile variation of his temper. But entering that car with him seems... lethal—to what remains of my pride, at least.

In the end, I decide that the prospect of him causing a scene in the middle of a crowded street—possibly by throwing his cell phone through the glass front of yet another establishment—is just a fraction worse than anything I might face inside the car with James present.

"Fine." I march past him and throw myself into the farthest corner of the Mercedes. He climbs in after me, keeping a wide swath of space between us.

"Drive," he tells James through gritted teeth, coincidentally without mentioning just where he might be driving to. I refuse to let myself panic over the potential prospects, though. The picture of calm, I settle my hands over my lap instead and try to regain control of my breathing. In. Out. My fingers start to shake, only to remind me of the tiny box still clutched in them.

"Put it on," Bellamy commands, following the line of my gaze. I can't shake the feeling that he was waiting all along for the chance to say those three words.

"Why?" My fingers glide along the plush velvet surface of the box. Some lines should never be crossed, even in the boundaries of an impulsive dare that leads to marriage.

"Because," Bellamy replies. "The world needs to know who you belong to." Such a heartfelt plea with decidedly possessive undertones.

I'm so touched by it, that deciding on my answer takes only a second of deliberation. "No." *Hell no*, I clarify mentally.

"Put it on." His enunciation sounds crisper this time, as if he merely suspects that I didn't hear him correctly the first time.

To dispel any doubt, I turn to face him, wrestling the stupid box into my fist. "No. As in—no, I will not."

"Yes." He blinks once, his expression unwavering. It's like he doesn't even know the damn meaning of a refusal. "Yes, as in, you don't have a damn choice—"

"You said I had to *marry* you," I interject. "You didn't say anything about having to wear... tokens of it."

"Wearing my ring is an essential part of your marital duties."

"Then where is your ring?" I nod pointedly to his naked finger, and a muscle in his jaw twitches. Almost a smirk in the right lighting.

"Were the reasons stated in my proposal not a sufficient enough explanation?"

Bastard. Summoning every ounce of calm I have left, I inhale through my nose and exhale a single statement. "Then let's pretend I have the same reasons, because I'm not wearing it."

Bellamy sighs. Closing his eyes, he rubs at his temple with the index finger of his right hand while the other gestures at me in the universal symbol of "hurry up." "Put it on, Evelyn."

"No."

His eyes open, blazing from beneath the shadow cast by his hand. "Put on the goddamn ring—"

"Make me."

His entire body visibly recoils. He blinks again and seems to have trouble regaining his composure. In the end, he has to adjust his tie, wrenching on the navy tail. "Evely—"

"I'm not wearing it," I snap. I don't know what makes me throw out a terse, "Husband," for good measure. Maybe it's to watch him squirm. But then, my lips keep moving before my brain can catch up. "Unless, of course, you earn it. Make me put it on."

"W-What?" His eyebrows shoot up an inch higher on his forehead. That notoriously callous mouth narrows into a dangerous, flat line. I know I'm in for it, even before the bastard inhales sharply, and then... he chuckles. "Challenge accepted," he declares with nothing but pure malice gleaming in those eyes. "Dearest *wife*."

Rather than try to force the ring onto my finger, he merely waits until the car stops before a destination I've become all too familiar with within the past week—a chic boutique.

*Uh-Oh.* A foreboding knot starts to gather in my stomach, but I do my best to ignore it.

"Did you want to do some shopping, Mr. Bellamy?" I ask while following his gaze to the front of Bristol's.

"Why, yes I do, wife," he calls back to me as he exits the car. As if in afterthought, he extends one hand in my direction, which I pointedly ignore as I follow him out. That doesn't stop him from dishing out another taunt. "And I would like for you to call me, Graeme."

"I think I prefer Mr. Bellamy." I keep my voice clipped, my posture tense just in case he decides to throw something. It's only when my fingers clench that I realize I have my own potential missile in hand—the ring box. I heft it, watching smugly as his eyes track every movement of the small shape. With the sweetest smile I can muster, I offer it to him. "I suggest you take this back, darling."

His eyes narrow into slits. "I suggest you put it on, Luv."

There it is again. I flinch unconsciously as the bastard smirks in triumph. Given that we're parked before a busy street in the thick of afternoon traffic, I'll humor him by not causing a scene. Yet. After all, if there is one thing I learned after my time in the corporate world, it's that the biggest fireworks were best put on where they could reap the most collateral damage.

"After you," Graeme prompts, stepping aside to usher me into the store. A shiver runs down my spine as I take in the racks of delicate lace and perfectly tailored satin that consume the spacious interior. Each garment feels like a live grenade, ripe for the throwing by none other than Graeme Bellamy, devious bastard extraordinaire.

Determined to maintain his throne, the bastard heads straight toward the back, where I know one section to be. "Come darling," he calls back to me. "I have something to show you."

*Oh god.* My stomach sinks down to my toes, but I do my best to disguise the reaction with a smile wide enough to put his charming grin to shame. Our gazes lock, trapping the poor sales associate between us. She nervously clears her throat and steps into the background. Smart girl.

"Interested in trying some lingerie for yourself, Mr. Bellamy?" That's the safest scenario that comes to mind as he stops beside a hanging display—a black bustier paired with a lacy scrap of fabric that I assume is meant to be worn as underwear.

"Not tonight." Suddenly, his voice becomes gravelly and thick. Dangerous. He steps toward me, and from the corner of my eye, I see his head lower, bringing his next words directly into my ear. "You told me to make you wear my ring, correct?"

*Oh no.* I wrestle my hands flat against the skirt of my dress, if only to hide the way they shake. "I think the discussion was more along the lines of never—"

"Let us propose a wager," he says over me. "A proper one. With... stakes."

"Like what?" I do my best to smother the tremor in my voice to no avail.

"Like... until the moment you put on that damn ring, we continue through this wedding day. Hmmm? You cannot refuse a single activity I propose." Thick fingers cinch my wrist, not tight enough to hurt. Just enough to reinforce the terms of the bet. "So, pick out your dress, darling. Our honeymoon suite awaits."

"No." I step back, wrenching my hand from his grip. No amount of space seems far enough, however. I set my sights on the front of the store and keep walking. "If you think this *marriage* means I'll bow down to your every whim—"

"You flatter yourself, luv," Bellamy says. The amusement in his voice alone stops me in my tracks. Like a predator, I sense him stalk up behind me, once again taking full advantage of my inability to resist a dare. "Sorry to disappoint, but this has nothing to do with bowing down, as you say. This is about one question and one question only—you, Evelyn King, can't even perform her wifely duty for one damn night. And here I was, convinced that you could at least last longer than twenty-four hours."

"Don't." I'm not sure exactly who I'm talking to. Bellamy? Or myself. *Not again. Don't fall for this again.*

"Don't what?" A piece of my hair is seized from behind and twisted around a crooked finger. A playful tug jerks my head sideways, closer to the warm lips grazing my shoulder. "Tell the truth. You can't even go through the motions, can you—"

"Fine." I pull away from him, scanning the priceless garments on display. My eyes narrow when they land over a fitting weapon. *Bingo.* "We'll play your game, Bellamy. I'll pick out a dress." My outfit of choice is one of white lace with delicate navy accents. "The blue seems rather fitting," I say as I run my fingers over the bodice. "Seeing as how that's the color you'll be when this night is over." I glance pointedly at the front of his slacks, pleased to see him stiffen.

"Is that so?" He flashes a smile that chills me to the core. "Funny. I envision a very different... happy ending."

*Son of a bitch.* I turn away as my cheeks catch fire. Deep breaths. It takes everything I have to school my expression into one that isn't glaring or venomous. If he wants to play this game again, he can have it his way.

"So, let me get this straight? I participate in your 'wedding day,' and if I don't willingly put on the ring by the end of the day, then we drop the topic once and for all."

"Done," he says, a little too quickly for my liking. I blink, caught off guard, as he approaches me in a few swift steps and snatches my selection from its hanger. "Ring this up," he tells the sales associate who appears from nowhere to do his bidding. To me, he... continues to smile. God help the nervous swallow that contracts my throat.

I can do this, sans any unintended consequences. I've survived Graeme Bellamy's antics up until this point. I can last a single day...

Can't I?

"Let us not dawdle a minute longer, wife," Bellamy says, his eyes reflecting a mischievous gleam. "The rest of the night awaits."

"Yes," I agree. Thank god my voice doesn't shake this time. "A *platonic* night." One where nothing gets naked except my ring finger.

"Of course," Bellamy says with a nod. "So, I suggest you change quickly, and then we'll be off."

Off? "Change?" Both questions seem equally as dangerous to voice. Does he intend to return to the suite? Perhaps he changed his mind about Adrian Riley's party and wants me to wear another goddamn evening dress.

But no... That quick, devious flick of his lips seems out of place in either of those options. "Into your wedding dress, of course."

When the saleswoman reappears with the white bit of lace draped over her arm, I can't stop my mouth from falling open. "You can't be serious."

"Oh, but I am," Bellamy assures. I've never seen him so damn smug—and that's saying a lot, all recent events considered. "I prefer that you just wear your ring instead, but if you insist..."

He raises a single eyebrow in what I assume is the closest thing he can get to a suggestive expression. "Then, by all means, dearest wife. My bride should wear something fitting as we celebrate our nuptials."

Fitting, as in barely-there lingerie to only god knew where. "You're insane…"

"And you have a choice," he reminds me, that terrifying smile still in place. Slowly, his eyes drift down to his ring box. "Your choice, darling."

A part of me screams to just give in. Put on the damn ring.

But lately, where Graeme Bellamy is concerned, all logic seems to take a back seat to stubborn pride.

"Fine." I snatch the lingerie and head straight for the dressing rooms. Regret can come later. After all, I only have to last one damn night.

And this time, I intend to win.

When I leave the dressing room, I'm sure several pairs of eyes swivel in my direction—but I only notice one. A fiery blue gaze sweeps over me with an intensity that raises goosebumps over my flesh. Given how much of said flesh is currently exposed, that is no understatement.

"Bloody hell!" In two strides, Graeme lunges from his seated position at the back of the dressing room. Using his body as a barrier, he herds me into the narrow stall I'd just come from. The velvet-lined door closes behind him, trapping us both inside. "Are you mad?" He gestures with a wave of his hand toward my current ensemble. "Just put on the bloody ring!"

"But I'm just doing what my dear husband requested," I counter with what I hope passes for an innocent flutter of my eyelashes. In the same motion, I lift my shoulder, straining the delicate bra cups that keep my nipples covered by sheer luck—and if I'm not mistaken...

He growls, a barely audible rumble that escapes his clenched teeth.

"If you don't think my outfit is appropriate for public view," I rush to add, "then maybe you should take me up on my offer."

"To wear a ring?" His voice lowers to a guttural rasp that makes my breathing hitch. "And if I do, you'll make sure that only your dear husband can see you in anything resembling this?"

The way his eyes ghost over me makes my belly quake. My skin heats, and I can't stop myself from swaying as his hands capture my waist. Deliberately, one of his thumbs nudges a dangerously thin bit of lace, and I'm grateful for the seclusion. Needling him is one thing, but flashing the entire, exclusive boutique wasn't exactly on my bucket list.

"Perhaps," I say in answer to his question.

"Fine." He leans in, letting his lips brush my throat as he says, "If you want me to wear a bloody ring, I will."

"Good, then we can go now." I shimmy out of his grasp and reach for my clothing.

"Yes," Graeme replies, but he beats me to the punch and snatches up my dress before I can put it on. As I watch, dumbfounded, he shrugs off his suit jacket and drapes it over my shoulders. "But I would hate for you to lose your leverage before said ring is on my finger. You can wear your ensemble to the store."

My upper lip quirks at the double-edged threat. "I suppose I'm not to remove this jacket."

"Not unless you want me to add another stipulation to our agreement," he says while guiding my arms into the sleeves of his jacket. Once I'm properly covered, he tilts his head, taking final stock of his prize. "I believe, Ms. King, that you and I will find this new arrangement suits us both."

I lick my lips. Hoarsely, I point out, "Don't you mean Mrs. Bellamy?"

His eyes gleam in a way that makes me suspect we won't be leaving this dressing room any time soon. "As you wish, Mrs. Bellamy."

Be the first to be notified when the next book in the Red Room Series is available, sign up for Lana Sky's newsletter!

https://www.lanaskybooks.com/newsletter

# about lana sky

Lana Sky is a reclusive writer in the United States who spends most of her time daydreaming about complex male characters and parenting her Cockapoo Joey. She writes dark, twisted romance across several genres. Her titles include everything from mafia romance to vampires.

www.ingramcontent.com/pod-product-compliance
Lightning Source LLC
Chambersburg PA
CBHW062102290726
48975CB00001B/77